Praise for *The Gardeners' Club*

'**Funny** and fresh. **Full of** ████████ █████ ████
genuinely root for. **Marnie R**███████████
Tammy █████

'Loved this **witty, fre**███████
Roz W███████

'Absolutely **loved** *The Gardeners' Club*. It has
everything **from murder and intrigue to award-
winning potatoes**. Fell in love with Gill and
Zak and was sad to finish – I miss them all!'
Rachel Wolf

'Such a **funny and clever** and dark cosy crime from
Marnie Riches, with **real and memorable characters**
you're invested in. I loved #TheGardenersClub.'
Louise Swanson

'Sometimes **hilarious**, sometimes **poignant**,
but **always compelling**. With **stand-out and
unforgettable characters**, Marnie Riches has crafted
a wonderful story. **Cosy crime at its best**.'
Julie-Ann Corrigan

'*The Gardeners' Club* is **a refreshing, heartwarming
mystery** blossoming with wit and charm. With quirky
characters harbouring secrets, a down-to-earth menopausal
woman juggling a hectic family life, and an intrepid
group of amateur sleuths unearthing clues, this is **a
perfect pick for plant-loving cosy-mystery fans**.'
Victoria Goldman

PENGUIN BOOKS
The Gardeners' Club

Marnie Riches grew up on a rough estate in north Manchester. Exchanging the spires of nearby Strangeways prison for those of Cambridge University, she gained a Masters in German and Dutch. Her bestselling, award-winning George McKenzie crime thrillers, tackling the subject of transnational trafficking, were inspired by her own time spent in the Netherlands.

Since her debut, *The Girl Who Wouldn't Die*, was published, Marnie has written prolifically, building a long backlist of critically acclaimed crime-fiction titles, as well as penning historical novels set in the north-west of England under the pseudonym Maggie Campbell.

When she isn't writing or teaching creative and academic writing for Cambridge University, the Royal Literary Fund, and New Writing North, Marnie loves to garden.

The Gardeners' Club

MARNIE RICHES

PENGUIN BOOKS

PENGUIN BOOKS

UK | USA | Canada | Ireland | Australia
India | New Zealand | South Africa

Penguin Books is part of the Penguin Random House group of companies
whose addresses can be found at global.penguinrandomhouse.com

Penguin Random House UK
One Embassy Gardens, 8 Viaduct Gardens, London SW11 7BW

penguin.co.uk

First published 2025
004

Set in 12.5/14.75pt Garamond MT
Typeset by Falcon Oast Graphic Art Ltd
Printed and bound in Great Britain by Clays Ltd, Elcograf S.p.A.

The authorized representative in the EEA is Penguin Random House Ireland,
Morrison Chambers, 32 Nassau Street, Dublin D02 YH68

A CIP catalogue record for this book is available from the British Library

ISBN: 978-1-405-96910-9

This book is dedicated to me, since I seem to be the only person who has never had a thanks, and let's face it, I did 100 per cent of the writing. In fact, this book and the others that preceded it could not have been written without my warped imagination, expensive gardening obsession and dogged persistence. So, thanks me.

I

For the last fifteen minutes, I've been looking at the clock on the wall and I could swear that time is actually going backwards. How can it be 5.42pm when it was 5.41pm about ten minutes ago? Surely there's only another five or so minutes of this corporate torture, featuring free bendy biscuits and lukewarm hot drinks, dispensed from urns that have probably contained Legionnaires' disease since the mid-nineties.

I sip the dregs of my coffee in a bid to wake myself up. It tastes like a cocktail of Bovril and petrol. When I slam the cup down a little too heavily onto its saucer, my boss, Colin, turns from the graph projected onto the whiteboard to lock eyes with me. He continues to speak in that nasal drone of his.

'So, the main worry-bead area is that average handling time of customer calls is too long, and we're getting very high call-abandonment rates. These figures show not just a drop in first-touch resolution, but . . .'

Like the eye of Sauron, his never-sleeping gaze has moved onto Jess, my opposite number in the Birmingham call centre, and I've already tuned out again. My heavy eyelids know it's time to drop the shutters for the day on the vagaries of servicing the nation's insurance policies.

'Gill! Gill, wake up!'

I feel a hand on my shoulder. My eyes snap open to see Jess standing over me. Everyone is closing their laptops and getting up from the meeting table. I see Colin has already left.

'Damn,' I say, glancing at the clock that shows 6.19pm. 'Did he notice I'd nodded off?' I hastily wipe my mouth and check I didn't drool on the lapel of my jacket.

Jess shakes her head. 'Nope. You're in the clear. Well done on perfecting the art of chair-snoozing, though.'

My pulse starts to race. Maybe it knows something I don't. 'Hang on. I didn't miss anything important, did I? Think I nodded off just as he was talking through that graph.'

'Only our new targets.' Jess chuckles but no smile reaches her eyes. I notice now that she looks harried. 'Check the last page of the presentation. He emailed it through to everyone.'

Barney from Glasgow is strolling our way, carrying his laptop bag and coat over one arm. Clearly he's overheard our little tête-à-tête, because he's singing that old Irving Berlin song about there being trouble ahead. 'Ready to face the music and dance, Gillian?' He exits the meeting room before I can interrogate him further.

I turn to Jess for clarification, but she just shrugs.

'Better batten down the hatches with those expect- ations,' she says. 'Storm's a'coming.' She pats my arm, her smile sympathetic. 'Anyway, I'll see you at the away day . . . assuming we're all still standing.'

I feel a bead of sweat running down my back to my waistband.

Left alone in the meeting room, I open the presentation and scroll through to the end to see the slide I missed – the slide that explains the gargantuan task I've been assigned; that we've all been assigned. Chislehurst Green Insurance is losing ground to its main competitors. There's a profit warning, according to Colin, supreme overlord of call centres. And I'm one of the seven senior lackeys who has to make sure the hundreds of people who spend all day answering phones to disgruntled policyholders do so as quickly and efficiently as humanly possible to put the company back in the black to the tune of millions. Cutting costs and raising productivity means only one thing: I have to conduct a witch hunt.

'Oh great. Just what I need.'

I know the coming weeks will be filled with my having to scrutinise the team managers beneath me and their teams beneath them, eavesdropping on colleagues' phone calls to earmark the slow and the unhelpful for a dressing down and/or retraining. At forty-eight, I realise that in return for keeping the roof above mine and Zak's heads, I have become little more than a corporate bully.

A super-heated wave washes over my body, and now my blouse, beneath my jacket, is like cling film wrapping my clammy skin. I wipe my top lip. 'God give me strength.' I snap my laptop shut. 'Come on, Gill,' I say under my breath. 'You've got this.'

Yet I'm not sure I have.

Returning to my desk and pulling on my coat, I pluck

my phone from my bag and check for messages. There's one from Zak.

What's for dinner? xxx

I've already told him there's a leftover portion of lasagne in the fridge. The boy never listens. He's in his first year of sixth form and he still seems an entire childhood away from being an adult, not to mention already being on the radar of the head of sixth form for the sort of disruptive behaviour that typifies a class clown.

Nuke the lasagne. Five minutes on full blast. Make sure the lid's not fully on. Xxx

My after-work engagement is a rarity and has been in the calendar for weeks. Zak knows I'm going to be late home. This evening, just for once, I really need him to look after himself. But he's typing . . .

What lasagne?

He treats me to a string of emojis that spell teen-aged bewilderment. Heading into the crowded lift and descending to the lobby, I thumb a response.

In the Tupperware container in the fridge.

The lift reaches the ground floor, and we're all released like caged animals. I make for the revolving doors, wave to the guy on security and head out into the early-spring drizzle. It's still light, thankfully. The days are getting longer. Finally, I feel able to exhale. I feel the tension start to leach from my shoulders.

Where?

'Come on, Zachary!' I shout at my phone. I glance around me, but nobody's listening to a middle-aged woman in a beige mac and sensible shoes, at the end of the working day. I lower my voice, but the frustration constricts my throat. 'On the bottom shelf. Use your eyes, son!'

I start to thumb a response, but guilt is pawing at me like a disappointed dog, reminding me that I'm a crappy mother and that my little-big-boy needs me or might set the house on fire or might start gaming and forget to eat and not do his homework and start surfing Pornhub.

Forget it. Am coming home. I'll cook fresh. Do your
homework. Love you. Mum xxx

Damn it. Sighing heavily, I reason that I didn't want to go to that stupid meeting, after all. The Bromley Botanists' gardeners' club almost certainly doesn't need another member – especially not one who manages to kill cacti. My therapist, Mandi-with-an-I, said gardening would be the key to starting fresh; to salving my shocking acid indigestion, the frequent bouts of insomnia that have me tossing and turning into the small hours, and perhaps even the anxiety that dogs my every decision. But attending a meeting of the Bromley Botanists is clearly not to be, thanks to my probably disproportionate worry over my son's kitchen-competence track record and my misplaced mumly guilt.

In the car park of the boxy sprawl that is Chislehurst Green Insurance's offices, with its tinted windows and depressing dark brown brick, I'm just about to start the engine of my old Volvo when my phone rings.

'Zak? You've not blown up the microwave, have you? I said I was coming home.' I visualise the fallout from an exploded lasagne, all over the innards of the appliance. It's only three months since Zak blew up two boiled eggs, because he'd lost track of time while doing his Maths homework and had left the pan to boil dry, filling the kitchen with black smoke. I'm still spotting rubbery bits of albumen on the kitchen ceiling and walls. Who knew eggs made good incendiary devices?

'Stop worrying, will you!' he says. 'I'm fine. I'm not a kid.'

'Okay.' I bite my tongue.

'I was just calling to say I've found the lasagne and I think you should go to the gardening thing.'

'But –'

'Mum, I'm an adult. Well, nearly. The eggs were a one-off, and you're using me as an excuse to avoid doing new stuff. Just go. You know you need this.'

Suddenly, my little-big-boy sounds wise beyond his years. I can see both him and Mandi-with-an-I in my mind's eye, judging me with arms folded and eyebrows raised knowingly.

'Oh, go on, then. Love you. Don't set fire to anything or fall down the stairs or hit your head. And keep off Pornhub. It's bad for the developing brain.'

'You're disgusting, Mum. Have fun.'

Ending the call, I take out the scrap of local news-paper from the zipped pocket of my handbag and plug the postcode of the Bromley Botanists' gardeners' club into my satnav.

'Let's give Marjorie a clap for her beautiful parrot tulips . . .'

A man's voice, followed by a sparse round of applause, drifts out to me as I stand on the threshold of the community hall at the side of an old red-brick church. This place looks like exactly the sort of mildewed hellhole that I don't want to spend my evening in. Yet I take a deep breath, acknowledge that I'm just looking for yet another way out of improving my life, and will myself inside. I know I'm late, but I hope I can slip in at the back, unnoticed.

I realise my plan is doomed when I see there are only six people sitting in the draughty hall, plus a stout, grey-haired man at the front, who is dressed in mushroom-coloured slacks, slung beneath a pudgy belly and paired with a yellow polo shirt with curling tips to the collar. He hasn't noticed me yet. Through his outdated tinted glasses, his gaze is fixed on an elderly woman in a pleated skirt and floral blouse. He beckons her over.

'Marjorie, why don't you come up to the front and explain your winning formula for such incredible . . .' He clams up as soon as he spots me and treats me to a faltering smile. 'Oh, hello. Can I help you?'

All eyes are on me now. I can feel the heat creeping into my florid cheeks, my recently acquired rosacea lighting up that dismal place. 'Er . . . I'm here for the . . . Is this the Bromley chapter of the Golden Trowel thingy?'

The man at the front pushes his tinted glasses up his nose with his middle finger and strides forward awkwardly. He extends his hand to me. 'Mike "Potato" Berisford, King of King Edwards. At your service, ma'am.' He clicks his heels, grins, and blushes. Behind the tinted lenses, I can see he is blinking fast. 'You can just call me Mike. Welcome.'

I shake his meaty hand, looking around at the others: two young people – a bloke in a designer hoodie and joggers, a girl with dreadlocks, dressed in tie-dye; two elderly women – the one with the pleated skirt (presumably Marjorie) and another, a punk-throwback Teletubby in her bright green jumpsuit and Dr Marten boots with dayglo green laces. There's an ordinary-looking woman of about my age in hiking gear, and a man in his late thirties or early forties, by the looks. He's wearing a straw trilby and has a Dalí moustache. What a peculiar bunch.

'And you are?' Mike asks.

'Gill,' I say. 'Gill Swanley.'

Everybody greets me in a hubbub of curiosity and friendliness. I feel like I'm in the midst of some kind of addiction support group or religious cult.

'So, I take it you garden, Gillian?' Mike says.

'Er, not really,' I say, picturing my dead IKEA cacti on the kitchen windowsill that look like deflated prickly penises, and the spider plant that I accidentally defenestrated at university in 1993. 'Not yet, anyway. When I was a little kid, I did a bit.' My green-fingered childhood, when I'd helped Dad with his veg patch, seems like an otherworldly dream now. I wish I could head for the door; head back to the safety of my son and his egg-terrorism tendencies in an otherwise empty, lonely house. 'But I'd like to take it up again.'

The old punk in the green jumpsuit gets to her feet and hastens towards me. 'Get out of the way, Mr Potato Head!' she says, pushing the King of King Edwards aside. She puts her arm around me. 'I'm Val. Come with me, love. Make yourself comfortable.' She ushers me to an uncomfortable plastic chair.

The others pull their chairs closer to me until I'm surrounded by seven pairs of enquiring eyes.

Val takes her seat next to me, wedging herself between me and Marjorie, the tulip aficionado. 'So, lovey. Tell us why you want to join the Bromley Botanists gardeners' club.'

I open my mouth to answer, but I don't honestly know where to begin.

2

'A neighbour told me about this place,' I lie. 'She'd seen the feature in the local paper and thought I might be interested.'

Will this be enough to satisfy their curiosity? They don't need to know my personal circumstances; don't need to hear about the pressures of work and bringing up a son alone and all the rest of the drama of the last decade. I force a smile.

The man with the Dalí moustache is sitting next to me. He leans over and pats my hand. 'It's a lifesaver. Certainly keeps me sane, though I'm not sure I'd say sanity and this lot go hand in hand.' He laughs at his own joke. 'I'm Neil, by the way.'

We shake hands.

'Gardening is God's work,' Marjorie says in a small voice, treating Neil to side-eyes. 'That's why the vicar lets us have this church hall for free.' She smiles sweetly. 'One does all the flower arrangements with one's home-grown flowers. You should see the harvest festival and Christmas displays.'

Val waves dismissively. 'Stop showing off for once in your life, Marjorie. You're always bloody boasting. Isn't that one of your deadly sins?'

Marjorie's smile sours to reveal a mouthful of

discoloured teeth. 'One can't help it if the good Lord blesses one with greener fingers than yours, Valerie. Maybe you should reconsider your heathen ways.'

In my peripheral vision, I can see the hippy girl and young guy in the hoodie trying and failing to stifle their giggles at the bickering old women.

Mike Potato gets to his feet. 'It's good, honest hard graft,' he tells me. 'Made all the more satisfying by the challenge we've got ahead of us as a group.'

Everyone falls silent, now. Nodding in unison.

'They're due to open entries for the Trowellies next month,' he explains, sticking his thumbs in his waistband. 'That's the Golden Trowel Gardening Association's annual awards. It's like the Oscars for amateur growers.' He folds his arms tightly across his chest. 'Last year we came in second, ahead of the Southwark Secateurs, but the Croydon Diggers and Dibbers snatched the Golden Trowel for club of the year from under our noses.'

The others start to grumble at the mention of these apparent rival clubs.

'It's ridiculous that Dotty Gloucester is both a member of the Southwark Secateurs and one of the patrons of the GTG Association,' Marjorie says, spraying indignant spittle as she speaks. 'Talk about conflict of interest! They get in the top three every year. Won in 2022.'

'Dorothy Gloucester, the Radio 4 presenter?' I ask, casting my mind back to all the times my mother made scathing remarks about the former presenter of BBC Radio's jewel in its horticultural crown, *The Lady Gardeners' Hour*.

Marjorie grimaces. 'She's not *that* famous. She and I mix in the same church flower-arranging circles. Believe you me, none of us is impressed by how much bosom she shows.' She shakes her head and tuts. 'Very ungodly behaviour. And her poppies are always droopy.'

'And Croydon's got Barnacle Betty,' Val adds, setting a Rizla on her knee and filling it with tobacco from a pouch. 'She's their most experienced gardener. Big pals with some of the judges, too.'

'Betty *Moule*?' Marjorie scoffs. 'Don't talk to me about that cheese-guzzling pétanque-fancier.'

Mike looks askance at Marjorie. 'Thank you, Marjorie. I don't think we need talk about the French in quite such disparaging terms.'

'Oh, she's not French. But she married a Frenchman.' She wrinkles her nose. 'Henri Moule – all boules, Boursin and Beaujolais.'

'Marjorie, *please*!' Mike holds his hand up and clears his throat. He turns to me. 'Now, Gill. Where were we? Yes, the Golden Trowel is the most prestigious prize a community gardening club can compete for. Ten thousand pounds to the winner. Ten *thousand*. Imagine all the tools and stock our group could buy with that. We could rent a dedicated smallholding and fill it with polytunnels, like the Dutch.'

'Yeah, or we could, like, totally blow the cash on a nice holiday.' The dreadlocked girl chuckles at her own suggestion and blushes. 'Like maybe a trip to Amsterdam.' She looks to the hoodie-wearing boy for approval.

The two bump fists and grin.

Marjorie merely shakes her head at the youngsters. Her lips narrow with disapproval, and she turns back to me. 'Last year, Bromley was voted best-in-bloom by the *Silver Sixty* podcast. I heard we lost the Golden Trowel to Croydon by a hair's breadth. Imagine! How frustrating not to have won.'

'One of last year's judges is married to a woman high up in Croydon Council,' Val says. 'I've heard she's big in the environment department or something. Recycling green waste.'

'It was a bare fix, man.' The upper-middle-class accent of the dreadlocked girl curdles with the council estate patois. Again, she looks to the hoodie-wearing young man for corroboration.

'They got all their compost for free, innit?' he says, taking her cue. His accent is genuine South-East London – all of the social currency with none of the cash. 'If I had all the compost I wanted . . .' His voice trails off. Given the smell of stale marijuana coming from his clothes, I can well imagine what his gardening aspirations might be.

The members of the group all start to talk over one another, keen to slander Bromley's competitors. Mike holds his hand up and clears his throat.

'Trowellers, can I have your attention please? Trowellers!'

But though Mike Potato is the self-declared King of King Edwards, he seems to have no dominion over the humans in the room, and I can see the collaborative purpose has been lost in a thirst for gossip about other community gardening groups and horticultural events I know nothing about.

I have never felt such an outsider. My very skin feels ill-fitting and itchy in this mildewed place.

'Hang on!' Neil says, getting to his feet. 'Surely we can do better than this as a welcome for our newcomer.' With some flourish, he points to a table at the side of the hall that is laden with biscuits, carefully arranged on plates, and plastic cups full of something dark and foamy. 'How about we take a break so we can talk to Gill properly?'

'Ah, yes,' Mike Potato says. 'Thank you, Neil. That's a good suggestion.' He pushes his glasses up his nose and pulls his trousers up. 'Please help yourself to some refreshments, Gill. Sample my dandelion beer home-brew and tell me what you think.' He grins. 'Don't pull any punches, now.'

And so, at just gone seven in the evening, when I would normally be at home, making dinner for my son, I find myself sipping dandelion beer out of a plastic cup and nibbling on a Bourbon biscuit that I neither need nor like.

'How's the beer?' Mike asks.

The beer tastes like earwax. 'Delicious.' In my peripheral vision, I can see the other Bromley Botanists pouring their beer out of an open window and topping themselves up with Diet Coke instead. 'What do you do for a day job, Mike?'

A red, blotchy rash starts to spread from Mike's neck to his face. He rocks back and forth on his heels and looks down at his highly polished shoes. 'Well, I'm, er, a planning enforcement officer in the department of, er, the local . . .' He looks up and smiles. 'And what do you do, pray tell, Gillian?'

I can barely bring myself to say it. 'I'm a team manager for an insurance call centre. Chislehurst Green.' It sounds even more boring when I say it out loud.

'Married? Children?'

'Widowed.' I swallow hard. 'With a seventeen-year-old son, who's probably setting fire to microwaved lasagne leftovers right now and gaming himself to a stump, instead of doing his homework. Ha ha.'

Mike Potato opens his mouth to respond, but Neil pushes in front of him and guides me by the arm away from Mike and towards the others.

'Come on, Gill,' he says. 'You need to get to know everyone. Just pretend you're in Narcotics Anonymous, except most people in here do Omeprazole and Fiery Jack on a Friday night.' He raises a plucked eyebrow. 'Although Auntie Val can probably get hold of some miaow-miaow, if you ask her nicely.' There's a mischievous smile playing around his lips. He lays his hand on his chest, muscular beneath a fitted blue shirt. 'So, let's start with me. I'm a secondary school English teacher, but I've just started taking the gardening enrichment classes. I came here to learn how to plant up a herbaceous border so I can teach the kids.' He places a hand on the shoulder of the middle-aged woman who has so far said nothing at all. 'And this is Cath. *Doctor* Cath.'

Cath raises her plastic cup of Diet Coke. When she speaks, her eyes look like still pools in the dark. 'Welcome.'

'Are you a medical doctor, then, Cath?' I ask.

She nods and sips her drink. 'On a sort of sabbatical. Very long Covid.' She looks away then, the conversation clearly over. Perhaps she's shy. I sense there's more to her story than Covid, but I'm hardly going to interrogate a stranger.

Now, I am faced with the white girl with the dreadlocks – the grubby, matted kind that I remember seeing on crusties in the nineties. 'Hello. I'm Gill.'

The girl touches a dread and smiles. 'Hi. I'm Phoebe.' She holds out her hand to shake.

Phoebe looks like the public-school kids I met at university, who would turn up to every march, every sit-in, every protest for Greenpeace and Amnesty in a bid to rebel against mater and pater. I see bitten nails on the ends of her child-sized hands and realise she's younger than I'd anticipated. Perhaps late teens like Zak. Overwhelmed by an unanticipated rush of mumly feelings, I shake her hand, wondering what she's pushing against. 'Pleased to meet you, Phoebe. How come you're here?'

'Well, I'd quite like to rewild a patch of land and I'm really into environmental stuff. So, my gramps said I'd best get off Insta and actually learn to garden. Dig for Britain and that?'

'Good on you. Got to start somewhere, right?' I'd put money on it that she's an Extinction Rebellion fangirl.

I turn to the hoodie-wearing young guy, but just as

I'm about to greet him, Mike Potato claps his hands together.

'Can we take our seats and turn our thoughts to the matter in hand now?' He looks around at us expectantly.

One by one, we settle in for round two of this chaotic gathering. I check my watch and wonder if my social going-through-the-motions has been worth missing dinner with my son. But in my mind's eye, I can see Mandi-with-an-I encouraging me to shelve my preconceptions. *Give it a go, Gill. Gardening is very good for your mental health and would be a better long-term strategy for dealing with your anxiety than endless therapy sessions with me, which you said you can't really afford. And you never know . . . you might enjoy it.*

'Now, do we have suggestions on how we can best Croydon this year?' Mike asks. He turns to me. 'We normally do traditional bedding displays, hanging baskets, troughs, window boxes. That sort of thing. Whatever the municipal planting budget won't stretch to, we try to cover, don't we, gang? Making Bromley beautiful.'

'One grows most of the plants in one's greenhouse,' Marjorie says, beaming and looking around for approval. 'One already has the seed from the previous year, you see, having left prize-winning annuals to set seed in autumn.'

'And I make the compost,' Mike says. 'My special recipe.' He taps the side of his nose. 'I call it "Berisford's Black Gold".'

The hoodie-wearing lad stretches out his legs, crosses them and puts his hands behind his head. 'You said you was gonna give us your recipe for "Berisford's Black Gold". You ever gonna share the wisdom? 'Cause I got entrepreneurial plans for a medicinal herbs business – on the side from my electrician's commitments, like.'

'Patience, young Seth.' Mike laughs nervously and pushes those glasses up his nose again. 'My magic recipe is only revealed to those members of the Bromley Botanists that have done a full . . . er . . . tour of duty.' He clicks his heels again.

Keen to contribute to the discussion about the gardening competition, I flip through the dusty, half-empty filing cabinet of my plant-based knowledge and remember that I have actually been watching *Gardeners' World*. I did go to the Chelsea Flower Show last year too, even though I wasn't entirely sure what I was looking for. I also remember pitching in with my father's gardening endeavours, when I was a child. He grew a mixture of fruit and vegetables and ornamental plants, grown from cuttings from other people's gardens. I'm inexperienced, but maybe I do have some horticultural thoughts worth sharing.

I raise my hand.

'Gill?' Mike says.

I can feel a blush spreading across my rosacea-pink cheeks. 'If you've not managed to win by doing traditional planting, how about changing it up? Wild planting's fashionable now, isn't it? Maybe scatter wildflower meadow seeds along grass verges so they don't have to be mown. Cornflowers and poppies; flowers for pollinators and whatnot. Maybe mix in edible plants with ornamentals? I heard bees like blue. Or planting for a drier, hotter climate since our summers are seeing higher temperatures and a lot less rain. Hibiscus . . . sedum . . . er, sea holly?'

'Oh, well . . . that wouldn't work, dear,' Marjorie says quietly. 'We, in the Bromley chapter of the GTG Association, have a reputation to uphold. One's dahlias, for example, have won best-in-show.'

'Er, Marjorie's right, Gill,' Mike says. 'You see, Croydon won with traditional planting, and we were runners-up, so we can't be doing much wrong.'

'Wild planting for pollinators would be way cool,' Phoebe says. 'I *love* Gill's idea.'

I am encouraged by her support. We exchange a smile. I turn my thoughts to how a business might triumph over its competitors. 'And publicity,' I say. 'Local papers will love to give you some positive coverage if you can find a heart-warming story behind the planting. Flower beds for the elderly and sick; hanging baskets on roads where there isn't even a tree. That sort of thing. The judges won't be blind to positive press, and it could give you the edge you need.'

Mike nods and then shakes his head. 'It's a nice idea, Gill, but what you need to remember is that the clubs are all being judged on their displays – design, flower quality, et cetera. We made a crown out of bedding for the Queen's Platinum jubilee.' He looks to the ceiling and puts his hands together in prayer. 'May Her Majesty rest in peace.'

'Yes. One's coleus was *marvellous* that year,' Marjorie

says in that small voice. 'So, I can't see how reputation or public image have got anything to do with horticultural prowess.'

'But you're a *community* gardening group, right?' I say, disappointed that everything I've suggested has been shot down by King Spud and his septuagenarian sidekick, Marjorie. 'Maybe it's not just about flowers. It's about community spirit too. That's where publicising the joy you bring to other people's lives could come in. The more community-focused you seem to be, the more you might be at the forefront of the judges' minds.'

'She's right!' Val cries, zipping the zip of her green jumpsuit up and down and up and down at the neck. 'You two couldn't organise a piss-up at a brewery, but you're always telling everyone else what to do, aren't you?' She has the beginnings of cataracts, judging by the cloudy edges to her irises, but she's pure punk spirit.

'I agree that Gill's ideas are interesting,' Neil says, adjusting the brim of his trilby.

'It's sustainability we should be going for,' Phoebe says. 'The planet's dying.'

Perhaps it's sustainability or the idea that the planet is dying that gets Mike and Marjorie's goat, but suddenly an argument erupts about old-fashioned versus new-fangled gardening styles and techniques, and all I can hear are insults being fired across the hall.

Above the hubbub, I hear Cath speak properly for almost the first time. Well, she's shouting, actually. 'Will you all just shut up?! How can we win against Croydon if you're all going to be so *pathetic*?'

Everybody falls silent and stares at her. Mike clears his throat but says nothing. I take a step back towards the exit, wondering if I've made a terrible mistake. I endure enough stress at work, after all. Do I really need this sort of strife in my private life, too?

3

'Well? How'd it go?' Zak asks, pulling his earbuds from his ears, his face lit by the ghostly glow of his monitor.

I kick off my shoes at the threshold to the living room and regard my beloved son, sitting in the little computer alcove I fashioned for him in the recess to the right of the chimney breast. He's five feet ten, sports the suggestion of a moustache, and has paused his game in the middle of close-range combat with a zombie, but he still looks very much like my little boy. 'I'm utterly drained. First things first. Tea!'

Zak and I gravitate from the living room to the kitchen, and he sits at our small kitchen table to eat a pre-bed snack of bran flakes, while I prepare to self-medicate with tannins and strong caffeine.

'So?' he asks.

'I thought there'd be loads of them, but there weren't at all,' I say, squashing a teabag against the side of my mug. I pour in a little milk, then put the carton back into a fridge that desperately needs restocking. Then I open the cutlery drawer to begin searching for the pack of ten cigarettes that I recently hid from myself, in a recess beneath the tray. 'There were seven of them. A couple of gardening prima donnas, bickering like mad. One of them actually introduced himself as Mike Potato, King of King Edwards!'

'Mike *Potato*? No way!'

'Yes way. Looks like a potato, too. His arch-rival looked like she might play the organ in church but had a tongue like a razor blade. There was an old punk and a young Extinction Rebellion type. Couple of guys seemed pretty normal – one was about your age – and a very shy doctor, who then completely lost it at one point. A bunch of lonely misfits.'

'You should fit right in then,' Zak grins. He shovels a spoon of cereal into his mouth. '*Joking.*'

I shake my head at him and take a cigarette out of the pack. I point it at him accusingly. 'Show some respect for your poor mother.'

'Sorry, Mum. Really sorry. Honestly didn't mean it,' he says, looking contrite. He eyeballs the cigarette. 'Should you be doing that?'

'Nope.' I open the kitchen window and light up, exhaling the smoke into the alley at the side of our semi-detached house, where the wheelie bins lurk, along with the rusting filing cabinet and the peeling old desk that I never have muscle enough to get into the boot of my Volvo or time enough to take to the municipal tip. Inside, cups and plates languish on every kitchen surface, though I left it in pristine shape when I went out this morning. 'Should I be trying to join a gardening club when I've got an ailing mother to take care of and a job from hell . . . and a *Zak*, who doesn't even put his dirty pots in the sink?'

My boy-child rolls his eyes at me and speaks with his mouth full. 'I was going to clear up just as you got back. Anyway, Mandi-with-an-I said –'

'Mandi-with-an-I didn't have to sit through an hour and a half of claptrap about winning a "Trowellie", led by the King of King Edwards.' I inhale the cigarette smoke and feel lightheaded. 'I'm not sure it's my scene anyway, community gardening. I haven't done anything remotely green-fingered since I was a kid. I mean, just look at our garden!'

I peer through the window that faces onto the water-logged mid-March back garden, but it's dark outside, and all I can see is my own reflection staring back at me. I look exhausted and dishevelled. I know that the back garden does too, with its muddy quagmire, where I've taken up the turf (but failed to do anything else since towards my grand landscaping plans), and the tumble-down shed that contains a possibly abandoned wasp's nest and spiders the size of my hand.

Zak starts to clear his various dirty pots into the sink, squirts washing-up liquid onto them, and runs the tap. 'You don't have to be Monty Don to dig a hole and put a plant in it. The point is, you do nothing but work and then come home and start all over again with me and Nan. You need to . . .' He's looking thoughtfully at the bottle of washing-up liquid. '. . . get out of your own head. Gardening's supposed to be brilliant for that, isn't it? Mindfulness. Meeting other people.'

'Meeting the green-fingered oddballs of Bromley Borough.' I pause and replay the part of the meeting where everybody in the group greeted me over earwax-flavoured dandelion homebrew. 'Actually, that's harsh. They were okay, I suppose. Friendly, mainly. I'm just not sure it was my scene.'

'I think you're too willing to give up 'cause you're scared to fail.' My own teenage son gives me a smug, knowing look.

'Woah! Where did that come from? I've got Mandi for that sort of cod-wisdom, thank you.' Kissing Zak on the side of his head, I extinguish my cigarette in the soapy water in the sink and throw the butt into the bin. I swipe my cup of tea from the worktop and sit at the table to watch my almost-adult son trying to make amends for his domestic sloth. I notice that his shoulders are hunched up and he's stooping again. 'Look, love, you've got to stop worrying about me. I'm the parent, you're the child. Not the other way round. Now, tell me how your day went.'

He dries his hands and turns around. 'I did okay in my Further Maths end of topic test. I could have got an A. I mean, I totally get what I did wrong.'

'What did you actually get?'

'I got about average. I was one mark off a C.'

'So, that's a D. Come on, Zak! You said you revised.'

There's pleading in his eyes. 'I did! It was such a hard test. I even beat Natasha Benson by two marks. Like I said, I could have totally got an A. Mrs Khan said so. It was just stupid mistakes.'

'You're doing well in normal Maths, aren't you?'

He doesn't quite look me in the eye. '*Further* Maths is next level.'

'Did you check over your work?'

He shrugs and scratches at his skinny arms. 'I tried, but they were shouting in the class next door, and I sort of got distracted. I dunno. But Mrs Khan says I could still get an A in the summer if I work hard. I got over eighty per cent in the last three homeworks.'

I see the optimism in my son's handsome face. There is nothing to be gained from making him feel bad about a result that can't now be altered. 'Well, the main thing is that you learn from your mistakes. Try to remember what you did wrong so you don't do it in the real AS exam.'

'Yes, Mum.' He stares sullenly at the fruit bowl on the side. Is he even listening to me?

'And read the mark scheme. See if you get extra marks for showing your working out in more detail. Maybe it's all down to exam technique and focus.'

'Yeeees.'

I snap my fingers in front of his face until he meets my gaze. 'Hey! You can do this. You've always been a maths genius. Even as a little kid. You get it from your dad.'

His full lips part in a brilliant gap-toothed smile, but the smile is fleeting, and the shine in his eyes dims. 'Do you think he'd have been proud?'

I get to my feet and cross the kitchen to enfold my little-big-boy in a bear hug. He smells of Lynx Africa deodorant spray with a slight whiff of school dinners. 'He *is* proud. I'm sure of it. He's watching over you, from wherever he is now.' I wave my hand vaguely towards the ceiling. 'And I bet he's thinking what an amazing man you're turning into.'

Zak nods. 'Cool. Love you, Mum.'

'You can tell Nanny Pat and Gramps all about doing well in those homeworks when we next Zoom.' I think about my in-laws, enjoying their retirement down the road from Dave's sister, Nicole, and her family, all thousands of miles away in Grenada. How desperately I wish that they still lived locally. 'They don't have to know about the D. Practice makes perfect, right? And summer's still a long way off.'

Zak seems reassured, but I can see frailty behind the smile. Nearly ten years on since Dave died, and it hasn't got any easier for either of us. Not really. We're both still treading water. I swallow down the regret that my boy is growing up without a male role model in his life, without a father's love. I try to be mother *and* father to him, but I know my efforts are two star, at best, despite my five-star intentions. Keeping this roof above our heads sucks more than its fair share of my energy, leaving less in the tank for Zak than I would like. And with the pressure on at work, I'm about to become even more thinly spread across my various commitments.

'Now, shouldn't you be getting to bed?' I ask. I glance at the sink. 'Leave that lot. I'll see to it.' I shoo him out of the kitchen. 'Go! Get your teeth brushed. I'll be up in a bit.'

I wish, how I wish, that I could tell him about my crappy meeting at work, but I bite my tongue. With AS-Level Further Maths looming this summer, and three A-Levels as well as applications to universities looming next year, he's got enough to worry about.

I'm just putting the last clean bowl in the draining

rack, thinking about Colin's presentation, when the landline phone rings. The clock's showing 9.45pm, and calls at this time of night are not usually good news. My heartbeat speeds up.

I dry my hands hastily and answer the call. 'Hello?' I'm fully expecting my mother, but hoping she's called to complain about something on the TV. I feel my gut tightening. The hairs on my arms stand to attention.

It's not my mother on the other end. 'Gail Swanley?'

'It's Gill. Gill Swanley. Who is this?'

'My name's Jim. I'm a paramedic. We've just arrived at your mother's flat.'

I can hear my mother shouting something in the background. The paramedic's voice sounds as if it's in another room as he obviously puts his hand over the phone's speaker and shouts, 'Don't worry, I'll tell her to feed the cat.'

His voice becomes clearer again as he refocuses his attention on me. 'Sorry about that, Gill. Your mother's quite distressed. She's had a fall. Her neighbour, Sandra, found her and called us.'

Closing my eyes, I try to imagine the carnage: my defiant, increasingly frail mother, covered in bruises. 'Has she broken anything? Did she hit her head?' I ask. We've already had a broken nose, this side of Christmas, from when she face-planted onto the hard floor of the Glades shopping centre. Last summer, we had a sprained wrist and a chip out of her ankle. But head injuries are always a nightmare. She's concussed herself twice in the last eighteen months.

'No obvious signs of a bump to the head.' He sounds hesitant. 'But I have to say, she's not making much sense at the moment. Anyway, we're going to take her into the Princess Royal University Hospital in Farnborough. You familiar with the PRUH?'

'Yes. Like the back of my hand.' I exhale hard.

'Well, if you meet us in A&E . . .'

My heart's beating so fast and my breath is coming so short that I feel dizzy. *Not making much sense* doesn't sound good. 'Sure. I'll get my coat on.'

'And she's worried about the cat. Mr Tibbs.'

'Mr Tibbs has been dead for three years,' I say. 'There is no cat.' I run through the scenarios in my head that might cause Mum to talk gibberish: head injury, lack of oxygen, urinary tract infection, just about anything else. 'But tell her I'll see to Mr Tibbs, if it calms her down.'

I end the call with the usual mix of desperation and panic. I take a pack of fresh-mint chewing gum out of my handbag and pop one in my mouth to dispel the cloying tea taste.

'I'm coming with,' Zak says, appearing on the threshold to the kitchen. He was already in his pyjamas, but he's thrown a hoodie over the top – the baggy grey one that Dave used to go jogging in.

'No, you're not, young man. You've got school in the morning.'

'Don't care. Nan needs you, and you need me.'

I shake my head vehemently. 'No way, pal. She's my mother, not yours. Nan wouldn't want you ruining your beauty sleep on her account. It's not like this hasn't happened before, and you know the drill.' I check the inside of my handbag. Car keys and purse are present and correct. I only need my phone, and that's almost out of charge. Damn it. I look around for the charger. 'We'll wait hours to see the doctor. They'll do a million tests, and they'll either kick her out, or admit her for a couple of days and *then* kick her out. None of that needs a teenage boy's input.'

'But what if Nan . . . ?' His voice trails off.

'She won't,' I say, barrelling past him and marching to retrieve my coat from the newel post of the staircase. 'Your nan's too full of hate and mischief to shuffle off her mortal coil. She'll be fine.' I kiss his forehead. 'Get to bed. No gaming on your phone. Get some kip. Don't answer the door to strangers. If there's a fire, get out, call the fire brigade, and go over to Afshan's at number thirty-six.'

The roads have emptied out in earnest now, but for a noisy orange Lamborghini SUV in front of me that is also indicating to turn into the hospital car park. Watching the owner of the Lamborghini straddle two spaces, directly beneath a streetlight, I opt to park in the adjacent space. I'm aware there has been a spate of car break-ins in Farnborough of late, according to the local rag, and I figure car thieves will target him before looking twice at my old Volvo.

As I watch the Lamborghini owner lock his car and walk away, his flashy footwear glowing in the dark, my heart is thumping like a frustrated prisoner hammering on a cell door. I reason that this will not be the end for my mother, but I'm also aware that you just never know.

'I'm here for Lily Fielding,' I tell the woman on the A&E reception desk, who treats me to a disengaged gawp. 'She's been brought in by ambulance.'

'You a relation?' She speaks with an estuary twang, and I remember that Farnborough is a sizeable demographic jump away from London and into Kent proper.

'Daughter.'

The woman looks through some paperwork and yawns as she does so. 'Bay three.'

'Has she seen a doctor yet?'

'Bay three, like I said. Nurse'll give you an update.'

Hastening through to the NHS's equivalent of purgatory, past the bust-up, foul-smelling drunks and the raving madwoman in her dressing gown, and the Lambo driver, who is surprisingly sitting in a wheelchair, now wearing a neck-support collar that glows blue-white next to his spray-tanned skin, I eventually find my mother. She is in an entirely different bay, trying to pull a cannula out of the crook of her arm. She looks starry-eyed and bewildered. With her white hair in a matted bird's nest that frames her pinched and sallow face, she reminds me of Doc from *Back to the Future* – a lady Doc, who swapped the white coat for a Primark nightie. I feel a rush of tender love for this cantankerous yet increasingly vulnerable woman.

'Mum!'

She seems not to have noticed my arrival. 'Get this bloody thing out of me,' she yells at the male nurse who is trying to tape the cannula to her bruised, wrinkled skin. 'I know your game. You're trying to kill me.'

'Hold still, Lilian,' he says, appearing unfazed by my mother's outburst. 'I'm just trying to —'

'You're trying to poison me!' It's now that she spots me, standing at the foot of her bed. 'Ah, at last. You took your time. Tell this arsehole to leave me alone.'

The initial relief that she's at least alive and kicking dissipates quickly, leaving me with my stomach in embarrassed knots. 'There's no need to speak to the nurse like that, Mum. He's just looking after you.' I turn to the nurse. 'So sorry she called you that. I'm her daughter, Gill. Can you tell me what's going on with her?'

Mum glowers at the nurse as he finally secures the cannula.

The nurse gathers up his phlebotomy equipment and turns to me. 'Your mum's been admitted with a suspected urinary tract infection. She was quite delirious.'

'Has the doctor seen her yet? I mean it's the third time she's been carted off to A&E in a month. First time, it was a terrible lung infection, where she could barely breathe. Second time a fall. Now a UTI. Every time, you just prescribe her some new antibiotics that don't work, or patch her up and kick her out.'

I move to the other side of the bed and take Mum's hand into mine. She has the papery skin of the severely dehydrated. When I kiss her knuckles, I note that she already has that institutional smell about her of hand sanitiser and hospital laundry. My heart is a leaden weight in my chest now.

'Her ECG was a bit erratic. Her blood pressure was in her boots when the paramedics first attended, and it's still a bit lower than we'd like. Both of those things could be connected to a UTI. Her bloods and a urine sample will go off now. Should get the results in a couple of hours.'

'Yes, but what about the doctor?'

'Doctor's going to come and take a look at her when we've got the test results back,' the nurse says. 'There's a four- or five-hour wait, though, I'm afraid. We're very busy tonight.' He turns to my mother, raising his voice. 'Do you want an extra blanket, Lilian?'

Mum waves him away dismissively and curls her lip. I can hear her mutter beneath her breath that she's not bloody deaf.

'Can we get her a cup of tea?' I ask. But I already know the answer.

'Doctor's got to see her first, I'm afraid.' His smile is professional and curt.

Over the next four hours, my mother settles for a while, only to grow agitated again, rambling and ranting in spurts.

'They're a bunch of bastards in here. They're trying to kill me, Gill.'

'They're really not, Mum.' I stroke her furrowed, clammy brow. 'They're going to make you better.' I can feel the heat of the fever radiating off her. 'Didn't you realise you had a UTI? You never said a word. Weren't you in pain? I could have got you an appointment at the

GP, and all this could have been avoided. You've got to drink more!'

'They're hiding in the walls, you know. Watching me. They drill peepholes in the plaster.'

I exhale hard and pat her hand. 'Don't worry, Mum. I'll check out your walls when you get home.'

Sinking back in my visitor's chair, I wonder how I could have been so stupid as to have attended a gardeners' club meeting. Since when do I have the time or energy for anything other than this?

4

'You look tired, Gill,' Colin says the following morning.

I stifle a yawn and my eyes start to water. 'I was at the hospital until about 3am.'

'Oh?'

'My mum's been readmitted. A kidney infection this time. She was delirious as hell. Took 'til the small hours for them to diagnose her properly and then find her a bed on a ward. When they did, she couldn't settle.'

'Sorry to hear it.' Colin doesn't sound sorry, though he's giving me his well-meaning face, which is almost identical to the face he pulls when anybody says something he disagrees with in a meeting. 'Take as much time as you need.' His well-meaning expression falters. 'But obviously, we need you to be making a start on the new targets, so I'd like to see your plan to cut costs and raise productivity in the London and South-East region on my desk by lunchtime today, please.'

Plan? I wonder. *I'm the senior manager of a regional call centre. I'm paid to manage staff, not come up with grand fiscal plans. That's a director's job.* 'Isn't this just an exercise in sorting the good performers from the bad and retraining those who need it?' I ask. 'I don't have jurisdiction over anything else. I mean, the IT platform is about a billion years old and runs like a dog, but it's not like I can change that, is it?'

'We've been tasked with turning the company's bottom line from red to black, so just deliver your brief, please,' he says. 'Write me a deliverable plan. And bear in mind the deadline on this, Gill. You'd best be doing a quality check on colleagues' calls by the end of today.' He claps triumphantly. 'Let's go!'

I nod and force a smile. I took a promotion so that I could put some extra money away for Zak's college fund. But becoming the Grand Inquisitor and squeezing even more out of already overstretched and under-appreciated call-centre staff is an unpleasant and unwanted side-effect of taking on more responsibility.

My concentration sputters in and out all morning. With Mum in hospital, I have rather more serious issues to worry about than Chislehurst Green's bottom line. But I call the hospital and am at least reassured by the sister on the ward that Mum's started the antibiotics and is already sitting up in bed, verbally abusing the other women. In spite of my family drama, I manage to cobble together a plan for Colin. Retraining sub-par staff takes me to half a page, so I pad my waffle out with a justified whinge about our woeful IT set-up, which involves navigating through about five different, clapped-out, and incom-patible systems, to find various bits of information regarding the caller, their policy, their claims history, and maybe even their preferred brand of toothpaste. If they fixed the damn IT, our call-handling times would be halved at a minimum.

At 12.56pm, I knock on his office door and enter.

He's sitting behind his desk visibly wincing like a man in pain. 'You okay, Colin?' I ask. 'Only I've done the plan you wanted.' I brandish the two pages that say very little in 14-point font.

'Close the door,' he says.

'Oh? Sounds serious. Am I in trouble?'

He gestures that I should sit in the visitor's chair. 'I need to level with you, Gill.' He laces his fingers together, glances at his computer monitor. 'I've revisited the figures. Looks to me like our salary bill is just too high. The easiest way of balancing the books would be shedding at least ten staff from each team – ideally without the expensive redundancy package.' His gaze is fixed on me now.

'Er, is it legal to do that?' I ask.

'To do what? Have I suggested you do anything illegal?'

'Sacking people . . .'

'Did I say anything about *sacking* people?' He rolls his eyes. 'Look, we have a high turnover of call-centre staff as it is, so there's no reason why we can't just fail to replace the ones who hand in their notice voluntarily. And the ones who aren't up to scratch . . .'

'I put them on a warning? And then if they still don't brush up, they're out the door?' I know I'm a senior manager but I've only ever had to fire one member of my staff before, and it was so excruciatingly difficult that I opened a bottle of wine at 10am to stop myself from shaking.

'We have a legal route to letting go substandard staff. Use the routes available to you, Gillian.'

'And voluntary redundancy?'

'As a last option . . . because of the cost. Look, we have to make difficult decisions in business. I've got targets. You've got targets.' Colin is waving his hands around like a cornered politician now.

'But –'

'Just do your job, Gill.'

I am dismissed without further discussion. *Just do my job*, indeed!

By 2pm, I have downed a disappointing tuna sandwich and have actually spoken to Mum on the phone. She sounded groggy and complained about the hospital food but at least admitted that Mr Tibbs is long dead.

Now, I'm listening in on a call between a colleague and an elderly woman in Shropshire, who wants to know if the contents of her shed are included in her policy.

'Well, opportunist thieves have just stolen next door's lawnmower, you see. And I've got a good one. It's a Bosch. Only a year old. My husband bought it just before he died.' She sighs. 'They just lifted up her garden panels and walked –'

'Can I take your name, first line of your address, and date of birth, please?' Darren Loveday, the colleague fielding the call, sounds bored. He makes a clack-clacking noise. I'm fairly certain he's chewing gum.

'Well, I just gave all that to your colleague.' The old lady is clearly flustered.

'Policy number.' Clack-clack.

'I gave that to your colleague, too. And I gave it to the automated woman when I first connected. You know,

I've been on this call, going round the houses for almost twenty minutes!'

''Fraid I can't open your record without your details. I need you to clear the security questions before I can talk to you.' Clack-clack. 'Imagine if you was a fraudster, like phishing for information and that. Would you want me handing out your policy information and address without knowing it was you? 'Cause that's asking for trouble, right?' Darren is now apparently gaslighting the customer. 'And you could lose everything.'

'Oh, dear! Good Lord, I hadn't thought of it like that.' The old woman sounds rattled. Speaking in a deferential tone now, she gives her details, including her policy number.

Darren Loveday faffs around longer than is necessary to look at the terms of the woman's policy and then cuts her off *before* he's managed to tell her that her lawnmower would, in fact, be covered – minus the excess, which is probably the price of the damn lawnmower.

I make a note in my notebook that this call has taken way too long, and Darren Loveday, the masticating colleague, is a candidate for retraining, at the very least.

Summoning his line-manager, Faith, to an impromptu meeting, I close the meeting room door softly and play back the recording of the call to her. She looks horrified by the end; blushing and pressing her lips together.

'I'll put him in for retraining,' she says, looking down at her beige-varnished nails.

'Does he have previous form for this sort of thing?'
Faith bites her lip. Her heavily drawn-in eyebrows

twitch like slugs poked with a twig. 'I'll be honest, Gill, his attendance and punctuality aren't great. He keeps going off sick, but never long enough to warrant a sick note. And he can be quite . . . difficult.'

'Why didn't you come to me with this? Has HR been involved?'

'No, no. I had a couple of informal chats with him because I wanted to see if I could deal with it myself before I escalated it.'

Exhaling heavily, I realise what I need to do. 'Okay. I'm going to speak to the new HR manager, and get this Darren in for a chat this afternoon. The way he conducted that call went completely against corporate guidelines, so I'm going to put him on a formal warning. You'll have to be in on it too, Faith.'

Beneath the heavy makeup and her polyester beige skirt-suit, I can see her blanch and shrink at the prospect of this confrontation.

'It'll be fine,' I say. 'This is a customer-facing department. We can't have people in the job who talk to older women like they're idiots. We're managers. If we don't pull him up, we're not doing our jobs properly.'

I'm acting like I have no compunction in stepping up to be the rottweiler, but in truth, I have a complicated relationship with confrontation. My mother has always been a powder keg of a woman, prone to explode with little provocation, and as a child I would always follow my incredibly beta father's lead and just yield, apologise, take cover. Dave, from a family of melodramatic shouters, couldn't abide any friction in his home life, so we rarely argued as a result. Only perimenopause has changed my conflict-avoiding DNA. Get me on a now-irregular PMT day, when my obnoxious neighbour has blocked me in with his van, and I'll happily scorch him to a crisp with fiery words. But I haven't had a period in four months. There is no PMT to rely on today. And I'm existentially bone-tired.

Even as I'm fixing the HR meeting up with Darren Chewing-Gum, like Faith, I am already dreading this particular confrontation.

'Do you want to tell us a little bit about how you talked to a customer on a call earlier today, Darren?' I look down at my notebook, where I've noted the woman's details. 'Belinda Harris. She rang about whether or not her policy covers her shed contents.'

Darren Loveday slouches in his chair and scratches at a spot on his stubbled jaw. He tries to make eye contact with Janice from HR, who is sitting on the other side of Faith. He seems to be studiously avoiding my gaze. 'Yeah, well . . . I tried to help her, but there was a problem with the line or something. Think she put the phone down on me. She was quite aggressive, actually.' He shrugs.

'Okay, well I've listened to the call, and I know that you actually cut her off, Darren.' I try to think of diplomatic ways of saying he was obnoxious. 'I think you sounded a little brusque on the call.'

'What?' He looks at me blankly.

'Your tone was a bit sharp.'

At my side, Faith chimes in, 'I have to say, I agree with Gill. You did seem to make that lady jump through some extra hoops she didn't really need to, didn't you?' As Darren sits up straight and glares at her, shunting his chair back and spreading his knees wide, I can see the delicate bones in Faith's throat rise and fall as she swallows hard. Her words become little more than a whisper. 'Well, I suppose it's always good to remind customers about identity fraud.'

'I'm also concerned about your absences, Darren,' I say. 'You had a conversation with Faith about them. I see you took a total of ten days in September alone. Five in October. Nine in November. Every month, there's at least three days where you're off for some cold or muscle strain or eye test.' I stare at his sullen face, expecting a reaction, but none is forthcoming. 'There's a pattern of absence here, Darren. Your attendance is just not good enough and neither is your performance. So I'm instigating formal disciplinary proceedings and putting you on a performance improvement plan. If you don't brush up your act, I'm afraid we have to take it to the next stage.'

Darren leans forward and now locks eyes with each of us in turn – Faith, Janice from HR, and me. 'This feels like bullying,' he says.

I wonder if he's about to threaten us with some kind of discrimination suit – Loveday strikes me as the type to manipulate a bad situation to his advantage. Instead, he bursts into tears. Not just tears, but wracking sobs like a small child.

'Oh, Darren!' I say, feeling like someone has reached

inside my chest and squeezed my heart. I rummage in my trouser pocket and pull out three pieces of unused toilet roll that I offer to him. 'Er, there's no need to cry.' I glance at Janice from HR and see she remains stony-faced. On my other side, though, Faith looks like she's just watched a bag of kittens being drowned. 'I only said "if". *If* you don't brush up your act.'

Loveday looks at me with doleful, bloodshot eyes. 'Please, Gill! Don't sack me! I'll try harder. I *need* this job.' His nose is a fountain of woe, streaming into rivulets of tears like the tributaries of a great river.

'Take the bog roll, Darren.' My mouth is dry. My stomach is knotted.

He clasps his hands together in supplication. '*Please.* I'm the eldest of six and the only breadwinner in my family since my dad lost his leg in an industrial accident. My mum's got cancer, and . . . if you sack me, we'll lose our house and everything.'

'It – it's fine, Darren. Honestly. Please don't cry. It's fine.' I glance at Janice, note her thunderous scowl, and realise that letting Loveday off the hook is the polar opposite of fine.

5

'Now, for the beginners among you, sowing seeds is not difficult and is highly cost-effective,' Marjorie says, taking an old supermarket strawberry container and filling it with handfuls of compost from a black plastic trug. 'One can reuse these dratted plastic things to keep expenditure down.'

I'm back at the gardeners' club, in a bid to salvage my sanity. Work has turned into an Orwellian nightmare since Colin gave me a dressing-down for exhibiting 'weak management' in front of the junior staff. Zak has had yet another detention for forgetting yet another homework. Mum is back in her flat, her low blood pressure confirmed to be a symptom of her humdinging UTI, except now she's threatening to stop taking her antibiotics mid-course because, according to her, 'they're giving me wind in my toes'. I have become a caricature of an overstretched sandwich-generation woman, complete with steam coming out of my ears, which is why I am now watching somebody else's aged mother pushing compost with bulbous arthritic fingers into the corners of a strawberry container.

Gone is Marjorie's sour, disapproving expression from the meeting in the church hall. In its place is a beatific smile that seems to light up the large conservatory in which we're sitting. She's working at a sturdy, scarred wooden table, and I get the impression that the fragrant lemon trees, garlanded with early blossom, the banana palms, the birds of paradise plants, and the orchids that sit in pots around the periphery of the place or that hang from the glazed ceiling, fat with buds and floral promise, are replacements for family, long since moved on. Here in this humid conservatory, they feel like sentient beings, appraising our levels of horticultural haplessness as we learn at the knee of this plantswoman.

'First, one wets the compost just enough,' she says, sprinkling a fine shower of water on the surface of the compost, dispensed through a small watering can.

To my side, I hear Seth whispering to Phoebe, 'I bet her compost ain't been wet since analogue times!'

Phoebe's shoulders shudder with mirth, and the heady scent of the lemon blossom is replaced by a guff of patchouli. She shushes Seth but snorts loudly only moments later.

Marjorie looks up and eyeballs Seth. 'I may be old, but my hearing and mental acuity are undiminished.' Her gaze moves to Phoebe. 'And you two would do well to remember that you are guests in my home.' She looks to Mike Potato for support.

Seated to her right, he clears his throat. 'Absolutely, Marjorie.' He turns to the two youngest members of the group. 'Can we have a little decorum, please? I know you Gen-Zers or Millennials or whatever you are think you know it all, but you don't. So how about you show some respect?' He shuffles in his seat, face flushed and arms folded tightly, clearly unaware that Seth just whispered, 'Okay, Boomer,' for Phoebe's benefit.

Mike looks around at the rest of us. 'Actually, now might be an opportune moment to point out that Marjorie is using "Berisford's Black Gold" compost tonight, aren't you, Marj? Made by my own fair hands, of course.' He's grinning now, and the cage of his arms falls away to reveal a sweater that looks like it was knitted by his mother, in the dark. He holds his 'fair hands' up and shakes them, then pushes his glasses up his nose.

'Thank you, Michael,' Marjorie says. 'Yours is admittedly very nutrient-rich compost, though not as fine and crumbly as one's own. Tonight, I've taken the liberty of mixing your far coarser product with vermiculite to aid root growth of the seedlings.'

I glance to my right and catch sight of Neil, covering his mouth with his hand to conceal a smile. He catches my eye, then nudges me conspiratorially.

I feel in on the joke. Even Val, who is filling a cigarette paper with tobacco at the rear of the conservatory (much to the chagrin of a glaring Cath), glances over and winks at me. Is it possible I'm going to become part of something beyond my tiny family unit and my team at work?

Finally, the group settles, and Marjorie takes out a home-made packet of seed. She holds it aloft. 'These are nicotiana seeds. Flowering tobacco.' She turns to Mike. 'Michael?'

Mike brings up a photo on his tablet of the star-shaped flower. He lifts the tablet and turns it towards us

49

so we can all see what is being sown. There is a murmur of enthusiasm around the table.

'One harvested these seeds at the end of last year's growing season,' Marjorie says, waving at Mike to put the tablet down. This small-voiced dictator is in full command of our attention once more. 'They're half-hardy annuals and release the loveliest fragrance in the evening. The bees love them.' The wrinkles around her eyes deepen as she smiles, softening her features.

'Cool,' Phoebe says, nodding. 'Save the bees, man.' She makes the peace sign, and I am momentarily reminded of Zak, who makes the peace sign in almost every photo taken of him.

Marjorie sprinkles the tiny seeds onto the compost. 'Some seeds need to be covered with up to a quarter of an inch of compost. These do not. They need the light to germinate. There! One simply covers the strawberry punnet with clingfilm now, to stop the compost from drying out.' With practised hands, she tears off a sheet of clingfilm and wraps it tightly over the plastic container. 'Next, we put it on a shelf or windowsill in full sunlight to warm up, and in ten or so days' time, hey presto, we will be delighted by an array of tiny seedlings.' She looks momentarily puzzled. 'Although here we are, starting to sow for the growing season, when what we really ought to do is conduct a little detective work to ascertain what our nearest rivals are planning to sow. We can start with the Southwark Secateurs. I know Dotty Gloucester personally.' She locks eyes with me. 'I see you have a car, Gillian. You'll take me, won't you?'

'Eh? Take you where?' I blink hard, bewildered at this turn of events.

'To Dorothy Gloucester's house, of course.'

'Me?' I thumb myself in the chest. 'Why me?' I look around at the others, who are all studiously staring down at the sweet pea seeds they've already sown in cardboard toilet roll holders.

Marjorie tuts and rolls her eyes. 'Mike says his car's loaded up with . . . What was it?'

'Equipment,' Mike mumbles, turning red.

'Neil's car's in for servicing,' Marjorie continues. 'Phoebe and Valerie don't drive, and I can't abide the fabric softener that Seth uses. It rather brings on my hay fever.'

Seth smirks, presumably at the prim veteran churchgoer not knowing the difference between the smell of Lenor and marijuana.

Marjorie fixes me with her small hard eyes. 'So that leaves you, dear.'

'But I thought you drove. You've got a Honda Jazz on your drive.'

The lines around Marjorie's mouth harden. 'I'm afraid my ban does not expire for another two weeks.'

Seth and Phoebe snort with mirth.

'You're *banned*?'

'Ageism,' she says, closing her eyes emphatically. 'One would think that all the tomfoolery one sees on the roads from youngsters would keep the police busy.' She opens one eye and then the other, looking directly at Seth before switching back to me with a sarcastic smile.

'But apparently, driving sensibly at fifteen miles an hour is a danger to other road users.'

'You were also over the limit,' Val says.

Marjorie tuts and frowns. 'Communion wine hardly counts as alcohol, and I'd been *in church*, for heaven's sake! Doing *the Lord*'s work.'

'You told me you got caught trying to do a three-point turn on the slip-road onto the Sidcup bypass,' Mike says.

Whatever the truth behind Marjorie's ban, she merely waves his comment away and turns back to me. 'So you'll drive me to Dotty Gloucester's.'

'I'm sorry, but I can't. I've got too much on.' I think of my work and mumly commitments and how I must drop in on my own mother twice a day, every day, until I've managed to find her a part-time carer.

'Nonsense,' Marjorie says. 'We'll go tomorrow. Pick me up at seven thirty.'

The next evening, after a hellish day at work, I cook a rushed meal of bacon and mushroom pasta. I gobble mine down hastily, leaving enough in the pot for Zak and my mother to eat later, as she has agreed to stay over at ours tonight. This allows me to go out, guilt free, while she and Zak enjoy quality time together, shouting dictionary advice at Susie Dent and answers at Rachel Riley in *Countdown*. At least Zak will ensure my old lady eats and hydrates properly.

At 7.40pm, I find myself pulling up outside Marjorie's house. Illuminated by the old-fashioned carriage lanterns affixed to the front of her house, only now do I see that her Honda Jazz is covered in bird droppings and a film of tree sap, in line with it not having been driven in a year.

Marj is already waiting for me in her porch, wearing a lavender zip-up old-lady anorak over a brick-coloured pleated skirt and walking boots. On her head, she's wearing one of those see-through plastic rain bonnets that I thought had been made extinct back in the early 1980s.

She emerges, pointing a tightly rolled umbrella at my Volvo.

'Onwards!' she shouts. 'Tonight we will gather planting intelligence from a Dulwich Village delinquent.'

On the journey from Bromley into South-East London, Marjorie regales me with tales of Dotty Gloucester's varying scandals: a lifetime of showing too much 'bosom'; a rumour of a teenage pregnancy, courtesy of a schoolboy heartthrob called Donald, that resulted in a 'prolonged stay in the countryside' from which she returned alone; allegedly poor garden hygiene and a resulting rose bed full of black spot.

'You'll see when you meet her,' Marj says as we breach the boundary of the A-listers' enclave of Dulwich Village. 'You can quite imagine she's the sort of woman who can be a patron of the Golden Trowel Gardening Association and yet have the temerity to compete for the Golden Trowel herself. Brazen! She even wears leopard print to church. Hard to believe it, but Dorothy Gloucester and I went to school together.'

We pass the spires of the stately private school, Dulwich College, which I remember is responsible for educating P. G. Wodehouse, Raymond Chandler, and Nigel Farage.

'Take the next left.'

I am instructed to pull up outside a grand, double-fronted Georgian villa. 'Is this it?' I ask, staring at the floodlit splendour of the stuccoed house and the perfectly symmetrical knot gardens out front, which are visible behind the tall wrought-iron fencing.

'Don't be fooled by the grandeur. Dotty Gloucester's all fur coat and no knickers. I'm told a gardener maintains that box hedging.'

We get out of my Volvo and press the buzzer at the gate. Nobody answers.

'Did you check she'd be home?' I ask.

Marjorie frowns. 'Yes. I called her yesterday, after you lot had gone.' She presses the buzzer and shouts at the intercom, 'DOROTHY GLOUCESTER! MARJORIE BLOOM HERE!'

When no reply comes, I suggest Marj calls her, but Marjorie merely tuts at me. 'At our age, an arrangement is an arrangement, even if one is a louche hussy.' She pushes the security gate. 'Ooh, I say.'

The gate swings open.

Listing slightly to starboard, Marjorie marches on scrawny, bandy legs up the pathway that bisects the knot garden. 'Follow me, Gillian! I suspect Dotty is entertaining a man and has forgotten all about us.' On the doorstep, she knocks smartly on the grand black front door, but it swings open. The lights are on. 'Oh?' She takes a step inside. 'Dorothy! Dorothy?'

'I really don't think we should go inside,' I say.

Too late. Marj is already striding down the hallway, which is decorated with flattering photographic portraits of Dotty Gloucester, taken throughout her career. 'Oh, Dotty! Dotty! DOROTHY! WHERE ARE YOU, DOROTHY?'

I feel uncomfortable, prowling around the old-fashioned but expensively furnished house of a complete stranger. 'Marjorie, she might have nipped next door to a neighbour's or gone to put the bins out. I really don't think we should be trespassing like this.'

'Nonsense.' Marj turns on her heel once she's given the ground floor the once-over. 'At our age, without well-meaning inquisitive souls, one might collapse and be found only weeks later, being slowly devoured by one's own cats.'

Thinking back to my mother's all too regular collapses in the last year, I concede that she has a point. We explore upstairs, which is in darkness until we turn on the lights. Marjorie seems miffed that there is no evidence of showbiz excess or unsavoury lifestyle anywhere to be found, but we are both nonplussed that there is no sign of Dotty Gloucester either.

Back downstairs, standing in the gleaming but somewhat outdated designer kitchen, Marjorie gazes blankly at her own reflection in the tall windows that back onto the garden. It is pitch-black outside, and a misting of drizzle clings to the glass.

'Maybe she's in the garden,' I suggest. I walk to the back door and find that though it's closed, it too is unlocked. 'She's bound to have a greenhouse or shed or something if she's a gardening guru.'

Behind me, Marj harrumphs. 'Guru, indeed.'

The chill air is sharp but fresh. I look around the pitch-black garden, trying to get my bearings. Blinking hard, I spot a dim seam of light coming from a structure at the bottom of the garden – a large shed. 'There you go! She's out here.'

Marjorie pushes past me and marches towards the shed. 'Yoo-hoo! Dorothy! It is I, Marjorie Bloom. We have an appointment.'

I follow, jogging to catch up with Marjorie's brisk pace. By the time she reaches the shed, where the door is slightly ajar, I am right behind her.

Pushing the door open, Marjorie begins to speak. 'Ah, there you . . .' Then there is a brief pause before she lets out a piercing shriek of alarm.

As Marjorie crumples against the threshold, I lay eyes on Dorothy Gloucester and clasp my hand to my mouth. 'Oh, bloody Nora.'

Marj doesn't even try to correct my language, because she, like me, is aghast at the sight of the beloved Radio 4 presenter seated on a chair pushed up against the wall, bent slightly over a rickety old table. Her skin is a deathly pale yellow-grey. She stares blankly ahead. Her lips are blistered. By her hand is a mug containing either tea or coffee.

'Is she dead?' I ask.

'J-just look at her! Of course she is,' Marjorie whimpers. 'Good Lord in heaven.'

I take note of the items on the table beside Dotty: one sheet of pink writing paper, a fountain pen with the lid off, and a small brown bottle bearing a yellowed label so faded that I can barely see what's written on it, but I do make out the ghost of a skull and crossbones. 'Ooh, what's that?' I point at the bottle.

Marjorie puts her reading glasses on and peers at the label. 'Paraquat,' she says. 'A herbicide. If she's ingested it . . .' I see her look at the mug and then grimace at Dotty's blistered mouth. 'What a gruesome way to go.'

I run my tongue over my teeth, staring at the pink paper and fountain pen, trying to look at the dead woman in the chair as little as possible. 'Maybe she took her own life, and the poison worked too fast for her to write a note . . . assuming she did swallow the contents of that bottle. Or is this something else dressed up as suicide?'

Inhaling sharply, Marjorie presses her hand to her mouth. She shakes her head. 'I can't bear it.'

'We mustn't touch anything,' I say, shivering involuntarily. 'Not here. Not in the house. Not 'til we know what's gone on.' I retrieve my phone from my handbag with trembling fingers. 'I'm calling the police.'

6

'Can I ask what you ladies were doing here?' Detective McGowan asks us, poised to write in her pad. She is in her late thirties, I'd guess: short haired and smartly dressed in a sober trouser suit. A no-nonsense type. I feel like a cell on a slide beneath her microscope and I catch a glimpse of how my staff must feel when they find out their calls have been monitored for signs of incompetence or some other misdeed.

'We were here to pick Dorothy's brains about a gardening competition,' Marjorie says, still visibly trembling. She fiddles ineffectually with the knot of the rain bonnet beneath her chin. 'We had an appointment, and she didn't answer when we buzzed the intercom. The gate was open. The door was open. The lights were on, but the house was like the *Mary Celeste*. Clearly, something was amiss.'

I instinctively reach out to help her with the knot. 'Here, let me –'

Marjorie swipes my hands away. 'One is quite capable of removing one's own headgear, young lady.' She wrenches the rain bonnet off and slaps it onto the kitchen breakfast bar at which we're sitting. '*Thank* you.'

The detective regards Marjorie with narrowed eyes. 'Did you know Miss Gloucester well?'

'We are . . . *were* . . . both in loosely affiliated gardening groups, and I've been moving in the same church flower-arranging circles as her for around . . . fifteen years, I'd say.' She leans towards the detective and lowers her voice. 'But Dorothy was not your average flower-fancier. These showbusiness types lead decadent lives, you know. One's hardly surprised she's met an untimely end.'

'Should we be speaking ill of the dead?' I ask.

Marjorie merely tuts in response.

'One of the lines of inquiry we're pursuing is that she took her own life,' Detective McGowan says. 'Was she depressed at all, that you know of?'

'Not that I'm aware,' Marj says. 'You might ask her co-conspirators in the Southwark Secateurs if you really want to know. Or her luvvie friends at the BBC. They might have a clearer picture of her mental instability.'

'So she *did* have mental health issues?'

'One didn't say that. But one wouldn't rule it out. Dorothy Gloucester was an unknowable spinster who had amassed a large personal fortune and adored her minor celebrity status. She saw no issue in being on the judging panel of the Golden Trowel Gardening Association Awards *and* being a competitor in her local chapter, despite the obvious conflict of interest. Who knows what was going on in the head of a woman who thought red and pink pelargoniums go together?'

The detective's expression is inscrutable. She scribbles something down and then flicks back through her notebook. 'Do you know anything about a substance called paraquat?'

Marjorie nods enthusiastically. 'Yes, dear. It's a weed-killer, and very effective at that. Banned in Britain a good fifteen years ago or more.' She screws her eyes shut and shakes her head. 'Health and safety gone mad, if you ask me.'

'So, you think it's a case of poisoning?' I ask. I clarify my comment before Detective McGowan thinks I'm somehow responsible for Dotty Gloucester's demise. 'Only, I noticed she had blistered lips and put two and two together when we spotted the bottle and the half-drunk cup of whatever.' I blush.

'How about you leave the police work to me, eh?' She raises an eyebrow. 'We won't know for sure how Miss Gloucester died until there's been a post-mortem examination and an analysis of the contents of that cup. Could have been suicide, could have been an accident, could be murder. But *if* poisoning is involved, I'd like to understand how a bottle of herbicide, banned over a decade ago, came to be next to Miss Gloucester's body in that shed.' She turns to Marjorie. 'Is it common for a gardening enthusiast to have a banned substance in their garden shed?'

Marj pauses momentarily and chews her bottom lip. 'Obviously, *I* don't have paraquat on my shelves. My Bromley Botanists are *fastidious* about horticultural hygiene.'

'But might Miss Gloucester have had such a chemical in among her gardening supplies?'

'Yes, yes. Older gardeners often keep contraband weedkillers and such like. You know, the regulations change so frequently that one would have no decent weapons in one's gardening arsenal at all if one discarded every bottle and tub deemed toxic or environmentally unfriendly by the foetuses that run the Department for Environment, Food and Rural Affairs.'

Detective McGowan nods and shuts her pad emphatically. 'Thank you, ladies. I might be in touch with further questions.' She gets to her feet, asks a constable to show us out but pauses, turns back to us, and holds a finger up like Columbo. 'One last thing. Do you know who Miss Gloucester's next of kin might be?'

I look at Marj, but she's shaking her head.

'As far as I know, she didn't really have anyone,' she says. She smiles sadly. 'All that success and she was totally alone. Her parents died decades ago. She never married. Her similarly childless sister passed away during Covid. Dorothy Gloucester had nothing but fans and fickle friendships . . . as far as I know. Perhaps you might try her agent? I presume she had one.'

The detective nods. 'Don't touch anything on the way out. Until we've established the circumstances surrounding Miss Gloucester's death, we have to treat the house and garden as a potential crime scene.'

'How will we find out what happened to her?' I ask.

'If we open an investigation, I'm afraid I won't be able to discuss the details of a live case with you. If it's suicide or accidental death, there's bound to be a report and an obituary in the papers, given she was famous. I'm very sorry for your loss.'

At last, we are allowed to leave. As we are escorted

through the hallway, past a bunch of forensics techni-
cians in white jumpsuits, coming just as we are going,
I can feel a headache start to thump away over my left
temple.

In the car, I start the engine to demist the windscreen,
puff air out of my cheeks, and grip the steering wheel in
a bid to stop my hands from shaking.

I turn to Marjorie. 'You okay?'

She's rummaging in her handbag. She pulls out a
hip flask, unscrews the lid, and takes a swig. She gasps.
'Better than Dotty Gloucester, at least.' She offers me
the hip flask and then takes another swig when I shake
my head.

I shrug. 'Well, that detective wasn't keen to commit to
anything, was she? Not even a cause of death.' I take out
my phone and google 'paraquat poisoning'. Checking
the results, I turn my screen to Marjorie and show
her image after image depicting people with blistered
mouths. Just like Dotty's. 'But sometimes, two plus two
makes four, right?'

Marjorie winces. 'Ugh, do put it away!'

I pocket my phone. 'And Dotty was about to write a
letter, judging by the writing materials on the table. How
could that have been anything but a suicide note, given
she's now dead?'

'It could just as easily have been a "Gardening To-Do"
list,' Marjorie says, raising a finely plucked eyebrow.

'Oh, come on! On pink paper? With a fountain pen?'

'Dotty was an ostentatious type who might well have
written her "To-Do" list on pink paper. And she was far

63

too pleased with herself to take her own life. Everyone in the GTG Association was in thrall to her; all the other church flower arrangers deferred to her, and she adored every moment. She was happy as a sandboy.'

'But I don't think depression works like that,' I say. 'People hide it well.'

'I can make enquiries in our mutual gardening and flower-arranging circles regarding her recent state of mind,' Marjorie says, tapping the side of her nose. 'But I'd be extremely surprised if she took her own life.' Her face wrinkles in obvious thought. 'And I can't see this being a tragic accident either. She would have known to keep something as pernicious as paraquat well away from her drink.' She shakes her head and sighs deeply. 'It's all too unseemly for words, and sitting in your uncomfortable car isn't going to help either us or Dorothy, so let's get out of this dratted inner London hellhole. Take us back to Bromley!'

7

Shaken, I drop Marjorie back and head home, where Zak and my mother have been entertaining one another for the last couple of hours. When I see my little family, I feel tears prick the backs of my eyes.

'Ooh, am I glad to see you two?' I hold my arms out for a hug. 'What a grim evening I've just had.'

'That bad?' Zak asks, getting up from the footstool he's been sitting on.

'You won't believe me when I tell you.' I embrace my son tightly. 'You been looking after your nan?' I plant a smackeroo on his cheek. He smells of buttery toast.

'We watched recordings of *Countdown*,' he says. He then points to the backgammon board that's on the card table by her armchair. 'And she's been slaughtering me at backgammon.'

My mother rattles dice in a cup and throws them onto the board wearing a look of triumph. 'I've been teaching the boy some tricks. We played poker for matches, too.'

'Mum! Please don't teach my son how to gamble.'

'I'll do what I like. I'm a grown-up.' She frowns at me. 'What's got into you? You look like a bulldog sucking on a wasp.'

I relate the tale of finding Dotty G dead in her super-shed.

'Her from the radio?' Mum asks. 'Never did like her. All tits and tambourines.'

'Well, there's no need to be unpleasant, because she's dead now.' I get to my feet and head to the kitchen, carrying the dirty plate that Zak had left on the floor beside him. There is a bad smell of burnt food. Detritus is strewn across the worktop like one of those models of a city used by architects and town planners, except this megatropolis of filth is rendered in dirty crockery, cookware, and glasses, stacked in teetering piles. 'Zachary, come here please!'

Zak dutifully bounds into the kitchen. He looks blankly at the mess.

I point. 'What is this?'

'What?'

'I made dinner for you and Nan before I left. How have you managed to go through almost every pot, pan, and glass in the kitchen? Why is the mixer out . . . and there's flour everywhere?'

My son rolls his eyes. 'Oh, yeah. Nan said pasta makes her parp like a trombone, so we did some "chaos cooking" with what was in the fridge instead. We made this pie thing, except it wasn't really a pie? And it sort of stuck to the oven and got a bit burnt, but it was okay because it tasted alright. And I know I should have cleaned up, but I forgot about that, too.' He pulls a contrite face. 'Sorry.'

I'd already filled the dishwasher before going out to Marjorie's, hoping to add only their pasta bowls and cutlery before switching it on. There is no room in the machine for an entire kitchen's worth of dirty crocks.

66

Sighing, I start to empty the stacked sink so that I can fill it with hot soapy water. 'What happened to the pasta?'

'Nan gave it to next door's dog.'

'*What?* You let her chuck my perfectly good home-cooked food? And then you used every pot in the cupboard to make . . . God-knows-what?'

'I told you. It was like pie.'

'"Like pie"?' I shake my head in disbelief. 'So, you made "Like Pie", *didn't* wash up, and then you returned to the scene of the crime to make toast, but you didn't notice the kitchen looks as if it's been hit by a tornado? Honestly, Zak. You're seventeen!'

'We got busy playing backgammon.'

'Just get a clean tea towel, assuming we can find one. I'll wash, you dry.'

We restore order and then head back into the living room. 'Mum, what in God's name did you do to my kitchen?'

My mother is gazing at the blaring TV. I grab the remote control and turn it off.

Finally, she looks up at me, defiant. 'All I was doing was making my grandson something proper to eat. If that's going to be your attitude, young lady, you can take me home.'

I notice that she still has the ghost of a black eye from her collapse on the landing. She looks so small and vulnerable in that moment, and I am so saddened by the thought of that lonely, dead old lady, Dotty Gloucester, that I want to hug my mother and keep her safe from the world. 'Forget it. It's fine. I want you to stay. I can't bear the thought of you struggling in that flat without any company or support unless I drop round. In fact, come and live with us, here.' Hang on. What the hell am I offering?

My mother glares up at me. 'Do fuck off, Gillian. I'm not a pigeon with a broken wing that you can play nursemaid to. I'm an adult woman who likes my own company and independence.'

'At least let me get a carer in for you a couple of times a week to help you get in and out the bath and tidy up a bit . . . have a chat, maybe help you make lunch. I'll find the money somehow.'

'I don't need your pity.' Mum scowls at me. 'I'm no charity case.'

'I was only trying to be considerate.'

By way of reply, my mother gives me a two-fingered salute – the perfect end to a perfect day: I'm *persona non grata* at work, my son is all at sea in sixth form, I've seen my first dead body since Dave died, and my mother's getting harder to look after and to love. I don't need a therapist to tell me I've been spinning too many plates for too long. My head feels like it's melting. Maybe I should put the kibosh on the gardeners' club before I get too involved.

I'm momentarily tempted to smoke one of my emergency cigarettes but realise that won't solve anything. Instead, I take up the jiffy bag that arrived in the post earlier but which I haven't until now had time to open. Inside are colourful seed packets, which I have no memory of ordering. 'Oooh, flowers!'

There are lavatera, with their candyfloss-pink, trumpet-shaped flowers; gerbera – the giant daisies that come in a nursery-school paint palette of tomato reds, hot pinks, and oranges; fluffy purple asters, which provide autumn colour (according to Marjorie); and dainty convolvulus blue ensign, which promise to be an electric shade of blue that will dazzle the bees. There are also packs of mangetout and peas. Some are for sowing now, in trays indoors, and some are for direct sowing outside, later in the season.

'Mind if I go outside to clear my head?' I ask Zak and my mother. 'Might do a bit of pottering in the garden. Recentre my chi, and all that crap.'

'Go for it,' Zak says.

'Suit yourself,' Mum says, moving her counter.

Leaving Zak and Mum to continue to bond over backgammon, I change into an old pair of leggings and a loose long-sleeved T-shirt, don Dave's old DIY hoodie, and go outside to clear my head.

The chill of winter still clings to Bromley, despite the fact that early spring is upon us. Night has fallen now too. Back in the depths of January, I'd tried to imagine my sad back garden – ramshackle shed and 1970s concrete slab paving plus a square of weed-infested, overgrown grass, marbled with cat shit from next door's ginger tom – relandscaped as a cruciform, Mediterranean arrangement. I pictured rectangular raised beds with a standard rose tree in the middle of each, encased by railway sleepers and edged with lavender or even miniature box hedging, if I can afford it. Shingle paths will crunch beneath our sandalled feet in summer.

In my head, it is an idyll in miniature, already blooming and fruiting with the seeds and plants I've bought. In reality, all I've managed so far has been to pile up the turf at the side by the fence in what Zak terms a 'midlife-crisis mud mound'. I've at least spray painted the four rectangles and built up the earth where the raised beds will be.

Tonight, in the glare of the security lights, I determine to work through my stress by planting the standard rose trees – four bare roots, ordered from an online supplier, which are currently sitting in a trug full of icy water by the back step. The instructions said I had to leave them soaking for twelve hours, and here they still are, three days later.

'Always a dollar short and a day late, Gill,' I say to myself.

From the shed, I take out the spade, the rake, and some thick rubber-coated electrician's gloves. I carry everything to the back door, leaning the tools against the house. Taking the kitchen scissors I'd brought outside with me, I cut the string that binds the trees into a bundle. 'Ow, damn it.' A thorn has plunged into the pad of my thumb. I squeeze the wound to check for a splinter and wipe the blood onto my fleece. 'Gloves! Bloody gloves!' I don the gloves and finally separate the rose trees.

I start to dig the heavy clay in the centre of what will be the first bed. I've read that rose roots need a hole well over a foot deep, and the bare roots are enormous, like the trailing, tangled locks of some swamp creature.

As I dig, I wonder about Dorothy Gloucester's demise. If the poisoning wasn't an accident, and it turns out that she hadn't been depressed, as Marjorie insists, it must surely be murder. Yet what sort of idiot would leave their murder weapon on show for the police to find?

My spade's progress is stopped by a dead old tree root from next door's long-since removed leylandii. I reach down and yank with all my might, growling with exertion until it comes free. 'They were dressing it up to look like suicide, weren't they?' I tell the piece of root in my hand before casting it aside. I look up at the moon, imagining Dave sitting on its surface, looking down at me, no doubt wondering what the hell I'm doing, gardening at night.

'Why would you kill someone and make it look like suicide?' I ask him. 'Maybe because you were known to your victim and didn't want the police to start digging, in case they suspected you?' I feel more questions bubbling up, but I shake my head in a bid to dispel them and the notion of Dave as the man in the moon. 'I just can't get involved. This is ridiculous. I've got my own fish to fry.'

I continue to dig, and my thoughts turn to Colin and my targets. I desperately need the paycheque and security that Chislehurst Green offers. I've worked too hard to have my tedious, soul-destroying career snatched away from me, just because I'm terrible at firing people.

'Confront Colin tomorrow,' I counsel myself. 'Fight your corner, Gill Swanley. Nobody else is coming to save the day.'

Eventually, I have dug four deep holes for the roses.

Surveying the muddy scene, I realise that I can't do the next bit unassisted.

I rouse my son from his backgammon. 'Zak, will you come out here and give me a hand with this, please?'

He appears at the back door, grimacing at the holes. 'You've been out here for an hour and a half, and all you've done is dig four holes?'

'In the dark! I'd say that's pretty impressive.'

'Mum, you're mental.'

Passing him the gardening gloves, I wrap my hoodie sleeve over my hand and grab a tree, thrusting it towards him. 'You hold it up straight while I plant it. Right?'

'I'll do it for a tenner.'

'You'll do it for free, because I'm big, and you're small, and last time I looked, I'm the boss of you,' I say, realising that he is, in fact, about five inches taller than me these days. 'Cheeky little sod.'

Zak grins and takes the tree from me. 'What kind of plant is this?' He holds the stem straight.

'It's called a Princess Anne rose. It should be covered in big deep pink roses, come summer. They're supposed to smell nice, too.'

Once I've spread out the roots, I remove a bag of mycorrhizal fungi from my pocket and start to scatter some of the white grains over the roots.

'What does that crap do?' he asks.

'It's fungus,' I say, trying to recall what I'd read about it on the rose grower's website. 'Apparently, it attaches itself to the rose's root system and helps transport nutrients to the plant.'

Zak's face lights up in the glare of the security light. 'A symbiotic relationship!'

I nod. 'Something like that. Val from gardeners' club says plant scientists are only just beginning to understand the important role that underground networks of fungus play in forests and that. Apparently, they help the trees communicate with each other when there's a threat.'

'Wicked.' There is genuine enthusiasm in my son's eyes. 'So, like, fungus is the AI of the plant world, and we're all going to get taken over and get our brains eaten by giant mushrooms, like in *The Last of Us*?'

'Just hold the sodding tree, Zachary. You need to spend less time online.'

Before long, we have planted all four rose trees and back-filled the holes. Zak has hammered wooden stakes into the soil, and I have cuffed the trees' slender stems to the supportive stakes. I firm the loose soil with my foot, taking care to level the soil off at the place where the tree has been grafted onto a wild rose rootstock. Val told me that bit is important. I water the base of each tree thoroughly.

'There. Job done.'

Zak has gone in, so I stand back and admire my handiwork, alone in the glare of the security light. What I now need are some climbers around the edges to clothe the bare fencing. Perhaps Clematis armandii or Jasminum officinale, both of which are supposed to smell amazing. Maybe I'll plant some Hydrangea Annabelle by the kitchen window, like they always have tumbling in giant beds, beneath the windows of the posh houses on the way to Chislehurst train station.

By the time I've finished, I feel much calmer and more resolute. I go inside and scrub the dirt from my hands and beneath my fingernails.

'Are you there?' Mum says, rounding on me as I stand at the kitchen sink, pulling garden detritus out of my hair. 'I want a word.'

I turn to her. 'I thought you were watching a film. Shouldn't you be resting?'

She lays her hand on my forearm. 'That carer you mentioned.'

'Yeah?'

'As long as you let me vet her first, I suppose it wouldn't do no harm to have someone coming in to give me a hand.'

I place my hand on hers, feeling my spirits soar with relief. 'Great. You've made the right decision, Mum.' I lean over and kiss her on the cheek. 'I'll line someone up.'

She licks her thumb and starts to wipe at my cheek. 'Come here, girl. You've got half the garden on your face.'

It could be a tender moment, but she notices me flinching involuntarily at the sensation of her spitty thumb landing on my cheek.

She tuts and shakes her head. 'I don't know why I bother, you heartless cow.' She turns away from me and shuffles back off towards the living room.

'I didn't mean anything by it, Mum,' I call after her. 'I just, I've never liked the sensation of –'

'Shove it where the sun don't shine, Gillian!'

I sigh, deciding that Dotty's demise and my various overcommitments aren't enough to stop me from gardening with the Bromley Botanists. With so much stress in my life, I acknowledge that I need them more than they need me.

8

'Listen up, turkeys,' Val says as she walks into the next meeting of the gardeners' club, where the rest of us are already assembled in Marjorie's enormous greenhouse. She's brandishing a copy of the *Guardian*. 'There's a report on Dotty Gloucester.'

Marjorie follows behind her, dressed in brightly coloured dungarees. 'One has already read a comprehensive reportage about her in today's *Telegraph*,' she says, closing the greenhouse door behind her.

Though the club hasn't assembled in person since Marjorie and I found Dotty's body, we have been discussing our grim discovery and the strange circumstances surrounding her death on our little Bromley Botanists' WhatsApp group. We're not the only ones, either. Marjorie says the entire amateur horticulturalist grapevine is apparently rife with speculation about how Dorothy Gloucester met her end.

Now Val flings her copy of the *Guardian* onto Marj's scarred old pine table, around which we're all seated like enthusiastic Biology students awaiting the start of a plant science practical. 'So you'll have read it weren't suicide?'

Marjorie takes her place at the head of the table. 'In the *Telegraph*, it said the coroner reported an "open verdict".'

'How can it be open?' Cath asks. 'Didn't you say there was a bottle of poison on the side and blistering around her mouth?'

Nodding enthusiastically, with all eyes on her, Marjorie has become the group's Miss Marple. 'There were indeed traces of paraquat in her coffee,' she says. 'I don't think the sinister nature of her death was ever really being called into question.' Marjorie fixes Cath with a hard stare. 'But there's clearly no evidence either way that confirms accident, suicide, or murder. That is the point of an *open* verdict, is it not?'

'Did you find out anything from Dotty's pals about the state of her mental health?' I ask.

Marjorie shakes her head. 'Nobody I've spoken to thinks Dorothy was suicidal. She was planning for the growing season and the Golden Trowel competition with her usual exuberance and bombast. Which is as I suspected. What I do know though . . .' Here, she treats us to a mischievous grin. '. . . is that the Southwark Secateurs have pulled out of the Golden Trowel competition entirely.' She claps. 'Praise be!'

'An official year of mourning?' Mike asks, pushing his glasses up his nose.

'Indeed,' Marjorie says, still beaming and rocking back and forth on her heels. 'They're apparently too bereft to compete, which will have Dotty spinning in her grave, since she was one of the most competitive women I've ever met. But this means that not only will Dotty's funeral be a rather more palatable affair than I'd anticipated –'

'Palatable?' Cath asks. 'Since when was a funeral palatable?'

Marjorie's smile falters. 'Well, we won't be putting hexes on one another during the wake, will we? If Southwark isn't competing, there's no bad feeling.' The smile returns, though I'm sure I can see the uncertainty behind her eyes. 'But it also means the only real challenge we now face for the Golden Trowel is the Croydon Diggers and Dibbers.' She turns to Val. 'Does that left-wing rag of yours mention Dotty's will?'

'Hey! *I* read the *Guardian*,' Neil says, twirling his moustache. 'Less of the "rag" please.'

'The *Guardian*? Left wing?! You're joking, aren't you? It's practically Tory propaganda, man,' Phoebe says, looking to Seth for a reaction. 'You can't trust mainstream media.'

Cath presses her hands to her ears. 'Oh, here we go . . .'

Before an argument can break out, I rap on the side of my teacup with my dibber. 'Er, can we let Marjorie get a word in edgewise, please?' Everybody looks at me as though I've been sniffing Jeyes Household Fluid, but I feel invested in Dotty Gloucester's death now. I lock eyes with Marjorie. '*Do* you know what was in her will?'

Marjorie holds her *Telegraph* up triumphantly. 'Yes, I do. And what's more, it has bearing on each and every one of us in this greenhouse.' She pauses dramatically, casting her gaze over us, one by one.

'Go on, then,' Mike says. 'Spit it out.'

79

'Dorothy Gloucester owned a golf course on the fringes of *Weybridge*,' Marjorie says, clearly looking for our reactions, as if we're all supposed to see this news as the terrific gossip it apparently is.

'So?' Seth says.

She rolls her eyes. '*So?!* Weybridge is one of the most expensive areas in Surrey, and what was an arable farm that had been in Dotty's family for generations . . . well, Dotty and her sister, Florence, turned the farm into a golf club once the area became chi-chi in the 1990s. I hear they charge astronomical membership fees because the locals can easily afford to pay them.' She tuts and points at Seth. '"Be on your guard against all kinds of greed; life does not consist in an abundance of possessions." Luke 12:15.'

'So?' Seth says again. 'Yo, Marj, man, can we get on with the dibbing and whatnot, yeah? Only I got to get back for a certain time.'

'Patience, young man!' Marjorie snaps her fingers at him. She quickly reverts to Miss Marple mode and looks around at the rest of us. 'The point is, Dotty had no surviving heir, so this golf course – prime land worth tens, if not hundreds of millions – is to change hands in a rather unusual way.' Her lips twitch into a smile as she flings the newspaper over to me, almost hitting me in the head with it. 'Read it aloud, Gillian.'

I take up the *Telegraph*, which is open on the page of the obituary. I scan through the details of Dotty's glittering career.

'There. The second to last paragraph.' Marjorie points at the spot with her arthritic index finger.

I start to read aloud: "'In a legacy befitting a long-standing patron of the Golden Trowel Gardening Association, ownership of the highly exclusive Chequered Lawns Golf Club will pass to this year's winner of the Golden Trowel Award for best community gardening club. Miss Gloucester stipulated, as one of the conditions of winning, that the golf club be converted back into a farm, where organic flowers must be grown for supply to the UK's florists. The farm must be open to the public several times per year at no cost. Members of the winning GTG Club may pay themselves a modest salary, but all net profits must be donated to Miss Gloucester's favourite environmental charities.'"

I puff air out of my cheeks. 'Blimey.'

The others all gasp in unison.

'That's like, totally sick,' Phoebe says, starry-eyed.

'That's a bit better than ten thousand and a weekly feature in *Wise* magazine,' Mike says, grinning. 'I wonder what a "modest salary" might look like . . .' His voice trails off, and his grin dissipates.

'That's a bit of a poisoned chalice,' Cath says. 'If *we* won, it would be way too much of a commitment for me. I'm on a sabbatical right now, but I go back to my surgery full time in September. I've got overheads and a Hippocratic oath to consider. I can't give up treating Bromley's sick and injured to become a bloody farmer.' She looks to Val, at her side. 'Could you make a commitment like that?'

Val shrugs. 'I ain't got nothing else on my plate, but there's no mention of where the money's coming from to convert a golf club to a farm. You'd need cash to set up, wouldn't you? Think about it! Earth-moving equipment, a couple of tractors and all the kit, stock, fertiliser, marketing budget to reach the florists. Way more than ten thou or whatever they normally give as the cash prize.' She pokes at an aerial-view photo in Marjorie's paper of the Chequered Lawns Golf Club. 'Don't matter that the land's worth a king's ransom if you ain't got no cash flow. And I sure as hell don't have any life savings. I just about scratch by on my state pension.' She tugs at the spikes in her thin hair – green today. 'And all them conditions and that. Comes with too many strings attached for my liking. I wouldn't fancy working no flower farm with Big Brother watching over me. You either win it or you don't.'

'I'm sure you can only impose conditions in a will *before* someone inherits, not lay down the law on how the estate is spent or managed afterwards,' Neil says. 'Bet you could challenge the details in court, so you could sell bits of it off to raise the cash and do what you want with the proceeds. I'll ask my philandering idiot of a husband.' He scowls. 'He's a barrister. He'll know.'

Opposite me, I can see Mike looking wistfully into the middle distance. 'Imagine, though . . . A fresh start on fertile land. Owning your own business.'

'I thought you were happy being a planning officer, Mike,' I say.

His cheeks flush red, and he looks down at the scarred wood of the table. 'I'd like to live in a world where not everything's about sitting in an office with disappointed strangers for eight hours a day. I'd like to do something more meaningful than object fruitlessly to poorly designed plans that end up getting the green light anyway, because some developer's greasing the right palms, somewhere higher up in the planning food chain.'

'That's the spirit, Michael,' Marjorie says, clapping her hands. 'This is a golden opportunity for us. If we won the land, we'd raise the money we need somehow. The Lord would provide.'

'The bank would have to provide,' Val says, 'and I ain't in the market for no business loan. Not at my age.'

'Oh, I think it's cool,' Phoebe says, toying with an amethyst amulet that hangs around her neck on a cord. 'This is what I've always wanted to do. Grow organic shit, yeah?'

'Thought you said you wanted to do rewilding,' Seth says.

'Pretty much the same thing. Think of the insect population you'd be supporting. All that wildlife, man.'

Seth nods and smiles. 'Yeah!'

Neil smooths his right eyebrow with a manicured middle finger. 'I suppose those of us who couldn't work full time on it could dip in and out when we can . . . like we do now. Evenings, the odd weekend? It's not like we'd end up arguing about money, if all profits have to go to charity. It's just a larger-scale version of what we do now . . . isn't it?'

I keep my thoughts to myself. On the one hand, the *Telegraph* reported that Dotty's will only offers a 'modest salary' for the flower farmers, and I have no idea what 'modest' constitutes. £25,000? More? Less? Pocket money to the sole breadwinner of a family in London's commuter belt. Likely, my financial responsibilities mean I must stay at Chislehurst Green Insurance until they kick me out, I retire, or I die, no matter how miserable I may be (especially since I've just engaged the services of a professional carer called Carol, who charges more by the hour than I had anticipated – she started last week and Mum hasn't sent her packing . . . yet). But on the other, oh, how wonderful it would be to be mistress of my own destiny. For only three seconds, I accommodate the fantasy of standing in the warm sunshine in a field full of swaying flowers, ablaze with colour and abuzz with bees. Then, the reality of Colin with his joke ties and Janice from HR's Sith-Lord powers and Armpits Alice's well-stirred WD40 coffee floods back in. Personally, I cannot afford unbudgeted flights of fancy.

'Well, I think the flower farm is a wonderful opportunity, and with a prize like that up for grabs, we'd better roll our sleeves up, hadn't we?' Mike says.

Outside, it's dark, and the spring evening air bites, but inside, it is warm, fuggy, and brightly illuminated with UV lamps and strung-about fairy lights. I can feel my pulse start to slow as Marjorie demonstrates how to nurture the seedlings we've created.

Bent almost double, like a mother stooping to comfort her child, Marjorie caresses the pristine young leaves with gnarled old-lady fingers. 'Now, I planted dahlia seeds several weeks ago, and already, we can see that the seedlings have germinated and they need pricking out.'

To my left, Neil snorts with laughter. He repeats '*pricking* out' under his breath and nudges me. I kick him beneath the table in collusion.

Marjorie scowls at us both. 'One is *not* in the school yard now, need I remind you?' She turns back to her seedlings and slaps a hand on some small black plastic pots. 'I filled these 9cm pots with moistened compost. Each of you must take your dibber and prick out the seedlings, following my lead.'

Neil leans over and whispers out of the others' earshot, 'I wonder what would happen if I offered to prick out Mike Potato with my dibber.'

'I suspect Mike's "Black Gold" leaves terrible stains,' I whisper in response.

'Pay attention!' Marjorie squeaks at us.

Contrite, I take a 9cm pot and copy Marj, taking my young dahlia delicately by its leaves with my right finger and thumb and digging the index finger of my left hand beneath the roots. I carefully lift the entire tiny plant free of the old strawberry punnet.

I gasp with admiration at the perfect little plant.

'See the roots?' Marjorie says. 'See how the compost is threaded with white veins? The plant is already putting on growth, and once it has a couple of decent-sized leaves that you can get to grips with, you can pot it on.'

Transferring the seedling to the palm of my left hand, I plunge my dibber into my pot filled with Mike's 'Black

Gold' compost and make space for the root ball. Then, just like Marj, I plop the seedling into the hole and firm it in with my fingertips. 'I did it!'

'Indeed you did! Brava, Gillian. All one does now is give the seedling a drink.' She pours water onto the contents of the little pot through the fine rose of a small watering can. 'Keep going until we've potted on the lot. And then, one must take cuttings of fuchsias, following the technique Valerie shared on our WhatsApp group.'

We have been allocated stations along the trestle tables that line the large greenhouse. We each have a strawberry punnet crammed with dahlia seedlings and a stack of 9cm pots. Slowly, I begin assembling my compost-filled pots, ready to pluck these terrifyingly tiny green babies from the comfort of their crowded nursery punnet.

When I've transplanted them all, I take a length of soft fuchsia stem that has been placed in a jug of water. I trim the stalk just above a leaf node, remove excess leaves, and then slice the top set of leaves horizontally in half. I dip the stem in rooting hormone powder and then poke it carefully into some damp compost. Then I place a small baggie over the pot and fasten it around the rim with an elastic band to provide it with its own little greenhouse.

'Good work,' Val says, peering over my shoulder. 'You've got the magic touch, Gill.'

I beam at her, feeling like a schoolchild who has just been given a gold star. I can feel my worries about Mum and Zak and work have all but slipped away. I know I am creating something new that will bring pleasure in the later summer weeks. Blousy blooms that will nod in the warm breeze on Bromley's streets, enticing the lazily buzzing bees with their sticky pollen. 'What kind of fuchsias are these?'

'These particular ones are upright doubles,' she says, chewing her nicotine gum noisily. 'Voodoo, they're called. Purple frill and a bright –'

There is a sudden loud crack and a pane of glass bursts inwards. We all yelp, jerking our arms aloft to protect ourselves and our plants from the flying glass; scrambling out of our seats in unison, unsure how to react in this fight-or-flight moment.

'What the fuck was that?!' Val shouts.

'Language, Valerie,' Marjorie says, but there's no conviction behind her criticism.

Mike bends over and, with a grunt, lifts up the offending projectile that has just punched a hole in Marjorie's costly greenhouse. 'A brick?' He locks eyes with Marjorie's and the colour drains from his face.

'Call the police!' Cath says.

I feel a disturbance in the air as Seth speeds past me in a blur of motion. With deft hands, he turns the key in the lock of the door onto the garden; flings it open wide.

'Seth?' Phoebe shouts after him. 'Where you going, dude?'

'Kill the lights,' I say.

Phoebe switches off the light, and we're plunged into darkness, giving us a clear view of the garden. I can see that Seth has already sprinted the length of the garden and has scrambled over the fence and out of sight. In my misspent youth, I saw slower greyhounds at Catford Dogs.

We breathe too fast and too shallow. Just for a moment, we have become one organism.

'They're gone.' Mike's voice, small and tremulous, breaks the silence.

The lights go back on.

'I'll call 999,' he says, fumbling with his phone. His hands are shaking.

'Why you calling the feds, man?' Phoebe asks.

'Because somebody just put a brick through Marj's window,' Mike says. 'That's criminal damage. Someone's got it in for her.'

'Or maybe,' Neil says, peering again into the dark garden, 'someone's got it in for *us*.'

9

'Police, please. I wish to report an act of vandalism.'
Mere moments have passed since the attack, and Mike
is through to the emergency services. His voice is
tremulous.

'Oh my God,' Neil says, staring at the brick now sitting on Marjorie's prep-table. 'I can't believe Seth's gone
after them.' He presses his hand to his mouth and looks
around at us all for a response. 'Talk about brave.'

Marjorie scoffs. 'More like, he doesn't want to hang
around for the police to get here. That wasn't strong
fabric conditioner I could smell on him all this time, was
it? Oh no. Our new, youthful vicar was highly amused
that I'd been mistaking cannabis for Comfort Botanicals,
but Marjorie Bloom won't be made a fool of twice. Just
the smell of young Seth is likely to give a positive result
on police drug detector tests.'

'Seth's not the one who put a brick through your
window,' Phoebe says, treating Marjorie to a withering
look. She scratches at the roots of her matted hair and
then sniffs her fingertips. 'But that's okay. You carry on
Gen-Z-blaming . . .' She seems to search for a fitting end
to her riposte. 'Boomer.'

'Do contain your misplaced disdain, Phoebe,' Marjorie
says, narrowing her eyes and folding her bony, wrinkled

arms over the bib of her colourful dungarees. 'One is fairly certain one has the measure of young Seth.'

Whatever unity of purpose we had pre-brick, it is quickly dissipating.

'Phoebe has got a bit of a point though,' I tell Marjorie. 'This isn't about Seth. It's about someone lobbing a brick through your greenhouse. We're lucky nobody was hurt. Any ideas who might be responsible?'

'Yeah, Marj,' Phoebe says, hand on hip like a child who just scored a point over a parent. 'You always act like you're all without sin and that, but someone literally cast the first stone in your direction.'

'*You* have the temerity to misquote the Bible at *me*, girl?' Marjorie shrieks. 'Have you never heard that cleanliness is next to godliness?'

'Hang on,' I say. 'Could this be connected to Dotty?'

Marjorie looks at me aghast, clasping her hand to her chest. 'Dear Lord. Don't say that!' The colour in her face has all but drained away and her features are sagging, like a melty Madame Tussauds. She grasps at the tabletop — white knuckles and the sinews in her hands standing proud beneath almost translucent, mottled skin. 'Oh, I say! One does feel a little . . .'

I can see her knees starting to buckle. 'She's going. Mike, grab her!'

Mike Potato reaches out to steady Marjorie. 'Oops-a-daisy. I've got you, Marj.'

'It's shock,' Cath says. 'Let's get her inside for a cup of sweet tea before the police arrive.'

*

By the time the police turn up, which takes a good forty-five adrenalin-fuelled minutes of checking the newly repotted plants for shards of glass and making hot, sweet tea, Marjorie has perked up. There is still no sign of Seth, however, and the mother in me hopes he's safe. My thoughts turn naturally to my own son, at home on his own. I'm acutely aware that I ought to leave. Yet, Marjorie's vulnerable, and the daughter in me feels obliged to see this through.

'So tell me what happened, Marj,' the female constable says, perching on the edge of one of Marjorie's 1970s sculpted velvet armchairs. She takes out a notebook. Her radio chatters and hisses ten to the dozen.

'It's *Marjorie*, dear. *Marjorie* Bloom. Mrs Bloom, to you.' Marjorie nibbles at a rich tea biscuit with tea-stained false teeth.

While Marjorie relates the pacy short story of a brick flying through the window of the greenhouse and landing on the floor, I peer through the window that faces onto the back garden and watch the second uniformed officer examining the damage. He leaves the greenhouse and starts to walk around the garden, presumably to look for a point of entry or to check no intruder is lurking. He returns to the house and comes through to the crowded living room, which is getting rather stuffy with all of us still squeezed onto the three-piece suite.

'Have you had any arguments with neighbours recently?' the female PC asks.

Marjorie wrinkles her nose. 'My neighbours on one

side are godless buffoons who have noisy barbecues – on a Sunday, of all days. I have complained to your lot and the council about the noise and the smell. Their children look as though they've never had their hair combed. And the father's beard looks unhygienic.'

'So do you think they might have thrown the brick?'

Shaking her head, Marjorie places a hand over her eyes. 'No! Of course not. I suppose my other neighbour might be responsible.' She takes a white handkerchief from her dungaree pocket and dabs at her nose. Then her eyes narrow. 'Gladys Melrose. A cut-through runs between our houses. She's my arch rival in flower arranging from the church. She covets my greenhouse.' Marjorie pokes the PC on her knee. '*Covets it*, I tell you!'

Mike clears his throat at this point. 'There is the slight issue of Gladys being eighty-five and suffering from gout, Marjorie. She drives a Motability scooter to the shops. I'm not sure she could have scaled your fence, let alone lobbed a brick through a window.'

I feel my pocket vibrating repeatedly. Checking my phone, I see it's Zak on WhatsApp.

U seen my Chemistry txtbk? Zx

I tap out a response.

I'm not the keeper of your schoolbooks, Zak. Weren't you using it to revise for that test last week? Have you had your mark? Done your homework? Back soon. Mum xxx

Revisited by mumly guilt, I interrupt the character assassination of Gladys Melrose. 'Shouldn't we be making the
greenhouse secure for the night? Only I've got to go.' I
tap the face of my watch.

'Don't rush the good constable,' Marjorie says, glaring at me. 'We're narrowing down the list of suspects.'
She turns to the female PC, and there's mischief evident
in her grin. 'Did I tell you about Walter Percy, the parish
counsellor who hangs bags of dog mess on the branches
of people's front garden shrubbery, presumably because
he thinks finding a bin is beneath him? He cheated in
last year's best-in-bloom show, and I *know* he covets my
greenhouse. He wears a *cravat*!'

The male PC sighs and answers a call on his radio
that makes it clear they're moving on. He barely looks
at Marjorie when he delivers his verdict: 'It's kids, if you
ask me, love. Just kids getting up to no good.'

Marjorie shuffles to her feet as the two uniformed
police make for the front door. She follows them into
the hall. 'Do you think this could be connected to the
death of Dorothy Gloucester?'

'The famous old actress?' the kindly female PC asks,
looking puzzled. 'National treasure, wasn't she? From
Dulwich?'

'I don't know about national treasure,' Marjorie says,
wrinkling her nose. 'She died from poisoning the other
week. My associate, Gillian, and I found her body, didn't
we, Gillian?'

I nod. 'Coroner reported an open verdict.'

'But that hardly rules out murder, and she belonged

to the Golden Trowel Gardening Association, just like me,' Marjorie says. 'If she *was* murdered, might the two attacks be connected?'

'I'll make some enquiries, but it's likely the two things are unconnected, Mrs Bloom. Dorothy Gloucester's file's closed, as far as I know. No proof that foul play was involved. And here . . . we've not got much to go on, if I'm honest. Get one of your pals to help you make that greenhouse secure, and the Crime Scene folks'll be here in the morning to take fingerprints off the brick. But even if you'd had CCTV, the chances of catching anyone . . .' She shrugs and takes her leave.

Within minutes of the police leaving, Mike Potato bodges a temporary cardboard covering for the broken greenhouse window to protect the plants from the cold. Meanwhile, Phoebe and Neil set about clearing up the debris from the attack in earnest.

The rest of us are in the house fussing over Marjorie when there's a sharp knock on the front door. Retrieving my door keys from my bag and wedging them between my fingers as a makeshift knuckleduster, lest Marj's greenhouse-coveter return, I peer through the peephole.

'Seth!' I open the door, and he steps inside. 'I thought you'd *gone* gone.'

Seth is smiling wryly. 'Thought I'd try to catch up with whoever threw that brick.'

We walk into the living room, Seth leading the way. All eyes are on him. Neil and Phoebe come back inside. Phoebe's face lights up at the sight of him, of course.

'Yo, Seth, my dude. Were you just waiting for the feds to leave?' she says, carrying a dustpan full of broken glass.

'Nah, man,' Seth says. He turns to Marjorie. 'Sorry I left without saying anything, Marj. Only I spotted whoever threw that brick climbing back over your fence, so I legged it after him.'

'And?' Neil asks.

'He was wearing a hoodie and a mask. I couldn't see his face, like. But I wasn't up for a fight, 'cause he's well bigger than me. I decided to hang back instead, so he thinks he's given me the slip. And I sees him drive off in a basic, pimped-up Astra. I gets into my A-Class and I follows him.'

We are all hanging on Seth's every word, with our mouths slightly open in disbelief and admiration. Well, I certainly am.

'And?' Mike says.

'Tracked him all the way down to Forest Hill. But then he pulls up outside a chicken shop and gets out his car. I didn't want to start no beef with him because I'm just hanging back on the other side of the road, doing reconnaissance, right? But once he's got his hood and mask off, I realise this geez looks familiar. He's got a tattoo on the side of his head, just above his ear.' He points to the place on his own head, then he scowls and rubs his stubbled chin. 'Only thing is, I just can't think where I know him from. A building site. College, maybe. The pub? It'll come to me.'

'Did you get a photo?' Neil asks.

Seth shakes his head. 'Wanted to stay on the down-low. I couldn't get the reg plate of the car either 'cause I couldn't risk getting too close, in case he spots he's being followed and starts a thing.'

Marjorie waves her half-eaten rich tea at him. 'Well, one might just call the police back and have them check their closed-circuit cameras along the route he drove. Those eyesores are on every street. Let them find this ne'er-do-well and fetch him into custody. Ask him why he's terrorising a good Christian like me!'

'Nah, man,' Seth says. 'You got no hard evidence it was him who threw the brick. None of you lot saw him. They won't get no fingerprint off a brick. Police won't do nothing on the say-so from me, and I don't want nothing to do with no cops. Keep this one under your hat for now, Marj. Let me think where I know this chump from. Then we can look into it ourselves.'

'Ooh, like private dicks?' Mike Potato says. He blinks hard, and even through the tinted lenses of his glasses, I can see intrigue in his eyes. It's clear that this is the most exciting thing that has happened to him since he found a King Edward that allegedly looked like the Virgin Mary holding Baby Jesus (I've seen the photo, and it did look impressively like the BVM, though Baby Jesus looked more like a deformed nub of potato).

'Just like private dicks,' Neil says, smirking.

I arrive home just after ten. The lights are still on down-stairs, and when I walk into the living room, I can see Zak is sitting in his computer alcove. He has his earbuds in and is completely oblivious to my presence. He's too busy playing online chess.

'Zachary.' I approach him and lay my hand on his shoulder.

He almost jumps out of his seat and automatically clicks to a tab that contains a Chemistry past paper. He pulls out his earbuds. 'Mum! I was doing my homework, honest.'

I kiss his head and ruffle his hair. 'I don't expect you still to be doing homework at bedtime, Zak.' I point to the screen. 'You don't need to hide online chess from me, son.' I collect up his empty squash glass and his empty tea mug. I give the glass a sniff to make sure it doesn't smell of clandestine alcohol. 'Learn anything?'

'Loads. How was the gardening?'

I walk through to the kitchen and plonk the glass and mug into the sink. Zak follows me in, clearly needing to unburden himself about something. The worktop and the sink are both full of dirty pots, as usual, and I brace myself for dishwasher-stacking. 'Don't ask. Every meeting is like a soap opera. I think I've got enough drama in my own life without taking on theirs.'

'Doesn't sound great.' He pushes his skinny frame up against the larder door and starts pulling at some laminate that's starting to peel away from the MDF. He's not looking me in the eye. 'Maybe you should –'

'Never mind me.' I open the dishwasher door emphatically. I start to take yesterday's clean pots out and stack them on the side. 'Out with it. What did you get in your Chemistry test?'

In my peripheral vision, I can see Zak looking down at his oversized feet. 'I didn't come bottom of the class.'

Now I straighten up and study my son's evasive body language in earnest. 'What's that supposed to mean? Is this a re-run of the Further Maths? What was your score?'

He's still looking at his feet. 'I could have got over fifty per cent if I'd finished and not made some dumb mistakes.'

'What was your score, Zak?'

He mumbles an answer.

'I didn't hear that. Speak up and look at me when you're talking.'

Finally he looks up, and I can see there are tears in his eyes. 'Twenty-one per cent. It's nearly a pass.' Then he starts to cry. 'I'm so sorry, Mum. I'm trying so hard, I promise, but . . . Chemistry's so dead. Doesn't matter how much work I do or how often I ask the teacher to go over stuff again, I still don't understand half of it, so the teacher gets impatient with me and the neeks make fun of me. Alright for them, because they totally get it first time. But it's just not clicking for me. And now I've lost my book and I'm going to get killed by Mr Eavis.'

I beckon him to me and embrace him tightly. 'Oh, bloody hell, Zak. Why didn't you tell me you were struggling this badly?'

In a clumsy tango of entangled arms, tears, and snot, we shunt over to the kitchen table, break apart, and sit facing one another. I take my little-big-boy's hand into mine, wishing I could do his schoolwork for him. 'Do you understand the basic content, at least?'

He nods. 'I just forget what I'm doing in the tests, and then I panic, and then I've run out of time.' He bites his lip, then produces a crumpled letter from his trouser pocket, addressed to me. 'Oh, and there's this from the head of sixth form.'

Feeling my heart sink, I take the envelope from him and open it. 'Is this about another detention?'

He doesn't answer, so I read.

Dear Mrs Swanley,

After Zak's repeated failure to hand homework in on time, his disruptive behaviour in the class, and his poor results in tests, I have consulted with his subject teachers, and we all agree Zak should be put on report for a fortnight, minimum. This is not a punishment for bad behaviour, but means that he will be given a card that you have to sign each evening, to say that he has done his homework in a timely fashion and that he is doing his utmost to focus on his schoolwork. His form teacher must sign the card at the end of each week.

We recommend that you oversee his revisiting topics that have been covered in class, to consolidate his knowledge. I am also recommending he be referred to our school Special Educational Needs Coordinator, who can test Zak's response times and reading ability, since there is a suspicion held by two of his teachers that Zak is perhaps neurodivergent in some way and/or suffers from dyslexia. Please call the SENCO as soon as you are able for an appointment.

If you have any questions, please call me on the main school number.

Regards,
Miss Crabtree
Head of Sixth Form

I sigh deeply, all thoughts of Marjorie's greenhouse and Colin and work relegated to the mental 'It'll keep' box. The letter from the head of sixth form confirms my suspicions that something more is afoot with Zak than mere teenage hormones and poor organisational skills. My son needs help, and with A-Levels and university applications looming, it's needed urgently.

All morning I've been surreptitiously googling ADHD symptoms and dyslexia in teenage boys when I should be working. Well, I am *sort of* working. While I'm scrolling on my phone to keep my work laptop's browser history clean, I'm still eavesdropping on call-centre conversations. Today, I'm listening in on the shoddy service being offered by a colleague, unironically called D'Arcy Mellon, to a man called Derek from Walsall, West Midlands.

'So am I covered for freezer goods, then? Only there's a full lamb and half a cow in my chest freezer what's defrosted,' Derek says. 'It pongs to high heaven. I wouldn't give it the dog. And that's quite a bit of money down the Swanee. Hundreds, in fact.'

D'Arcy sounds like she's filing her nails on the other end of the call. Across the vast floor of hot desks and call booths, if I stand up, I can just about see her faded pink hair and the piercing through her septum. 'No.'

'Why not? I thought freezer contents were covered.' Derek sounds belligerent.

'But you just told me you blew your electrics by drilling holes in the ceiling? You hit a cable, you said? That's why your freezer went off?'

'I was looking for the joist to hang a light fitting.'

'No, but, yeah. That's why you're not covered, 'cause you caused the damage yourself?' She ends every sentence with a rising inflection that would break me out in hives, if I were Derek.

'Yes. But I've got accidental damage.'

'Sorry, but . . . er . . . it wasn't accidental. It was your fault? But look on the bright side, that much meat's really really bad for you and greenhouse emissions?'

Derek breaks into a bout of swearing.

'Sorry, but . . . er . . . that's quite abusive, and there's a company policy against –'

D'Arcy Mellon doesn't have time to explain the company policy in any detail, because Derek has already told her where he'd like to shove his rotting lamb carcass and has hung up. I mark D'Arcy as a candidate for retraining, followed by a formal warning if she antagonises a customer like that again, yet I know instinctively that I'd struggle to dole out the necessary discipline, just as I did with Loveday. Maybe I can just do a Faith and tell D'Arcy off informally. That might be enough to push her to resign. She's young. She'll find more soul-destroying work to do badly. I, on the other hand . . . if Colin sustains the hump indefinitely and gives *me* the push, would I even be able to find more work at my age, in a job market that counts anyone approaching fifty as past it?

I caress the shiny leaves of the peace lily plant I've brought into work with me in a bid to make my work environment healthier and more calming. I turn my thoughts back to Zak. I've got to make sure he gets help.

At lunchtime I find an empty meeting room, dial his school, and ask to speak to the SENCO. The receptionist puts me through to a woman who sounds like she smokes sixty a day. I explain Zak's predicament.

'He's working pretty hard,' I say. 'But he's struggling. You know? Really struggling.'

'In what way, Mrs Swanley?'

I list Zak's teenage challenges. 'He's so disorganised. Always has been. Only now, he's also doing badly in his schoolwork. His concentration's worse than terrible. He keeps losing his textbooks. He's always late to things. He's always forgetting things.' I wince when I remember the giant egg on his forehead that Zak returned home with the other week. 'And you name it, he'll walk head-first into it. Columns. Lampposts. The edges of doors. I'm always running with frozen peas. I just don't think he watches where he's going. He keeps getting detentions for distracting the other kids in class – cracking jokes, asking them to explain what the teacher just said because he hadn't been listening properly. His mind wanders, you see. And then, of course, when he gets into trouble or does badly in his schoolwork, he gets *really* upset.'

'Okay. Well, his Physics and Chemistry teachers have actually emailed ahead about how he's been struggling with focus and falling behind a bit, even though he's a bright lad. Is there anything else that you've noticed?'

'He's read one full book in the ten years since his dad died. Is that relevant?'

'Could be. Dyslexia often goes hand in hand with ADHD.'

'I mean, his teachers have regularly mentioned all this at parents' evening, but we agreed to put it down to immaturity – like, a wait-and-see approach.' I cast my mind back to the many excruciating almost-confrontations with his subject teachers, where I've insisted Zak's the model pupil, and they've politely but firmly disagreed. 'It's not like he's ever been *bad*, as such. And until sixth form, he'd always scraped along in the middle set in arts subjects, but he did really well in his Maths and Science GCSEs.'

'Bright and able, then.'

'Exactly.' My motherly pride and loyalty are warring with guilt at having ignored the signs for so long. Can Mrs Cigarillo hear it in my voice? 'Look, I'm a widow and a single parent. I was hardly queuing up to spend thousands I didn't have on assessments for a boy who was ticking along and maybe just needed to grow up a bit. But I appreciate we've got to the point where it's time to look into why he might be struggling.'

On the other end of the phone, she coughs a rattling, phlegmy cough, and I imagine her sitting with her feet up, cradling a Jack Daniels with a cigarillo between her fingers. I wonder fleetingly if she looks like Val from gardeners' club. 'We'll get him in for some response time testing,' she says. 'Can you make it in for a chat, too? We really need to talk to you as well as Zak, and you'll have to fill out some paperwork.'

I look at my Outlook calendar and realise that the only opening I have, between visiting Mum, attending once-weekly gardening sessions, and seeing Mandi-with-an-I, is after work today. 'I don't suppose you're free this evening, are you? Only, I work full time.'

'I can make 3.15pm, when school finishes. No later than that, I'm afraid.'

I agree to the meeting and then immediately message Colin about it, promising I'll make up the time lost by staying late one evening or even going in on a Saturday morning. Next, I thumb out a message to Zak, telling him to come to the SENCO's office after school.

Eventually, 2.45pm swings around. Colin's response to my having to duck out of the working day early to fulfil my parental obligations was a curt emailed reply of, 'If you must.' I'm keen to slip away unnoticed now, to avoid being on the receiving end of his disapproving looks or loaded comments about the difficulties of working mothers short-changing both their families and the company (always dressed up as sympathetic feminism, though his subtext is anything but).

Checking that his office door is firmly shut, I snatch up my bag and head for the lift. The lifts are within sight of Colin's internal-facing window, but his blinds are closed, so perhaps he's busy in a meeting or beating his meat over some spreadsheet.

No sooner have I pressed the button for the lift than my personal phone blasts the office with Tone Loc's 'Funky Cold Medina'. My fingers are clumsy, and I can't turn the damn volume down. Could it be Mrs Cigarillo calling to cancel?

'Gillian. Are you there?' It's my mother, shouting as

if she's calling me from Australia, using the medium of a plastic cup and string. 'I've had an accident.'

I catch sight of Colin's closed blinds being cracked. Worse still, the regional director, Gordon Mitcham, is walking over to the lift, flanked by two sharp-dressed women I don't recognise. They come to a standstill only three feet away. I turn the volume on my phone as low as I can, pressing the device hard to my ear.

'What seems to be the problem?' I say, trying to make it sound like a business call. 'Is it an urgent issue?'

'I've shit my pants,' Mum shouts, I suspect loud enough to be audible to the others waiting by the lift. 'I don't know what to do. It's gone everywhere, I've got no clean kecks, and I'm panicking, Gillian. Can you come over and sort me out? I feel faint.'

In my peripheral vision, I'm sure I catch sight of one of the women looking at me, wearing a horrified expression. She clearly doesn't have infirm parents.

'Sorry, I can't make that right now, but I can call someone to come and help you, or I can tend to the problem . . . later.'

'Why are you talking like a fucking robot, Gillian? I just told you, I've filled my drawers, and I'm out of clean kecks. I think that mackerel you bought me was off.'

The lift arrives and we all step inside. 'Can you just hold the line for a moment, please?'

'Gillian, are you there? Gillian, are you ignoring me? *Gillian!*'

The doors close, and my mother's voice is momentarily silenced as reception is lost. I smile sweetly at the regional director and his colleagues, dying inside with embarrassment.

When the lift finally arrives at the ground floor, I hasten away from the eavesdropping senior colleagues and out of the building. I get into my car and switch to the speaker function on my phone, setting the device down onto the dash as I buckle in. 'Jesus, Mum. Why's Carol not there?' I check my watch. 'She's supposed to come in for an hour in the morning and then again in the afternoon. She should be there now.'

On the other end, my mother cackles with mischievous delight. 'Oh, she turned up, alright. I told her to sling her hook.'

I clasp my hands to my head. 'Why?' It's taken me *months* to get Mum to accept care from someone who isn't me, and it was no mean feat finding someone who came with impeccable references and still had space in their schedule.

'She smells like a shed. You know? That damp, musty smell. I decided I can't have someone who smells like a shed touching me.'

'She's not there to creosote your nether regions. She's a bloody professional carer. Does it matter what she smells like, as long as she makes you a cuppa and helps you get washed and dressed?' I glance at the time showing on my phone. I'm going to be late to my meeting. 'Mum, I'm going to call Carol and beg her to come back. *If* she agrees, you're going to let her in, and you're going to let her clean you up. Unless she can't come, I am *not* coming over until tomorrow, after work, because I've got a job to hold down and a teenage son to look after. Right?' Mandi-with-an-I would be proud of my excellent boundary-drawing.

Before my mother can respond, I end the call and get in touch with Carol. It takes her a while to answer. Has she gone on to another job? Finally, she picks up.

'Gill.' There's little warmth to her voice. In the background, there's a rhythmic thrum and car noises. Where is she?

'Hi. Oh hi, Carol? Look, I've just spoken to my mother and I'm calling to apologise.'

'Not being funny, Gill, but it's her who should be apologising. She was very rude.'

I wince. 'I know, I know. It's . . . she's –'

'I don't get paid to take no abuse. And I don't smell of shed, neither. Your mother's a very difficult woman. You know that, don't you?'

'Yes. Yeah, well, she's lonely and in poor health.' I hold up my hands in surrender though Carol can't see them. 'It makes her short-tempered. But you're absolutely right, and there's no excuses. Look, she's had a toilet accident, and I just can't be there for her. I've got an important thing at my kid's school. Please come back, Carol. *Please. Pleeeeaaaase.*'

I hear tutting at the other end. Carol reveals she has not yet gone on to her next job and has stopped just around the corner to fill up with petrol. She mercifully agrees to try again with my mother, and I say a silent prayer of thanks, just in case God's listening or Dave has lobbied God on my behalf. Switching on the engine,

I look up to Colin's office window and see him staring down at the car park, giving me daggers, even though I have his permission to leave early in return for working a Saturday morning.

At school, I am shown to the SENCO hub, and meet with Zak.

'Why are we here?' he asks, planting a hasty peck on my cheek. He smells of school dinners and sweaty feet. There's a new biro mark on the sleeve of his pale grey suit jacket. 'Shouldn't you be in work?'

'We're doing what we should have done years ago. The signs were there.'

He shrugs. 'Well, Dad died.'

I shake my head and stroke his cheek. 'This isn't just about Dad. Look, I can tell it's all been getting you down – getting told off constantly, getting distracted, falling behind. It's not right.'

'It's fine.'

'It's not fine, and I'm partly to blame. I dropped the ball on you.' I then tell him about the note from the head of sixth form and his being put on report.

He rolls his eyes. 'Oh, great.'

'Hey! Listen, this is our chance to see if there's something undiagnosed that you could be getting help with. School's being proactive about this, and that's no bad thing.' I want him to see that we're taking the right action; that this trip isn't designed to stigmatise him in any way; that he isn't in any kind of trouble.

Mrs Cigarillo comes out to greet us. She looks nothing

at all like the noirish gumshoe or salty seadog in elasticated trousers that I'd imagined, but her voice and her yellow smile betray her obvious smoking habit.

'Mrs Swanley, thanks for coming in.' She turns to Zak. 'Hello, Zak. I hear you've been having trouble with your schoolwork. Why don't we all sit down and have a chat? Then we can go through a little questionnaire. Depending on what we find, we can have a look at your response times.'

Zak looks nonplussed, but I'm relieved to be unburdening myself. We take our seats on an old sofa, have the chat, and then fill out the questionnaire together, ticking all the boxes about poor concentration, shocking organisational skills, and fidgeting. Zak then sits an initial test of his response times.

When he's done, and Mrs Cigarillo has checked his results, she smiles her yellow-toothed smile. 'Well, Zak does have rather poor response times and is almost certainly neurodivergent in some way.'

'Really?' Zak and I say in unison. Does he feel the same sense of relief as me?

Cigarillo nods. 'I'll recommend him for more in-depth tests — we've got a lady comes in to do them — and if he scores as I suspect, he'll qualify for extra time in exams straight away. Up to fifty per cent plus rest breaks, if he needs them. You might want to get Zak formally assessed by a psychiatrist for suspected ADHD, as well as getting him tested by a dyslexia specialist. ADHD and dyslexia would explain his slow speeds and poor test results in the comprehension section.'

'So you think he needs formal diagnoses?' I ask.

She nods, screwing and unscrewing the cap of her fountain pen with nicotine-stained fingertips. 'Better to get diagnoses and sort the paperwork and any support he needs while he's in school. Then it's all in place for when he goes on to university or future employment.'

At my side, Zak is grinning. 'Cool. That explains so much.' He high-fives me. 'Hey, Mum. Thanks for arranging this. I'm really glad we did it. Just in time for my AS-Level, too.'

For the first time in a long while, I feel like I have done something right. We take our leave of Mrs Cigarillo and head for the car park, arm in arm, discussing the possibility of fish and chips as a celebratory dinner. We are so deep in conversation about the merits or evils of vinegar on fish that I don't initially respond to my name being called.

'Gill! Gill! Is that you?'

I finally realise someone is calling out to me and turn to find the voice's owner. At first, I can't quite place the man in the green polo shirt, embellished with the logo of Dobbies garden centre. He's standing by an old Ford Mondeo, two cars along from where I have parked the Volvo. But then I notice the way he pushes his steel-rimmed glasses up his nose.

'Mike?!'

'Hiya.' Mike is waving. 'I thought it was you.' He turns his attention to Zak. 'So this is your son?'

Zak's face is flushed. 'Yeah?' Is he that horrified that his mother should know an adult man outside of work?

But then Mike grabs Zak's hand and shakes it. 'Greetings, Master Swanley. I'm Michael Berisford, King of King Edwards, but you can call me Mike. At your service, sir!' He salutes and clicks his heels, of course.

'Mike's one of my gardeners' club pals,' I say, feeling a hot flush rolling in, brought on by Zak's reaction to Mike, and Mike's ridiculous greeting. 'What are you doing, standing outside the school? Do your kids go here?'

Mike nods and laughs nervously, placing a hand on the grubby white bonnet of his Mondeo so that his whole body forms a barrier between me and a view of the car's interior. 'Hugo and Katie are in the lower school. Not big sixth formers like Zak.' Is he hiding something?

I crane my neck to get a better view of what's on his passenger seat and behind the driver's seat, wedged on the rear shelf. Then I realise. 'Mike, have you got your car set up as a bed?'

His nervous chuckle says more than he is clearly willing to divulge. 'Oh, ha. It's just a pillow and a duvet. I'm taking them to . . . the laundrette . . .' His features freeze, as though he's pressed pause on his facial expression while he wracks his brain for a plausible excuse. Then his face softens slightly. 'Because they don't fit in my washing machine. Ha ha.'

What he doesn't take into account in telling this blatant fib is that I've had a lifetime of reading the true meaning behind my mother's deliberately obfuscating words and my teenage son's excuses. 'You're sleeping in your car? Has your wife kicked you out, Mike?'

He presses his hand to his chest. 'Me?' His voice is on the high-pitched side. 'Don't be silly.'

He's looking away from me, and I get a distinct sense of sorrow emanating from him. I reach out and place my hand on his arm. 'Mike? Are you alright?'

Finally, he turns to me and there are tears in his eyes.

11

'Zak? Come on! Homework, pal,' I tell my son, once our plates are empty. He groans, but I clap my hands. 'Chop-chop. I've got to sign that report card to say you've done it, remember?'

The three of us are sitting at my kitchen table, staring in a carb-induced, semi-fugue state at the empty chip-shop wrappings. The bottle of pinot grigio that I cracked open is now half empty, and I can tell from the way that Mike's shoulders are slightly less hunched that I have done the right thing in offering him a bed for the night.

Zak yawns. 'Yeah, whatever.' He scrapes his chair back noisily, carries our three plates and cutlery to the sink, and then slouches off to the living room.

I turn to Mike. 'So, are you going to tell me why you're sleeping in your car?'

Mike cradles his wine close to his chest and peers through the kitchen doorway with narrowed eyes. He pushes the door closed so that we are alone. 'I've recently split from my wife.'

'Oh, Mike. I'm so sorry to hear that.' I top his glass up, and then my own. I decide not to mention the fact that on our first meeting, I'd pegged him as a lonely bach-elor, still living with his mother. 'Did you just drift apart or was there a catalyst?'

He opens his mouth, poised to answer, and then seems to think better of whatever he was about to say. He frowns, pats his lips with his fingertips, then finally starts to speak. 'I don't really like to speak ill of Donna to other people.'

'No. Of course. If you don't want to tell me, that's –'

'Her plan was to run off with a younger model and leave me with the kids,' he says, speaking quickly as if the words burn his tongue. 'Except now she wants the house for her and lover boy, so I'm in the car, and Hugo and Katie are stuck with a disengaged parent until I can find somewhere new and affordable for the three of us.'

I'm certain surprise at his wife's behaviour is showing on my face, despite my intention to appear non-judgemental. 'Were there any warning signs that she was going to leave you all in the lurch?'

He shrugs and looks wistfully towards my cooker. 'Probably, if I'm honest. Maybe even from the start. We were quite young by today's standards. We'd only been going out for three months when I proposed to her. I didn't expect her to say yes, but our parents wanted it, and everyone around us was tying the knot.'

'Peer pressure and being in love with the idea of being in love?'

'I guess. By the time she realised who I *actually* was and she decided that she was disappointed with her choice, it was too late. The same happened with motherhood. She really wanted it, right until the moment when Katie came.' Even the tinted lenses of his glasses cannot mask the happy glimmer in his eyes when he speaks about his children. 'Katie's fourteen, by the way. Hugo's just turned twelve. Such amazing kids. I'm a very, very lucky dad.' Then the shine dulls again. 'Anyway, the reality of first-time motherhood didn't match with Donna's expectations. She never seemed to bond properly with Katie.'

'But you had a second?'

He sighs and waves a hand dismissively. 'Donna's mother persuaded her to have another to see if she might grow into motherhood, over time. Hugo came along, and . . . well, you know what boys are like. Little bundles of testosterone.' He looks to me for a reaction.

'Oh, yes!'

'Then Donna *really* couldn't cope. To me, the children are a blessing.' A smile flickers on briefly and then off again like a spent lightbulb. 'To her, they're an . . . "impediment to her self-fulfilment," she says. Now I'll be left holding the babies, so to speak. Raising a tween and a teen on one manual worker's salary is no laughing matter. They're *so* expensive. They keep asking me for all this tech gadgetry and big-brand trainers –'

'Sounds familiar,' I say. 'Shame Marjorie doesn't have the seeds for a money tree, eh?'

As he looks up to contemplate the trailing ivy that sits on the shelf above the table, along with the cookbooks I rarely get time to use, I see his Adam's apple bounce up and down. His eyes are sorrowful pools now. 'I wish.'

I'm tempted to reach out and place a comforting hand on his arm, but then I contemplate what he's just said about a manual worker's salary and realise something is off about his story. 'Hang on. Didn't you say you worked for the council as a planning officer? That's an executive job, right? Not manual.'

Mike's wan cheeks are suddenly bright red. He roughly wipes an escaped tear away and sniffs; sits up straighter and folds his arms over his chest. 'Well, er . . . I *did* work in the planning department. That's true. But I was pushed out because I didn't agree with some big development of overpriced, faceless apartments that was given the green light. It meant knocking down a row of large, historic houses in a conservation area, right on the edge of green belt land. They were going to pave over the mature gardens and a copse of apple trees to make a car park, would you believe?'

'So you're a Nimby?' The words tumbled out before I could bite my tongue.

He unfolds his arms. 'Not in my back yard? Yes, I suppose I am.' He clicks his fingers and points. 'But did you know there are five hundred and twenty thousand hectares of residential gardens in Britain?' He raises an eyebrow, clearly delighted at being able to share this obscure town-planner's factoid. 'That's a lot of green space to cultivate into something beautiful or . . . just leave to nature.'

'There's an urgent need for more housing,' I say. I think of the grand balance of £547.30 that sits in the Bank of Mum – a risible contribution towards a deposit on Zak's first home. 'At this rate, my Zak might have to wait until I fall off my perch before he can own his own place.'

'Yes, but if every developer got his way, Gillian, we'd have hundreds of thousands of acres of car parks instead of gardens. Believe you me, I was just doing my bit for Bromley by objecting to thoughtless designs.' He looks ruefully into his wine glass. 'Except caring about our borough made my life so intolerable that I felt forced to hand in my notice. I couldn't bear the constant jibes and filthy looks from colleagues anymore. If someone was making the team a cuppa, I was the only one who wouldn't be asked. That kind of thing. My line-manager seemed to encourage it – singling me out for ridicule in front of the others, leaving me out of meetings so that I'd make mistakes because I wasn't privy to the right information. Ostracised, from the bosses to the recep-tionists. Makes you wonder if they weren't all in the pay of the developer in question. I hear he's a nasty piece of work and has his fingers in a lot of council pies.'

I'm forced to think about what is unfolding at my own place of work, where I am being compelled by my slimeball of a boss to conduct daily witch hunts, just so we can deliver a better dividend to shareholders.

The soul-destroying crappiness of the contemporary work environment seems to thicken the kitchen's air, and I feel light-headed. 'That sounds like constructive dismissal.'

'Constructive dismissal?' Mike looks at me quizzically. 'Do you think so?'

'Oh yes,' I say. I swirl the wine around in my glass and take a gulp, wishing the alcohol would anaesthetise my professional anguish. 'My husband was an employment lawyer, so I've heard my fair share of anecdotes about hardworking, loyal employees being pushed out by ruthless bosses just because they've raised justifiable concerns. Even at a big, reputable insurance company like Chislehurst Green, they might stay on the right side of the law, but they're only interested in who's easiest to cull when the books aren't balancing.' I clutch the bottle of pinot grigio as if it's a lifebuoy saving me from drowning. 'What did your wife make of you losing your job?'

He chuckles without mirth. 'Aha! So, this is where we come back full circle.' He runs his finger along the open collar of his garden centre polo shirt. 'My unfaithful wife is so disgusted by my inability to keep what she deems a "proper" job . . .' He does air-quotes with his fingers, '. . . she's using it as an excuse to kick me out to live in my Mondeo. Meanwhile, she installs lover boy in the house *I've* been paying the mortgage on, all these years.' He finishes his wine and sets the empty glass back down on the table. 'I'm the ultimate cuckold. And there you have the full story.'

What exactly do you say to someone who has been treated so badly, when you hardly know them at all? I run through a few options in my head. 'What happens next? Will you divorce?'

'Yes. That's inevitable, and I don't doubt I'll have a battle on my hands to get some equity out of the house, because Donna's got a horrifically expensive divorce lawyer lined up and waiting to hammer me into the ground.'

I wince sympathetically. 'Ouch.'

'Indeed. But one step at a time. I've got to concentrate on keeping my new job at the garden centre and I have to find somewhere affordable for me and the kids to rent. Luckily, I've scratched together a little rainy-day fund that will do nicely for a deposit and the first month's rent. I'm looking at two places tomorrow.' Mike gets up from the table and walks to the kitchen window so that he has a view of my horticultural work-in-progress. 'In the meantime, gardening's keeping me sane.' He points to the giant pile of turf sitting against the garden fence and the mud bath that is punctuated only by four standard rose trees and spray-painted rectangles. 'What's going on here, then?'

I shrug. 'Well, I've started landscaping the garden. I want to do some raised beds. That's what those white rectangles are. You can see the rose trees I've planted, right?'

'You put the trees in before you built the beds?'

'I already built up the soil a bit. I just haven't got to a timber merchant for sleepers yet.' I wonder how knowledgeable I sound about landscaping, given I'm pretty much busking.

'Okay. Well, you know the rain is likely to wash all that flat again? Earth moves if you don't hold it in with a retaining wall. But you don't necessarily need sleepers, you know. They're expensive and they rot after about ten years. If you've got any bricks knocking about though . . . I can lay them for you, if you'd like. You'd only need them one or two courses high.'

I nod enthusiastically. 'Ooh, good idea! My neigh-bour's had a pile on his drive for a couple of years, ever since his extension was finished. He offered them to me a few months ago, when I started with my grand garden plans.' I bite my lip. 'I'll nip over and ask him if he still wants rid of them.'

'Perfect. If he says you can have them, I'll wheelbar-row them over. Laying them won't take me more than a weekend.'

'Are you sure?'

'Oh, yes.' He flashes me a smile and then turns back to the garden. 'But first things first. What's happening with the big mud pile?'

'I practically gave myself a prolapse digging the turf up. And now . . . now it just looks like Jabba the Hutt in a green wig. Will it eventually rot down?'

He gazes out at the mess. 'Have you got a compost bin?'

'Nope. I blew too much money on roses and some other bits and bobs. Compost bins are expensive!'

'Got any tarp or some old carpet?'

I nod. 'Carpet.'

'Any old bits of wood lying about?'

'Come and look in the shed.' I eye his smart uniform with a degree of scepticism. 'You might want to change out of your uniform, though. I'm pretty sure I've got some of my husband's stuff still knocking about.'

I think about the few items of Dave's clothing that I couldn't bear to part with – his precious U2 *Zooropa* tour T-shirt, his favourite cable-knit jumper, his DIY hoodie and jogging hoodie, the old Arsenal-liveried joggers that he lived in at the weekends, and, not entirely inexplicably, a pair of his pants, which I occasionally sleep with like a safety blanket. The items that no longer see any use now sit neatly in a plastic bag in the bottom of our chest of drawers. Over time, Dave's half of the chest of drawers has filled up with more of my own clothes, as if I've been hoarding my own superannuated underwear and socks to plug some kind of drawer-based existential hole. Could I really offer Dave's remaining clothes to Mike? After ten years, am I ready to let go?

'Don't worry, Gill. I've got my gardening rough stuff in my overnight bag,' Mike says.

I exhale slowly with relief.

Now that spring is upon us in earnest and the evenings are lighter, when we step into my deconstructed back garden the air is almost warm, and the birds are singing their evensong. I even see a brave bumblebee bypassing my barren work-in-progress on its way to next door's crocuses.

'What exactly are you planning on doing with an offcut of carpet and some wood?' I ask.

'You'll see. Just show me to your equipment, ma'am.'

I open the shed door and immediately, three or four giant spiders scuttle out. 'Help yourself.'

Peering inside the tiny 3x6 shed, Mike finds some old 4x2, left over from the construction of a vanity unit in the bathroom, when a twelve-year-old Zak killed the old pedestal sink with a fast cricket ball, whacked along the landing.

He takes hold of one of the lengths of wood. 'This looks in decent condition. Do you need it?'

I shake my head. 'Not a DIY kind of gal.'

'Don't suppose you've got any chicken wire?'

Pushing him aside, I heft the lawnmower out of the way to reveal a part-roll of chicken wire which has been here since Dave constructed a rabbit run for Tub-Thumper, the escapologist rabbit, who died unceremoniously on Zak's fifth birthday beneath the Winnebago wheels of my neighbour, who had been 'driving with the wrong glasses on'.

'Here you go. Will this do?'

'Perfect.' He points to an old, rather mildewed roll of carpet. 'And can I use this?'

'Sure.'

Curious to see what will become of my odds and ends, I follow Mike to a corner of the compact garden that cannot be seen from the windows at the back of the house.

'I'm going to make you a compost box,' he says. He points to the wood. 'First thing we need to do is get some posts into the ground. Have you got something like a lump hammer? Some nails, too. A staple gun, ideally.'

I bring him the necessaries, and presently, I'm holding a piece of wood upright while he bashes it deep into the ground. 'Don't hammer my hand, will you?' I flinch every time the hammer comes down. My wrists jar with the reverberations.

'Don't worry. I'm imagining lover boy's head, ha ha. My aim is true.'

When the first makeshift pillar is sunk, we put in three more so that they form a neat square. He reinforces them with wooden offcuts, tacked on horizontally. The neighbour (not the Winnebago idiot, but the one on the other side) comes out for a nosey over the garden fence. I wave him away with reassurances that I'm not murdering Zak.

With the structure in place, Mike starts to unfurl the chicken wire. 'Now we've got to wrap this around the stakes and fasten it on tight.'

Together, we wrestle the sharp chicken wire into place, and Mike attaches it using the staple gun. Shovelling Jabba the Turf Hutt from one corner to the other is something Mike seems to undertake with relish.

'The more tired I am, the less energy I've got to fret over my situation,' he says, panting while carrying the fourth spadeful of heavy, waterlogged turf.

My thoughts turn to the time I've missed at work today. 'Listen, I've got to go and log in. If I don't check for urgent work emails, my boss will have my guts for garters. Are you alright to crack on without me? I feel guilty that I'm not helping,' I say, my gut tightening at the thought of owing Mike a favour.

'Letting me stay over and feeding me is contribution enough. I am at your service, ma'am.' He salutes. 'And maybe you could start working on your planting plans for the group.'

I smile. 'Good idea. That sounds perfect.'

Inside, having logged in and dealt with the most pressing work issues, I start to google summer-blooming annuals – tall for the back, medium height for the middle, and small for the front of a border or trough; climbing, bushy, and trailing; single specimens and clump-forming workhorses that will suppress weeds. I surf the main online plant retailers to look at their photography for inspiration, and I try to get behind the paywall of various upmarket gardening magazines, though the best source of inspiration seems to be Monty Don's Facebook feed, since he has about a billion distinct parts to his garden, which look completely different as the seasons change. I feel my mood lifting with each photo I peruse. I jot down notes about how the deep blue of delphiniums or eryngium can be successfully paired with, say, yellow roses for a Scandinavian-inspired scheme, or else with flashing red and hot-pink dahlias – except, I realise, dahlias come out far later in the season, and this pairing business is not as easy as I thought it would be . . .

The spring sun is all but down by the time Mike calls me back outside to inspect his handiwork. Wiping his sweaty brow with a muddy hand, he stands over our creation, which is now full to the brim with discarded turf.

'You can do the honours,' he says, inclining his head towards the carpet offcut.

I pick up the carpet and lay it ceremoniously over the top of the turf. 'I now crown this bin Queen Compost of Swanley.' I tuck the carpet in at the sides as though I'm putting a child to bed. 'A challenger to "Berisford's Black Gold".'

Mike puts his arm around me gingerly and gives me an awkward squeeze. He lets go and pushes his glasses up his nose, looking sheepish. 'We're a great team, Gillian. Ha ha. Maybe we should go into business.'

'You're funny,' I say.

'But if we win the Golden Trowel and Dotty Gloucester's golf club, we *could*.'

I shake my head. 'Dotty Gloucester's not even in the ground yet, Mike, and we've got some brick-lobbing, tattoo-headed crackpot maybe trying to sabotage our group. Let's see what we find out at Dotty's wake before we start fantasising about building a horticultural empire!'

12

'Well? How did the funeral go?' I ask Val as we nab the only remaining free table, right near the exit of the Horniman Museum's grand Victorian conservatory. At this time of year, the ambient temperature inside is pleasantly cool enough to accommodate any incoming hot flushes, and it's fitting that a celebrity gardener should have her wake here. I pray I won't get grease from the vol-au-vents on my dark-blue work suit. 'I felt bad not going, but if I ask my boss for any more time off, I think he'll spontaneously combust.'

With a mouth full of breaded jalapeño, spraying crumbs onto her black leather biker's jacket and black crushed velvet leggings, Val fills me in. 'It was very sad. You know. No such thing as a fun funeral. But she must have left instructions for her trustees to spend a bomb on it. Coffin looked nicer than my flat.' She grins. 'I hear the interior was purple satin, too. I love a bit of goth purple, me. Class.'

'What about the church? Was it a big turnout?' I bite into a mini quiche, wishing I could swipe some leftovers for Zak, who is eating pizza at my mother's this evening and will inevitably be hungry again before bedtime. 'Anyone there who looked like a poisoner?'

'Place was rammed,' Val says. 'And the flowers . . . !'

129

She looks over to where Marjorie is weaving her way towards us through the crowd of elderly people and obvious media types, carrying a plateful of food at a rakish angle. 'Here she comes,' Val says. 'Pissed as a newt on her hip flask, and it's only five in the afternoon.'

Marjorie takes a seat at the table, leaving a space between us as if I smell. 'Did one hear mention of flowers?'

'Yes, one did,' Val says. 'They were out of this world, weren't they?'

'How very *BBC* of Dotty to pay a celebrity florist instead of trusting her fellow flower arrangers to give her a good floral send-off,' Marjorie says, eyeing the media mourners with naked disdain that tugs the corners of her mouth downward. 'Even in death, she thought she was too good for the rest of us.'

The rest of our club jostle their way through the crowd and weave past the other tables to sit with us.

Mike points to the spare chair to my left. 'May I?'

I slap the seat, noting that he looks every inch an ex-council worker in his ill-fitting brown suit, which is shiny at the knees and the elbows. I want to ask him how his house-hunting is going and to tell him how my day at work went (mercifully without drama), but the personal chit-chat will have to wait. 'So what have you guys found out so far?'

Neil, who is seated on the far side of the round table, leans towards me. 'No sign of anyone with a head tattoo, but we did hear something interesting from some old codger in the Southwark group.'

'Cecil Braintree?' Marjorie says. 'He's hardly old. He's only seventy-three.'

Cath side-eyes her, looking flummoxed by Marjorie's notion of 'old', then joins in. 'Yes. Apparently on the night the brick was thrown through Marjorie's greenhouse window, Dorothy Gloucester's house was burgled. About half an hour later in fact. How about *that*?!' Normally so serious and taciturn, Cath looks animated, like a woman who has been at the free bar for an hour.

'How about what?' I shrug.

'Two attacks on the property of two lady gardeners on the same night? Within half an hour of each other?'

'Well, it could be a coincidence. Dotty's place is pretty grand.' I remember the stucco Georgian façade, floodlit and fronted by knot gardens like a small manor house. 'And it is empty.'

'But get this,' Neil says, tugging at the ends of his Dalí moustache. 'Old Cecil spoke to Dotty's cleaner the following day. The only things that were taken, according to her, were a hairbrush and some old diaries. Pretty weird spoils for a burglar, if you ask me. They're normally all about the jewellery and electronics and things you can sell easily down the pub. But this . . . ? This isn't your common or garden burglary.'

I look up at the delicate cast-iron latticework of the conservatory's vaulted roof, where the late-afternoon sun is streaming through the glass after an unseasonably fine spring day. I cast my mind back to Seth having run after Marjorie's attacker, and turn my focus back to our youngest member. 'Seth, didn't you say you chased the tattooed brick-thrower back towards Dulwich?'

He nods slowly, toying with the cuffs of a sharp suit that transforms his appearance entirely, from dope-smoking youth to respectable young professional. 'Yeah. For real. I lost him near here, in fact. Right close to Forest Hill station.'

'So the brick-thrower could have been heading to Dulwich?' Mike says. 'And if Dotty G was burgled on the very same night – half an hour later, which is the time it takes to drive from Bromley to Dulwich Village – that would mean her death, Marj's greenhouse attack, and the burglary *could* all be connected.'

'What did this Cecil say the cops are doing about it?' I ask Cath and Neil. 'Will they reopen Dotty G's case because of the burglary?'

They both shake their heads.

'That's incredible negligence,' Mike says.

'Is it though?' Val asks. 'It's a lot of "ifs" and "coulds" and guesswork. Don't surprise me the fuzz ain't looking into it further.'

'Come on! You've got to admit the three things happening close together – Dotty G's death, Marj's brick, and the burglary – they're all a bit fishy,' I say, scanning the room for people behaving suspiciously, except most of the guests are just jostling each other out of the way to get to the buffet. 'I mean, if Dotty *was* murdered, maybe the murderer wanted something from her house. Damning evidence in those diaries, maybe . . . not that I can see how a hairbrush fits in. Trophies, maybe?

Killers take trophies, don't they?' I look around at the others, but their faces are blank, apart from Mike, who is nodding enthusiastically. 'And what happens if Mike's right and the police *are* letting a murderer get away with it?'

'What are you saying, Gillian?' Marjorie asks.

I shrug and bite into a fish goujon. 'Dunno. I mean, look at the common denominator. Between Dotty G . . . and you.'

Marjorie unscrews the lid of her hip flask. 'Both esteemed lady gardeners, both church flower arrangers.' She balks. 'Could the tattooed oink be someone with a . . . a *fetish* for godly, green-fingered women of a certain age?'

'What, like the Kentish Gimp-Suit Flasher?' Phoebe suggests, bursting into a fit of giggles. 'Was he ever arrested?'

'Did that oink steal hairbrushes?'

'*Oik*, Marjorie,' Mike says, wagging his finger. 'Not "oink".'

'Oh, do be quiet! Fool!' she says. She takes a swig from her hip flask and gasps. 'One is dealing with the serious matter of a murderous pervert in one's midst.'

I point to the people at the other tables and those standing by the buffet table. 'Do you spy anyone here who might have a vendetta against you or Dotty G?'

Marjorie narrows her hard blue eyes and looks at the people at the next table. 'Well, there are the Southwark Secateurs.' She scowls. 'Hmm, that battle-axe Lizzie Butterworth isn't among them. She's their rare breed specialist. She went to school with Dotty and I. Strange that she isn't here.' She shakes her head. 'But I've always been under the impression that the other Southwark Secateurs all worshipped the ground Dotty trod.' She eyes the media types on the other side of the conservatory. 'I suppose one might expect the sorts to carry *man*-bags and wear clompy shoes that befit people decades younger *might* lack moral fibre enough to commit a crime.' Her powdery, liver-spotted brow furrows. 'But none of the BBC lot know me, do they?'

'What about other gardening groups?' I ask. 'Who else is here?'

'Croydon Diggers and Dibbers.' Marjorie's lips suddenly curl like a sandwich left in hot sun. 'There's Barnacle Betty Moule.' The name drips like poison from her tongue. 'Look at her, with her *French* husband and her sequins and chignon. How unseemly for a funeral to wear sequins! How FRENCH! Who does she think she is, Prue Leith?!'

I follow the direction of Marj's gaze and catch sight of Barnacle Betty. She is indeed a glamorous older woman, dressed in a black beaded top that looks perfectly suitable for a celebrity funeral. Betty is sitting next to a silver-haired man with Gallic good looks, whom I presume is her husband. Others at the table include a couple of older men and a large-bosomed woman in a low-cut red dress. I notice quite a few of the older male mourners looking admiringly at her, and I wonder who she is. Then I spot an orange-faced man with grey blow-waved hair, who puts me in mind of nightclub-owner and erstwhile playboy Peter Stringfellow, except this guy is not dead and he looks very familiar.

'Who's he?' I ask, pointing. 'I've seen him before.'

'That's Luke Cromarty,' Mike says. 'He's one of the Croydon lot, though ironically, he lives out in Farnborough, which would have made him eligible for our group.'

I snap my fingers as the fog lifts and the memory becomes clear. 'I know where I've seen him. He was at the Princess Royal Hospital in Farnborough, when my mum was taken ill. Drives a giant orange four-wheel drive.'

'Shit. That's my boss,' Seth says, sinking lower in his seat. 'Or at least, my boss's boss's boss.'

'*He's* an *electrician*?' I ask. 'Do electricians earn enough to drive cars like his?'

Seth shakes his head and holds the order of service from Dotty G's funeral up in front of his face. 'Developer. Owns Sunset Pastures Homes. You know? The retirement flats.'

'Oh, I know Sunset Pastures and Luke Cromarty alright,' Mike says, glaring in the direction of Croydon's not-dead answer to Peter Stringfellow. 'I objected to the plans for one of their soulless developments.' He locks eyes with me and raises an eyebrow. 'And it landed me in a world of pain.'

'It was *him*?' I mouth, jerking my thumb in Cromarty's direction.

'Yes,' Mike mouths back, rubbing his thumb and forefingers together to indicate money. 'The puppet-master of the planning department. Or should I say, "pay-master"? Same thing, if you ask me.'

I puff air out of my cheeks. 'Well, I don't think having a car that matches the colour of your tan-in-a-can is harmful to anything but eyes, but given we've got one dead, burglarised gardener and another singled out for vandalism, I'm wondering if we shouldn't do a bit of snooping into the backgrounds of the rival Trowellers – just to make sure the police haven't left a killer on the loose.'

'What, you want us to do a turn as gumshoes?' Val asks.

'Just . . .' I shrug, wishing I hadn't made the sugges-tion, especially since I barely have time spare to attend the gardeners' club once per week. 'Maybe in a *know thine enemy* kind of way? See who out of the Southwark and Croydon lot might see Dotty and Marj as a threat. They moved in the same circles, after all, so this might not even be about gardening. It might be about the church flower arrangers or . . . well, anything really. We won't know 'til we look into it.'

'How do you propose we do that then?' Val asks.

'Gardening gossip grapevines and Google would be good places to start.'

At my side, Mike is practically vibrating with excite-ment. 'We could also make door-to-door enquiries in Dulwich to see if Dotty had any visitors the day she died. Her close neighbours and such like – someone must have seen something.'

'The feds should have done all that, man,' Seth says,

kissing his teeth. 'They're bare useless. But I ain't down with getting up in posh people's grills about Dotty's final movements. A guy who looks like me is going to attract too much heat, knocking on doors in Dulwich. You feel me?'

Phoebe snaps her fingers. 'Mike would make a really good snoop. He's got that old-square-in-a-flasher-mac vibe like Jackson Lamb in *Slow Horses*. If anyone can get Dotty's neighbours to spill, Mike can.'

Mike's cheeks are aflame. 'Thanks, I think.'

'Suppose I can ask around about Cromarty, at least,' Seth volunteers. 'Think some more about where I know that brick-flinging idiot from.'

'So we're doing this?' Neil asks.

I nod. 'One Troweller's dead. One Troweller's greenhouse was sabotaged. And now, a burglary. Maybe there's worse to come. I don't see that we have a choice. Do you?'

13

'No, thank you,' the man says, looking us up and down. He starts to close his front door.

'But you don't even know what we want,' I say, frustrated that Mike and I have given up an evening with our families to have doors slammed in our faces by the wealthy denizens of Dulwich Village. If his expensive-looking pin-striped shirt, gold cufflinks, and Swiss watch are anything to go by, Dotty Gloucester's next-door neighbour is the sort used to having his bidding done without question.

'Look, if you're Jehovah's Witnesses or canvassing for the local elections, I'm not interested,' he says, shaking his head. He glares at Mike. 'You're trespassing, and I've got dogs, so . . .' As if on cue, I hear dogs barking inside his detached Victorian gentleman's residence.

'Oh, we're not politicians or religious types.' Mike pushes his hand against the man's door to stop him from closing it entirely.

'Get your hand off my front door.'

Before the man can unleash his hellhounds on us, Mike brandishes his tablet. 'Please. We're from the planning office of Southwark Council. We're here to ask you about some vandalism to . . . er . . . planning notices that were affixed to the lampposts on your street.'

'It won't take a moment,' I offer, hopeful that we've bought ourselves a reprieve.

'I want to see some ID,' he says.

Mike flashes him the pass that he assures me is realistic, though given he admitted to having cobbled it together with some careful colour photocopying and lamination, I doubt it would hold up to much scrutiny. At least the lanyard neck strap is the real deal.

The man seems convinced since he opens the door a fraction. 'What? The notices about number 56's extension?'

'That's the one,' Mike says.

'Someone's been ripping them down?' A smile plays around his thin lips. 'Good on them, I say. Mercer thinks he owns the street. He only had a new double garage built a couple of months ago, and his builders were always blocking my driveway.' He nods towards the house opposite. 'I wouldn't mind, but there's more than enough space for four cars on his drive.'

'Well, the thing is,' I say, glancing over at the neighbour's place, which is a hulking contemporary pile behind tall gates; the two-storey garage is the size of my entire house. 'If there are unsavoury types in the area, tearing down notices, it's potentially a security risk for the whole neighbourhood.'

'That's right,' Mike says. 'I'm sure you heard that Miss Gloucester next door passed away recently.'

The man blinks hard at us and scowls. 'Yes. Her house is standing empty, and she didn't do anything to it in all the time I've lived here. Thankfully, though, because it's a beauty.'

'It is a very good example of London's Georgian stock,' Mike says, pushing his glasses up his nose. 'You have good taste, sir.'

There's that suggestion of a smile again. The man stands up straighter and puffs his chest out a little. 'I hope to hell whoever buys it doesn't think they can tear it down and throw a Travelodge up like Mercer.'

'Not if I have anything to do with it,' Mike says, clicking his heels together and clutching his tablet like a rifle.

'Good man.'

I'm relieved Mike's established a rapport with Dotty's neighbour, but I check my watch and realise we haven't got long before I have to get home to Zak. 'So, er, have you seen any suspicious comings and goings recently?' I ask. 'Around the time of Miss Gloucester's death. That's when the vandalism was reported to us, as coincidence would have it.'

The man scratches at the roots of his thinning silver hair. Has he bought our nonsense story?

A woman's voice comes from within. 'Darling, who is it?'

He shouts down the hallway, 'Planning types. Asking about nefarious goings-on at the time of Dorothy's death.'

There's the sound of dogs barking and then footsteps. A glamorous blonde woman in her early forties, maybe, appears at the door. She looks us both up and down and treats me to a sympathetic smile.

'Have you told them about the white Golf?' she asks, clearly excited by the council-sanctioned gossip.

'White Golf?' Mike writes on his tablet.

'Yes. A *Volkswagen*.' She spits out the brand name as though she's just said 'pork scratchings' or 'nylon gusset'. 'I saw it parked outside Dorothy's house several times just before she died. Blacked-out windows and alloys. Unsavoury types drive cars like that, don't they? Chavs.' Her nostrils flare with obvious disgust. She turns to her husband. 'I mentioned it to you, darling, remember? I kept seeing it when I came back from walking Portia and Milo.' She treats us to a dazzling, professionally whitened smile. 'Everybody drives a Range Rover or a Tesla round here.' The wattage of her smile dims. 'Only the cleaners drive *Volkswagens*.'

I think about my old Volvo which I've been duti- fully keeping on the road for fifteen years. What would this woman make of its passenger footwell, full of the detritus from transporting a teenage boy? Empty crisp packets. Long-forgotten drinks bottles. A mysterious supply of odd sports socks. 'Do you have CCTV by any chance, madam?' I ask.

'Why? We haven't contravened any planning laws, have we?'

Mike clears his throat. 'We're after some vandals who have been removing planning notices. If you think a white Golf is involved, it might be useful to see foot- age of it arriving and leaving . . . if you have footage, of course. Perhaps we can get a number plate or a glimpse of its owner.'

The woman laughs. 'Don't be absurd! We don't mon- itor our own CCTV footage. We pay a security company to do that. And as far as I know, they only capture what lies within our property's boundaries. Anything beyond that is illegal. *You* of all people should know that.'

The last I see of her husband is his bemused expression as she slams the door in our faces. We get to the end of the pathway and pass through the garden gate.

'Blimey, she was a piece of work,' I say, looking back at the beautifully manicured house and garden with its twin Range Rovers sitting out front, gleaming in the red-orange light of the sunset.

'Well, we've made a start,' Mike says. 'We know we're potentially on the lookout for the driver of a white Golf with blacked-out windows. Maybe it's the ruffian who threw the brick.'

'I'm sure Seth said he drove an Astra.'

'Hmm. The plot thickens. But if we can get a look at CCTV footage . . . who knows what that will reveal about the circumstances surrounding Dotty's death?'

'So, getting access to people's CCTV is the holy grail?'

He nods. 'If we're doing this, we might as well do it properly.'

We walk along to Dotty G's empty house. Mike looks beyond the tangled hedge of roses, just coming into leaf on the other side of the railings that edge her front garden.

'I personally can't believe the police didn't go door to door, asking these questions,' he says.

I rummage in my handbag and check my phone absently. 'Maybe they did and they hit a dead end, because the neighbours were all out doing rich-people things. Or maybe they're underfunded and couldn't afford to put detectives on a door-to-door thing when the death wasn't suspicious enough to warrant it. Or *maybe* . . . and I reckon this is the most likely . . . the death of an elderly woman – however famous – isn't too much of a priority.' I remember the Georgian house as Marjorie and I had found it – unlocked and brightly lit, as though Dotty G had just nipped out of her life, only for a moment, with every intention of returning.

'That's a lot of maybes, Gill.' Mike starts walking towards the neighbouring property on the far side of Dotty's plot.

I follow him. 'But why wouldn't leaving your door open be considered weird in a place like this, where everyone seems to have top-notch security?' I turn to take in the sight of Dotty's elegant house. This evening, the sinking sun has turned the white stucco pink. There are no floodlights; no signs of life inside. For all its splendour, it looks sad. I sigh deeply.

Mike glances back at me. 'Cheer up! The next neighbour might give us some information that sheds light on what happened.'

'You sound unhealthily chipper, Michael. Like a scout leader.'

He snaps his fingers and points triumphantly. 'You never know your luck in a big city. The other week, I was homeless. Now, I've got a twelve-month rental contract on a lovely little terrace for me and the kids. Things can turn on a dime, Gill. You'll see.'

There is only an open driveway next door — no tall gates, no intercom — though the house is still a grand double-fronted affair.

'Art Deco with the original Crittall windows,' Mike says. 'Very nice. They must have built it in the garden of Dotty's house in the thirties. Glad to see they've not replaced the originals with uPVC.'

I have no real idea what Mike's talking about with such audible enthusiasm, so I just nod. 'No lights on. No cars on the drive.' I push the bell.

We stand almost too close together on the doorstep, staring pointlessly at the leaded lights in the glass of the front door. A minute or so passes. Mike knocks. I press the bell again. Nothing.

'They're out or away,' I say. 'Let's give this one up.'

Back on the pavement, Mike peers up and down the street. 'Okay, by my reckoning, there's no sense in going any further afield on this side of the road. The plots are so wide that two doors down wouldn't get a good view of Dotty's frontage.'

'So, our next port of call should be the people opposite,' I say, pointing at the hulking Travelodge that cufflink man had spoken so disparagingly about. 'The Mercers, didn't he say?'

We cross the road. Obviously, the gates are locked, and there's an intercom built into one of the pillars. Mike presses the buzzer. After about twenty seconds, we hear a woman's voice.

'Hello?'

'We'd like to speak to Mr or Mrs Mercer please. We're

from the planning office of Southwark Council.' Mike nudges my shoe with his.

'They not here,' the woman says. 'They gone on holiday. I'm housekeeper. You come back in ten days.'

There is a click, a buzz of static, and then silence.

'Well, that's the end of that,' I say. I take several steps back and look at the roofline of the house. I follow it down to the charcoal-coloured barge boards and fascia, and I smile. 'Look!' I point up at the black orbs that hang at regular intervals from the fascia. With red winking lights and lenses like little black all-seeing eyes, I know they are looking down at us, recording everything. Turning around to survey Dotty's house, I nod, feeling hopeful. 'If they've got access to their own CCTV footage, and those cameras have taken more than just what's inside the boundary, chances are we'll see who's been visiting Dotty.'

Mike pats me on the shoulder. 'Meanwhile, we've got the white Golf to go on. Let's see if anyone in Golden Trowel gardening circles has a car that matches that description. Find the driver, and I think we might just find a murderous saboteur.'

14

'One does hope you've all brought your plans for planters with you,' Marjorie says at the following gardeners' club meet.

She treats us all to a tea-stained smile and waves a sheaf of magazine cut-outs vigorously, wafting the fusty, damp smell of the church hall's stale air towards me so that I sneeze.

'Yes,' we murmur in unison.

Dutifully, I rummage in my bag for my USB stick, taking the opportunity to check my phone for any messages from Zak, though it's the Easter holidays, and he's supposedly busy revising for his summer exams. Supposedly. There are no messages. Not even from Mum, who told me she's rewatching an old film with Robert Redford *and* Brad Pitt tonight, which is about as much wholesome excitement as my mother can endure without throwing her back out.

Mike gets to his feet and clears his throat. He's dressed in borderline fashionable chinos and a stylish shirt tonight. 'Thank you, Marjorie. I'll take it from here.' He pulls his chinos up, either ignoring or unaware of Marjorie's disdainful glare. 'Now, I've set up our interactive IT centre.' He points to a rickety table which bears a laptop – evidently so old, I can barely hear him speak over the noisy fan, cooling its overtaxed processor – and a whiteboard, mounted precariously on a painter's easel. 'Thank you to Neil, who is lending us tonight's whiteboard.'

'Well, the kids won't miss it while it's the holidays,' Neil says. 'I won't tell if you don't.' He nudges me, as if I'm his co-conspirator. 'But if you break it, you pay.'

Mike takes a step away from the haphazard easel rig-up. 'And thank you to Valerie for lending us her easel.'

Val looks up from rolling a cigarette and nods. 'Last time that easel saw light of day, I was painting a life model. Young man, he was.' She grins. 'Buck naked. There was barely enough room on the canvas for his –'

'Yes. Thank you, Valerie.'

Phoebe and Seth chuckle and whisper to one another behind their hands.

'I'll go first, shall I?' Mike says. Ignoring Marjorie's fistful of magazine cut-outs, he sits at the IT table and brings up a duplicate of his own laptop screen. Realising he's left several tabs open that are visible behind the file search, he hastily clicks on each in turn to shut them down. We now all know he's been reading about the legalities of constructive dismissal in the workplace, a personal trainer's guide to losing excess belly fat, and how to rid yourself of excessive ear hair. His face turns fuchsia. 'Oh, dear. Sorry, I . . . Hang on. Whoops. Ah. Ha. Right.' Finally, we are able to see photographs of his planting ideas.

'So, in my presentation, I wanted to concentrate on the various large troughs around the borough that we've installed over the years. We've got ten of these to fill.' He clicks his mousepad, and a map of the area appears on the whiteboard. He pushes his glasses up his nose and focuses in on me. 'Believe me, when they're in bloom, they make such a wonderful difference to the residents.'

Marjorie raises her hand. 'Except the one we put on the border with Downham, where the neighbours either stole the plants or killed them, because they used the trough as a dumping ground for dog-mess bags and empty alcohol receptacles.'

Val turns to Marjorie and almost vaporises her with a death stare. 'You being a snob, Marj? Because blaming the country's ills on the working classes and immigrants would be totally out of character, wouldn't it?'

'Oh, Valerie, one finds your leftist rhetoric rather wearing. The fact remains that the Downham trough was desecrated by the local oinks.'

'*Oiks!*' Mike, Cath, Val, and Phoebe all chime in unison.

Neil claps his hands, as though he's addressing his pupils. 'Jesus Christ, calm down, everybody! Let Mike get on with his presentation, or we'll all be here long enough to take root. We've got to allow time at the end to give updates on our internet sleuthing.'

'*Thank* you, Neil,' Mike says. He brings up a series of photographs next, which show his suggested planting scheme. 'So, I propose black canna Tropicanna in the middle, paired with dahlia Apache, so that we've got dazzling tomato-red flowers, lasting well into September, early October. And I'd offset that with bright blue lobelia and those lovely purple petunia Tumbelina.' He clicks the mouse again and brings up a picture of some flowers that I vaguely remember sowing seeds for during the last practical session in Marj's now-repaired greenhouse. 'Some nice burgundy coleus to complement the canna's black foliage.'

Marjorie holds her hand to her eyes. 'One finds those colours rather clashing, Michael.'

'I don't think the red goes with the blue,' Cath says.

Mike Potato looks utterly crestfallen.

'Looks gorgeous, Mike,' I say, looking around to see if I've committed a faux pas by backing up the King of King Edwards.

He smiles at me. 'Thank you, Gillian. I thought so too. Given we've got all these troughs, I don't see why we shouldn't have a little variety.'

'Couldn't you put in some perennials too, like those lovely blue sea holly thistles – isn't the Latin name "eryngium"?'

Mike snaps his fingers at me. 'Yes. There's a cobalt-coloured eryngium called Blue Steel. That would look spectacular, and the bees would love it.'

'And those weird red and yellow lily things, that look like upturned claws,' I say, feeling emboldened by Mike's enthusiasm.

'Gloriosa superba Rothschildiana, or flame lilies, as some call them. Lovely idea.'

Next up is Seth, who shows us his ideas for an impressive tall display, built around a bamboo obelisk filled with sweet peas, coupled with flowering tobacco and scented begonias. 'All these plants I've chosen, yeah, will smell really nice,' he says. 'I think it's a good idea to go for nice-smelling stuff, so people will want to sniff them, and the bees will like them and that.'

Marjorie stands up and addresses us all, in turn. 'This is a lovely idea, Seth,' she says, 'and scent should definitely be a consideration. But A . . .' She holds her thumb up. 'Sweet peas need constant dead-heading, and we can't get round often enough to stop them from going to seed. And B . . .' She holds an arthritic index finger aloft. 'There's the small issue of our plans being restricted by the seeds we've sown this year and that which has overwintered success-fully. We're also overdue starting off the dahlias this year.'

'Yeah, why is that?' Val asks.

Marjorie fiddles with the pearly cuffs of her peach polyester blouse. 'Given the cold snap we've had, down to three degrees at night, and the gale that was gusting through one's broken greenhouse window, I thought we should delay by a few weeks.'

'Good point,' Val says. 'Gill, would you like to show us your ideas?'

The room falls silent again. Already, I feel my pulse accelerating from a steady plod to a wild, galloping beat. 'Yes. Sure.' I approach the interactive IT table and take the hotseat, praying my USB stick works – more nervous than I have ever been when giving a presentation to the regional directors at work. I open my file. As soon as I see the photographs of the flowers on the whiteboard, my pulse begins to slow once more, thanks to the bright colours and intricate form of the petals releasing a hit of dopamine (or so Mandi-with-an-I would say).

'Right, well, having trawled the internet for gardening porn . . .' I ignore Marjorie's tutting and Phoebe's sniggers. '. . . I realise the colour scheme that makes me happiest is a multicoloured one. So I've selected a multicoloured million-bells mix – cal-i-bra-choa.' I struggle to read out the Latin name. 'And then, I'd pair these with cascading fuchsia Voodoo, because those colours pop, and maybe some giant fuchsia marbeller Orange King because they're a bonkers clash.'

'How would you build height for the centre of the trough?' Mike asks.

I click through to the next photograph. 'Well, I was wondering if you could have a ring of big gladioli, maybe. Purple, pink, and orange?'

'The problem with that,' Marjorie says, 'is that gladioli need staking, ideally, and they're over too quickly. One would need something coming up in front . . . er, delphiniums per se, which come in delightful blue and purple shades.'

'Ooh, I adore those,' I say. 'The intense colour and ruffled flowers are gorgeous. But don't they need staking too?'

'Indeed.' Marjorie nods. 'And the dratted slugs simply adore them.'

'Yeah.' Val pulls some tobacco off her tongue thoughtfully and rubs a heavily kohled eye so that she looks like a panda. 'And whatever early-summer-flowering tall plants you put in, you need something for when those are finished.'

I click through to the next photos. 'How about dinner

plate Emory Paul dahlias or maybe a tower of alstroe-meria, growing through a support? You can get those ones that grow a metre and a half.'

Mike gets to his feet again and gives me the double thumbs up. 'Some excellent ideas for a vibrant display, Gill. Thank you.' He beams at me and mouths, 'Well done.'

I feel like a kid who's been given the class prize. When the others have finished presenting their ideas, Mike clears his throat and claps his hands.

'Great work, people. I think we should incorporate everyone's ideas. Maybe everyone gets a trough each. There's certainly enough to go round this year.'

We all murmur our agreement.

'Now, shall we turn our attention to our little sleuth-ing sideline?' he asks.

Mike looks at me expectantly, so I fill the others in on the upshot of our jaunt into Dulwich Village. 'So, we won't know for over a week if we can access CCTV and potentially get a look at Dotty's mystery visitor,' I say, enjoying the experience of people actually listening to me when I speak. 'But in the meantime, we can be finding out if anyone within our rival groups drives a white Golf.'

'Surely we don't need to look into the Southwark Secateurs,' Marjorie says. 'They've withdrawn their entry into the Golden Trowel Award.'

Shoving his thumbs inside his waistband, Mike rocks on his heels. He's wearing nice brogues this evening too. They look brand new. 'I think we should be thor-ough and not make any assumptions.' He chuckles and touches the collar of his shirt. '*Assume* makes an "ass" of "u" and "me".' He looks to me for a reaction.

I stifle an eye roll at a hackneyed corporate maxim I've heard Colin come out with, time and again. 'Yep. Absolutely right.' I turn my attention to the others. 'Have you guys found out anything interesting about the Croydon lot, apart from Luke Cromarty being Seth's boss's boss's boss and having terrible taste in cars? Anything that might point to one of them being a murderer with motive for poisoning an elderly Radio 4 presenter?'

'They added a new tab in the "About Us" section of the Croydon Diggers and Dibbers website,' Seth says. 'It's got little biographies of the members.'

We huddle around the table, craning our necks to look at Seth's phone.

'Here's your pal, Marjorie.' Seth raises his eyebrow, turns the screen towards us, and shows us a photograph of Barnacle Betty. 'She's Croydon's most senior Troweller.'

'If they're involved in this skulduggery, *she'll* be the ringleader.' Marjorie bites the claws off a Monster Munch paw (Mike brought pickled onion flavour, sadly) and then points the remnants at us. 'Mark my words.'

Seth brings up the biography of the next Croydon member. 'Barty Bing.' He clicks his fingers and chuckles. 'That name, man! Priceless. Says here he's a retired solicitor. Looks like his false teeth be too big for his head. Anyone?'

'Oh, Barty, yes. He's a nice enough chap,' Marjorie

says, almost smiling. There's a wistful look in her eyes. 'I had tea with him once after we bumped into each other at the Chelsea Flower Show. One had heard through the grapevine that he used to have a large home in Oxshott with some outstanding hydrangea borders. One can't imagine what on earth he's doing in Croydon. He must have fallen on hard times. But I feel certain he's completely benign.'

Seth clicks through to the next biography. 'What about *this* old geez? Neville Studley. Retired GP.'

Cath frowns. 'Oh, wait a minute. I know that name.' She cocks her head to the side momentarily, and then her face lights up. 'I *do* know Neville Studley! He got struck off about fifteen years ago for manhandling his female patients' boobs.' She snorts with derision. 'Neville bloody Studley. Ha. What a turn-up! But I don't think a disgraced GP is behind all this, unless he's moved on to groping used hairbrushes and poisoning BBC radio presenters.'

Marjorie and Val peer at the photo of the handsy GP that Seth is now showing us. They both curl their lips and shake their heads.

'Never trust a man with Liberace hair,' Val says.

Seth clicks on the biography of a middle-aged woman. 'Louise Lampard? Anyone? Says here she's a part-time university lecturer and a "writer of erotic fiction".'

At this point, Mike turns a noticeable shade of red.

'Michael, have you got anything to share with us?' Marjorie asks.

Mike looks at his hands. 'Er, I may have come across her online.'

'Been reading her dirty bedtime stories?' Seth asks. 'Or did you swipe right on Tinder?' He throws his head back and guffaws with laughter. 'Mike, you a player, man!'

'Actually, it was *Guardian* Soulmates, but I sincerely doubt she'd have any involvement with bullying tactics. She didn't strike me as the type, although our exchange was admittedly brief. She stopped returning my messages after a day or two. I think she may have ended her membership.'

'Ooooooh! She ghosted you.' Seth claps his hands together triumphantly.

'Oh, no. I don't think so.'

'Yeah, right!'

I stare at Mike Potato with incredulity. He didn't mention online dating when he stayed over at mine or when we were out playing detectives in Dulwich. But then, why would he? Am I being fair in expecting him to confide in me to that extent? Would I even want to know if Mike's nicer clothes and better shoes are for my benefit or some other woman's? I take a sip of my drink and dismiss the crushing sensation in my chest as trapped wind from the bubbles.

'Now *this* guy!' Seth says, having clicked on the next biography, which bears the photo of a surly-looking young man with terrible hair and a scruffy beard that makes him look like a poorly shorn sheep. He taps his finger on the screen. 'Taylor Jones.'

'Looks like a ne'er-do-well,' Marjorie says.

'Well, this numpty is working on the same new building site as me. An apprentice joiner. He don't seem to recognise me, and it took me a while to place him, because he's shaved off that beard and he's been wearing a beanie to work. But I realised the other day he was on the last big Sunset Pastures Homes development I worked on.'

'So there's a connection between Cromarty and this Taylor lad,' Mike says. 'Neither of them strikes me as gardening types, if I'm honest.'

Seth nods. 'Right?! That ain't all, though. Listen to this! When Taylor took the beanie off when we was having our break – this is the other day, like – I seen he's shaved his hair off, and . . . wait for it . . . he's only got the same head tattoo as the guy in the Astra – Marj's vandal.'

We all gasp in unison.

'Why would an apprentice joiner have beef with someone like Marjorie?' I ask. I look at Marj. 'Did this young guy do some woodwork for you, and maybe you forgot to pay?'

Marjorie's lips thin in clear indignation. 'What are you insinuating about my honesty, Gillian? One *always* pays one's bills in full and on time. I have *never* used the services of this oink. With or without a beard and that degenerate haircut, I *never* forget a face.'

'Sorry, Marjorie. I didn't mean . . . We should pass this on to the police, right?'

Seth wags his finger at me, looking aghast. 'Nah, nah, nah! Don't start a thing with Taylor Jones until we got proper damning evidence.'

'If you knew all this,' Mike asks, 'why didn't you mention it sooner?'

'Give me a chance, man. I only put two and two together yesterday. And we definitely shouldn't rush in with the feds, accusing Taylor of all sorts, until we're sure we can *prove* he threw that brick, and we can say why he did it. I know his family, yeah? From New Addington. They're nasty people, man. His dad's got a real reputation, and his brother's been inside for armed robbery. And I ain't keen to end up labelled as no grass. They'll turn up on my doorstep. Know what I mean? So, leave it be for now. I'll watch him at work and see what I can find out.'

Mike looks around at us all. 'A dodgy developer and his sidekick, eh? Assuming one of them drives a white Golf with blacked-out windows, I think we might have our first two suspects.'

When we break for a fresh drink and more snacks, I stand by Mike and down one of his horrible dandelion beers.

'I'm so glad the presentation went well,' I tell him. 'I was worried Marjorie would rip my ideas to shreds.'

'But she didn't, did she?' Mike says. 'You did great.' He claps me on the back. 'You're getting the hang of this. We'll all have *bona fide* green fingers by the end of the season.'

'Maybe I'll have a back garden I can sit in and enjoy by the end of the season,' I say. 'Partly thanks to you.' I picture the raised beds Mike has promised to fashion for me once we're all planted up for the Golden Trowel.

Mike drains a cup of his disgusting homebrew and

visibly twitches, as though somebody has attached live electrodes to him. 'That'll put hairs on my chest. Ha ha. You'll have to have a grand opening when it's all planted up.' He holds his cup aloft. 'I'll supply the fizz.'

'Maybe I'll get this lot round.' I chuckle at the thought of having such a bunch of near-strangers in my home. 'Maybe not.' I'm not sure I'm ready for that. 'Mind you, I might not be able to afford anything else for the garden this year. The NHS wait to see a psychiatrist for suspected ADHD is a couple of years long, so I'll have to fork out for a private assessment for Zak. And the NHS doesn't cover dyslexia assessments at all, so going private for both is going to run to a couple of thousand. Stumping up for a new Chemistry textbook because Zak lost his last one just adds insult to injury.'

I feel a hand on my shoulder. 'You looking for an A-Level Chemistry textbook?'

I turn around and see Seth looking at me expectantly. 'What?'

'Chemistry A-Level textbook. Is that what I heard you talking about? Only, I got one in good nick if it's the same as what he's using at school. You can have it for free.'

Blinking repeatedly, I try to make sense of what I'm being offered. 'AQA exam board? New syllabus?' Has Seth, the aspiring cannabis-growing magnate, got a side-hustle in stolen textbooks, I wonder?

Seth nods. 'Yeah, man. I finished at night school last year, like, so I don't need it no more. You feel me?' He frowns and bites his lip. 'I would bring it with next time, but I always come straight from work. So, as long as you come round my house to pick it up, it's yours.' He takes a short pencil from behind his ear and scribbles an address on a pad. 'I'm in after four.'

I'm delighted that I won't have to find almost fifty pounds to replace Zak's lost textbook. I'm also touched by his kindness. But part of me – a part that I'm ashamed of – is wondering how safe I'll feel heading to Seth's place. The kid constantly reeks of marijuana, and the address he's given me, on one of Bromley's few council estates, is not particularly salubrious. 'Brilliant. Thanks. Great. Yes.'

'Or you could get it after this meeting, if your kid needs it. Follow me in your car?'

15

My windscreen wipers whine in anguish as I hurtle after Seth through a torrential April downpour. When the detached houses give way to small 1930s semi-detacheds, and the semis give way to boxy blocks of flats, we turn into a side road that is full of ugly 1960s terraced housing, maisonettes, and one high-rise. I feel exposed as a single, middle-aged woman, venturing into uncharted territory, alone and in the dark. At least I've told Zak where I'm going.

I see that Seth has pulled up some way ahead outside a house. When I slow the Volvo and park opposite, I can see that there is a bare bulb illuminated in one of the bedroom windows. The curtains in the living room are shut, but there is a net curtain hanging at a wonky angle in front of the curtains. Is this a drug den? Does Seth live alone or with friends? Who is in the bedroom?

'You don't half get yourself into some fixes, Gill Swanley,' I tell myself.

Seth gets out of his car and beckons me to follow him. I get out of the car into the pouring rain, lock up, and sprint over to the open door. The smell of marijuana hits me immediately, and I say a silent prayer that the house isn't raided by the police or a rival drug gang while I'm there.

'Jesus, Seth,' I say, covering my nose. 'What a guff!'

He hasn't heard me. He's already inside the hallway, shouting, 'I'm home, Mum!' He flings his door keys on the side.

What greets me, as I gingerly cross the threshold, is unexpected. First, there is a volley of barking, and a giant golden Labrador bounds down the narrow hallway to meet me. Not the Rottweiler I had anticipated, but a big, soft Lab. Tongue out and panting, the dog is friendly. He barks once and sits in front of me, clearly expecting a reaction, tail wagging, paw raised, as if he's been trained.

'Shake his paw. Go on. And give him one of these. He'll love you forever.' Seth throws me a dog biscuit. 'He's the worst guard dog in the world, aren't you, Rebel?'

I tentatively shake Rebel's paw, let the dog gobble the biscuit, and pat him on the head. 'Good doggy.' Dave always hated dogs, so I've continued to eschew them, even though there have been many times over the last ten years when the company of a dog would have been nice for me and Zak.

'Come through,' Seth says.

The second unexpected thing is that the house, despite looking like a crack den from the outside, is pristine inside. It does reek of weed (and a little bit of wet dog), and it is terribly old-fashioned, with furnishings that look like a charity shop showroom, but there is not a speck of dirt or clutter to be seen. The only items of ornamental value are houseplants and photographs of Seth at varying ages. As I take in the living room, my gaze comes to rest on a woman, who is sitting perfectly still in an armchair with her feet on a footstool, staring at a television that is on but without sound; the large floral pattern on her top an almost perfect match for the wallpaper behind her. Small wonder I hadn't noticed her.

'Mum, this is Gill,' Seth says.

The woman slowly turns towards me. Her eyes seem unfocused, and her face is drawn. 'Alright, Gill? Sit yourself down.' She raises a shaking hand and gesticulates at the sofa.

As I sit down, I notice that a large joint is burning in an ashtray at her side. I also clock a wheelchair, folded and propped against the wall behind the door.

'My name's Mary,' she says. 'I'm Seth's mum.' She shouts after Seth, who has disappeared into the kitchen. 'Make a cup of tea, darling? Gill'll have one, and all, won't you, love?' She speaks with a pronounced Estuary twang.

I nod with a smile, keen to find out more about this shaking shell of a woman.

'I hadn't realised Seth lived at home with his mum and dad,' I say.

Mary scoffs. 'Ain't seen his dad in fifteen years. But my Seth's a good'un. He's on a good whack as a spark. He could be living in some flat-share with his mates, by now. But he's stayed at home to look after his ma.' She leans towards me. 'I got MS, you see. Diagnosed a while back. Just before his dad shipped out.' She tuts.

'Oh, that all sounds dreadful. I'm very sorry to hear it.'

Seth returns carrying a tray holding our drinks and a plate of biscuits. 'That's the real reason why I'm at the gardeners' club, ain't it, Mum?' He stuffs two biscuits into his mouth at once and speaks with his mouth full. He squats beside his mother's armchair, placing his hand protectively on the broad armrest. 'Learning proper plant breeding and composting to a pro standard. I grow cannabis for Mum's pain, see? Got an amazing hydroponics rig-up in the spare bedroom and the loft, but I want to go into medicinal cannabis full time. Start my own business, like.'

His mother pats his hand and smiles. 'He's such a clever boy, my Seth. He was terrible at school – couldn't wait to leave – but he went back and did Biology and Chemistry A-Levels at night school and got all A*s.' She ruffles his hair.

'That's right, Mum. I got plans.' Seth's eyes find mine, and it's like looking at Zak when he enthuses about some chess game he's been playing. 'I've been playing with cross-pollination and that, and I'm breeding the perfect marijuana for pain relief without the grogginess. Mum's my lab rat, ain't you, Mum?'

Mary laughs. 'Yeah. Gladly. You're a lifesaver, darlin'.' She grabs his face and plants a kiss on his cheek. Then she turns her attention back to me. 'He's gonna win a Nobel Prize one of these days, my boy. And I wouldn't mind, but he doesn't even touch it himself! Can you believe it?!'

'Wouldn't do my asthma much good,' Seth says, scratching the patchy smattering of stubble on his chin. He gets to his feet with knees that crack disconcertingly for a young man of his tender years. He takes a seat opposite me. 'Bad enough, working on building sites. All that damp and dust . . .'

It becomes clear, then, that the smell of weed on Seth is not from his own cannabis consumption but from his chronically ill mother's. Seth is no drug dealer. In fact, his South-East London council estate patois has been replaced with an accent that more closely matches his mother's, now that he's on his home turf. I realise that he's been putting on a hardman front, perhaps to impress Phoebe, who has also been wearing an ill-fitting 'street' persona, undoubtedly to impress Seth.

The sheer silliness of youth brings a smile to my lips. 'So that's why you want to learn how to make Mike's "Berisford's Black Gold" compost?'

He nods. 'I'm gonna give it my best shot: breeding a special strain of medicinal cannabis, getting it patented, and then growing it commercially.'

'But you need a licence, don't you? And the market's already cornered by drug dealers or pharmaceutical companies. Aren't you worried you're going to get tangled up in trouble?'

He simply shakes his head uncertainly, and I can see that his aspirations are fuelled by a combustive mix of desperation, optimism, and naivety. Mary clearly has enough on her plate, if she's ill enough to be reliant on a wheelchair in her late thirties or early forties (it's hard to tell which). She also doesn't strike me as the sort of mother who would know much about the world of big pharma, licensing, and organised crime. I privately wonder if I should mention Seth's sideline business project to one of the others in the group.

'I steer well clear of the dealers round here,' he says. 'I ain't looking to sell on the street.' He blushes and looks at his feet momentarily. Then he shoves his hands in his pockets and meets my gaze once more, raising an eyebrow. 'Anyway, maybe I got more to worry about with you lot. Turns out community gardening ain't no picnic, what with bricks through Marj's greenhouse window and dead old ladies and whatnot.'

I take a sip of my tea. It tastes worse than the muck from the urns at work. 'You're going to have to be very careful on the building site with that vandal, Taylor, working in close proximity. If he finds out you're keeping tabs on him . . .'

Seth blanches visibly, and I wonder why.

His mother is staring at the side of his face. 'What's this? You never said nothing to me about playing private dick. What you getting involved with, son?'

'Someone started with one of the old ladies from the gardening club, Mum, and I just followed them to see who they were. At a safe distance, like. And then I recognised he works on my site. I'm just keeping a bit of an eye on him. All on the down-low. No confrontation, like. It's nothing to worry about. Honest.' Seth gets up from his chair and walks over to a bookcase, where the shelves are sagging beneath the weight of what appear to be sagas and romance paperbacks, judging by their titles. On the bottom shelf, however, are a few crime thrillers and some chunky textbooks.

'Seth Robbins, you better not be lying to me.' Mary leans forward in her chair, frowning.

'Honest I'm not. I swear, Mum.'

Seth picks out the textbook that I've come here for. 'Here you go, Gill.'

I take my purse out of my handbag. 'How much do I owe you?'

He shakes his head. 'Nothing. Put your money away.'

Undeterred, I stuff twenty into his hand. 'Take it. I insist. You're still saving me thirty quid.'

He puts the twenty back into my handbag. 'Come on. I'll show you out. I been wiring up those retirement flats since half seven this morning and I'm knackered. Early night for me.' He yawns pointedly.

With my tea half drunk, I bid farewell to Mary, aware that Seth either wants rid of me or else has something to say to me in private. In the hallway, I hook my bag over my shoulder and tuck the textbook under my arm.

'You alright?' I ask.

He bites his lip. I recognise the same sort of fidgety body language that Zak displays when he's about to blurt out something he's been sitting on for a while. 'Yeah. Only don't tell the others none of my business. You know. My mum being ill, and me being her carer, and the weed farm and that. I don't need people feeling sorry for me or lecturing me.'

I nod. 'My lips are sealed. Promise.' I pretend to zip my lips closed.

'I should have kept my mouth shut about the brick, and I don't want to worry Mum. She's got enough on her plate.'

'She's right. You shouldn't be chasing violent strangers

into parts of London you're not familiar with. I mean, I know he turned out not to be a stranger, but you didn't know that at the time. It could have gone quickly sideways if he'd spotted you.'

He walks me out to my car. The rain has stopped.

I pause by my Volvo, key in hand. 'Listen, I don't suppose you'd do tutoring, would you? For Chemistry A-Level, I mean. An hour a week, just to help my Zak go over what's been done in class so he "gets" it and keeps up.'

Seth frowns and looks up at the pink, light-polluted cloud cover. 'I suppose I could. Yeah.'

I think about the cost implication of what I've just asked, knowing other parents spend as much as £50 an hour for a good tutor. *More* money, on top of Mum's carer and the various private assessments Zak must undertake. I'm getting myself deeper into a financial hole, but how can I let my boy's prospects suffer?

'How about fifteen an hour?' Seth says. 'I can swing by yours after work on, say, a Wednesday?'

'Fifteen pounds? That's too little. That'll barely cover your petrol.'

'Mates' rates, innit?' Seth says. 'I'm happy to help. I love Chemistry. Make me a sarnie while I'm there, if you feel funny about the price.'

I clasp his hands in mine, flushed with gratitude and relief. 'Oh, Seth. God bless you. You're an angel.'

His phone pings loudly in his pocket. He takes it out and frowns. Then his eyebrows shoot towards his hairline.

'Everything alright?' I ask.

'A message from Phoebs,' he says. He turns his phone towards me to show me a photograph she's sent of a white Golf with blacked-out windows, standing on a driveway in the dark in front of an unremarkable boxy house. 'She's found Dotty G's visitor.'

'Who?' I look at the photo, wondering if perhaps this Taylor Jones had been driving a Golf, rather than an Astra.

As I'm looking at the screen, a new message bearing a name pops through. And it's certainly not Taylor Jones.

16

'Lizzie Butterworth?' Mike asks. 'But she's one of the members of the Southwark Secateurs, isn't she?'

'She is,' Marjorie says, peach lipstick on her teeth. 'And had one known she drives such a *showy* vehicle, one might have suspected her sooner as a potential *murderer* and saboteur. Golf GTI, indeed! With tinted windows and black alloys!' Her mouth arcs downwards over a chin wrinkled in disgust. 'Who does she think she is? A septuagenarian drug lord?' She's shouting indignantly now, a fine shower of spittle spraying over her pain au chocolat.

'Keep your voice down, Marjorie,' I say, peering around at the elderly clientele in the coffee shop of the garden centre where Mike works (though he's spun Marjorie a yarn that he's here as a weekend palate-cleanser, following a hard week of town-planning). It's 11am on a Saturday, but the place is already full of white-haired gardening enthusiasts in their pastel-coloured anoraks and orthopaedic shoes. I drain my coffee, set my cup down, and dab my lips with a napkin. 'We don't know the circumstances behind any of this. Best not to go accusing someone of murder on the basis of a Golf that was spotted outside Dotty's house and a photo of a similar-looking car that Phoebe took on a detour home after a gardeners' club meet-up.'

'But Lizzie has motive!' Marjorie says, slapping the table.

'Marjorie, please calm down,' Mike says. 'I have to work here and people are looking.'

She finally lowers her voice. 'I'll have you know that Lizzie is married to a rather dashing man called Donald.' She gazes over at the novelty gift section with a faraway look in her eyes. 'Donald cut a fine figure in his youth. He was at St Olave's Grammar when I was at Chislehurst and Sidcup Girls' Grammar with Dotty Gloucester and Lizzie – North, as she was back then. We were all in the same year, and *every* girl had a crush on Donald. He looked like a young Tab Hunter.'

'How does that give her motive for murder and maybe getting Taylor Jones to attack you?' I ask.

Marjorie's peach lips thin to two mean lines. 'Remember I told you Dotty disappeared to the country with a rumoured pregnancy? She returned some months later, as trim as ever, and nobody asked questions?' She nods and raises an eyebrow.

'Are you saying Dotty Gloucester had Donald . . . what's his name?'

'Butterworth.'

'She had Donald Butterworth's child in secret?' I look to Mike for a reaction. Can he see how absurd this sounds? 'That's a bit of a leap.'

'Is it?' Marjorie breaks off some of her pain au chocolat and takes a tiny bite with sharp-looking teeth. She chews in silence momentarily. 'Dorothy was not the only young gal to fall for Donald's charms.' Eyeing the people sitting at the next table, she shunts her chair further towards us and almost whispers, 'And that's something I never even disclosed to my own husband, so I'll thank you two to keep that to the confines of this tryst.'

'What goes on in Dobbies stays in Dobbies.' Mike salutes. 'But what are you saying about Lizzie?'

'She's jealous, of course! Assuming Dotty had Donald's love child, and given Donald and I also had a . . . youthful dalliance, maybe Lizzie has suddenly got a taste for neutralising her rivals.'

'But Lizzie and this Donald have been married . . . how long?'

'I should think it's approaching sixty years. But Lizzie's a very dumpy and plain woman.' Marjorie's cold blue eyes harden. 'Imagine if you discovered you'd been drawn as the short straw by someone you thought adored you.'

I study Mike's face and see hurt etched around his eyes. Clearly, Marjorie's words resonate with him, given his wife's preference for a younger replacement.

Marjorie is oblivious to his apparent inner turmoil. 'Imagine if you'd just discovered there's a love child out there . . . Your husband's progeny. Wouldn't you be incensed that the person you loved had kept their former indiscretions secret for decades?'

A blotchy rash spreads up Mike's neck. Blinking hard, he checks his watch. 'Right, well, we need to decide what to do with this information – the motive for murder, the Golf that matches the description of the one outside Dotty's the night she died. Do we go to the police and let them take it from there?'

'That's a good idea,' I say. 'They're the professionals. We can pass the information on.'

'Nonsense,' Marjorie says. 'The police will have no interest in reopening a case that the coroner deemed unworthy of investigation. And I am not going to delude myself that they'd look into a possible connection between Dotty and my greenhouse.' She pushes her plate aside.

'Your working theory is Lizzie might have paid Taylor Jones to throw the brick?' I rub the handle of my teaspoon, as if I'm trying to polish up the memory of Seth's revelation, just two days earlier.

'Quite.' She purses her lips. 'Why else would Taylor Jones target me? One hasn't needed the services of a joiner since one replaced one's kitchen in 1987, and it's still as good as new. Cottage-style oak doors, I'll have you know. And I have very little to do with the Croydon lot, except when everyone meets for the annual Golden Trowel Awards ceremony at Wisley.' She taps on the table. 'Lizzie Butterworth makes sense. I can see the connection there, as she and I went to the same school along with Dotty, and Dotty and I moved in the same flower-arranging circles. But Taylor Jones? I can't see the connection there unless Lizzie employed him as her henchman.' She takes her phone out of her handbag. 'Perhaps I shall report him to the authorities even so.'

I reach over and put my hand over hers. 'Seth said Taylor's the wrong sort to start a confrontation with. Let's do a little digging first.'

Mike checks his watch. 'I'm going to tell my manager

I've got a migraine and need to nip home.' He lays his napkin down emphatically. 'I say we pay Lizzie a visit and ask her a few searching questions about her movements just before Dotty's demise.'

As we pull up in my Volvo in front of Lizzie Butterworth's neat 1960s box, with its hanging baskets full of blousy purple pansies and late-blooming red, white, and blue primroses, I begin to wish I'd gone to Bluewater shopping centre with Zak. Yet as I take off my seatbelt and put on my unwieldy stop-lock, I catch sight through a gap in the privet bushes of the white Golf GTI sitting on the drive. Sure enough, it has blacked-out windows and alloys. I swallow hard, wondering how I've gone from hoping to do a spot of community gardening in what little spare time I have to playing at detective.

'Are you sure about this, Marj?' I ask my prim passenger, who is clutching her hard-framed handbag in a white-knuckled grip.

'I am. And don't call me Marj.'

Mike and I exchange a knowing glance through my rearview mirror.

'Just try not to make any assumptions until we've spoken to Lizzie,' he tells her.

We alight from the Volvo. Marjorie marches smartly up to the front door and pushes the bell. Nobody comes to the door. She presses it another three times.

'Take it easy!' I say. 'Looks like they're out.'

She takes a step back and points to the open window upstairs. 'Oh, they're in alright.'

A shadow finally looms behind the obscure-glazed door, and it opens to reveal a stooped and weary-looking elderly man, wearing heavy-framed spectacles and baggy old jeans. Whatever Tab Hunter might have looked like, I feel certain it wasn't this. He seems to recognise Marjorie and blanches.

'Marjorie Bloom? Do my eyes deceive me?'

'The very same, Donald Butterworth.' Her cheeks are even pinker than usual. 'It's been *eons*.' She stands there expectantly while he regards Mike and me with a puzzled expression. 'Well, aren't you going to let us in?'

He shakes his head. 'Much as such a blast from the past is a lovely surprise to find on my doorstep, Marjorie . . . er, what do you want? Because I'm rather —'

Marjorie places her hand on Donald's shoulder and pushes him aside. 'We're here to speak to Lizzie on horticultural business. Where is she?' She marches in and disappears off down the hall shouting, 'Lizzie! Elizabeth Butterworth? It's Marjorie Bloom!'

Donald frowns at us fleetingly. 'Are you her handlers? I suppose you'd better both come in.' He then turns to follow Marjorie. 'Marjorie, please stop shouting. Lizzie is napping.'

'I'm dying of embarrassment,' I whisper to Mike as we enter a house that smells of medicinal alcohol wipes and dust. I catch sight of a wheelchair, collapsed and stacked against a radiator cover in the hallway. 'This feels like an intrusion too far.'

Marjorie comes to a halt by a doorway towards the back of the house, and Mike and I pull up short just behind her.

'Oh,' she says. 'Dear Lord.'

Beyond the threshold, I catch sight of a dining room, perhaps, or what once was a dining room, because now, it's been set up as a bedroom and in it is one of those adjustable hospital beds that I've seen my own mother lying in too many times.

'Lizzie?'

Donald places his hands on Marjorie's shoulders and shunts her out of his way. 'Marjorie, please!'

He walks into the makeshift bedroom and sits on the end of the bed. It's only when he grabs a bony hand at the end of a thin, wrinkled arm that I see there's a woman in among the pile of bedclothes. She raises her head off her pillow and tries to talk but her speech is unintelligible.

'It's okay, darling. It's just Marjorie Bloom. She's come to say hello.'

Marjorie clasps her hand to her mouth and gingerly walks ahead of us towards the woman in the bed. With cracking knees, she squats by the side of the woman. 'Lizzie, my dear. I had no idea you were ill.' She looks enquiringly at Donald.

He beckons Mike and me into the room. 'Please. Sit!' He gestures at two dining chairs that are pushed up against the wall.

'Whatever's the matter with you, Lizzie?' Marjorie asks.

Lizzie tries to speak, but her words are too slurred for us to understand.

Her husband gently removes a stray lock of white hair

from her forehead. 'Lizzie had a massive stroke about two months ago. She was in the house on her own when it happened. I'd been out having a game of bowls with the boys and didn't find her for a couple of hours. And then the ambulance . . . well, you know how long it can take them to arrive nowadays.'

I nod. 'It's shocking. I know from my own mother's experience. I'm so sorry we're intruding on you.'

He shakes his head sorrowfully. 'It's quite nice to have visitors who aren't our children, if I'm honest. It can be quite lonely. And Lizzie gets very frustrated. I'm afraid her chances of rehabilitation aren't good.'

I try to reconcile the pimped-up car that's sitting out front with the frail woman in the bed. 'Tell them why we're here, Marjorie.'

'Yes, why *are* you here?' Donald asks.

Marjorie relates the tale of how we discovered Dotty's body, the break-in, the brick-based greenhouse sabotage, and the mystery of the white Golf-driving visitor to Dotty's house in the weeks preceding and shortly before her death. 'So you see, when one looked at all those connected to both Dorothy and oneself, and when one discovered that your car matches that description . . .'

Donald's bristly grey eyebrows and the hairs poking out of his nostrils twitch with indignation. 'What? You thought you'd casually drop by after years of ignoring us both at the Golden Trowel Awards and casually accuse my wife of murder? You can see she's completely incapacitated. Didn't you wonder why we never attended Dotty's funeral?'

Smiling uncertainly, Marjorie inclines her head to the side. 'One might have been mistaken about Lizzie, but *you* are still able to drive, Donald. And there are still rumours flying round church circles surrounding your relationship with Dotty, all those years ago.'

'Ah, well, there you're wrong on both counts, you bad-minded woman.' He keeps his voice calm and friendly, all the while stroking his wife's hand. 'Our car has been sitting on the drive, unused, since Lizzie had her stroke. And if you don't believe me, go and have a look at the tree sap and droppings that have accumulated on the paintwork.'

'Why? You've been driving since you were a young man,' Marjorie says. She flushes pink. 'I remember you taking your father's Wolseley for a spin, and I particularly remember because you were quite adamant you wanted to show me the cream leather upholstery *on the back seat* after we'd been to the cinema.'

He lets go of his wife's hand and folds his arms. 'I lost my licence. You of all people should understand that, Marjorie, since I hear through the grapevine that you were banned for doing a three-point turn on the Sidcup Bypass.'

'Who told you that?' Marjorie's eyes are little cobalt slits.

'Except in my case, no sherry was involved.' Donald takes off his glasses and waves them at her. He puts them back on and the beer-bottle-bottom lenses, which I hadn't previously noticed, are immediately apparent. 'I have visual impairment, which means I've been relying on taxis since Lizzie had her stroke. Uber is making a fortune out of me.' He sniffs. 'And as for Dotty, she and I have never been anything but acquaintances. Her friendship was with Lizzie and revolved around the work they did together as Southwark Secateurs.'

'So you haven't been making clandestine or otherwise visits to her house in Dulwich Village in that car?' Mike asks.

'Didn't you hear a word I said?'

'It's a terribly flashy car for an elderly woman.'

'We got a good deal on it, not that that's any of your business.'

Mike persists, despite the frost in Donald's voice. 'Why haven't you sold the Golf if you can't use it?'

'I had hoped my wife would recover.' Donald gets to his feet. 'Look, I understand why you might be looking into Dotty's death, and I think it's good that someone cares enough to make doubly sure nobody took advantage of a wealthy elderly woman who lived on her own, but I do think it's time you went. Lizzie gets very tired.'

As I take one last look at the incapacitated woman in the bed, I am sure she is scowling at Marjorie. 'You don't know a man called Taylor Jones, do you?' I ask, studying Donald for a reaction.

He looks blankly at me. 'Should I?'

'So that's a no?' Marjorie asks.

'*Goodbye*, Marjorie Bloom.' He slams the door behind us.

We walk past the Golf, and I can see that it does indeed bear all the hallmarks of not having been used in a long, long while.

Back in the Volvo, I take the stop-lock off my steering wheel and fling it into the footwell of the rear passenger seat. 'I feel such an idiot. That was such a waste of time.'

Marjorie places her liver-spotted hand on mine. 'Nonsense, dear. Gardening has become suddenly dangerous. We must solve this riddle if we're to compete in this year's Golden Trowel without fear.'

I sigh and shake my head. 'I definitely never signed up for this. What do you propose we do next?'

Mike locks eyes with me through the rear-view mirror. 'When did that housekeeper say the Mercer family get back from their holiday?'

'They're due back this coming Tuesday, I think.'

'We need to go back and ask to see that CCTV.' I can see his face has a luminescence to it, or maybe he's just sweaty. Either way, it seems Mike is enjoying himself.

'No can do,' I say. 'Certainly not 'til the back end of next week.' My stomach churns. 'I've got family commitments, and then there's my work's team-building away day in Suffolk, which is actually two full days of torture.' I swallow hard, wondering which is worse: the threat of a possible murderer turning his sights on our little gardening group or being cooped up at Center Parcs with the likes of Colin and Janice from HR.

17

'Where the bloody hell is this place?' I mutter as I crawl along the A11 in terrible traffic, behind a tractor (are tractors even allowed on major A roads?), a couple of dumper trucks, and a heavy goods vehicle, carrying two brand-new combine harvesters. I feel like I'm in a scene from *Deliverance* with worse weather and more boring topography.

The only distraction from the hee-haw of my windscreen wipers and the acres and acres of flat land on either side of the road is Radio Suffolk. Chris de Burgh has finally stopped warbling about his 'Lady in Red' and now, the local news is on. Apparently there's been a serious collision up ahead. Something to do with a runaway sow from a pig farm getting onto the road and causing a heavy goods vehicle to jack-knife and plough into a campervan, which had been ferrying its ill-fated passengers from Center Parcs – the place where I'm headed. It doesn't bode well for Chislehurst Green Insurance's Annual Staff Away Day. I feel a pang of visceral pain for the campervan occupants, but I can't help but vaguely wonder if the pig made it out alive.

My phone rings. It's Zak.

'Hi Mum. Don't worry. Nothing's wrong.' He sounds far cheerier since he's qualified for extra time in exams – an interim support measure, thanks to his abysmal results in the SENCO's response time tests, which will tide him over until he's had his ADHD and dyslexia assessments. Seth has also started tutoring him in Chemistry for an hour per week at those all-important mates' rates, and what a difference that's making to his confidence! 'Can you talk?'

I turn the volume up on my bluetooth headset, because he sounds like he's calling from a toilet. 'I'm in rotten traffic. Shouldn't you be in lessons?'

'So, like, Nan called me?'

There's a pregnant pause, where he's waiting for a reaction, and I'm waiting for bad news.

'And?'

His tone is light enough to allow the knot in my stomach to ease. 'She says she's thinking about trying Tena pants and she's having trouble getting a repeat prescription for codeine. Oh, and she says Carol smells of onions this week.'

'Carol can sort the repeat prescription, or I'll deal with it when I'm back tomorrow night.' I glance at the car's slow clock. 'Are you alright? Shouldn't you be in Maths?'

'No, I've got a free. I just wanted to say . . . I love you, Mum.'

Part of me is so touched by this announcement that I feel tears pricking the backs of my eyes. Another part of me wonders which bit of the house or school he's set on fire by accident. 'I love you with all my heart, boy-boy. Have a brilliant time at Imran's.'

'Mum . . .' There's more, clearly.

I see an opportunity to get ahead of the tractor and the combine-harvester-carrying HGV. I flip on my indicator and pull out, accelerating two whole cars in front. 'What? Look, Zak, I'm in terrible traffic, in torrential rain, and you're supposed to be –'

'You realise what today is, don't you?'

I wrack my brains for significant milestones. Then I feel my blood run cold as the enormity of what I've missed hits home. 'No! Zak. I'm . . . I'm . . . fuck.' The car suddenly feels too hot and airless. I open a window and feel the cold rain pelting the side of my face. 'Are you okay?'

'I'm fine. I just thought it was weird that you hadn't even mentioned it.'

Exhaling hard, I think about the reasons why I might have forgotten a date I think about all year, and have done for ten years. The anniversary of Dave's death. 'Zak, I . . . How could I forget? I was thinking about Dad only the other day. Literally last night. It's this damn perimenopausal brain fog. My brain . . .' I slap my forehead. 'I think about things and then they just . . . go. They disappear. I'm so sorry. I should be at home with you, getting Dad's favourite pizza for dinner. But I'm here on the A11, going to the idiot away day. And I had it in the calendar and everything.' I picture our calendar, pinned to the wall in the kitchen. I can see my own handwriting clearly, in my mind's eye: *Dave's DD*, embellished by a heart with an arrow shot through it. 'We were supposed to go to The Tree after school to talk to him.'

I picture the tree in Highbury Fields, close to Arsenal's Emirates Stadium, where we scattered Dave's ashes. 'I'm so sorry, Zak. We'll go at the weekend, I promise. And I love you with all my heart, son, and this doesn't mean I've forgotten your dad.'

'I know, Mum. I love you too. Don't worry about it. Me and Imran are playing a ranked game on *Siege* after school. I would have missed it if we'd gone to Highbury. I just wanted to check you're okay.'

Can Dave see us now? Is he disgruntled that I've forgotten to mark the anniversary of his death, and Zak is happy to be gaming at a friend's house? Does spinning too many plates and dropping Dave's make me a bad wife . . . well, widow? Does Zak living his life somehow invalidate the gut-wrenching memory of the bereft little boy who was left without fifty per cent of his entire world and a male role model? Would Dave be affronted by Zak's resilience in some strange way? I make a mental note to discuss guilt yet again with Mandi when I next see her.

The call comes to an end, and finally, we file past the grim fallout of the car crash. A lorry is tipped on its side, half in a field and half out. The motorhome is a mangled wreck. No sign of a pig. I say a silent prayer of thanks that I was not caught up in the crash, and pray not just for the campervan's occupants, but also for mine and Zak's continued safety.

'Gill! At last!' Jess shouts, waving to get my attention. She slaps the empty seat next to her in the Sports Café – the venue where we're all meant to congregate before the first stultifying group exercise. 'Come and sit over here, you Cockerney freak of nature!'

Barney from the Glasgow office is sitting to her left. He waves blithely, and I trudge across to join them. Jess stands to embrace me, but I can see that the others around the table – some of Colin's cronies from my branch – are looking less enamoured with my arrival.

I hug Jess. 'How you doing, you scruffy Brummie cow-bag?'

'Well, I brought a bottle of gin for the room and a family pack of Alka-Seltzer for the morning.' She winks. 'Aren't you glad you're sharing a cabin with me?'

'Er, I dumped my stuff in the cabin, and I see you've already commandeered every available surface with your crap. You *owe* me the gin and Alka-Seltzer. Danger money.'

It is then that I spot Colin himself, flanked by Janice from HR and Faith, my subordinate. I can see them all looking at me and then whispering among themselves. I feel the temperature in the Sports Café lower by several degrees, and it's like I'm back at school and the last three or four decades haven't happened.

Colin looks at his watch and gets to his feet and claps his hands. 'Right, everyone. Can I have your attention, please?'

All eyes are on our regional leader, who is oozing smarm this afternoon. My stomach growls, and I regret not having eaten yet today.

'Now that the last person is *finally* here – welcome,

Gill – we can begin. Welcome to the Chislehurst Green Insurance Annual Away Day. For those of you who are new to the company, this is a chance to get the regional managers together from Bromley, Birmingham, and Glasgow, so that we can get to know each other, get up to speed on the latest corporate plans, and . . .' He goes red in the face and clicks his fingers like a cocaine-fuelled Channel 5 game-show host. 'Crucially, have *a lot* of fun!' Colin points to Jess. 'And just as a disclaimer, ha ha, any spin the bottle game that Jess starts after dinner is definitely not a Chislehurst Green-sanctioned event.'

My colleagues are all laughing along, but at my side, though Jess is smiling, I can see her mouthing the word, 'wanker'.

Colin raises his hand. 'First up are the icebreakers. We're moving to a function room, where many of our activities and presentations will take place. Janice, our HR angel, has got some cracking exercises lined up, haven't you, Janice?' He gestures that Janice should get to her feet and speak.

Janice puts her glasses on and reads from a sheet in a tremulous voice. 'Hello, everyone. Right, first up, we're going to split into five teams of five and do "Lost at Sea", where you've got to decide *as a team* on survival tactics, et cetera.'

Some of the more long-standing staff groan at the prospect of doing 'Lost at Sea' yet again.

'No mutinies, now! Colonel Colin will make trouble-makers walk the plank.' Janice beams at Colin, and I wonder for the first time if she and Colonel *Colon* are actually boinking on the sly. 'Then, we've got the quiz. I know you all love the Chislehurst Green corporate quiz, so you'll be glad to hear I've scheduled that.'

Her list of tedious icebreakers continues, and then she passes back to Colin.

'Thank you to the lovely Janice.' He encourages us all to give her a round of applause.

'They're at it, aren't they?' Jess whispers in my ear.

'I'd put money on it,' I say. 'Bet you he manhandles her when we do the tree trekking.'

Colin interrupts our theorising. 'After the icebreakers, we've got dinner, followed by a presentation on the new call-handling platform we're rolling out. Karaoke at 8pm. I've got first dibs on Bryan Adams' "Summer of '69".' He grins and runs his sausage fingers around the collar of his Guns N' Roses T-shirt. 'Tomorrow, though, you lucky people . . .' He gives us all the thumbs up. 'We've got outdoor activities designed to get our communicating, motivationary, negotiating, and problem-solving juices flowing.'

'Motivationary's not a word, Colonel Colon,' I say beneath my breath.

'But for now, let's give ourselves a round of applause and then swiftly make our way to the venue for the icebreakers.'

I feel a headache rolling in.

'I think you should get up and do a song,' Jess says, as the karaoke from hell rolls around later that evening.

The room has an institutional feel to it, even though they've rearranged the seating and tables and they've

189

switched off the bright lighting, replacing it with the karaoke man's disappointing LED display. His giant TV screen is already playing a video of a glamorous young Korean couple, holding hands by an urban waterfront, as a rendition of Tiffany's 'I Think We're Alone Now' plays, with not quite the right lyrics flashing up on screen.

I shake my head. 'No way.' I take another large sip of my third glass of wine, still dimly aware that I must stop drinking; that the away day is no place for drowning my sorrows on the tenth anniversary of my husband's death.

'Oh, go on!' She nudges me. 'It'll be a laugh.'

'Who for? This lot, at my expense? No thanks.'

Yet, within an hour, a number of colleagues, including Jess, have got up to sing tuneless duets and solos, clearly fuelled by cooking wine and the strangeness of being holed up with people you barely know and don't really like.

Jess sits back down, after having murdered 'Total Eclipse of the Heart' by Bonnie Tyler. 'Go on, Gill. Let your hair down. It's okay to make a complete twat of yourself. It's away-day rules.'

Now feeling pleasantly numbed by alcohol, I drain my glass. 'Sod it. I'm going to sing a song for Dave.'

I walk up to Colin, who has been hogging the book of songs for a good ten minutes. I've already seen him put about six request slips in, though his Bryan Adams, accompanied by frenzied air-guitar, admittedly went down well.

'Hi Colin. Do you mind if I grab the book?' I ask.

He ignores me.

'Colin, can I have the book, please?'

Janice glares at me. 'Hardeep has got another book over there. Can't you see? Or don't you want to handle it because he's Asian?'

Despite the alcohol making everything that bit more tolerable and fuzzy around the edges, her words bite. I feel the blood cool in my veins. 'Are you drunk, Janice? I'm absolutely not racist. My late husband was Black. My son is mixed race, for God's sake!'

'I never said that. You said that, not me.' She waves her finger at me and there's a lack of focus to her eyes.

Not only is she not making sense, but I can hear she's slurring, and this is no place to get into a slanging match with the drunken head of HR. So I write out a slip and hand it in, knowing the karaoke guy will definitely have the song in question.

Two performances later, he shouts my name. I can see my song is cued on the screen. Everybody whoops as I stand and make my way to the front.

'Go, Gill!' Jean from Glasgow shouts, clapping her hands.

What the hell am I doing? I grab the microphone and turn away from my colleagues. I picture Dave, before he got ill. In my mind's eye, he's in the park, teaching a four-year-old Zak how to ride his bike without stabilisers. Dave is wearing the terrible acrylic snowman jumper that my mother bought for him for Christmas – the one from Primark that melted a month later, when he hung it to dry on a very hot towel rail.

My thumping heart is the only thing I can feel or hear when the keyboard introduction ends, and I must come in with vocals, acapella and in tune. I'm terrified of looking an idiot, but I've committed to performing this song in front of the people I work with. So, I will myself to channel also-dead Whitney Houston and try to do 'I Will Always Love You' as much justice as I can. Once I hit my stride and realise I'm actually having fun, I turn to face my colleagues. They are totally rapt. In my Chardonnay-fuelled head, I hit not one single bum note, and I manage to sustain the last 'you', right to the end. When I finish, there is rapturous applause. Even Gail, the notoriously dour tank of a finance manager, gets to her feet to give me a standing ovation, wolf-whistling her approval. When she stands, so do Jess, Barney, Hardeep, Maisie, Beth, Gavin, and Saima. In fact, a good half of the room is on their feet and clapping.

'That was for Dave,' I say, flushed warm with the approval. At least I have marked Dave's Death Day in some small way. He loved a bit of Whitney.

Still buzzing with adrenalin and fully tipsy, when I bump into Colin on the way to the toilet, I forget how he has recently behaved. I smile and wave. 'Loved the "Summer of '69", Col. Great air guitar.'

But Colin's magnanimous response and returned compliment don't come. He merely grabs my forearm and pulls me close enough that I can smell his beer breath. 'We all know you just milk being a widow for sympathy.'

I shake him loose. In my head, I'm telling him exactly

where he can shove his sour grapes, but my mouth won't collude. I merely stand there, baffled. 'What did you just say, Colin?'

He doesn't respond. I watch him slalom drunkenly along the corridor, back to the away-day revellers.

It's as if I dreamed the exchange, but I didn't. I really didn't.

'Jesus, could that have been any more tedious?' Jess says, once the evening's high jinks are over and we're back in our cabin, shoes off and drinking strong G&Ts.

I shake my head. 'I wouldn't say tedious is quite how I'd describe it.' I tell her about my encounter with Colin by the toilets, and she is aghast.

'What a total dick!' Jess's eyes are wide and disbelieving, though bloodshot. 'Report him.'

I laugh without mirth. 'Who to? Janice in HR? Do me a favour.' Tears are threatening. There's an invisible hand around my throat.

Jess rubs my arm sympathetically. 'Are you alright?'

Dabbing at my eyes, I exhale hard. 'I was just so taken aback by his unfiltered nastiness, you know? But what's the point in whingeing? There were no witnesses to it, and there's no one I can tell. It's his word against mine.'

'I'll stick up for you, babe.'

I shake my head vehemently. 'Don't you come within a mile of this. I don't want my crap sticking to you.'

'That's not how friendship works, love.' Jess, the amazing human distillery, tries to top up my glass. 'If you can't report him to HR, take it higher. Take it to the board.'

I wave the gin bottle away, vaguely aware of the prospect of post-breakfast tree trekking and a geo-cache treasure hunt that both demand more than alcoholic poisoning and the eye-hand-leg coordination of an earthworm. 'Can you imagine the CEO being remotely interested in some hearsay bullshit, where his pet gofer comes over all *small-dick-energy* with a middle-aged female manager – a woman who's put her own personal discomfort above the needs of the company? Forget it.'

I get to my feet and make for the sliding patio doors, not wanting her to see the true extent of my anguish. When I open the door, the smell of pine trees and wet soil envelops me and pulls me outside.

'You okay, mate?' Jess asks.

'Fine. I just need some air.'

There is a plastic patio chair under the heavy canopy of a mature tree, not far from the door. The seat is dry, so I sit down and take in a lungful of fresh air. I look up through tears to the branches.

'I've got to get out,' I whisper to the stars, one of which is definitely Dave. 'This is killing me. I just can't take it anymore and I've had enough.'

For the first time in hours, I take out my phone and there's a WhatsApp message from Mike.

Went back to Mercers. Sorry. Couldn't wait. Found this on their CCTV. Mx

My heartbeat picks up pace. I feel a cold sweat break out on my forehead and upper lip when I see the attached slightly pixelated still of a white Golf GTI. There is a 'play' arrow over it. Mike has sent me a video clip, quite possibly of Dotty G's murderer.

I press play.

18

'Righty-ho, can I have your attention, everyone?' Mike claps his hands together. 'By now, you should have all seen the footage from the CCTV of Dotty Gloucester's neighbours.'

The following early evening meeting of the gardeners' club is upon us, hot on the heels of my return from Center Parcs. We have taken our seats on the little square of decking outside the shed on Mike's allotment. He has brought a battered old table out from the shed and has set his tablet and a large blue plastic trug on top of it.

First, he picks up the tablet and turns it around so that the screen is facing us. He pokes at the screen, and the short clip he sent to me while I was at the away day starts to play. Once again, I watch as a white Golf with blacked-out windows and alloys – almost identical to that owned by Lizzie Butterworth . . . *almost* – pulls up outside Dotty G's house. The digital clock in the top right-hand corner shows the time as 18.27. It is the evening that we found her; twilight, with the footage still in colour for the first twenty or so seconds, then switching to black-and-white night-vision as the light levels fall.

A figure wearing a black hoodie and trousers emerges from the driver's side. They are wearing a baseball cap pulled low and a black FFP2 mask, completely obscuring their hair and face.

'This is the last person seen going into Dotty's house before Gill and Marjorie found her in her shed,' Mike says. 'If she was murdered, it's entirely possible this visitor is responsible, and I found three other earlier instances within the week leading up to her death, where the same car pulls up after dark, and the same person gets out.'

'So, Dotty knew whoever it was, right?' Seth says.

Mike nods. 'It would appear so. I couldn't go back more than a week before she was found, because the footage on the CCTV hard drive gets recorded over every so often with fresh material. As it was, I was in the Mercers' loft reviewing footage for three hours or more.' He pauses the footage just as the driver has fully emerged from the car. 'Now does anyone recognise this shady-looking gentleman?'

I look at the shoes on the driver's feet. 'Scroll back to when the footage is still in colour?' I ask Mike.

He pokes at the screen and then runs the footage from the top. I watch again as the driver emerges from the car.

'Stop! Wait! Look at those shoes!' I point to the flashing lime-green fabric, embellished with cartoon neon orange flames, on the side of . . . are they sneakers? Trainers? Lace-ups of some description? It's hard to tell. 'Can't be many people with shoes that loud. They look limited edition.' I turn to Seth. 'Could this be that guy from your building site? Taylor?'

He shakes his head. 'Nah, man. Taylor's ripped and much taller than that.' He points to the footage. 'This geez on the footage ain't no bigger than five-nine, I'd reckon.'

'And his feet be small too,' Phoebe adds in her cut-crystal accent.

'Hang on,' Neil says. 'We're assuming this is a man, but if I'm honest . . .' He peers at the frozen image on the tablet screen and shakes his head slowly. 'It's hard to tell from the footage. It could also be a woman?'

'She'd have to be reasonably tall,' Val says, nodding. 'But Neil's right. It's not out of the question.'

'Well, the answer lies with finding those shoes,' I say.

'And how exactly do you propose we do that?' Cath asks, frowning at me. 'Go round South-East London and Kent asking to cross-reference everyone's footwear with whatever car they're the registered owners of?'

Strangely, her vitriol brings a lump to my throat. 'There's no need to have a go,' I say. 'I've come here to get away from stress. If I want to feel attacked, I can stay in work later.'

Cath glares at me. Then her expression softens. 'Sorry. I'm just angry at the thought of someone going around attacking vulnerable older women and getting away with it. I shouldn't be taking it out on you.'

I pat her arm and feel the tension dissipate. 'We're the Bromley Botanists' gardeners' club. Teamwork makes the dream work, right?'

'Very inspiring, Gillian,' Mike says, setting down the tablet. 'So in conclusion, we're looking for an average-height man —'

'Or a tall woman,' Val says.

Mike nods. 'Yes, and someone with those very distinctive shoes, *plus* the white Golf, which should also be easier to spot because of those black windows and alloys.' He tugs at his earlobe and wrinkles his nose. 'How are we supposed to investigate the shoe collection of every single person who sits at the centre of the Dotty Gloucester and Marjorie Bloom's social circle Venn diagram?'

'One can't, realistically,' Marjorie says. 'Both Dorothy and I have always been *deeply* popular.' She closes her eyes emphatically. 'And there must be at least one hundred old school friends, gardeners, and flower arrangers that we had in common.' Her eyes snap open. 'The most sensible course of action is to think about who, in the centre of that Venn diagram, might stand to gain from hurting Dorothy and oneself? Is their aim to remove the competition so they can win the Golden Trowel or are they harbouring a grievance of a more personal nature? Only once we have those answers and we've identified suspects can we legitimately take them to task over their footwear and automotive choice.' She punches the air. 'Then, we shall demand entry to their homes! The Lord wills it.'

'Well, we can ruminate on that during breaktime,' Mike says, 'but right now, let's turn our attention back to gardening.'

Mike reaches into the blue plastic trug and pulls out a fistful of black matter, letting it crumble through his fingers. On the air is a tangy botanical smell with a vague whiff of mildew.

'Right, folks. Now, I promised you back in the autumn that I would reveal the secret recipe for "Berisford's Black Gold", and here we are. I have a huge finished batch, ready to be used in potting on and planting up.'

'At last!' Seth says, clicking his fingers in that way that anyone under twenty-five can do with aplomb. 'I'm only here for the BBG, man. Bring it on.'

Mike chuckles. His cheeks flush pink as he pulls up his jeans. 'Right. Now, for you beginners, the secret to good compost is a good mix of organic material going in. You need nitrogen, so you'll get that from grass clippings, but you also need stuff to give it some fibre. Dead leaves, hedge clippings, food waste, but not teabags.' He eyes us all like an enquiring teacher. 'Who can tell me why we don't use teabags?'

Cath's hand shoots up. 'Is it because they're full of tannins? Are tannins bad?'

Shaking his head, Mike makes a wah-wah-oops noise, reminiscent of a game show. He ignores Cath's crest-fallen expression and turns to Seth, who has both hands in the air like the show-off kid in reception class.

'Seth?'

Seth grins. 'It's 'cause there's plastic in teabags what don't rot down?'

'Exactly, Seth. Well done.' Mike then locks eyes with me. 'Gillian, can you tell me what else you might put into compost to make it nutrient rich?'

I feel the others staring at me, and my skin is suddenly itching with embarrassment. Forcing myself to focus on the question, I think about the things we have knocking around at home that might rot down. 'Coffee grounds?'

'Yes.'

'Coffee grounds are excellent for acidifying your compost and soil,' Val says. 'I put 'em around the base of my camellias, and my hydrangeas love 'em.'

Marjorie laces her hands together on her lap. 'Valerie, if you scatter coffee grounds onto the stems of your plants, you will kill them. Don't teach these fledgling horticulturalists your bad habits.'

Val gives Marjorie the finger. Marjorie gasps audibly, clutches at the beads around her neck, and is clearly about to erupt with a tart comeback.

'How about newspaper and egg boxes?' I blurt out, trying to head off any arguments.

Snapping his fingers, Mike shouts over Marjorie so that we can't hear her retort. 'That's quite right, Gill. Paper's great for adding texture. And we can add fruit and vegetable waste, though I can tell you from personal experience . . .' He starts to rock on his heels and titter. '. . . that there's nothing like bacon rinds and meat off-cuts to bring the rats sniffing. So, no meat products or anything synthetic and sweet, because you really don't want to be chasing rats out of your compost heap on a Saturday morning.' He runs his clean hand through his hair, and I suddenly realise he's had a haircut. A border-line-fashionable haircut. And he's looking at me again.

My latest hot flush starts at my toes and works its way up to the very follicles on the top of my head, and I wish Mike hadn't had his hair cut and hadn't worn nice jeans, instead of his usual old-man slacks. And I wish he wasn't looking at me.

'I bet Seth could tell us the chemical process for making compost,' I say in a bid to distract the others, who may or may not be staring at me and Mike, wondering if the compost's not the only thing where chemistry is afoot. Ugh. Mike Potato. Just, ugh.

Seth gets to his feet. 'Oh, yeah, man. I can totally chemistry the shit out of this.'

'Language, Seth!' Marjorie shouts. 'I can't withstand the industrial language. It gives one indigestion.'

'Soz, Marj.' Seth starts to explain things like oxidisation producing carbon dioxide and fungus and heating up and microbial growth. He says words like thermophilic and nitrifying bacteria. We all nod sagely at the mention of phosphorous and potassium, and 'ooh' and 'aah' at his animated talk of high temperatures accelerating the breakdown of plant matter.

Mike pushes his glasses up his nose – new glasses? Yes. New glasses. Nice glasses. 'Can I interrupt there, Seth? Thank you for that illuminating explanation of the chemical processes of composting.' He turns to address us all. 'What's really important here is that the compost gets hot enough to kill off viruses and weed seeds. I'm always very careful not to put perennial weeds like dandelions in my compost, because those horrible taproots have a way of regrowing, no matter how valiant your efforts.'

'Dandelions are a scourge,' Val says. 'Like those thugs, spear thistles. They've got a taproot too. If you can't dig them out in their entirety, just keep hoeing the buggers.'

Marjorie slaps her thighs. 'Language, Valerie! How many times must one say it?'

Val tells Marjorie where to shove her linguistic guidelines, and the two women start to bicker in earnest.

'Simmer down, ladies,' Cath says. 'You aren't doing your blood pressures any good.'

'Not being funny, Cath, but mind your own business,' Val says. She points to Marjorie. 'I'm sick and tired of this old baggage, shouting the odds out and telling us all how to behave. Who do you think you are, lady muck?'

'Michael! Michael! Take charge!' Marjorie is looking to Mike for support, holding her hands up, as though she can physically fend off Val's words.

'You forgot to tell this lot that me and you grew up in the same neck of the woods. Convenient, eh?' Val folds her arms and crosses her legs. There is a glint of mischief in her eyes. 'She's a Peckham wanderer, is Marj, just like me. Take no notice of her Lady Bountiful routine. Her old dad had a veg stall on Peckham market. He sold stuff that was on the turn for top whack, and all. Cheating old bar-steward.'

Marj clasps her liver-spotted hand to her mouth and gasps dramatically. 'You must be mistaking me for someone else. My family moved to Beckenham in the 1930s, after my grandfather lost the family money in the depression. One grew up in a rather grand Victorian gentleman's residence in the smart end of BR3, I'll have you know!'

'Bullshit,' Val says. 'You didn't move over the border into Kent 'til high school, and then we never heard nothing from you again once you got a place at Sidcup Grammar. I knew your dad, Len, because I did a Saturday stint on Almira's bric-a-brac stall, over the way. We called your old man "Lechy Len". Leaned on the scales while he was weighing the produce, and peaches weren't the only soft fruit he couldn't keep his mitts off.' Val laughs too heartily. 'And I remember you. You were a stuck-up, toffee-nosed cow back then. You still are.'

Marjorie looks away, the fury and hurt in her now watery eyes visible to all. She opens and closes her trembling lips, as if contemplating a cutting comeback. Unexpectedly, she shrieks.

'Michael, what is *that*?!' She points to a clump of green, in among Mike's flourishing dahlias.

'Oh my days, Marj. You sound like an actual dog whistle?' Phoebe says, clamping her hands to her ears.

Mike sets down his trug of compost and, frowning, walks out to the green clump. I can still see his face from where I'm sitting, and I can see that his colour has drained away.

'Oh, I don't believe it.'

'What?' we all ask in unison.

'Is that what I think it is, Michael?' Marjorie asks, her voice thin and reedy with evident panic.

He looks up and locks eyes with her, then turns to Val. 'Every gardener's worst nightmare.'

'What is it?' Neil asks. 'What could be so bad?'

'Get the Roundup and stand clear,' Mike says. 'This is an emergency that only strong chemicals can fix.'

19

'Japanese knotweed,' Mike says, standing over the clump. 'One of the most invasive things you can get in a garden, and it costs an arm and a leg to get rid of – professionally.' He thumbs his stubble. 'Strange. I definitely didn't see it last time I was over here.' He frowns and cocks his head to the side. 'Definitely not.'

'Well, it looks pretty settled in to me,' Marjorie says, hanging back, as though the very sight of the knotweed will infest her own garden, over a mile away. 'What are you waiting for? Spray it or dig it up, man!'

Phoebe crouches by the interloping plant, scratching at her dreadlocks. 'Nah, man. I don't think you should spray. That's like environmental homicide or something. And the soil around this stuff does look freshly disturbed.'

I stare at the offending clump and then glance at Seth, who has eyes on me. Clearly, he's thinking the same thing. 'Could it be another act of sabotage?'

Everyone else is suddenly looking at me, oohing and aahing, as though I have the wisdom of Gandalf.

Mike takes up the spade he's retrieved from the shed and plunges it into the earth. 'Why did this have to be in the middle of my Café au Lait Royal dahlias? My late-summer favourites!' He turns to me. 'Get a rubble sack, Gill. There's a roll on the shelf in the shed. I'm not stopping 'til every last piece of root is gone, and then I'm going to burn this far, far away from here, where it can't do any damage. This stuff is worse than running bamboo.' He thrusts the spade's blade into the soil with a grunt. 'And I should know, because my old neighbour's running bamboo started pushing through the floor of our conservatory. It almost pulled the entire construction down.'

I retrieve the heavy roll of rubble sacks and peel one off. Inside the shed, it is dark and musty like every shed (well, not like Dotty's – hers was almost habitable, apart from the dead body), yet each gardening tool that hangs from the wall is gleaming. Every shelf is orderly. There are no giant spider webs or wasps' nests or damp and slightly buckled boxes of crap, carelessly shoved into a corner with a rusting pair of lawn shears and a grass-encrusted mower that has a blunt blade. It's almost nicer than my living room. What does this say about Mike Potato? Is he a proud man? A hard worker? A super-nerd? I can't decide.

When I return with the bag, he is beaming. He holds the offending plant on the end of his spade.

'It came up all in one piece, easy enough. See the root ball? It has blunt edges as though it's been dug up from somewhere else and then newly planted in my bed. Thank heavens Marjorie spotted it before it got established.' He places the knotweed into the rubble sack with great care.

'Someone planted the most invasive plant in the UK

in your flower bed in the hope it would take root.' I twist the end of the rubble sack shut and pass it to him. 'They must know it costs thousands to remove, once it gets a grip. So, this has got to be deliberate, and it's got to be garden-based sabotage, rather than personal. It's not just about Marjorie and Dotty anymore. This is about the Golden Trowel.'

Mike nods, silently takes the bag, and plonks it into his wheelbarrow. 'No doubt about it.'

Everyone gasps.

'You think this is the Croydon Diggers and Dibbers?' Cath asks.

'Who else?' Mike says. 'The Southwark Secateurs are out of the game since Dotty died. Seth identified Marjorie's brick-throwing vandal as Taylor Jones. He's a member of Croydon. Our group's other nearest competitor for the Golden Trowel is Harrogate. They always perform to a high standard in the Trowellies, but I can't see them travelling all this way to intimidate us out of the competition by means of planting Japanese knotweed in my allotment. No, I think Croydon must be where the threat is coming from. Think about it. It makes sense.'

'We've got to go back to the police and demand action,' Neil says, sitting back down. He unscrews the flask that has been sitting by the legs of his golf stool, and the smell of coffee wafts over to me.

'What's the point, man?' Seth runs his hands through the 'Berisford's Black Gold'. 'The cops won't reopen Dotty G's investigation because the coroner couldn't make his mind up between accident, suicide, or murder.

We think it was murder, but we can't prove it. We can't prove Taylor smashed up Marj's greenhouse either.'

'You said you saw him leave!' Cath says. 'You can identify him by his tattoo.'

Seth shrugs. 'My word against his, though, innit? I ain't got no legal proof, at the end of the day. And I'm not about to start beef with someone I work with, when I know it'll just get me labelled as a grass. My life would be hell on-site. We can't prove who done this, either,' he says. He stares at the crumbly 'Berisford's Black Gold' mixture in the blue trug, which Mike has set back on the table. Scooping out a handful, he holds it to his nose to sniff. 'No CCTV, right? And if one of them's clever enough to cover up a murder, they'll have made sure there's no eyewitnesses to this either, I bet.' Unexpectedly, he sticks his tongue into the compost and grimaces. 'Shit, Mike, man. This tastes of salt.'

'Salt?' Mike hastens over to the trug and takes a pinch of compost between his forefinger and thumb.

'Ugh! Why are you licking the compost, you weirdo?' Phoebe asks Seth.

'Dunno,' Seth shrugs. 'I just thought it smelled nice and wondered what it tasted of.' He smiles as if a genius thought has just occurred to him. 'I'm like one of those detectives on the telly, yeah? They always lick things.'

'You ain't right, fam,' Phoebe says, shaking her head.

Like Seth, Mike pushes out his tongue, scrunches up his eyes, and tastes the compost. 'Ugh.' He spits into the trug repeatedly and grabs the flask of coffee that Neil's cradling in his hands. He glugs it down and spits again.

'Seth's right.' His voice is wobbly. 'There *is* salt in my compost. They've salted "Berisford's Black Gold".' He makes for his four compost bins, lined up like fat black plastic sentries on the sunny side of his shed. He takes off the lid. 'Dead slugs! Oh my giddy aunt. Come and look at this.'

Everyone but Marjorie repairs to his side.

I stare into the bin and balk. 'Eeuw. That's a lot of slime. Are you sure it's dead slugs?'

Mike nods ruefully. 'Absolutely certain.' He takes a pen out of the breast pocket of his shirt and picks up something that looks like a melted Hershey's Kiss. He holds it out towards me. 'See this? These are leopard slugs.' There is tenderness to his voice. 'These are the good guys. Were.'

I back away and return to the decking. I don't need to see any more slime and oomska this evening. I spent the day with my semi-continent mother, after all. After having cleaned up and changed the incontinence pad and clothes on a nine-stone reluctant patient, not once but twice, I can confirm that Carol the carer is earning every penny.

'I thought slugs were bad for the garden,' Phoebe says, wide-eyed at the sight of the spotted and striped, very dead slug. 'My mum says they decimate her echinacea and hemerocallis.'

Mike still sounds utterly crestfallen. 'These fellers – leopard slugs – eat the bad guys. They're omnivores. They eat dead plant material *and* pests, other slugs, and . . . they're quite lovely, really. These were my little helpers.

A key ingredient in the manufacture of "Berisford's Black Gold".' His voice is almost a whisper. 'And now they're dead.'

Neil lifts the lid on the third bin and peers inside. 'All dead in here, too. Just a load of snot and obvious signs of salt. I'm not bloody tasting it though, because I'm not mental.' He closes the lid solemnly, takes off his straw trilby, and rubs his bald head. 'But I do think it's time we squared up to these Croydon sabotaging dirtbags.'

'One surely can't be suggesting retribution?' Marjorie, who is sitting on the decking with me, smooths her skirt over her knobbly knees. She blinks hard as she speaks, like a schoolma'am trying to talk sense to a classroom of five-year-olds. *'Bless those who persecute you; bless and do not curse. Do not repay anyone, evil for evil. Leave room for God's wrath, for it is written: "It is mine to repay. I will avenge," says the Lord.'* She nods at me and raises her eyebrows, as if the matter is settled.

The others are making submissive noises as though the matter is out of their hands. But I find myself thinking about my own situation at work – about how I'm being steamrollered into finding ludicrous financial savings for the company; about my situation at home – where my mother tries to rule my life like some despotic Greek god with rheumatoid arthritis, emphysema, and a ruined pelvic floor.

'Wait a minute, Marjorie,' I say. I peer around at the orderly patchwork of allotments, with its late-spring vegetable patches full of grey-green cabbage and yellow-green lettuce and bamboo canes full of runner bean seedlings. I take a deep breath and exhale slowly. 'We can't just roll over. There's land worth tens of millions at stake and a career change up for grabs, for a start. That could be life-changing for those of us who are still working age. And given how well you guys did last year, if I'm not mistaken, we've got a good shot at winning.'

'Oh yes,' Mike says, looking down at his hideous gardening Crocs. 'Our plans are excellent, and our stock is first class. Croydon won last year, so they're favourites to win again, but we're *seeded* number two, if you excuse the pun.' There is no mirth to his voice as he stares forlornly into his compost bins. 'And Southwark's withdrawn.'

'Ain't there hundreds of entrants?' Seth asks.

Mike nods. 'Yes, but only a handful of serious contenders for the Golden Trowel – the same clubs that have been in the top five every year, for a good four or five years.'

'Then why should we be bullied into giving up?' I ask. The group's murmur of collective agreement makes me feel emboldened, so I continue. 'It's not just the money, either. What are we doing this for, if not to make Bromley a nicer place for its residents? Flowers bring real joy. They add value to areas. They let people who aren't that mobile or who aren't lucky enough to have gardens connect with nature. Are we going to let Croydon trample over their enjoyment and quality of life?'

20

'Follow me,' Marjorie says, striding away from the allotment with renewed determination in those slightly bandy,
varicose-veined legs. She raises her hand and points
towards the road, where we are all parked. 'Onward!'

We all get to our feet and hasten after her.

'You said you were gonna leave it to Jesus,' Val calls
after her. 'Now you're storming off on the warpath?'
She picks up her pace to gain on the surprisingly rapid
Marjorie. 'Where the hell are you going, Marj?'

Marjorie pauses and turns around. There's mischief
etched into every crevice of her papery skin. 'Betty
Moule's. She's Croydon's senior member, so she needs
to accept responsibility for this chicanery. The day that
Barnacle Betty Moule gets one over on Marjorie Bloom
is the day hell freezes over.'

Swept up in Marjorie's fever, we all make for our
cars – Phoebe hitching a ride with Seth, and Mike, who
had cycled to the allotment, hitching a ride with me.
Following Marjorie's Honda Jazz (now she's finally got
her licence back), travelling in convoy at a breakneck
twenty miles per hour, we travel a full half-mile down
the road and over the postcode into Shirley, Croydon.
Marjorie leads us onto a street where there is no easy
parking, because every resident has had the kerb dropped

in front of tight little driveways that were meant to be small front gardens.

'We could have walked this quicker,' I tell Mike, as I search frantically for a space that can accommodate the old Volvo. 'By the time we've parked up, the wind will have gone out of our sails.' I find a space that looks about right, almost half a mile in the opposite direction, and start to reverse into it.

'Back a bit . . . back a bit.' Mike is looking over his shoulder, beckoning me to inch towards a gleaming BMW behind me.

'Er, Michael, I know I have a womb, but I've been driving and parking this car successfully for many, many years. You don't need a penis to master spatial awareness.'

He colours up and blinks repeatedly, pushing his glasses up his nose. 'Yes, ma'am.'

'And don't call me ma'am. I'm not the Queen or a police inspector.'

'Sorry, ma— Whoops. Old habits and all that.'

Finally, we congregate outside a 1930s detached house – standout for being the largest house on the street with by far the biggest plot. The place is crisply rendered in ivory, sporting immaculate low-profile wooden windows in Farrow & Ball pale mushroom – the sort that cost more than I earn in a year. The original stained glass seems to have been encapsulated in triple-glaze. This is undoubtedly Betty Moule's lair, not least because the front garden is stunning, ablaze with alliums, giant oriental poppies, lupins, peonies about to pop, early roses, and late rhododendrons, all basking in the unseasonably warm sun. The block-paved driveway is guarded by two sinister-looking garden gnomes, who leer, rather than grin, at us and who are completely at odds with the otherwise expensive-looking exterior. There is a brand-new blue Jaguar SUV on the drive. No VW Golf, though there is a garage which could contain one.

'Oh my days, this is a sick front garden, yeah?' Phoebe says, bending to sniff a pink peony that is just beginning to show its ruffled fuchsia centre.

Marjorie grimaces. 'One's own front garden is significantly better.'

Val kicks over the first gnome as we advance towards the front door. 'The pruning on her roses wouldn't win any awards,' she says, patting Marjorie's upper arm. 'And she's getting black spot on the leaves already. Poor rose husbandry, that is.'

Marjorie looks pointedly at Val's hand and pulls away from her touch. 'Don't underestimate Betty Moule.' Her pursed lips thin to a peach lipsticky line. 'She won Best In Show for her sweet peas at the Surrey Flower Show in 1996. And I heard she voted Remain because of that Frenchman of hers.'

The door opens and we are confronted by the tall, attractive woman I last laid eyes on from a distance at Dotty G's wake. Today, her white-blonde hair is pinned into a bun. She's wearing an expensive-looking pale blue denim sundress with a white cardigan over the top and looks like an advertisement for *Wise* magazine's infamously middle-class Rhine cruises or Italian Lakes mini-breaks – the sort

of ageing perfection that my own mother loves to decon-
struct with class-A swear words, hate, and a little spittle.
I can't see Betty Moule owning a pair of dayglo shoes or
concealing a pimped-up Golf GTI in the garage.

'Can I help you?' She looks alarmed until she clearly
recognises Marjorie. There's a smile, but it's faltering. 'Marjorie Bloom? Whatever are *you* doing on my
doorstep?'

I glance upwards and catch sight of CCTV orbs
hanging from the eaves, staring down at us and silently
recording everything we say and do.

Marjorie takes a step towards Barnacle Betty. She
reaches out and grabs the trunk of a perfectly clipped
and fragrantly blooming standard lilac tree, planted in
a contemporary pot by the front door. She yanks the
plant over at an angle so that compost starts to scatter
onto the ground. Clutching it in her white-knuckled fist,
as though it is her hostage, she speaks through gritted
teeth. 'One wants a word with you, Betty Moule.'

'Put my lilac down, you horrible woman.' Betty points
to the standard tree, her face a picture of concern. 'What
you're doing is criminal damage, and in fact, you're trespassing.' She turns to the hallway behind her. 'Henri!
Henri, call the police!'

We all shunt forwards to give Marjorie our support.

'Go on, Marj. Tell her,' Val says, pushing Marjorie in
the back with her knuckle.

The tips of Marjorie's ears are bright red. 'How dare you
have the temerity to lecture me about criminal damage?'
Her normally timid voice is gathering power and depth,

like coalescing storm clouds. 'You and your oinkish acolytes are guilty of sabotaging the Bromley Botanists' stock and equipment . . . perhaps even more serious misdemeanours, when one considers Dorothy Gloucester's sinister fate. We are here to warn you to back off or else.'

Barnacle Betty folds her arms across her chest, glancing nervously at the lilac. '*Oinkish*? What's oinkish? What do you mean, sabotage? And Dorothy Gloucester? You're babbling, woman. Are you demented?'

'One is nothing of the sort,' Marjorie says, now maxed out on fire and brimstone, which she's clearly able to brew from within, like a biblical superpower. 'And I'm talking about the brick through one's greenhouse window, thrown by the oink.'

'And the salt in my compost and the Japanese knotweed in my prize dahlia bed,' Mike adds. 'We're under assault, and we know it's you lot.'

'You always did have the hallmarks of an evil puppetmaster, Betty Moule!' Marjorie says. 'I certainly wouldn't put Dotty Gloucester's poisoning past you.'

Barnacle Betty frowns and marches from her threshold to where Marjorie is standing. She wrenches the lilac free and rights it. 'I have no idea what you're talking about, and actually, Marjorie,' she places a manicured hand on Marjorie's shoulder and pushes her backwards, 'you're slandering me.'

Marjorie stumbles backwards – her fall broken only by Mike grabbing her.

'Now, now, Mrs Moule,' Mike says. 'There's no need to get physical.'

Barnacle Betty fixes him with a piercing, venomous stare. 'Oh, there's every need. Marjorie is besmirching my good name. Give me one good reason why I shouldn't call the police and press charges.' She points to the CCTV orb. 'Because I have the ultimate witness. The camera doesn't lie. You're on my property without my permission, and I have no idea what you're talking about. Brick-toting *oinks*, indeed! What a fabrication.'

I step forward, channelling not only my sense of injustice at the attacks we've been subjected to but also my own personal frustrations. 'We *know* Taylor Jones threw a brick through Marjorie's greenhouse window, because he was seen and recognised.' I raise my eyebrows pointedly. 'That tattoo of his – not exactly discreet, is it?'

'You're grasping at straws!' Barnacle Betty says, waving her hand dismissively. 'Most young men nowadays are covered in tattoos.'

'On their heads? Come on! Pull the other one! And Taylor's mugshot just happens to be on your Croydon Diggers and Dibbers website.' I clear my throat and am aware that Marjorie is smiling in my peripheral vision. 'Also, Mike here has covert CCTV installed at his allotment, don't you, Mike?' Obviously, I'm lying now. Well, not lying so much as calling her bluff. 'What have you got to say about *that*, Mrs Moooooooule?'

I can see Barnacle Betty's cheeks flush, and her right eye starts to twitch. 'I don't have to put up with this nonsense on my own doorstep. You're all insane. Criminally insane.' She turns to the hallway again. 'Henri! Henri! Help! I'm being attacked.' There's anguish in her voice but when she turns to us, there's mischief in her spark-ling pale blue eyes. 'Come quickly, *cher*!'

'You're the head of the Croydon club, so you must shoulder the responsibility for this sabotage,' Marjorie says, stepping forward again, though Val is trying to pull her back. 'You have a short memory, Betty Moule. Don't forget that *I* know what you're capable of. *I* know what you did to Norman Pinter's sweet peas in 1996.'

There is no '*one* knows' now. Marjorie is owning this confrontation, and I admit, I feel a little proud of her.

She continues, pointing and pointing. 'And don't think that the Bromley Botanists are going to take this lying down, just so that you under-achievers in Croydon . . .' There is an audible sneer in her voice, '. . . can snatch the title and the prize without having the requisite talent or putting in sufficient effort.'

The last of her words are swallowed by the sound of a siren – a police car, advancing up the street. It likely isn't anything to do with us, but Val grabs Marjorie's upper arm. 'She's got the message, Marj. Come on. It's time we split. Just in case her husband's called those fuzz for us.'

Like a gaggle of easily spooked armchair anarchists, we scatter to our respective cars, but not before Val has flipped Barnacle Betty the bird.

'Right. We need a plan of action,' Mike says, sipping the foam from his pint of ale. He writes 'IDEAS' on a paper napkin in biro. 'Well?'

I watch the bubbles rise in my lime and soda, feel-ing certain I should be at home, watching something

Scandinavian, subtitled, and improving, rather than sitting in the Bickley Arms. We have repaired here to regroup and draw up a battle plan, travelling in convoy behind an intensely skittish Marj, who clearly wanted to get as far from the Croydon boundary as possible, judging by how she drove here at an uncharacteristically breakneck speed of forty-five miles per hour.

'We need to establish a proper connection between Dotty's murder, these acts of vandalism, and Croydon,' I say. 'Enough to warrant handing over to the police so they can make a case that would stand up to legal scrutiny. So I think we need to look into the other members properly and see if there's anything they're hiding. Try to see if there's maybe a motive for killing Dotty G that goes beyond winning the Golden Trowel.'

Seth frowns at his Coke. 'Winning land worth multimillions is motive enough to corrupt the Pope, man.'

'No need to bring the Vatican into this conversation,' Marjorie says, curling her lip.

'Let's choose a member each to investigate,' I say. 'You guys decide between yourselves which of you takes Moule, Studley, Lampard, and Bing. Seth's on Taylor Jones.'

He nods.

I picture Luke Cromarty in A&E on the night my mother was admitted, wearing a collar that he hadn't been wearing only minutes earlier in his car; sitting in a wheelchair after having practically bounced across the hospital car park. I know shifty behaviour when I see it. 'But leave Cromarty to me. I've got an idea . . .'

21

'Shereen! Remember you said you were dying of hot-
ness?' I ask at work the following morning. I am standing
behind the typing chair of our supreme database overlady. It is only 9.47am, and she is already fanning herself
with a piece of photocopier paper, despite the office
aircon being set to a modest twenty-two degrees.
Outside, the late-spring sun has risen unseasonably warm
over Bromley yet again, and I know Shereen beats me
hands down for internally combustive body heat, even in
winter, because we frequently moan to each other about
our sweaty perimenopausal torment. Today, I have the
perfect gift for her. 'Well, I brought you a present.'

I set down my coffee, put the portable fan on her
desk, plug it in, and switch it on. The cool air starts to
shift around Shereen's workspace.

'Ooh, that's *lovely*.' She tugs at her collar to allow the
fresh gust to reach her ample bosom. 'Aren't you a darling?' She gasps with delight and slaps her large belly
beneath her smart linen shift dress. 'I know I'm booty-
licious, like, but it's no fun carrying weight when the
inside of your car is like a sauna. My sodding aircon
bust at the weekend, and I've been flaking out on the
way in. This fan's a godsend.' She then looks at me with
undisguised suspicion and narrows her eyes at the sweat

patches beginning to form around my armpits. 'Hang on. Why you giving me your fan when you're melting? What you after, Gillian?'

I perch on the edge of her desk and give her the print-out of all I could find about Luke Cromarty on the internet, which wasn't much beyond his being the owner and the face of Sunset Pastures Homes. 'Do us a favour. Can you see if this guy has lodged a claim in the last couple of months?'

'Only if I get full custody of that fan.' Shereen studies the photo at the top of the homemade fact sheet. She cocks her head to the side inquisitively. 'Hey, I know this guy.' She pokes at his face. 'The one who advertises in the *Bromley News Shopper*. My auntie bought one of his retirement places in Purley, and it's well small. Cheap and nasty. Toilet broke when she sat on it, first week in, and she's small like my mum. Apparently they got undersized furniture in the show home to make it look bigger, too. My auntie says her shower stinks of rotten eggs whenever she uses it, and nobody ever comes out to fix it.' She kisses her teeth. 'I don't care for people who try to swizz old folks out of their hard-earned cash.'

'Well, he's driving round in a four-wheel drive worth as much as some people's homes, so your auntie's clearly not the only one funding his lavish lifestyle.' My heart is pounding as I anticipate what my colleague might find in the database. I can almost feel the electricity coursing through my body. I switch Shereen's new fan up to number three and pray that Colin isn't headed our way. 'Cromarty – C.R.O.M.A.R.T.Y. Luke.'

Shereen nods, plugs his name into the insurance database, and clicks the search icon.

Immediately, I can see that a record for him has indeed come up.

'Let me guess. Injury claim?' I ask.

She scans the information on the screen and whistles low. 'He's claiming for a neck and back injury. Apparently fell off a ladder on a building site and now he's near-paralysed. Says he can barely walk. Can't get out of bed or wash himself without assistance. Can't drive. All that malarkey. He's claiming against Sunset Pastures' public liability policy *and* he's trying to claim on his life and critical illness policy.'

'How much?'

'Five mill.'

She delivers this news as I am mid-mouthful of coffee, and I manage to spit the coffee all over myself. '*Five million?*'

Shereen hands me a box of tissues. Patting down my giraffe-like coffee blotches, rueing my decision to wear a pale blue shirt-dress to work, I replay yet again the memory of the property developer loping across that hospital car park in those Gucci loafers. He hadn't looked like a man who had just sustained life-threatening injuries. And he had managed to drive there in a car so high off the ground, you'd need a diploma in rock climbing to get in and out of it, so his claims of barely being able to walk and drive don't track. Similarly, he'd looked every inch the Peter Pan of property at Dotty Gloucester's wake. 'Has all of this been signed off by one of our medical team?' I ask. 'Any report from A&E or a specialist?'

She shakes her head. 'It's under investigation now. A&E couldn't find nothing on the initial X-ray or CT scan when Cromarty first went into the PRUH. He's seen his own private physician since, who's saying . . .' She moves her face closer to the screen and turns up the brightness. Kisses her teeth again. 'Can't see through these bloody varifocals, and they cost me over four hundred quid.'

I read over her shoulder. 'His own orthopaedic consultant is saying he's got hairline fractures on three of his vertebrae – one in the neck and two further down – and significant bruising. So, broken back, broken neck. Yadda, yadda, yadda. Got to wear a collar and have complete bed rest.' I bite the inside of my cheek, wondering if Cromarty's claim is, in fact, bona fide. 'Possible wheelchair confinement?' Might he have gone to A&E, initially unaware of the extent of his injuries, I wonder? Had he brought a walking stick with him to Dotty G's wake? 'When's his appointment with our medical guy?'

'Three weeks' time.'

I pat Shereen's shoulder. 'Thanks for this. Can I get a print-out?'

'Whatcha gonna do with it?' Shereen narrows her eyes at me. 'You ain't going vigilante on me, are you? We do have fraud investigators, you know.' She prints out the report.

I take the paperwork from her and fold it neatly in two. 'I know. I know. I'm just doing a little managerial digging. Due diligence and all that. You just enjoy your lovely cool fan and remember you're my favourite supreme overlady of the database.' I move over to my own workstation, then I catch sight of Colin in my peripheral vision. I turn back to Shereen and tap the side of my nose. 'Oh, and keep this to yourself for now.'

Shereen nods and waves.

By the time I'm properly ensconced at my desk, a plan is starting to shape up in earnest, and I realise I must pay a lunchtime visit to another of my fellow Bromley Botanists. I dial his number. He answers just before the phone goes to voicemail.

'Yo.' The sound of hammer drills whining and banging in the background almost drowns out his voice.

'Seth? It's Gill. I need to visit you at your building site. Ping me your address?'

I arrive at the building site for the latest development of Sunset Pastures' 'luxury assisted living for seniors', where the tradesmen sitting out front on the giant stacks of breeze-blocks all seem to be crushing their drinks cans and screwing their paper lunch bags into balls.

'Do you know where I can find Seth?' I ask a middle-aged man with a kindly face.

He looks me up and down, grinning. 'You his mum? You're way too good-looking to be *his* mum.'

'I'm his auntie. And that kind of flattery gives a woman indigestion. Know where I can find him?'

Now looking crestfallen, the builder nods towards some parked cars. 'Well, your nephew's antisocial, love. He never eats with the rest of the lads. He's in his car.'

When I reach Seth's gleaming A-Class Mercedes, he gestures that I should get in the passenger seat. Inside, the car is immaculate and there are plastic covers on the seats as well as pieces of cardboard lining the pale carpeted footwell.

'I need a favour,' I say. 'I want you to keep tabs on Cromarty. Let me know when he turns up to the site. Take photos if you can – especially if he's walking around, climbing ladders, driving . . . that sort of thing.'

Seth looks at me askance. 'You could have asked me that on the phone. Why'd you come in person?'

'I was hoping Cromarty would be here so I could see him for myself.' Have I made this journey for nothing? 'Is he?'

Seth points to something visible through his windscreen. I follow the line of his finger to an imposing, blindingly flashy orange Lamborghini four-wheel drive. 'Car's here. I know Building Regs are on site today to sign off on some stuff. But I ain't laid eyes on him myself.'

I feel a hot flush building with the excitement of stalking a potential insurance fraudster, and momentarily imagine that I'm a spy, rather than an administrative functionary – albeit managerial – in the call centre of an insurance company. 'Brilliant.' I take out my phone and photograph the car. 'I just need to wait for him to reappear.'

Seth frowns. 'Not in my car you can't. Building trade has lunch at midday, and I'm already five minutes late getting back to work.' He shows me the time on his cracked and dust-encrusted phone screen. 'You'll have to sit in your own car, and don't let him see you.'

I take my leave from Seth and repair to the Volvo. The sun beats down on the car so that pretty soon, the interior feels like a furnace. My chicken and pesto sandwich has gone limp, even inside its tinfoil wrapping, and the orange squash in my hand flask tastes of dishwasher soap.

Just after 1.45pm, there is still no sign of Cromarty, but a young(ish) woman dressed in expensive-looking gym wear and wearing a hard hat appears, two floors up. She clambers down from the scaffolding like a woman used to building sites and ladders. Her descent is accompanied by wolf whistles from the builders above. She waves merrily at them, reaches the ground, and takes off her hard hat with a flourish to reveal a head of long, tonged, brassy blonde hair. More wolf-whistling for this performance. For an encore, she sashays with a pronounced wiggle to the Lamborghini, whereupon she unlocks the car and, with a final wave to the tradesmen, climbs in on the driver's side.

Will Cromarty follow? I cross my fingers, my heart pounding, waiting for the shady developer to show. But he doesn't.

Have I just witnessed Cromarty's wife conducting a meeting with Building Regs in her husband's stead? If so, he's clearly being careful in case nosey insurance humps like me are watching from a distance. And why wouldn't he be, with millions at stake?

'Damn it,' I say beneath my breath.

It's time for me to go. I peer at the now departing Lamborghini feeling stupid for having given up my

229

lunch hour, when I could have been listening in on more calls or going through some more spreadsheets in a bid to salvage my job. I could even have rung my mother to ask if she needs me to fetch anything from the supermarket, ahead of this evening's visit. But I did none of those things, and I'm left wondering how my life has ended up with me using my free time failing to spy on a spray-tanned man with bouffant hair. Then, I remember that my quarry might be involved in a murder and is merrily, blatantly trying to defraud Chislehurst Green Insurance to the tune of five million pounds, while I must fire people on tenuous grounds or else risk incurring the wrath of Colin.

'Screw you, Luke Cromarty.'

I tap out a text to Mike.

> Hi Mike. Hope the allotment is still knotweed free.
> How easy would it be to access financial information
> like solvency about a businessman like Cromarty? Any
> ideas? You seem like the sort of man who would know.
> Gill x

Why have I put a kiss after my name at the end of my chatty message to Mike? I erase the kiss and then replace it, erase, then replace it several times. Do I want to give Mike the impression that there is more to our connection than shared professional angst and an interest in plants?

I leave the kiss in and wait for the reply.

22

'I don't want pasta. It makes me fart all night long,' my mother shouts over the television. 'Stop making me fucking pasta, Gillian!'

'But mum's "creamy-pasta-thing" is the best,' Zak says.

'Don't lecture me about my own digestive tract,' comes my mother's retort.

'I wasn't, Nan! I wasn't.'

I emerge from her small kitchen, and through the mirror on the hall wall, I can see the mini-drama unfolding in the living room. I watch my son putting his feet up on my mother's sofa and wince, knowing how she will react to this perfectly innocent move. He's not even wearing shoes.

'Get your bloody feet off my sofa, young man,' Mum says. 'Show some respect.'

'Sorry, Nan.'

Clearing my throat, I step into the fray. 'Mum, I've brought a lovely, nutritious salmon, spinach, and mushroom pasta dish that I prepared at home before we came over. Fresh as a daisy. I'm just going to put it in the microwave to reheat, and we can eat in five. I even brought some grated parmesan in a pot.'

Mum turns and fixes me with a disgruntled look. 'Well,

don't bother on my account. I don't fancy farting myself into next Tuesday.'

I lean against the wall and sigh. 'You've got to eat, Mum, and it's this or nothing.'

Mum rolls her eyes and switches the television off. 'I don't even have any control over what I eat, do I?'

I lock eyes with Zak, and I feel certain we are silently communicating our frustration with one another. 'Zak, you've not had a chance to tell Nan about your ADHD and dyslexia stuff. Why don't you tell her now?'

I repair to the kitchen to set the pasta dish to heat in the microwave. While I'm taking three plates out of a kitchen cupboard, I eavesdrop on Zak, talking to my mother about his neurodivergent journey of self-discovery.

'So they've given me extra time at school, Nan.' The grin is audible in his voice. 'And Seth from gardening is tutoring me in Chemistry now, and it's, like . . . wow. I mean, what a difference! I got an A in my last end-of-topic test. Legit, about fifth in the class.'

Again, I peer through the mirror in the hall to see what is going on just around the corner in the living room, and I note my mother's bored expression.

'So you're a reject like the rest of us, are you?' she says.

I can see the ebullience of Zak's expression fade until he looks like someone switched off the light behind his eyes.

'Mum! That's enough.' I march into the living room, hand on hip, vaguely recalling Mandi's advice not to lose my temper with my mother. I fail. 'Why do you have to suck the joy out of everything, for God's sake?'

'It's fine, Mum,' Zak says, ever the diplomat, just like his father.

'No, Zak. It's not fine.' I turn to my mother, who is looking studiously at the film section of the *What's On TV* guide, as if she hasn't just insulted the very fabric of my son's being. 'Mum, look at me! Don't pretend you haven't just said something despicable to your grandson. Untrue, as well.'

Sighing, my mother slaps her TV guide onto the arm of her chair and rolls her eyes. 'I didn't mean it as an insult,' she says. 'I just mean . . . well, come on, Gillian. Let's call a shovel a shovel and a spade a spade. I've got dementia.'

'You haven't got dementia. You've been told by the GP before. Bipolar disorder or anxiety and depression, maybe? But we still don't fully know, because the last time I took you to the GP, you told him where to go, didn't you?'

Mum is digging deeply into her molars with her tongue. She does this when she's considering some witticism or character assassination. 'I believe I called him a lanky twat, because he was, and I told him to fuck off, and he did.' She chuckles mischievously. 'I don't like those do-gooders, like that silly cow you pay through the nose for advice. Mand-*i*: so full of herself, she couldn't possibly have the normal spelling of Mandy. These overpaid charlatans can't get their own affairs straight, let alone anyone else's.'

Studying Zak's hangdog expression and defensive body language, I feel my spine hardening to steel. 'Apologise to Zak, or we're leaving.'

Mum shoots me almost dead with a glance so venom-ous she could wilt the anthurium on the coffee table. 'I don't owe no apologies to a snot-nosed kid.'

'You're stigmatising the boy for something he has no control over. He's neurodivergent.'

'Woke bullshit. Everyone needs a trendy label, nowadays.'

'And neurodivergence has to come from somewhere, and I can't see it being Dave's side of the family, because they're all the most unremarkable, uncomplicated people you could hope to meet.' I look at the sun-bleached framed photo of my father on top of the television. I feel certain that, had my dad lived to see the new century, his social awkwardness and hyperfixation on growing vegetables and fixing up old cars would definitely have been explained by an autism spectrum disorder diagno-sis, had he sought one. 'Everyone said Dad was shy or the strong silent type, but he wasn't just that, was he? He was definitely on the spectrum.'

Mum is up and out of her chair faster than a grey-hound out of the gate at a dog race. She snatches up the photograph of my father and clutches it to her chest. 'Don't you dare speak ill of that man,' she said. 'Your father was a king among men. And he was clever.'

'Zak's clever,' I say. 'Zak's just like him. And the gar-dening I'm doing now . . . Dad would have loved it. Growing things from seed and getting your hands dirty with good honest soil and compost.'

Tears well in my mother's eyes, and she sits down on the sofa next to Zak, clutching the photo with one hand

and squeezing his knee with the other. 'Sorry, boy,' she says. 'I didn't mean what I said. You're a good kid. And my Ron was a good man. The best.' She turns to me.

I nod, privately musing that I have lost not one but two men in my life who have been the best. I don't know if I'm cursed, or if that constitutes an embarrassment of riches. Many women don't know a single good man their entire life.

The microwave dings, so I return to the kitchen to serve dinner. As we eat, it's clear the atmosphere has lightened somewhat. Mum asks Zak about school and actually listens to his answers. I talk about my ongoing woes at work with my belligerent boss expecting me to ruin people's lives for the sake of the company's bottom line. Mum moans heartily about Carol, the carer.

'She's got nothing but hairspray between her ears, has Carol,' Mum says. 'It's like talking to a tumble dryer. All she watches is *Love Island* and *The Real Housewives of Cheshire*. A woman of her age should know better.'

I nod and spoon the pasta into my mouth, realising that the greatest challenge my mother faces is the one that, until recently, I also faced: loneliness.

When we've eaten (and amazingly, I didn't get a single complaint), Mum shuffles off into the cupboard where she keeps everything from the hoover to coats, to books and old lampshades and the paraphernalia of almost eighty years of life. After some clattering about, she returns bearing a photo album that I recognise from my childhood. Princess Diana is on the hard, shiny cover – a photo taken when she'd still been 'Lady Di'.

'What have you got there?' I ask, bemused. 'Have you looked out childhood pics to embarrass me in front of Zak?'

Mum grunts as she takes her seat in the middle of the sofa and beckons that Zak and I flank her. She opens the album and flicks through several pages. 'Here we go.' She pokes at the cellophane-covered old 6x4 photos, which entirely lack the definition of today's easy snaps but are no less precious for their graininess and the ubiquitous scourge of red-eye on anything taken inside or at night.

I trace a finger lovingly over the image of my father, digging in the small back garden of my childhood home. He is wearing a tartan shirt and old mud-encrusted jeans, tucked into black wellies. His thick steel-grey hair is dishevelled and his cheeks are ruddy, but he's smiling at the camera — at Mum — and I am at his side, on my knees in the soil, pulling a seedling out of an upturned pot.

'If only I could step back into that photo,' I say.

'That's your granddad, Zak. My Ron,' Mum says, pride and sadness in her voice. 'He looks the picture of health, doesn't he? Slim, handsome. Hard to believe he was diagnosed with a dicky ticker, not all that long after this picture was taken.' She tuts and clasps my hand as if in solidarity, that we are the women who loved and lost. 'But the garden . . . He always grew the loveliest-tasting veg, did your granddad. We were never short of something to eat. Remember his carrots, Gill?'

I nod. 'Massive, they were. And sweet. You never tasted more carroty carrots than them.' I rub Mum's back and feel warmed by affection for her . . . though it could just as easily be a hot flush rolling in. 'Remember how he used to have that long length of twine attached to two sharp sticks, and he'd shove the sticks in the soil, pulling the string taut to mark out a straight seed drill?'

'He got you to trowel out some of the soil, didn't he, so you felt involved?'

'Yes. And then he'd let me put the seeds in. I used to love watching the carrot tops come up, all frondy and green. Didn't take long.'

In my mind's eye, I am back in the 1980s, wearing my dungarees and freezing cold wellies. I am peering into our compost bin, which was tucked away at the side of the house, rather like mine is now. Wrinkling my nose, I can still see the writhing centipedes and wriggling worms and scurrying woodlice, making the compost seem as though it was moving; almost a sentient organism. I can see my father in that tartan flannel shirt, tying in wayward runner beans that would wrap their delicate tendrils around whatever they could reach, in a bid to accelerate their way up the six-foot-tall bamboo supports. In my mind's eye, the heavy trusses of tomatoes we'd grown together from seed are still ripening. They are green, orange, and red jewels, and I can still smell the pungent chlorophyll on my father's clothes when we hug.

'Nice memories,' Mum says. She turns to Zak. 'You should get into gardening too, son. It's good for you. Keeps you on the straight and narrow, my Ron used to say. "Plants are more demanding than kids," he'd say. Ha. Not sure I agree with him there.' She looks at me with undisguised judgement in eyes that sport white cholesterol rings around the irises. Her lips thin. But instead of doling out another anticipated jibe, she leans over and kisses me on the cheek. I can feel her chin hairs tingle on my skin, and for a moment, Mum smells like she used to of talc and baking and clean washing.

I take her hand into mine and stroke the varicose veins that stand proud beneath her loose, liver-spotted skin. Planting a kiss on her knuckles, I glance at the photo of Dad, where he's holding a bunch of homegrown sweet peas that dazzle like tropical butterflies on a summer's day. 'Come with me to the gardening club, Mum,' I hear myself say. 'There's a couple of women around the same age as you, and I think it would do you good. I think they'd like to see these pictures of Dad, and I think you might enjoy yourself.'

Mum snaps the album shut. 'Fuck off, you silly girl.'

'You totally should, Nan,' Zak says. 'I can help Mum get you in the car. I'll come too, if you'll come.'

Getting to her feet with a grunt, my mother shakes her head and marches back to the cupboard full of junk with the photo album tucked under her arm. 'I'm not some psychological experiment, son, and your mother's no shrink.'

Ordinarily, I would find my mother's rejection frustrating and disheartening, but I am minded to ignore her barbed comments when there's a ping from my phone, and I see Mike has sent me a message.

Hi Gill. No more knotweed, thankfully. We need to talk at the next meet. I have news on Cromarty's finances. Looking forward to seeing you. Mike. X

23

'Common pests,' Val announces as her theme at our next meet. She takes a drag from her roll-up and points to the next slide projected onto a plain white wall, her index finger only slightly yellowed from nicotine.

We are gathered in Val's maisonette, which is comprised of the lower two floors and garden of a four-storey Victorian house near Bromley North station. As I anticipated, her place seems to be furnished with mid-century and 1930s thrift shop finds: a tiled coffee table on spindle legs; a heavy carved Deco sideboard; a crocheted throw covering an old gold mid-century settee. Uranium glass ashtrays everywhere. On the walls, there are aluminium-framed posters from various band tours. The Sex Pistols, The Clash, Siouxsie and the Banshees. And there are plants. Scores of plants on every windowsill, every side table, hanging in tubs from hooks screwed into the ceiling.

'First up is dahlia gall,' Val says.

'We've already talked about this,' Mike says. 'Everybody knows about gall.'

Marjorie turns to Mike and smooths her pleated skirt over her knees. 'Well, seeing as half of our stock *has* turned out to have gall this year, perhaps one should take a look at Valerie's photograph. "The Lord detests all the proud of heart," Michael. Proverbs 16:5.'

I am aware that my eyebrows are heading for my hairline. I hadn't anticipated that Marjorie would stick up for Val under any circumstance, yet I have just witnessed a show of solidarity with my own tired eyes.

We all focus our attention on the projected photo of a dahlia tuber blighted by ugly fused growth.

'What do you do if you spot gall?' Val asks Phoebe.

'Bin it off,' Phoebe says.

Val nods. 'That's right. Bag it and bin it or burn it. Don't be tempted to put the tuber in the compost, because it will affect all your other stock. And gall travels, so make sure you quarantine the affected plant, if you're not sure and you're waiting to see how it goes.'

I put my hand up like an eager schoolchild.

Val points at me with her cigarette.

'Val, what happens if you just leave the gall?' I ask.

Mike jumps in with an answer. 'Flower yield will be very low, and it will get lower and lower until the plant dies. Everything else will get infected and . . . death, basically.'

'Didn't know you'd turned into my doppelganger, Michael.' Val regards Mike over the top of her glasses, like an unimpressed schoolteacher. She turns back to me. 'But yes. He is right. It's just not worth keeping a plant with gall, and it spreads like butter on a hot summer's day.'

I grimace as Val changes the next slide and shouts, 'Hygiene, people. Keep your tools and pots pristine. You are surgeons, and your plants are patients. If you would wash your hands and surgical instruments between removing appendixes –'

'Appendices,' Marjorie says.

'Thank you for the lesson in English, Marj,' Val says. '*One's* always grateful to be Marj-splained to.'

And there the truce between the doyennes of the group seemingly ends.

After a lecture on mosaic virus, about which Cath seems to know a good deal, we all head into Val's garden to admire her oriental poppies and late-flowering peonies. Mike steers me off towards the bottom of the garden, where two enormous, mature rhododendrons – one, hot pink, and the other, bright purple – have merged to form a secluded nook. I feel the hairs on my arms stand to attention in the breeze – or is it being alone with Mike Potato in his new glasses?

'Well?' I ask. 'What did you find out about Cromarty's finances?'

Mike glances back at the others, who are gathered around a clump of the biggest tomato-red oriental poppies I've ever seen, listening to Val wax lyrical about them. He turns back to me.

Leaning forward, Mike almost whispers in my ear. 'I couldn't find anything about Cromarty personally, but the yearly accounts for Sunset Pastures are published online, and get this: according to what Cromarty's accountants have lodged with Companies House, the company has hardly any cash in the bank.'

'What do you call hardly anything?'

'Just over twenty thousand.'

I breathe in sharply. 'Oof. That's peanuts for a big concern like that, right? And there's me, thinking only millionaires drove cars like that.' I think about the elevated price of just one of those retirement flats. 'I don't understand. Where's all the money going? Cromarty's thrown up developments all over the South-East. I thought he'd be sat on a fortune.'

Mike sticks his thumbs into the waistband of his trousers and rocks on his heels. 'Ah, well, this is par for the course with the likes of Cromarty. Developing is a high-risk game, you see. The land, planning, and building costs are astronomical, so what you generally find is that the clear profit is often all in the last couple of units to be sold.'

'But how on earth is he keeping a huge building site running if he's cash-poor? He's still got to pay his workers. Can you imagine the weekly wages bill on that apartment block Seth's working on?'

Mike's eyebrows wander north. 'No doubt he's servicing huge debts. Don't forget, we recently started a new financial year, and he's mid-building project, so those online year-end accounts will show only what his accountants want to show from *last* financial year. Someone like Cromarty will hire top-drawer accounting staff who know all the tax loopholes. By the time his expenses are deducted and he and his directors have claimed a salary . . .' His eyes widen. 'And this is where my research got *really* interesting.'

'What do you mean?'

'Ask me who the directors at Sunset Pastures are,' he says, grinning.

'Go on. Who are they?' I feel the thrill of discovery fizz inside me.

'Cromarty, obviously,' Mike says. 'His wife, Lexi. They've been directors since the company was started, fifteen years ago. But a handful of people left a year ago and have been replaced recently with newly registered directors.' Behind the lenses of his glasses, his eyes are shining. He's rocking on his heels like a child desperate to share a secret. 'Guess who they are.'

'Spit it out, Michael.'

'Betty Moule, Taylor Jones, and Neville Studley — three members of the Croydon Diggers and Dibbers.'

Just as I'm about to react to this momentous bit of gossip, Val shouts over to us.

'Oi! What you lot doing over there? My garden, and you're leaving me out of whatever it is you're hatching? What a bloody cheek! Get yourselves over here and tell your Auntie Val what's so important you need to discuss it at the bottom of my garden!'

I wonder briefly why I ever tried to keep my investigation into Cromarty to myself. I have no boundaries with my own mother, so why did I ever think I could set boundaries with this lot?

'Not here,' I say, peering up at the windows above and either side, behind which neighbours might be eavesdropping. 'Inside.'

We repair back to Val's front room, and within five minutes, I've filled everyone in regarding Cromarty's attempted insurance fraud to the tune of five million pounds, and now everybody also knows how Cromarty has recruited three other Croydon Diggers and Dibbers as company directors for Sunset Pastures Homes.

Phoebe scratches at her matted hair and then sniffs her fingers. 'But why would a couple of olds get involved in a property development company? I can understand Taylor Jones, because he's in the business anyway, but Betty Moule and Neville Studley are retired, right?'

'They must be investors,' Mike says. 'Or maybe they lend a pretty shady company some respectability. Sunset Pastures doesn't exactly have a good reputation for planning transparency or value for money.'

'That's hardcore, man,' Seth says. 'Especially if those two old codgers know bad stuff's going down – I mean Dotty G and the attack on Marj.'

'If they didn't know skulduggery was afoot before, they most certainly do now we've threatened Betty Moule on her own doorstep,' Marjorie says. She grins mischievously. 'I'm glad I manhandled her lilac.' She says, '*Putain!*' not quite beneath her breath.

'Right, I get it!' Val holds her hands up. 'I get it. Listen up! Here's my theory: Cromarty's a straight-up conman, preying on the elderly. He sells substandard flats to them for sky-high prices, and he's fiddling money out of Betty and that Studley feller to boot.' She straddles the arm of her sofa, next to which Marjorie is perched on the edge of a seat cushion. 'And either they've fallen for it, because they're gullible berks, or else Cromarty's making big, empty promises about returns on their investment.'

'One noticed that Betty Moule had those windows that cost a small fortune,' Marjorie says, scowling.

Seth is standing by the sideboard. He shovels a biscuit into his mouth and speaks while chewing. 'Yeah.

Her house did look like it had been newly renovated, so maybe Cromarty's not fiddling them, and they're getting building services rendered in return for their cash injection. Taylor Jones works for Cromarty, so maybe Cromarty's promising to bung him a ton of extra money out of profits to act as his muscle. Maybe all the new directors stand to make a wedge of cash if Cromarty gets the insurance cheque, yeah? And if the Croydon Diggers and Dibbers win the Trowellies, Sunset Pastures is bound to get a load of new buyers off the back of the year's free advertising in *Wise* mag.'

'That's not the only motivation,' I say, waving my hands with a surge of adrenalin as realisation dawns. 'Certainly not motivation enough for murder. My guess is Cromarty wants to build over Dotty Gloucester's golf club.'

Everyone inhales sharply as if they're a single organism. 'Of course!' Neil says.

'If he can get the usage of the land changed from the flower farm that Dotty stipulated in her will to residential . . .' I look at Mike. 'He can get the best lawyers so he can change use, can't he? And if he's got five mill seed funding from his insurance scam, he'll have a hefty chunk of change to bribe obstructive planners to wave through a housing estate, right?'

Mike nods. 'Oh, yes. That stuff does go on. More often than you'd think.'

'The insurance money must also be his building fund,' Seth says. 'Bricks and mortar don't come for free — especially when you've got that many acres of land.'

'Then if he invests five million in a development of, say, fifty or more executive houses that sell for two to three million each, he'll make a hundred million, easy,' I say, feeling jigsaw pieces arrange themselves to slot neatly into place. 'The three members of the Croydon club will all be on a percentage cut of the profits for enabling Sunset Pastures to keep on its feet and for helping to win the Golden Trowel and all that prime real estate . . . by any means necessary.'

'It's skulduggery on a grand scale,' Mike says. 'But *if* Cromarty is guilty of all this, how on earth did he know about Dotty Gloucester's legacy of the golf club in the first place *before* she died? And we still don't know who her visitor in the mystery white Golf was . . .'

24

'Well, it's clear to me that you've got ADD, yes?' the psychiatrist says the following morning. 'Not ADHD, but ADD. Attention deficit. No hyperactivity.'

'But he's always fidgeting,' I say. 'His foot's always going like Thumper the rabbit.'

The psychiatrist shakes her head. 'It's not like he's climbing things and putting his life in danger or jumping from great heights with no fear. He's not refusing to sit in class, is he? Those are the sorts of behaviours that normally come with the hyperactivity element of ADHD. A bit of a twitchy foot isn't quite the same.' She locks eyes with my son. 'But you are definitely neurodivergent and always will be, even if you take medication, yes?'

Zak has just undergone his official ADHD assessment, and the psychiatrist is awaiting his response to her diagnosis with an expectant half-smile.

'Cool,' Zak says, looking to me for a reaction.

I merely exhale hard and nod. 'Good. Good. So, this is good, right? Getting him diagnosed before he does A-Levels and applies to universities is brilliant timing. Isn't it? All the support he'll qualify for?'

Zak nods uncertainly, clearly hoping for some reassurance from the psychiatrist that doesn't come.

'A diagnosis of ADD should help you answer a few questions about yourself, yes?' She then goes into some rapid-fire detail about the medication available, should we opt to go down that path, and the potential side-effects that scare the hell out of me.

'So, what do you think, Zak?' the psychiatrist asks. 'Would you like to try medication?'

Zak glances over at me. 'Yeah?'

'I've heard it can be transformative, so we could give it a go, and just stop if it doesn't agree with you,' I say, wondering if I'm the best mother in the world or the worst.

We come away with a prescription for low-dose stimulants, the name of which I can barely pronounce. I register a pang of sadness that I have to put chemicals into my child to give him the best chance of succeeding in a world that doesn't tolerate the dreamers, the restless, the ones that colour outside the lines. I also feel self-loathing at not having joined the dots up sooner, because I've been too tied up in my grief, my work, and my mother. Ah well, better late than never.

'How do you feel?' I ask my son when we're back in the car, and the pink private prescription is safely folded in the zipped compartment of my handbag.

'Brilliant,' he says, grinning. Even on a cloudy day, the interior of the car feels warmer and brighter for the optimism radiating from him. 'Oh my gosh. So much makes sense, Mum. I feel like none of it was my fault – all those times I did badly in class or got shouted at by teachers or made to feel like a loser by the other kids . . . you know?

It's just I'm wired different. I'm *neurodivergent*.' There's pride audible in his voice, as if he's just announced he has a superpower.

I grab my boy-child into a bear hug and kiss the top of his head. 'Great. I'm so relieved.' I think about the substantial four-figure sum that I've had to scrape together for this private assessment, with further payments in the pipeline, each running into the hundreds, for private six-monthly medication reviews. With the NHS waiting time to see a child psychiatrist for treatment running to as much as seven years, I count myself lucky to have a regular paycheque going into my account, however tedious and stressful my job might be. 'Money well spent, kiddo. Maybe these meds will help you – with your schoolwork, with getting your head around the practicalities of adulting. But even if they don't, you'll find your path, because you're a wonderful boy.' I swallow down a hot geyser of emotion. 'Your dad would be proud of the young man you're turning into. So proud.'

'Yeah. Cheers,' Zak says absently. He's staring through the windscreen of the Volvo at a sports car roaring down the street towards us. 'Oh my God. Look at that! A McLaren 720S Spider. Sick!'

I smile at the proof that the assessment was absolutely the right course of action to take for this wonderful, highly distractible boy.

Having dropped Zak back at school, I return to work to find Colin hanging around by my desk with arms folded.

'Ah, Gill. At last,' he says, no trace of warmth in his

smile. He looks at his watch and his eyes narrow. 'Can you follow me to my office, please?'

And just like that, after feeling the burden of mid-life lift somewhat following Zak's diagnosis, I am shackled anew to the lead-lined corporate mould that Chislehurst Green demands I squeeze into. When I see that Janice from HR awaits us in his office, I realise serious trouble is afoot.

'Ah, Gillian.' She is wearing her poker face that I've seen her don before for sackings. Her cloying floral scent is almost certainly called 'The Perfume of Betrayal'.

'Take a seat, Gill,' Colin says. He's fiddling with his tie. He closes the door behind him.

'This all sounds a bit serious,' I say. 'I hope nobody's died. Especially not if they don't have life insurance. Ha ha.'

Their faces are unyieldingly hard.

Colin sits behind his desk. 'Now, Gill. I know you've had a parental commitment this morning, but we've been reviewing the targets against each regional manager's performance, and Janice and I thought we should apprise you of the latest.' His face looks shiny, as if he's either enjoying or hating every minute of this. It's hard to tell. 'Janice?'

'Yes. Thank you, Colin.' Seated next to me in the visitor's chair, Janice turns to me wearing a Dolores Umbridge grin. She speaks in a soft, high, kitten-fancier's voice, though she is anything but soft or kitteny. 'You know, Gill, this company sometimes offers staff voluntary redundancy packages, or we ask that people reapply for their old position or accept an internal move, if we're . . . reorganising.'

'Yeah. And?' I feel a flush rolling in. I know exactly what's coming.

Janice crosses her hands on her lap. 'Well, Gill, I'm afraid that since your attendance record is so poor, and what with you refusing to put people on a warning where appropriate, we have no option but to put *you* on a warning . . . or perhaps we could consider a voluntary redundancy package.'

My anger glows white-hot inside me. I turn to Colin. 'How can you do this to me when I'm trying my hardest to up my staff's productivity? I put Loveday and D'Arcy Whatsherface down for retraining. I am trying, Colin!'

He is the smiling assassin now. 'You've always been a valuable member of the team, Gill, but a manager's got to manage, and I'm not sure your managerial skillset is complete. We have to be able to dole out bad news, as well as good, especially when company profitability is at stake.'

I grip the arms of my chair tightly. 'Are you asking me to actually sack people?'

He shakes his head and shrugs. 'I would never ask you to cull staff without following company procedure.' He toys with a photo of his cockerpoo, which sits in a small bejewelled frame next to a photo of him posing in fisherman's waders, holding a giant tench. 'I seem to remember just asking you to identify ways that we can put the company back in the black. You suggested ear-marking staff for retraining and issuing warnings, where appropriate. Yet you haven't demonstrated you can actually do that.'

Janice exhales heavily. 'Nobody likes doing this, Gill, but . . .'

I feel the red mist descending but realise I'm not my mother and I'm in no position to antagonise these ghouls, even if they are doing a switcheroo on me. *Come on, Gill! Think!* I think of Luke Cromarty, gaming the system to benefit himself, and then I realise what I must do. 'Look. I need this job, and I've worked at Chislehurst Green for donkey's years. What if I was to save you an absolute ton of cash? Way more than the directors initially asked you to claw back.'

'How?' Colin says. He sits back in his chair and steeples his fingers together like a Poundland Gordon Gecko.

'I know of a five-million-pound injury and critical illness claim that's bogus. It's in the assessment process. It looks like it's going to go through, and I know it's a fraud.'

Colin's barely there eyebrows bunch up. 'How? Who? Have you got evidence?'

'If I brought you enough evidence to warrant a proper investigation by our fraud team – guaranteed success – would you drop this "managerial skillset" crap and wipe the warning from my employment record?' I lock eyes with Janice. 'Come on, Janice. You're the HR director, for Pete's sake. I'll bet I could take Chislehurst Green to the cleaners, and *both of you* would get the order of the boot.'

'You're expensive and you're cherry-picking the parts of your job that you're prepared to do. We've got legitimate grounds for suggesting you take voluntary redundancy.'

'Wanna risk it in court?' In my mind's eye, Dave is giving me the thumbs up, and Mike salutes my bravery.

I'm vaguely aware of Janice accusing me of holding them over a barrel, but I'm too busy watching the sweat suddenly shine on Colin's face. I'm willing him to accede to my request.

He loosens his tie, wipes his top lip, and gets to his feet. 'I'll be very happy to hear details of the claim so I can pass it to the investigators, but you can't use it as a bargaining chip to keep your job.'

'Suit yourself,' I say, willing myself to maintain a show of bravado. 'But it doesn't look good to the shareholders if the staff is allowing the company to be defrauded on such a grand scale, does it?'

I leave Colin's office, grateful that I've managed to hold back my tears. I save them up, all the way to the disabled toilet at the opposite end of the floor, where I can lock myself in and let the anguish out, unobserved.

'Er, Gill, this is Mandi. Hiya. Hi.' When I arrive home from work and listen to my sole message on the old answering machine, my therapist's voice sounds nasal and crackly. 'I'm just calling because I'm concerned that you cancelled the last couple of sessions without rebooking. Er, can you give me a call, please, and let me know you're okay?'

I fling my handbag onto the kitchen worktop and am poised to call her back, even though it's later than her advertised office hours. I know I should make an appointment and stick to it. I know that course of top-up sessions I booked back in the new year, to quell my mounting anxiety over the dizzying merry-go-round of my life, has only helped. Yet, for the first time in a long time, I'm actually relishing the opportunity to see if I can get through my various trials without a professional crutch.

'Don't be a knob, Gill. You can't do this alone. Just call her,' I tell myself.

'Nope,' my alter-ego says. 'Stop being a coward and stand on your own two feet for a change.'

Stepping back from the phone, I fight the urge to out-source my bravery to someone else. What I do instead is dial Mike. He picks up on the third ring.

'Gill. What a lovely surprise. How are you?'

I swallow down the anguish and loneliness and frustration that threaten to choke me. 'I've had the worst day.'

'Oh, I'm sorry to hear that. How come?'

'Long story. What about you?'

'Mine was rather good, actually.' He sounds genuinely chirpy. 'I rearranged the large terracotta pot display in the garden centre so it looks so much better and I've made an appointment tomorrow morning to see an employment lawyer at the Beckenham branch of Biggins Broadacre and Levy.'

'Oh, they're supposed to be very good,' I say, remembering hearing Dave mention that they were a rival outfit to the firm where he was an associate.

'Yes, Marjorie recommended them. Apparently all the church flower-arranging brigade uses them. She's getting me a ten per cent reduction on fees. Might as well sound them out.'

I contemplate how unfairly I was treated earlier by Colin and Janice. 'I'm glad you're going ahead with the tribunal, Mike. Win it for me?'

He chuckles, falls momentarily silent, and I can hear him clicking his tongue against the roof of his mouth in contemplation. 'Fancy meeting me for lunch after my meeting?'

I picture the busy roundabout that Biggins Broadacre and Levy is on, just across from the old Odeon cinema. 'If memory serves, there's a nice Turkish place opposite.'

'Great. Let's meet there at one? You can tell me about your terrible day, I can tell you how my meeting went, and we can bash our heads together over Luke Cromarty and the contents of Dotty Gloucester's will.'

25

'I'll just have a Diet Coke and a Greek salad please,' I tell the waiter in the Turkish restaurant.

I'm sitting at a table for two by the window, so I catch sight of Mike as soon as he leaves the solicitors. He strides across the road like a man whose morning has been filled with promise. Either his meeting has gone extremely well, or he's excited to be lunching with me. Was I right to meet up with him?

The doorbell tinkles, and Mike enters, squinting in the restaurant's murky artificial light.

'Mike! Over here!' I wave.

He walks towards the table, grinning. 'Gill! You made it.' He flops down into his seat. He's wearing a suit, rather than his garden centre uniform – not the shiny brown town-planner's double-breasted thing that I've seen him in before. This one looks new and actually fits him properly. He looks dapper.

'Well? How did it go?'

'I've got a very strong case.' He picks up the menu with some flourish. 'They're taking me on as a client on a "no win, no fee" basis. I signed all the paperwork. We're suing for constructive dismissal.' He looks younger today. 'How about *that*?!'

'Brilliant. I hope they haul your former bosses over the coals. No less than they deserve.'

He orders, and we chat as we're waiting for our food. I tell him about my dreadful run-in with Colin and Janice at work.

'If we win the Golden Trowel, will you take the voluntary redundancy and start over as a flower farmer?' he asks, pouring iced tap water into our glasses.

I puff air out of my cheeks. 'It's a huge risk for me personally. I've got enormous overheads. It's not just me and Zak any more.' I picture my mother, sitting in her armchair, hooked up to an oxygen machine and barking breathless orders at Carol. 'I'm having to pay for a carer for my mum. She's not ill enough to qualify for any free support. She's not well enough to be left to her own devices.' I press my hands to my eyes and sigh. 'And she will never ever *ever* go into a care home, because she's the feistiest, fightiest, most truculent woman I've ever met. I doubt they'd tolerate her for more than an afternoon, even if we could afford the exorbitant fees. So, I'm not sure about jacking in my day job, however much I hate it.'

'Dotty's golf club would be quite a commute from Bromley, too.' He downs his glass of water and gasps. 'Over an hour on the M25, and that's in good traffic. Imagine if Harrogate wins! They'd have to sell the land . . . assuming they were allowed to sell up because of the covenants in her will . . . or all move down south. Dotty didn't think any of that through, did she?'

'I don't suppose Dotty gave any of it much thought.'

I gaze out at the street, barely registering the unremarkable figure dressed all in black and wearing a baseball cap pulled down low, walking towards Biggins Broadacre and Levy. I turn back to Mike. 'The terms of her will were probably just an abstract concept when she had it drawn up. Unless she did take her own life, she couldn't have known death was coming for her in her garden shed.'

Our lunch arrives, and I am suddenly self-conscious eating in front of Mike. I've become so used to gobbling food down, alone and unobserved by anyone but my son or mother, that I consider my table manners for the first time in years.

Happily, Mike clearly has no such compunction and has just shovelled in the largest forkful of kebab he can feasibly fit in his head. I silently thank God he doesn't chew with his mouth open. He makes a strange humming sound, as though he's about to speak, but then holds his finger up and chews dramatically. He makes the noise again and then points to his mouth. Finally, he swallows with another satisfied gasp.

'I'm going to have to redo my will when Donna and I divorce. Assuming she leaves me and the kids with more than the shirts on our backs.' He looks over to the solicitors' firm and raises an eyebrow. 'I should have asked them how much their divorce lawyer charges by the hour.'

I follow the line of his gaze to Biggins Broadacre and Levy's front door. Just as I'm about to ask Mike if he'll be involving Katie and Hugo in any of next week's planting out, I see the black-clad figure emerge. Now, I can see that it is a man, though he's wearing sunglasses.

'What prat wears sunglasses in a solicitors' office?' Mike rips a piece from his pitta.

I see the man's dayglo green trainers with the cartoon orange flames licking up the sides. Mike and I lock eyes, as if the same thought has occurred to us both at the very same moment.

'Is it him?' Mike asks. 'White Golf man?'

'Those shoes . . . It's got to be him, right?' I snatch up my handbag and rummage with urgent, shaking hands for my purse, pulling out a twenty.

'You want to go after him?' Mike takes out his wallet.

'It's too good an opportunity to miss. Don't you want to know who Dotty's mystery visitor and potential murderer is?'

We throw the money onto the table, shout our apologies at the bemused-looking waiter, and hurry outside.

'Which way did he go?' Mike asks, peering down the street that leads away from the roundabout towards Elmers End.

A long-wheelbase van obscures our view of the man, but I spot our quarry emerging on the far side. 'There!' I point.

Together, we dash across the road, barely dodging a beast of an Audi SUV that is going way too fast.

Mike pulls me out of its path.

'Where's your car parked? Mine's at the back of the cinema.'

I feel my chest complain, tight from lack of fitness,

but my heart is pumping delicious adrenalin around my body. 'Same direction he's going in. Side street just after Kwik Fit: Westfield Road.' Reaching into my handbag, I grab the keys to the Volvo. 'You're not suggesting we chase him, are you? What would we do if we caught up with him? Ask him, "Oh, hello. Are you Dorothy Gloucester's poisoner?"'

'Let's judge it as we go.' Mike grabs my hand and pulls me along.

Yet, just as I acknowledge a frisson of excitement that Mike is holding my hand, I notice the black-clad man look through the large side mirror of another parked van. He speeds up and somehow dips out of view.

'He knows he's being followed.' I pull my hand free of Mike's. 'Bugger. Where's he gone?'

I start to run towards Westfield Road and pull up short at the top. Looking down towards the identikit Edwardian semis and the double-parked cars, I catch sight of an indicator flashing on a car way ahead. Someone's pulling out.

I point. 'Could that be him? He's damn fast if it is!'

The front end of a white car that looks very much like a Golf swings out, its black alloy wheels an immediate giveaway.

'Black alloys on a white hot-hatch; blacked-out windows; dayglo trainers? It's him alright.' Mike's nodding and breathless.

Now, it's my turn to grab his hand. 'Volvo's over the road. Come on!'

We pant and puff our way to my old estate car – so old

that I have to unlock the doors manually. She has over 150,000 miles on the clock, and I pray my trusty steed won't give me any hassle today. *God, I'm starting to sound like Mike in my thoughts*, I muse, pulling out and following the Golf, which is already near the bottom of Westfield Road, indicating that it's turning left onto Hayne Road.

'He's turning left,' Mike says.

'Yes, I can see.'

'Was it Cromarty, do you think?'

'Who knows? Same height as Cromarty, roughly, but there was no sign of that awful bouffant mullet. Was he orange?'

I can feel Mike staring at me. 'What do you mean?'

'His skin. Did that guy have a bad spray tan?'

'Yes. No. Don't know. I can't remember. It all happened so fast.'

I put my foot down as the Golf accelerates to get away from us. 'Take down his number plate.'

Mike squints through the windscreen. 'BV69 R –'

'Get a photo! Get a photo!'

Rummaging in his pocket, Mike takes out his phone just as the Golf turns left again onto the leafy Victorian splendour of Cedars Road.

'He's gone. Damn!' I slap the steering wheel. 'Did you get his full reg number?'

In my peripheral vision, I see Mike shaking his head and staring blankly ahead.

'I didn't get the last two digits. And it didn't even occur to me to take a photo until you said.' He slaps the dash. 'Shitbiscuits!'

'Michael!' I say, half laughing, because I've never heard Mike swear before. 'You're full of surprises today.'

We slow up to the junction. I peer left down Cedars Road, but there's a troupe of nursery school children crossing the road hand in hand, guided by their teachers. I stop, knowing that our quarry will be long gone by the time the children are safely on the other side.

'So close,' Mike says.

'We've got something to go on, though,' I say. I feel a mixture of thrill and dread prickling icy along my spine. 'We know we're looking for a man. We know he's got business at your solicitors. We know he's guilty as hell, judging by the way he ran, and we have a good chunk of his car registration. It's a brave start. We're onto him now, and if he knows who we are . . .' My gut tightens, '. . . my guess is he'll come looking for us next.'

26

'Feels so good to finally start planting, doesn't it?' Neil says, pinching the sides of three petunia pots between the fingers and thumb of each hand and carefully setting them into one of the cardboard vegetable boxes that Phoebe has liberated from Tesco.

In the few days since Mike and I engaged in our unsuccessful car chase, doing a breakneck twenty-seven miles per hour through the congested backstreets of Beckenham, there has been frustratingly no more progress on our hunt for the man in the Golf. We handed details of the partial number plate in at Brixton police station, asking that they be passed on to Detective McGowan, but we have heard nothing back from her yet. At work, I have given warnings to two more call-centre staff, yet not a single salary has so far come off Chislehurst Green's bottom line, and the threat of my being pushed to take 'voluntary' redundancy continues to hang over me like a Kafkaesque sword of Damocles. I am convinced that Colin and Janice hate me.

Happily though, I have the Bromley Botanists to keep me sane, and the risk of frost has entirely passed, according to Marj. Now, I'm holding up two electric blue lobelias jubilantly to show to Zak, whom I have brought with me on this most momentous of mornings: planting day.

'I grew these from seed,' I tell my son. 'Me! Can you believe it? The queen of dead cacti.'

'That's way cool, Mum.' Zak's laughing and shaking his head, as though he's just discovered that his mother has been body-snatched by an evangelical fledgling horticulturalist, crossed with a clown in gardening clogs. 'Well done. Dad wouldn't believe his eyes.'

Together, Zak and I place the lobelias into the box marked in Sharpie with 'Trough #1', along with the address where the big wooden trough is situated.

'And I actually planned the troughs that they're going into. *Me!*'

It is 6.30am. We all turned up to Marjorie's early, as we have to get everything planted up by the end of the day, if at all possible. Though I haven't been sleeping well of late, I've mentally shoved the Pandora's box full of stress into the dusty far corner at the back of my mind, along with a recent parking ticket, the need to clean the bathroom, and the overdue visit to Dave's tree with Zak. 'If nothing else, I can grow beautiful things that bring joy: one teenaged boy and a hundred and fifty lobelias! Ha.'

'You are doing God's work, Gillian,' Marjorie says, appearing seemingly from nowhere. Since we arrived, she has been stalking around her house, brandishing a trowel like a horsehair fly-swat, as though she's some royal shaman, barking instructions at us all in her small but steely voice. 'Now make sure you don't spill any compost on the Wilton as you carry the plants through to the front. One will be charging for a professional carpet cleaner, if there are stains, and those fellows don't come cheap, mark my words.'

Wearing baggy red shorts and a faded Spandau Ballet T-shirt, Mike is carrying large tubs containing dinner-plate dahlias out to the van. I can see black liquid dripping from the bottom of the recently watered pots, but merci-fully, Marjorie has covered the temporary thoroughfare with those horrible ribbed plastic carpet protectors from the 1970s, with the gripper spikes underneath.

I nod towards them and whisper to Zak, 'See those disgusting plastic runners? Your nan used to have those when I was a kid. She was always putting them upside down by accident because she was too vain to wear glasses. I had feet like colanders.'

'Nice.' Zak clearly doesn't think the runners are nice. I can see he thinks Phoebe is nice, though. He follows her around the room with his gaze.

'Stop ogling the girl and fill a box with lobelia,' I tell him. 'Come on, son. You said you were going to be helpful.'

'Give us a break, Mum. It's the crack of dawn.' Zak yawns, as if to demonstrate his point.

'The early bird catches the worm,' Marjorie says. 'And let's not forget that "Good kings and armies rise early for battle." Isaiah 37:36.'

With our veg boxes full of lobelia, Zak and I escape Marjorie's Bible lesson. We follow Mike outside. 'Wait up, Mike!' I call after him.

He dumps the dahlias into the roomy van that Seth has borrowed from a plasterer workmate. He turns to

267

me and smiles. 'This is one of the best bits,' he says. 'I adore this stage, when we start to see all our plans coming to fruition.' He takes the veg box from me and stacks it carefully on top of the others destined for the same address. He takes hold of Zak's. 'Thank you, young man. You know, in a couple of weeks, with moderate sun and rainfall, everything will be twice the size it is now and fully in bloom.' He looks down at his chunky bare legs and the new-looking deck shoes that he's mis-guidedly wearing with grey mid-length socks, and he looks back up at me. 'Let's hope it's not cracking the pavestones or tipping it down for weeks. Three years ago, we had torrential rain, and almost every bloom just rotted on the stem or got eaten by slugs.'

When Zak sidles off to speak to Phoebe, Mike's smile sputters on. He lowers his voice. 'Biggins Broadacre and Levy are *brilliant*. They've already sent over all the draft paperwork. They're ready to go to Defcon One with the council.'

'They're convinced you'll win?' I ask, noting the excitement in his eyes.

'Yes, siree. Solicitor thinks we'll be allocated a tribunal date this side of Christmas, and I stand to get *very* good compensation,' he says.

'Would you go back to your old job, if they apologised and asked you nicely?' I think of the psychological tor-ture I'm being subjected to at work.

Mike shakes his head. 'No, I want to win on principle and I need the money. My little nest egg has all but gone on the deposit and first month's rent for the house. But

I'm happy at the garden centre for now, because I can fit it round Katie and Hugo. While I'm going through this divorce with Donna, I want as little stress and upheaval for me and the kids as possible. Unless we win the Golden Trowel, of course. Then *everything* changes.' His face is incandescent with a smile that seems to emanate from deep inside him. I realise Mike Potato is an optimistic dreamer.

'You're assuming Croydon won't try it on with us again and scupper our chances.'

He shrugs. 'It's all gone quiet since we confronted Betty Moule. Long may that continue.'

'Amen to that.' An image of Dotty G in her shed flashes before my mind's eye. I bite my lip, musing on how joining the Bromley Botanists seems to have introduced more risk into my life, along with all the friendship. What would Mandi-with-an-I say about risk-taking?

'Anyway, even if we don't win, I do have a business proposition to put to you at some point.'

'Like what?'

'Let's save that conversation for down the pub, eh? Or perhaps we could go for something to eat – pick up where we abruptly left off at that Turkish place. But maybe after work and somewhere a bit more . . .'

Immediately, I feel my face burn red hot. 'What, like dinner?'

'Oh, or Sunday lunch,' he says, almost stumbling over the words.

Is he desperately backtracking on asking me on a date, or is he nervous that he's gone too far, too fast? Am I in the 'friend zone', as Zak calls it, or is Mike Potato finally suggesting something more?

'You could bring your Zak – he's a fine lad – and I could bring my two. I think he'd get on very well with Katie and Hugo. Shame they went to their mum's today.'

I'm poised to answer, but Cath and Neil emerge from the house, carrying veg boxes full of osteospermum – African daisies, already in bloom with jewel-coloured flowers of hot pink, dark red, bright orange, lilac, and yellow.

'Talk about it later?' I say, side-eyeing our compatriots. Now I realise I am contributing to this connection between us. I try to imagine myself kissing Mike Potato and feel itchy, not just for having such a thought, but for having it with Zak in the immediate vicinity. I look up to the cloudless blue sky, wondering if Dave is about to call on the elements to strike me down in a freak lightning storm. Maybe I deserve it.

We continue to load the van until the very last plant is on board.

'That's it,' Marjorie declares, tottering out of her front door, bearing a tray laden with glasses of orange squash. 'One's greenhouse is empty. Drinks for the workers!'

'I ain't your worker, your ladyshit,' Val says, swiping a drink and downing it in one. 'Just remember, there ain't no "I" in team, and there certainly ain't a "*one*".' The 'one' is said in a high-pitched, upper-class squeak.

'Oh, do try to keep a civil tongue in your head for once, Valerie,' Marjorie says. 'And don't lecture me about teamwork.' She closes her eyes dramatically. '*I* have been part of the church's flower-arranging team for many, many years.' When she opens her eyes, they are hard little balls of lapis lazuli.

'Which I heard you rule with a rod of iron,' Val says, sitting on Marjorie's garden wall to roll a cigarette. 'So, hardly teamwork, is it?'

Marjorie shoves the tray into a surprised-looking Seth's hands. She turns back to Val and points with an arthritic-jointed index finger. 'Listen, Valerie Novak! If *we* are to take on and triumph over the likes of Croydon – highly talented gardeners who are seemingly hell-bent on winning at any cost, even if that means playing dirty – *we* need to pull together. So, can *we* please stop bickering?'

I flop down next to Val. 'She's offering you an olive branch. Just take it.'

With pursed, downturned lips, Val nods at Marjorie. 'Have it your way.' She smiles wryly. 'Croydon won't know what hit them.'

For the first time since I have been coming to the group, Marjorie's smile reaches her eyes. She takes the tray back from Seth. 'Biscuits, everyone?' she shouts and looks into the distance, as though she's addressing a crowd of hundreds that fills the street. 'I have baked the loveliest fig rolls, with figs I picked and dried myself – from my own tree in the side-garden. Not that one likes to brag, but one's fig rolls won first prize at the regional Women's Institute's baking competition in 2007, 2008, and 2013, don't you know?'

Mike puts a fig roll into his mouth, chews for about five seconds, and then spits his mouthful surreptitiously into a dahlia pot that is still waiting to be put on the van. He examines his glass of squash dolefully. 'Shame I forgot to bring my *delicious* dandelion homebrew. It would have been perfect for cleansing the palate after that fig roll.'

He seems unaware of the relief on Neil's and Seth's faces. And mine. Poor Mike.

After our watershed Val-and-Marj-truce moment and this award-winning figgy repast, we drive in teams to our planting spots.

Neil is with Cath and Val, ferried by Cath in her people carrier. Mike, Phoebe, and Marjorie are squashed together in Marjorie's Honda Jazz. Zak and I are with Seth, travelling in the borrowed van. We have been tasked with dropping off everyone's plants at their designated planting locations. We will then travel to our own troughs, beds, and streets full of hanging baskets. 'Will we really get this done in one day?' I ask Seth.

'Only one way to find out.'

27

'What am I supposed to do?' Zak asks as we head off to our first destination in the filthy van that smells of plaster dust, stale cigarettes, and wet dog.

'Help unload,' I say, squeezing his hand. We take a tight left, and an empty Coke bottle rolls into my foot. I kick it away and find myself toe-deep in discarded crisp packets. 'Keep your eyes peeled for trouble. You're our lookout in case Croydon tries any funny business again. Oh, and I was hoping you'd have a go at planting yourself.'

'You'll enjoy it, mate,' Seth says, changing gear as he glances over at my son. 'Good to get a break and get some fresh air. There's only so much revision a bro can do, yeah?'

Zak withdraws his hand from mine. 'Fine.'

Our first stop is a long street of 1930s terraced housing, where there is a hanging basket suspended from every streetlight. This is Neil, Cath, and Val's first port of call. We pull up behind Cath's people carrier, and Seth and Zak start to unload their veg boxes full of showy bicoloured petunias in hot pink and livid purple. The first open blooms wave in the breeze. They are to be paired with trailing Voodoo fuchsias, bearing giant double blooms in the same livid purple and flashing pink, and the lime-green foliage of golden Creeping Jenny. We unload canisters of water, bag after bag of compost as well as a special mix of feed and water-retaining granules that will keep the displays fresh in between watering.

Neil claps his hands together. 'Right, let's get cracking, because it's meant to be a hot one today, and I've forgotten sunscreen for my poor bald head.'

Val reaches into her canvas handbag and holds out a yellow bottle. 'Factor thirty do you?'

Seth and Zak take a ladder out of the van.

Cath looks at it with obvious uncertainty etched into her furrowed brow. 'Really? We're going to be climbing ladders?'

'How else we gonna get the baskets down, fill them, and get them back up?' Val asks. 'You got no option. Ladder duty's part of being a community gardener, and everyone's got to do their bit. Don't worry, though. You'll get used to it.'

We bid the team farewell and head on to the next destination, where Mike, Marjorie, and Phoebe are arguing about how Marjorie has parked the Honda Jazz.

'Blimey, small wonder you were banned for twelve months, Marjorie. You can't just leave it at that angle,' Mike is saying, pointing to the car, which looks like it has been stolen for joyriding and then abandoned in haste. 'You're a good two or three feet from the kerb. Someone will take off your wing mirror.'

Marjorie, dressed in her floral dungarees and tartan gardening clogs, with a floppy brimmed hat that almost covers her entire face, lifts her head up so she can see

Mike. 'Nonsense. I have been driving for more than fifty years —'

'Give or take twelve months wearing the driver's cone of shame.'

'One is perfectly capable of parking one's own vehicle, and one is entirely confident that one's wing mirror will remain intact.'

'Don't say I didn't warn you,' Mike says.

Marjorie marches up to the van and peers inside. She tuts. 'Those dahlias have been poorly installed. Look!'

I follow the line of her finger and see where some large potted dahlias have fallen over. For a moment, I am gripped with fear that the plants will be damaged.

'Flaming Nora!' Mike says, manoeuvring me out of the way and scrambling into the van. 'If these have been disbudded or the stems broken, we'll be scuppered for the big troughs.' He grabs the large black pots, with the stems and foliage nodding gently as he carries them at an angle. 'Take it easy when you're driving, Seth!'

'Chill, man. I wasn't doing no more than thirty-five.'

'Thirty-five!' Mike's voice is shrill. 'Around corners too? No wonder the cannas are on their sides. Get them out! Get them out!'

I haven't seen Mike this uptight since those first few meetings I attended, when — as I now know from our subsequent meet-ups — he was still in the grip of anxiety about losing his job and his wife.

I place my hand on his upper arm. 'Mike. It's just plants.'

He turns to me with panic in his eyes. 'It's not just

plants, though, is it?' He scratches at his throat. 'It's months and months of work. It's the competition. It's everything we've worked for as a team, and everything we're striving for for the future.'

'Yo, dude,' Phoebe says to Mike as she's taking a veg box full of nicotiana from Zak. 'You're being really uptight, yeah? Seth doesn't need this pass-agg BS. He's doing his best. He got us a van for free, and he's doing all the heavy stuff.'

Marjorie flaps her hands at Mike. 'Do calm down, Michael. You're giving one indigestion, with your parking advice and your transport criticisms.'

'But the plants are getting damaged, Marjorie! It's my responsibility to –'

'Right now, Michael, your only responsibility is to plant plants and remember that nobody has appointed you our leader. Not that *I* am personally a fanatic of teamwork because one's wisdom and mature years make one better suited to directing others, but we *are* a team. And much as one loves each and every one of God's beautiful creations that we've grown and nurtured for months, we do have plenty of spares. Kindly take a deep breath, calm down, and crack on.'

Mike's cheeks are aflame. He takes off his glasses and looks thoughtfully at the smudgy lenses, opening and closing his mouth, though no witty words emerge. He shoots me with a contrite glance.

'It's going to be brilliant, Mike,' I say.

'Is it?'

'Absolutely. We're going to ace it. We've got the most

beautiful plans and the best, best stock.' I slap a hand on my son's shoulder. 'We've got Zak, here, as an extra pair of hands and our trusty lookout.'

'Yes, but he can't be everywhere, all of the time,' Marjorie says, lifting the brim of her sunhat so she can see me. 'We're splitting into groups.'

'Everyone'll just have to be vigilant,' I say. 'It's been quiet for weeks. Croydon will be busy with their own planting, right? I can't see them being brazen enough to attack us in broad daylight. Can you?'

Marjorie's mouth arcs downwards. 'Never underestimate Betty Moule.'

'Come on. You showed her who's boss. Let's think positive!' In some strange quirk of fate, I feel like I have become the group's Mandi-with-an-I. How on earth did that happen?

Mike presses his fingertips to his temples. He speaks with a theatrical, fruity voice: *'They can, because they think they can.'*

'Exactly! That's the spirit!'

We unload the rest of Marjorie's, Mike's, and Phoebe's plants, water, planting matter, and ladders, wish the three of them luck, and climb back into the van.

'Our turn,' Seth says, starting the engine. 'Where we headed?'

I read out our destination address. We have been tasked with filling large troughs and hanging baskets on a triangle of land by Widmore Green – land to the north of Bromley town centre that the council have never sold for development but have neglected to do anything much with.

'Can't you just drop me home?' Zak asks, looking up from the game he's playing on his phone.

'No. Stop moaning. The fresh air will do you good. You can be in the moment, doing something physical, for once. And put that phone away, young man. The psychiatrist said gaming puts you in a permanent state of fight or flight.'

'Yeah. *Okay*, Mum.' The sarcasm in Zak's voice acidifies the air in the van. I observe him trying to make eye contact with Seth.

Happily, Seth is not playing ball. 'Your mum's right,' he tells Zak. 'Gaming's not real, man. And you've got attention deficit, right? Blowing stuff up and killing zombies like a kid ain't gonna help with your focus. But getting your hands dirty and creating something might.'

I am happy to see Zak put his phone away. I pull him to me and kiss the side of his head, thankful to make this incremental gain in helping a good boy to grow into a great man, when I have no adult male role model to guide him.

When we arrive at our troughs, they are filled with the remnants of the spring growing season – overgrown, slug-nibbled pansies, spent primroses, the brown strappy leaves of ex-daffodils, and discarded beer cans.

'Let's get this cleared out,' I say, opening a bin liner. 'Get some gloves on, Zak.'

My son buckles his lanky body into a shape that spells reluctance. 'Aw, come on, Mum. That's like community service or something. Crims get sentenced to that as a punishment. There's all crap in there. Crisp packets and that.'

'Do you think we should be growing crisp packets and beer cans in troughs?' I ask.

'But *we* didn't put all that rubbish in there.' He pulls on one of his tight curls.

'Do you think that's nice for the little kids and the old folk round here to look at?'

He shakes his head and wrinkles his nose. 'Nah. It's minging.'

'Exactly. And this is a *community* gardening group.'

Seth interrupts. 'You get rid of community, and suddenly nobody cares about no one but themselves. It's a dog-eat-dog world. No neighbouring. No loyalty or sense of duty. Nobody gives a monkey's about the vulnerable folks like my mum. Community's where it's at, man.'

Zak chews on his lower lip and dons a pair of gardening gloves. 'I didn't take you for no activist type.'

'Don't have to glue yourself to the M25 and stop taking a shower to know right from wrong. You feel me?'

As we pull the spent plants, weeds, and rubbish from the large troughs, separating the plant matter into one bag and the cans, bottles, and crisp packets into another for recycling, I smile to myself, amused at how my son and the not-much-older Seth speak to one another. The slang that they use and the rhythms of their speech are reserved only for their fellow young. When Zak speaks to me and Seth speaks to his mother, gone is the affected

South-East London council estate hard-man patois, leaving only the truth behind. These are both Bromley boys. Half London, half Kent. Half capital-city fast lane, and half Garden-of-England slow lane. I am reminded of how important it is to preserve some of England's gentle, rural slowness in a world that worships at the altars of immediate gratification, economic growth, and the relentless grind of technological progress.

The troughs are soon half empty.

'Right. We need to top these up with about ten inches of fresh compost,' Seth says. 'It's a shame Mike's special brew was ruined by all that salt. That stuff's like magic.'

'What do you reckon he puts in it that makes it so special?' I ask.

Seth slashes open a 100-litre bag of multipurpose peat-free compost and heaves it into the trough. He upends the bag and pushes the black, crumbly, woody matter into the space we've created. 'He's well secretive about the recipe. I think he would have told me, if he hadn't found his gear had been contaminated. But now . . .' He raises his eyebrows. 'He just won't talk about it. You'd think that Croydon lot had murdered his kids. And I needed that recipe for my crop at home.'

I help Seth to spread the compost around. 'Should you really be looking to make a career out of *that*?' I don't refer specifically to his cannabis farm, because I don't want Zak getting ideas that Seth is his go-to man for illicit substances. I know what seventeen-year-old boys can be like.

Seth shrugs. 'Why not? It's gonna benefit my mum,

and medicinal crops are the future.' He turns to Zak. 'Start bringing out the plants, will you, mate?'

'How do I know which ones?' Zak asks.

'The ones labelled "Widmore Green",' Seth says. 'Anything else is spares.'

I rub the fresh compost from my hands. I've left off my wedding and engagement rings. I feel naked without them, but that's not a bad feeling today.

While Zak is out of earshot, I take the opportunity to talk frankly to Seth. 'You seen Cromarty on the building site?'

He shakes his head. 'Nah. He keeps sending his missus to do site meetings. He ain't stupid. He must know he's got to keep a low profile, what with this insurance claim and all.'

I tut and inhale sharply, frustrated at how impotent we are to stop a bully and a fraudster. My thoughts turn to two-bit gangsters and Seth's chosen career path. 'Medicinal crops might be the future, but right now, Seth, you're swimming in the same pool as some really unsavoury types,' I say. 'The last thing your mother needs is you getting into trouble with bad, bad people, or with the police. If you get a criminal record, you'll struggle to find legitimate work. Isn't there something else you could do with your gardening talents?'

'What? Like become a landscape gardener, working in all weathers for sod-all cash? No thanks.'

I pour a heavy canister of water into our watering can, splashing my feet accidentally. I heave the watering can aloft and start to wet the compost. 'But you've got these amazing talents for growing things. Gardening and horticulture bring billions into the country's coffers, *legitimately*. People want plants and flowers that have been cultivated here in Britain, and the medicinal cannabis market is already crowded with all sorts of products your mum can use. If we win, wouldn't you be tempted to start again as a flower farmer?'

'I only know how to grow one thing,' Seth says, taking the first black-leaved canna Tropicanna out of its pot and placing it in the centre of the trough.

I'm about to make some more suggestions that will fall on wilfully deaf ears when Zak returns from the van looking distraught.

'Mum, I'm *starving*.' He screws up his face in a look of calorie-deficient teenage anguish.

'Fine,' I say. 'Get some money out of my handbag. It's in the passenger footwell of the van. There's a chippy if you go left at the junction. Literally around the corner. If it's not open yet, there's a newsagents in the other direction and maybe a bakery, I think. I don't want anything yet.'

Zak's anguish is replaced by a beatified grin. 'Sick. Want me to get you anything while I'm there, Seth?'

Seth grabs a fistful of loose change from his pocket and puts in an order for chips or crisps or a ham roll or anything feasibly edible at all, within a £5.64 budget.

With Zak on a snack-run and the troughs finished, Seth and I can now start on the hanging baskets.

'How are we going to do this?' I ask, balking at the height of the nearest basket that is full of last season's dead flowers and weeds. 'Only, I'm with Cath on the heights thing.'

Seth frowns. 'Well, you're going to have to face your fears, Gill, 'cause I've got a dodgy ankle. Sorry.'

I feel my stomach flip and a cold sweat break out beneath my T-shirt. 'Don't say that.'

He throws his head back and laughs. 'Ha! Got you there good and proper! Your face! Classic.' He claps his hands together.

'So I don't have to be the one who climbs? Only I do get a bit of vertigo if I stand on anything higher than a chair.'

'Nah. You're alright. You just hold the bottom of the ladder, yeah? I'll go up and do the honours.'

He extends the telescopic ladder and leans it against the lamppost in what I would call a precarious arrangement, though he bounds to the top without evident qualm. We chat companionably about phobias and gardening and the cost of Nike trainers. Every time I look up, I become convinced Seth is going to fall on top of me, so I gaze off in the direction of the chippy, wondering if it was open after all and when my Zak will return.

Seth is unhooking the spent hanging basket from its bracket when I spy a dark shape moving in my peripheral vision. The hairs on my forearms stand proud as I clutch the sides of the ladder. I turn to see a burly figure sprinting towards us from the nearby bushes.

I yelp and take a step towards him, trying to defend Seth on the ladder. But my attacker barrels into me so hard that I lose my footing. I fall awkwardly, knocking my head on the bottom rung of the ladder. My heart thumps and my ears ring. The world spins.

'Oi!' I hear Seth yell, above me.

The scene is a dizzy blur of colour and confusion. I try to scramble to my feet. Above me, the attacker is shaking the ladder from side to side.

'Get off him!' I yell.

I reach out to grab the leg of the attacker, hoping to destabilise him, but he kicks out at me and suddenly, Seth crashes to the ground. The attacker sprints off.

'Seth! Seth!' I crawl to where Seth is lying only feet away, but he doesn't respond. His eyes have rolled back into his head, revealing only ghoulish whites. 'Help!' I cry, looking around frantically for someone to come to our aid. But we are alone. 'Seth! Wake up!' I pat his cheek gently. Nothing. Not even the flicker of an eyelid. I feel for his pulse in his neck and am relieved that his blood is still pumping strong beneath my fingertips.

Zak comes haring towards me, then, carrying a bulging plastic bag.

'Mum! I heard you calling for help. What's happened?' 'Call an ambulance!' I shout. 'And the police. Quickly.'

Zak flings the bag down, ashen faced, and takes out his phone with a violently shaking hand.

While he dials 999 and makes a garbled, panicked request for an ambulance and the police, I call Cath. She's just around the corner, and if anyone can administer emergency first aid until the paramedics arrive, it's going to be a GP.

'Hi, Gill. How's it—'

'Cath, come quickly!' I glance at Seth, lying in an untenable position, with limbs skewed at odd angles. 'Seth's fallen off the ladder. He's . . . he's out cold, and it doesn't look good.'

28

I clasp Seth's hand in mine, but it's cold and clammy. 'Seth, can you hear me?' It's no use. His facial features remain slack and unresponsive.

'Leave him. Don't move him,' Cath says.

It took Cath, Neil, and Val only minutes to get to us. Cath has taken the phone from Zak and is now talking to the woman at the emergency call centre. 'He's still breathing.' She checks for Seth's pulse again with two fingers; frowns as she delivers her verdict. 'Pulse is running a little ragged, and I'm worried about his spine and a possible head injury. Suspected fracture in the left forearm. It's already swelling. How long until the ambulance arrives?'

As Cath negotiates with the emergency services, Neil sits down cross-legged on the ground next to Seth.

'What the hell happened?' he asks.

I press the cloth handkerchief he's given me to my head. It quickly grows wet beneath my fingertips. I remove it briefly to see a colour-clash of my vivid red blood against the snowy white glare of the cotton fabric. I hastily press it back to my wound, though not before a crimson drip blossoms on my T-shirt.

'Well, one minute, I'm holding the ladder at the bottom. Next minute, this guy comes out of nowhere and rugby-tackles me. I went down like a sack of potatoes; hit my head on the bottom rung of the ladder.' I can hear my speech is a little muffled. There is the metallic tang of blood in my mouth, and I realise my teeth pierced the inside of my bottom lip when I fell. I touch my lower lip tentatively. It is twice its normal size.

'Split my lip on the inside as I went down, didn't I?' I take the handkerchief from my head again and examine the giant carmine rosette. 'I can't believe I wasn't knocked out, but I've got a clonker behind the eyes.'

'What about Seth? What happened there?'

'Well, once I hit the deck, the guy started shaking the ladder. Seth tried to kick him away, but . . . he fell. I couldn't get up fast enough. It all happened like that.' I snap my fingers.

'Did you get a look at his face? The attacker?'

'No. He was wearing a mask and had a hood on. Built like a brick outhouse though.'

'Where was Zak while all this was going down?'

'Gone to get us food, thankfully. I think this guy must have been watching us. Waiting 'til there was just me and Seth.'

'Do you think it was the same guy that lobbed the brick through Marj's greenhouse window – Taylor Jones?'

I wipe a tear from my cheek, appalled that my Zakky could so easily have been the one on or holding the ladder. 'No idea. That picture of Jones on the Croydon club webpage is only a headshot. You wouldn't get a sense of his build from that. But I'd say this one was young, judging by his agility and body language. No paunch.'

I sigh, glancing over at the van where Zak is perched up front (at my insistence), whey-faced and likely wondering if Seth will die. Val is sitting on the kerb, speaking to Mike on the phone, and I can hear that she is shaken. All the while, the residents facing onto the scene of the crime look through their windows, keen to find out what has happened but evidently not keen to get involved.

I become aware of the grating sound of multiple sirens coming closer, and a police car is the first emergency vehicle to drive onto the street, followed within moments by an ambulance.

All of a sudden, the area beneath the streetlight is mayhem. Two paramedics are speaking encouraging, friendly words to an unconscious Seth while they shine a light into his eyes and check his vital signs. A third conducts various reflex tests on me to check I'm not badly concussed and, when satisfied, cleans and dresses my wound, reassuring me that it 'looks worse than what it is, because head wounds bleed like stink'. There are also police officers, speaking into their radios and getting the low-down from first-responder Cath.

'Tell me what happened?' a baby-faced male officer asks me, taking notes in his little pad.

I give rough details of the burly man in black who seemed to lurch at me from nowhere. I am easily distracted by the walkie-talkie strapped to his shoulder, which is alive with the thrum of police call-centre chat and static.

'And you can't describe his face?'

'Nope. He was masked up. All I know is he was white, big, seemed young. That's it. It all happened so fast.'

'Any idea who could have done this?' He raises an eyebrow.

'He seemed to want to stop us doing the hanging basket. If it helps, there's been problems with our rival gardening group in Croydon.' I explain about the vandalism to Marjorie's greenhouse and Mike's allotment. I mention Cromarty potentially committing insurance fraud, and I allude to Dotty Gloucester's untimely death. 'Maybe if you get in touch with the detective who worked on Miss Gloucester's case. McGowan. That was her name. Detective McGowan. She was from Brixton police station. Tell her what's going on. I mean, Dorothy Gloucester's death was recorded with an open verdict, but maybe after these other attacks, she'll reopen the case and –'

'But no eyewitnesses to any of it apart from you and your friend who was knocked off the ladder?' the officer asks, poised to write on the blank page of his pad. 'This is all you, putting two and two together about separate incidents, months apart, and a closed case?'

'Well, I, er . . .' I glance at Zak, sitting in the van, hoping he's calming down. 'I, er . . .'

In the confusion of paramedics and flashing lights and walkie-talkies, I start to feel quite faint. I reach out to steady myself on the lamppost as I talk to the police officer.

When Marjorie's Honda Jazz weaves into view, I am

surprised to find myself weeping openly with relief, as though Mike and Marjorie will know exactly what to do.

Marjorie parks at a dislocated angle and staggers out of the car. She is wearing a look of fierce determination. Mike emerges from the passenger side, slamming the door too hard. His colour has drained. Phoebe climbs out of the back and makes straight for the tangle of people surrounding Seth.

'Gill. What on earth . . . ?' Mike asks me.

'Another attack,' I say. 'Seth . . . He got knocked off the ladder. He's still unconscious.'

I look over to where the paramedics are bolstering Seth's neck and body with padded supports to stop him from moving. His lips move, his nose wrinkles, and then his eyes open properly, focusing first on the paramedic bending over him and then managing a weak smile for a distraught-looking Phoebe.

'Oh, thank God for that,' I say, clasping my hands to my face. 'He's coming round.'

Mike and I take a step forward in unison to hear Seth speaking in a weak, befuddled-sounding voice to Cath, one of the paramedics, and another police officer.

'How long have I been out? No, I didn't see who it was. Just some guy.' He is told to keep still, but I can see him trying to reach out to Phoebe, taking her hand. 'Oh, Phoebs! It was mad.'

'Thank God you're alive, dude,' Phoebe says, tears rolling onto her cheeks. 'If you'd died on me, I'd have had to kill you.'

I turn to Mike. 'This has got to be Croydon,' I say. He nods. 'They've gone too far.'

I inhale deeply and exhale sharply. 'We've got to put a stop to this.'

29

'Are you sure this is where he lives?' Mike asks Seth.

'Oh, yeah. No doubt,' Seth says. 'That's his car.'

Five days have passed since the attack. Seth was discharged from hospital within hours of being admitted, having undergone a satisfactory CT scan and X-ray, mercifully being given the all-clear on all fronts by the A&E registrar. He was lucky to walk away from the fall with only a slightly sprained arm and a clanging headache. He has since had time to rest. I am back to normal, save for the neat dressing on my head that covers the gash caused by the ladder. It is healing well, albeit tender to the touch.

Now, at 9pm, it is still light outside. We are sitting in Seth's borrowed van, staring out at Luke Cromarty's mock 'Tudorbethan' mansion, which sits on an eerily quiet, tree-lined boulevard, full of giant houses behind tall fencing and electronic gates. Cromarty's orange Lamborghini is sitting on his driveway, though there's garaging for at least two more cars at the side of the house.

'He's surely in if his car's there,' I say.

'Only one way to find out.' Mike's lips are set in a determined-looking line. 'Let's finish this.'

In unison, we clamber out of the van. I eye the neighbouring houses, hoping we're not being observed through the sophisticated-looking CCTV cameras that spy on us from multiple vantage points. I'm glad Zak is safely tucked up at home. There is no knowing how this will go, and I don't want my son involved if things go pear-shaped.

Seth pulls on his hoodie and presses the buzzer on the intercom, mounted on one of the bulky brick-built gate pillars at the boundary of Cromarty's property.

'Can I help you?' A woman's voice on the other end. She speaks with a Kentish twang and sounds irritated, as though we've ruined her evening simply by buzzing.

Only Seth is visible to the fish-eye lens of the intercom's in-built security camera. He is careful to angle himself so that his face cannot be seen. Mike and I are hiding just out of sight.

'Oh, hi. I'm one of Mr Cromarty's electricians. There's a problem on site. I wondered if I could just have a few words with him, please.' Seth speaks confidently. Only his twitching fingers show how he's really feeling.

'Can't you just ring him?' the woman asks. 'It's late.'

We can hear a man's muffled voice in the background, and suddenly, Cromarty's voice is on the intercom. 'What's this? Who are you? Look into the camera, please.'

Seth ignores his request, offering the lens a view of his shoulder and neck. 'Yo, Mr Cromarty. I'm one of the sparks on your site. Gavin Davies? I wanted a quick word, man. A few of us was working late, and there's been a problem. Something urgent. I need to show you photos.'

'Can't this wait 'til Monday?'

'Nah, man. It's urgent, like I say. A problem with the wiring that could hold the whole job up.'

There's an audible tut. Several seconds of silence pass. Clearly Cromarty's mulling over whether or not he should allow his evening to be disturbed by work matters. But suddenly, there's a click and a buzzing sound as the gates unlock and start to move apart. 'Come up to the front door. And make it snappy. I'm a busy man.'

Mike and I slip in behind Seth and scurry up to the house, taking cover behind some tall potted camellias that are in full glossy leaf near to the entrance. I glance at the garaging; notice that one of the doors is cracked open by a third. I can just about see the number plate of the car within. Though I try to take note of the letters and numbers, I become distracted by Seth, who is approaching the large portico that's all faux-Grecian columns and colourful terracotta planters. Rather than stepping up to the front door, he remains standing on the driveway.

When the front door opens, I pop my head out from my hiding place just enough to catch sight of Cromarty. I glance over at Mike, hidden behind his bush. We nod to one another; silently raise our phones in unison to film the encounter.

'What do you want?' Cromarty asks Seth. 'What have you got to show me?'

'You'd better come over here and have a look,' Seth says, pointing to the screen of his own phone. He beckons Cromarty close. 'It's serious. Thought you should know.'

'Bring it to me.'

'The signal's better over here. Come and see.' Seth takes a step further away from the house and beckons Cromarty to him.

Finally, Cromarty comes outside. I film him walking some five metres from the front door to Seth, who is backing away, backing away. It is absolutely clear from Cromarty's sprightly gait and the absence of any supportive collars or crutches that there is nothing physically wrong with him.

He peers down at Seth's phone and frowns. 'Wait. What's this?' He tries and fails to snatch Seth's phone from him. 'That's not a picture of my building site. That's some young feller, lying in a hospital bed. What the hell?' He meets Seth's gaze, and even from my hiding place, I can see there is thunder in his eyes. 'Hang on a minute. You're not Gav Davies.' He pokes Seth in the shoulder. 'You're that kid from the Bromley gardening club.' He snaps his fingers. 'Steve? No. Seb? And that's *you* in the picture.'

Seth holds the phone aloft so that Cromarty can get a good look at the screen. 'Yeah. It is. This was me, five days ago. I was knocked off a ladder by either you or someone you paid to be muscle. Out for the count, I was. They took me to hospital with a bad concussion and a sprained arm. Lucky I didn't break my neck, else you'd be up for murder.'

Cromarty blanches. 'I've no idea what you're talking about, son. I haven't left the house all week. I'm a sick man, see? And you should know it's a very serious thing to accuse someone of attempted murder.'

Seth's nostrils flare. The tendons in his neck protrude. He pockets his phone and balls his fists, speaking through gritted teeth. 'Maybe you already got a murder under your belt, because me and my gardening mates, we been putting two and two together about Dotty Gloucester's poisoning, right? And we're onto you, man.'

Cromarty points to the gate. 'Get out. Get off my property, now. I'm calling the police.'

'Was it your dude from New Addington then?' Seth continues, stepping backwards. 'The one you sent to throw a brick through Marjorie Bloom's greenhouse window? You know? Taylor Jones. Yeah. That's right. We know his name, and I'm no grass, but it wouldn't take much for me to identify him to the police.'

From my vantage point, I can see the tendon over Cromarty's orange jaw flinching away. He takes out his own phone and holds it up, presumably to photograph Seth. 'Keep going with your baseless accusations. I've got lawyers who'll make you wish you'd never been born, son.'

Seth pulls the collar of his T-shirt up and over his nose so that his face is obscured. He's backing away, fast.

At this point, Mike bursts out from behind his camellia. 'We know what you lot are up to,' he shouts, his voice sounding thin and stringy with adrenalin. He's filming all the while, with his phone held out in front of him, as though he's challenging Cromarty to a digital duel.

Cromarty looks puzzled. 'What the hell? Where in God's name did you come from?' He turns back to his front door and yells, 'Lexi, help! Call the police! I'm being assaulted. Let the bloody dog out!'

I emerge from my hiding place and see that all of Cromarty's swagger has gone. He looks smaller, older, more vulnerable. 'We've got evidence your insurance claim is fraudulent, Luke Cromarty,' I say, feeling like I'm powered by a ball of white-hot energy in the pit of my stomach, though I'm shaking all over. 'And we also know you're behind the sabotage of the Bromley Botanists' gardeners' club.'

I hear barking coming from the garage block. I glance back at the part-opened door, which is rolling up, up, up. It's then that I catch sight of the white Golf GTI, with its blacked-out windows and its number plate that begins BV69 R . . . I know for sure then that we have our man. And when I turn back to face Cromarty, one look at his feet confirms it. 'We know you killed Dorothy Gloucester, because you're wearing exactly the same dayglo trainers with the flames up the sides that you had on in the CCTV footage taken just before her murder, when you stepped out of that Golf GTI you've got hidden in the garage.' Now it's my turn to feel like Columbo, but without the raincoat. 'You were the last person to see Dotty alive, and you had motives coming out of your ears, Mister Greedy Developer with dollar signs in your eyes.'

Cromarty's striding towards me. 'I don't know what you're talking about, you silly moo.'

'How dare you call my friend a "moo"?!' Mike shouts. 'I'll give you "moo", you big orange cheesy puff of a man!'

'Dorothy Gloucester took her own life,' Cromarty says, his attention fixed on me. 'Everyone knows that, including the police. She was a lonely old woman with a shed full of poison and a death wish.'

The barking is louder now. The electronic gate clangs into life and starts to close, threatening to trap us in Cromarty's front garden.

'Think you're so clever, don't you?' Mike says, picking up his pace as he walks towards the swiftly closing gate. 'But we've got your ticket, pal. We saw you coming out of Biggins Broadacre and Levy, wearing those self-same shoes. We saw you get into your Golf and drive off. The exact same Golf that was caught on CCTV the night Dotty died.'

'*You* were the one who chased me in that knackered old Volvo?' Cromarty scoffs. 'Well, you're persistent, I'll give you that.'

'Oh, there's no flies on us, sir,' Mike says, treating Cromarty to a self-satisfied smirk. 'And you mustn't underestimate the power of the grapevine, either. Did you know, for example, that there's a strong rumour going round that Dotty fell pregnant in her youth and had the baby put up for adoption?' I see the realisation spread across Mike's face, as he solves this conundrum in real time. 'It's you, isn't it?'

'You're her long-lost son,' I say, pointing at Cromarty. 'When you realised who Dotty was and that she was worth a mint, you tracked her down, didn't you? Tried to get her to change her will to benefit you. And once you thought she had, you murdered her in cold blood.'

Mike's nodding enthusiastically, then he's shaking his head. 'But she didn't, did she? Dorothy left her multimillion-pound golf club to the Golden Trowel Gardening Association, as first prize for this year's top trowellers. Which means you'd have to eliminate the competition to guarantee a win for Croydon, and even then, if you won the Golden Trowel, that would mean sharing your spoils with the others. So, the only surefire chance of getting your hands on that prime real estate would be if you could successfully challenge her will *by proving you're her long-lost son.*'

Cromarty scoffs. 'Rubbish.'

'Is it, though?' I ask. 'I'd say it doesn't take Sherlock Holmes to work out that that's why you had Dotty's house burgled. A hairbrush and some old diaries? You needed her DNA and maybe some old, confessional journal entries to prove she was your mother, so you could have her will overturned and inherit everything.' The truth is so blinding, it is as if I have been hit by a bolt of illuminating lightning.

Every last drop of blood seems to have drained from Cromarty's face. The hand in which he's holding his phone has dropped limply to his side. He shouts back towards the house. 'Lexi! Let Titan out, right this minute!'

'So, now you're keeping your options open, aren't you?' Mike says. 'Trying to prove she's your mother, and at the same time, trying to eliminate the competition for the Golden Trowel, just in case you can't overturn the will. Ha!'

'You've got no proof,' Cromarty says, a slight wobble in his otherwise gruff voice. 'And I'm a man who's used to winning. Throw your worst at me, because I'm getting that Golden Trowel and that land, no matter what.'

'You're going to rue the day you picked a fight with the Bromley Botanists . . .' Mike shakes his fist defiantly at Cromarty. 'Because we're going to take you down to Chinatown, sir.'

A Doberman bounds out from the garage, snarling and barking. It makes straight for Mike's trouser leg and latches on tight with its dreadful fangs.

'Ow! Call your dog off!' He kicks out, trying and failing to shake himself loose from the dog's determined grip. 'Get off me! Bad Titan. Get off!'

I spy a tennis ball on the neat lawn. Snatching it up, I wave it at the dog and throw it towards the Lamborghini. The ball bounces on the bonnet and triggers the car alarm. It's enough to distract the dog, and when it releases Mike's trouser leg, I grab his arm, and we run. The gate is closing, closing, almost closed. Seth is already on the street clambering back into the van.

As I sprint towards freedom, I glance back and catch sight of a trophy blonde at the front door. Lexi Cromarty. The woman from the building site. Strangely, she doesn't look even remotely startled by the scene that is unfolding on her driveway. No. Lexi Cromarty is no stranger to trouble knocking on her door. But Cromarty himself is well and truly spooked. His orange spray tan has now paled to a sickly yellow-grey, like spent cigarette smoke. He has a haunted look to him.

'Don't think I'll take this lying down,' Cromarty says. 'I know who you are. I know where you all live.'

Fear chills me as if my bones have been dipped into liquid nitrogen, but I don't want Cromarty to see I'm rattled. 'See you on the front page of the *Daily Mail*,' I shout. The gate clangs shut behind us, liberating us from the threat of the Doberman. 'They love a good true-crime exposé.'

30

'We're here to see Detective McGowan,' I tell the officer on the front desk at Brixton police station.

At my side, Mike is still breathless, presumably with adrenalin after our confrontational showdown with Cromarty and his Doberman. He's polishing his glasses on the hem of his T-shirt, and I can see his hands are still trembling. Poor Mike. I, however, am invigorated by the adrenalin that is still coursing through my veins.

'Can I ask what it's regarding?' the officer says, one eye on a loudly protesting youth who has just been marched in, apparently by his mother (judging by his pleading), who has him gripped by the ear.

'The murder of a Miss Dorothy Gloucester,' I say.

The officer on the front desk frowns at us. 'The Radio 4 presenter? Oh, that case is closed, madam.'

'But we have new information that points to her having been murdered in cold blood,' Mike says, waving his mobile phone before the desk sergeant's cynical eyes. 'And it's not just that either. We have reason to believe the man who killed Dorothy Gloucester was also behind the attempted murder of one of our friends.'

'Yes. I was knocked to the ground.' I point to the dressing on my head. 'And our friend was knocked off a ladder. He landed up in hospital. He could easily have died.'

Mike puts his hands together. 'Please. Can you tell Detective McGowan that we need to speak to her urgently?'

When the officer looks beyond us and beckons the outraged, somewhat terrifying mother and her cowed son to come forward, I realise he thinks we're idiots. 'Step aside, please.' He's already focused on the mother. 'Yes, madam?'

The mother barges me out of the way and slaps her free meaty forearm onto the counter, still gripping her son's ear though he wriggles and tries to contort his way out of her grip. 'Hello, officer. I'm here because this rarseclart, my feckless son, thinks he can steal the shopping money out of my purse to fund his addiction to collectible trainers. Teach him a lesson, officer. Throw him in the cells for the night.'

Tears start to roll onto the youth's cheeks. He struggles, but his lanky frame is all arms and legs and no match for his mother's middle-aged solidity. 'Mum! You're *so* unfair.'

Much as I'd enjoy seeing this family drama play out, Mike and I can't be fobbed off by the officer. 'Sorry.' I hold my hand up to the mother. 'So sorry, but we hadn't quite finished with our enquiry. Can I just . . . ?'

The front desk officer's eyes widen and he treats me to an incredulous look. '*Yes*, madam?'

'Look, we have compelling evidence that a vulnerable elderly woman was deliberately poisoned in her own home, and we *have* to see Detective McGowan. Today . . . as in *now*. *Please*.' I peer around the waiting area and see two free seats in among the desolate-looking locals who are sitting on the blue, bolted-down chairs, waiting to see what fate the Metropolitan Police has decided for them in their hour of need. 'We'll wait. Yes?' I catch the front desk officer's eye. 'Yes?'

'I'll see what I can do, but obviously, this is a *very* busy station and Detective McGowan might not even be available.'

'I'm sure you'll try your best.'

Mike and I take our seats on the unforgiving blue chairs and the long wait begins, during which we observe some of the choicer domestic dramas and disasters of South-East London.

With arms folded, Mike inclines his head towards me. 'So, I notice you didn't mention the fraud when we spoke to that officer.'

'No.' I stare blankly at a notice about domestic abuse that's stuck on a pinboard on the wall. 'I'm saving that one for Chislehurst Green's fraud squad. They'll bring the police in anyway, as soon as they review the footage we took of Cromarty strutting around his front garden. But by using Colin . . . my moron of a boss . . . by going through him and our fraud team, I get points for saving the company five million. I get my HR slate wiped clean.'

There's a look of surprise on Mike's face. 'I thought you might take the voluntary redundancy they're offering and start fresh. You seem so unhappy.'

I sigh. 'Like I told you, I need money because people rely on me. I am mortally unhappy at work. That's true. But right now, there's a lot of things need to happen before

I could make a huge decision like jacking in my job and starting over. I need a financial safety net before I jump.'

'But if we win the Golden Trowel . . . ?' Mike looks positively crestfallen.

'We still wouldn't have start-up funds unless we got a huge business loan. And I'm not in the market for that kind of extra financial burden and risk.' I shake my head. Then I realise I'm squashing the hope out of him, so I pat his arm encouragingly. 'Let's see how the Trowellies pan out first, eh?'

'Excuse me. You two!' There is a female officer on the front desk, now. She's peering out at us from behind her protective booth. 'You're the ones waiting for Detective McGowan?' she asks.

We nod.

We are ushered away from Brixton's crime-afflicted residents to a room that has an institutional smell of fear, second-hand bodily whiff, and disinfectant. Detective McGowan is already sitting down behind a table that's bolted to the floor. She's wearing a pained expression that suggests she'd rather be chalking out a dead body than speaking to two gardeners-turned-amateur-sleuths.

'I know you, don't I?' She points at me. 'I never forget a face. You're one of the women who called in Dorothy Gloucester's death.'

I nod. 'Gill Swanley. That's me. And this is –'

'Mike Berisford.' Mike sticks out his hand, which remains unshaken. His smile quickly falters. 'Oh, er . . .' He pushes his glasses up his nose and runs a finger around his collar. 'Hmm.'

Detective McGowan closes her unadorned eyes, and her fine, pale eyebrows make for her hairline. I recognise the look — it's one of an exasperated parent. Her eyelids snap open suddenly. 'You'd better not be wasting my time.'

'We're not,' I say.

'Come on then. Give me what you've got.'

Half an hour later, Detective McGowan is reading over the notes she's made in her notebook with a furrowed brow. She leans back in her chair and purses her lips.

'It's a compelling case you've put together here,' she says. 'And that's just as well, because there's no way on this good earth that my boss will reopen Dorothy Gloucester's case without a convincing case for murder.'

I feel excitement spark within me. 'So you're going to look into Luke Cromarty? See if our theory holds water — that he's Dotty Gloucester's long-lost adopted son and he killed her, thinking he'd inherit?'

'And we reckon he's now trying to overturn her will,' Mike chimes in.

'Yeah. Our working theory there is that he had her house burgled,' I add. 'Stole her diaries and a hairbrush so he could prove Dorothy's parentage through a DNA test and maybe through her written confessions, too.'

'Leave it with me,' she says. 'It's all a bit circumstantial at the moment, but if we can link the white Golf to Miss Gloucester's house, and link Luke Cromarty to the white Golf *and* the sabotage of your group, we've got motive.' She taps the end of her pencil thoughtfully on her book.

'We *should* be able to get Biggins Broadacre and Levy to tell us what he wanted when you saw him the other day. If we're just looking at Dorothy Gloucester's murder, he'll be protected by client confidentiality, because she's already dead. But if there's a possibility that you or your friends are in mortal danger from this man . . .' She cocks her head to the side and looks thoughtfully up to the ceiling. 'We might be able to override their confidentiality commitment.'

'Seize his computer!' Mike says, slapping his knees. 'Analyse his browsing history to see if he's looked up how to prove his genealogy. Maybe there are damning emails between him and Taylor Jones. You'd have to seize his devices to access WhatsApp and Facebook Messenger. That's all end-to-end encrypted, isn't it?'

At this point, Detective McGowan chuckles and shakes her head. She throws down her pencil. 'I'm going to be out of a job if I'm not careful.'

Mike salutes. 'Ma'am.'

I treat him to a disapproving look. Mike blushes to the tips of his ears. He retires his saluting right hand to his left armpit and mouths, 'Sorry.'

'Do you think you can do anything with the information straight away?' I ask. 'Only, we're all frightened, if I'm honest.' I think of Zak, home alone after school, when I haven't yet returned from work; the two of us in that house overnight with no defence beyond a mortice lock and the hockey stick next to my bed. 'Like I said, we're pretty sure Cromarty's behind one of our number winding up in hospital.'

'A blight on the good name of the Golden Trowel Gardening Association,' Mike says. 'Such wanton violence.'

I nod and lock eyes with the detective. 'If we're right, Cromarty's ruthless and dangerous. We're all fair game.' A liverish feeling roils around my gut. 'Me and Mike are single parents with kids at home. We don't live together . . . obviously.' My skin feels ill-fitting at such a suggestion. I rub my arms.

'Leave it with me.' Detective McGowan gets to her feet and collects up her notebook and pencil. 'Don't take the law into your own hands anymore. Lock your doors and windows at night and when you're out, and let the police do their job. No more vigilante stuff. Okay?'

Monday morning follows another sleepless night. I tossed and turned the hours away, wondering if the masked and hooded man would be paying Zak and me a visit in the night. Every creaking floorboard had me sitting up and listening for the footfalls of an intruder. Yet the new week has rolled in, and we are still mercifully unmolested.

'Promise me you won't do anything dumb,' Zak says as he pulls on his shoes for school.

'I won't. Promise me you'll call the police if you see anyone suspicious hanging around.'

Zak shakes his head. 'God, Mum. You got into gardening to chill out and meet people, not get into a fight with some local hardmen. Dad would have run a mile.'

I look down at my beautiful son and see so much of his father in him – a mild-mannered man, who disliked conflict intensely. 'I'm not your dad, Zak. There's just me and you, now. I have to stick up for both of us.'

'But this isn't about *us*, is it?' he says. 'It's about your gardening pals.'

'It's about what's right, Zak. People are getting hurt. Dorothy Gloucester's dead. Marj was terrorised in her own greenhouse. Me and Seth wound up with a concussion each – it could have ended up way worse. None of that sits well with me. And your dad was an employment lawyer. He couldn't bear to see injustice. If he could have done something about suspected murder and sabotage, he would have, I'm sure.'

'I don't want you getting hurt.' He stands up and clasps me in a bear hug, then turns to the wall, no doubt to hide the fearful tears I see standing in his eyes.

'I won't.' I pat him on the back and kiss his ear. 'And I would never jeopardise your safety.' I break away from him and take his chin gently in my hand, forcing him to look me in the eye. 'Now, stop worrying and go to school. I've got this.'

He nods, and all that remains of the tears are some rogue broken capillaries on the white sclera of his youthful eyes.

I make a beeline for Colin's office as soon as I get into work. My heart is pounding, and I am drowning in a hot flush that has been going on for the last ten minutes. But my skin prickles, not only with perspiration but also with exhilaration. I feel like a spy.

Through the glass panel in the door, I can see that my boss is alone and trying to get something out of his teeth with his fingernail, using a shiny ball on his Newton's cradle as a mirror. Today, he is wearing a *Spongebob Squarepants* tie. With a slightly trembling fist, I take a deep breath and knock on his door. I open it without waiting for a reply.

'Gillian.' Colin looks up at me. His expression is one of mild disappointment and distaste, as though he is sitting in someone else's lingering fart.

'Have you got a minute?' I am already inside and have closed the door. It's tough if he hasn't.

He looks at his watch. 'Well, I have a meeting in –'

'Remember I told you about that huge fraudulent claim?' I take a seat in front of his desk, not waiting to be asked.

He nods and steeples his fingers together. 'Yes. You tried to blackmail me into expunging the warning from your employment records in return for information. I seem to remember saying you had a duty to report it anyway.'

Sighing, I take out my phone and place it on his desk. Somehow, the sleep deprivation has emboldened me, and rather than feeling tired and guarded, I am energised and seem to have lost my Sensible-Gill filter. 'Cut the crap, Col. I've known you for ten years. You used to be pragmatic and principled. I don't know what's happened to you to change all that . . .' I wave my hand blithely. 'Maybe Janice has got to you?'

Colin is suddenly bright red to his receding hairline, and I know my suspicions that he knows the Dolores Umbridge of HR in the biblical sense were correct. I shudder, visualising them in bed together, and I say a silent prayer that they never breed and produce a sugar-voiced despot with a penchant for joke accessories.

'What are you trying to say?' he says.

I tell him about the £5 million claim, though I keep Cromarty's name back for now and refer to him only as a 'successful local businessman'. 'If you save the company all that money,' I continue, ignoring him, 'and we're not talking chump change – it's a feather in your cap. The books balance. Nobody needs to be culled. Problem solved, and *you* come up smelling of roses.'

He stares at me blankly for rather too long. 'I want hard proof.'

I wave my phone just close enough to his face for him to try grabbing at it. Then I snatch the phone back. 'Promise me that you'll make things right. You'll clear my record and stop forcing me to push people out.'

'Show what you've got, Gillian.' He has a greedy look on his face.

'*Promise!*' I bite my lip, the blood rushing in my ears.

His nostrils flare and he slow-blinks, nodding almost imperceptibly. 'Give it here.' He reaches out for the phone again.

I clutch it to my chest. 'I need your assurances, Colin. I need to hear you say it.' My heartbeat is thunderous. I feel light-headed. But I smell victory. 'Think of the accolades for you. Everyone's a winner. My clean record for this footage?'

'*If* the footage is hard evidence of a major fraud, then you have my word.'

Thumbing my phone into life, I turn it towards him and play the clip of Cromarty walking across his drive, taken from two vantage points by Mike and me. 'This guy . . .'

'Luke Cromarty? The property developer?' Colin raises an eyebrow. 'Always in the local rag, trying to peddle his retirement flats? My dad bought one of those flats and he pays an astronomical management fee. Such a rip-off, and so tiny and shoddily built.' He starts to rub the lapel of his jacket between his nail-bitten thumb and fingers. 'It's my inheritance up in smoke.'

My hot flush gives way to a warm rush of satisfaction. 'Exactly. Except this guy's trying to bankroll his lavish lifestyle and his next build with money from the Chislehurst Green coffers.' I keep the information about the police investigation into Dotty G's death to myself. Better to keep the two prongs of our attack separate, in case one goes awry. 'The guy's lying through his bleached teeth.'

The corners of Colin's mouth twitch upwards into an unequivocal smile. 'I shall take great pleasure in making sure this fraud case goes to court. Well done, Gillian. It seems you've been exonerated.'

'Fancy a cup of coffee, Gill?' Armpits Alice asks when Friday afternoon rolls around. 'My turn to make it.' She waves her mug at me and then smiles sympathetically. 'You look like you're about to nod off.'

She's got a point. Sleep has continued to evade me at night, despite having my trusty hockey stick propped against my bedside cabinet in anticipation of a visit from our masked attacker. Yet there has been no brick thrown through our window while Zak and I are watching *Police Interceptors* on TV, no obvious attempted break-in in the dead of night or trespass in my garden – not that I'm aware of. The wait for news is killing me. I remember from the times between Dave's consultant's appointments and scans and surgeries that waiting is nothing short of agony.

'Yeah. Go on then. I'm absolutely shattered.' I can't help but yawn, covering my gaping mouth with my now-rugged gardener's hand. 'Ta.' I pass her my 'World's Best Dad' mug. 'Better make it a strong one. Long time 'til the clock strikes five, God help us.'

Taking my mug, she bends over my partition, almost dangling the oversized bow of her blouse into my pen pot. I can smell her pungent armpits. 'I've found a new technique for stirring. You have to stir it one way, then the other – hard, like whipping it – and then add extra milk. It's all in the wrist. Makes it taste like actual coffee.'

'I don't think that's biologically possible, Alice. But A* for optimism.'

'I'm telling you. There's a knack to it.' She takes her armpits and our mugs to the kitchenette.

I look at my overly bright monitor, barely able to concentrate on my mundane task of preparing an agenda for a weekly meeting. Item number four. What the hell was I about to write before Alice walked over with the offer of a non-delicious, catering-wholesaler-own-brand, instant-caffeine hit?

I am poised to type nothing at all when my phone rings. I can hear it inside my handbag, getting louder. Rummaging in among the unlikely bits and bobs in my 'mumly bag of requirement', as Zak calls it, I answer just before voicemail kicks in.

It's Seth. 'Can you get away?'

'Why? What's happened?' I can hear my own breath-lessness as I speak. *Now* I'm awake.

'It's all kicking off here,' he says, clearly at pains to

keep his voice down, despite a hammer drill and an angle grinder being used somewhere in the vicinity. 'Cromarty turns up for a site inspection about twenty minutes ago, right?'

'Did he recognise you?'

'No, no, no. Anyway, the cops have just rocked up. You'll wanna see this.' He ends the call.

Again, I peer at the clock. It's gone two. Alice is just visible in the kitchenette, stirring my coffee like a woman possessed. Can I get away with slipping out, even though I've only just finished my lunch hour?

Instinctively, I call Mike, dialling his number with shaky fingers. He picks up quickly.

'Gillian?'

'It's on,' I say. 'Seth just called me. Cromarty's at the building site. Sounds like he's about to get arrested.'

There's the echoing, rapid squeak, squeak of Mike's trainers moving across a concrete floor in a lofty space, and then, suddenly, he sounds like he's in a cupboard. 'I'll meet you there in ten, ma'am.' He hangs up.

What choice do I have but to go and watch the demise of our orange nemesis? Alice's extra-whipped WD40 will have to wait.

The ten-minute journey to Sunset Pastures' latest building site seems to take twice as long, with every light turning red, but I pull up alongside Mike, pleased to see two squad cars and a police van still parked outside.

Grinning, I lower my window, reach out, and knock on the passenger window of Mike's car. He stretches to manually roll down his window, and suddenly, we are no longer Gill from the insurance company and Mike Potato from the garden centre. We are undercover agents, exchanging sensitive information in a clandestine car park meet.

'Well?' I ask, feeling a hot flush rolling in. 'What have I missed?' I start to fan myself with the MOT invoice from my glovebox.

'Nothing. I just got here. But –'

'Shush. Someone's coming out.' I point to the entrance to the building site, which is just a discreet plywood door displaying health and safety signs, set in a tall plywood fence that wraps around the entire site, painted black and covered in Sunset Pastures Homes logos. It looks impressive. But the man who emerges from the door doesn't.

'Cromarty,' I say. 'He looks like he's about to puke.'

Mike rubs his hands together. 'Here we go.' He grins at me and gives me the thumbs up. 'Good lord. He's in cuffs!'

I watch as Cromarty is frog-marched to the waiting police van by two burly uniformed officers. Detective McGowan follows behind. The construction workers are hanging off the scaffolding on the upper floors, smoking and nudging each other as they revel in the gossip about their employer. There are a couple of wolf-whistles. I spot Seth, who locks eyes with me, and I wave. He doesn't wave back but looks pointedly to his left at some young tradesman who is pulling on the hood of a black plaster-splattered hoodie as though he has something to hide. Taylor Jones. Almost certainly the ladder-shaker who felled Seth and me, given his build is identical to that of our attacker.

'You did it, Gill!' Mike says, interrupting my thoughts.

'*We* did it.' I clap my hands together, allowing myself the satisfaction of having brought down Cromarty's house of cards. '*We* took down a probable murderer and a bully. Taylor Jones is still at large, but . . .'

'We've dug out the parent weed by the roots,' Mike says. 'That's no mean feat.'

He reaches across, offering his hand, and I find myself straining through my window and his passenger window to grab it. I succeed only in cricking my neck. 'Ow. Back atcha, Mike.' I rub my stinging neck. 'Maybe, now, we can just get on with this competition and make Bromley beautiful.' I glance at the time on my phone. 'Look, I'd better get back. I don't want to push my luck by going AWOL for the afternoon.'

I'm about to close my window when Mike shouts, 'Wait! Gill, wait!'

'What?'

'W-would you like to meet up later? At the troughs in Widmore Green maybe? You said you didn't finish those because of the attack. But the stock's still there, isn't it?'

I nod. 'Neil hid it all behind some trees, and it's rained for most of the week, so it should be fine.'

'Well we could do a little planting up and then find a nice pub to have a spot of dinner.' He looks at me hopefully; smiles uncertainly. 'My treat, of course. What do you think? Celebrate our triumph with a glass or two of prosecco?' He pushes his glasses up his nose.

'What about Katie and Hugo?'

'They're at their mum's tonight.'

I consider that Zak is off to his friend's house after school, and they have plans to meet up with others to convince the Wetherspoons bouncers that their IDs aren't fakes off the internet at all. He won't be back until his curfew at 10pm. 'You bet.'

32

'Pass me those surfinia,' Mike says, pointing to the wilted casualties hastily stashed behind the troughs after the attack.

'These look shot to bits,' I say, tweezing three 9cm pots between my fingers and thumb. 'Aphids on them, too.'

'Don't worry. They'll perk up with a good watering and a spray with some neem oil. I made up a bottle at home and brought it with.' Mike takes the bedraggled plants off me, removes them from their pots, and pushes them into the holes he's made in the compost. 'I tell you what, though, this replacement compost is pretty sub-standard.' He sighs and shakes his head. 'It's ended up costing us over a thousand pounds to replace "Berisford's Black Gold" with this multipurpose muck. The group's kitty's completely empty now. Croydon's got an awful lot to answer for.'

While Mike waters the trailing hot-pink and purple surfinia, I hunker down to deadhead the fuchsia Voodoo that have already started to produce bean-like seed heads. I am busy thinking about how our dinner in the pub might pan out when I become distracted by an old brown and beige Rolls-Royce, making a deafening grumbling noise as it heads up Plaistow Lane. The Roller stops abruptly with a screech of brakes, causing the drivers behind to toot their horns angrily. Garnering sweary rebukes from the other drivers, who hang out of their windows to turn the air blue and offer a range of one- and two-fingered salutes, the Roller backs up a way and pulls into the little parking space at the troughs, hemming in both Mike's Mondeo and my Volvo.

I stand up straight to see who the owner of this 1970s time warp on wheels might be. An elderly man swings a Sta Prest-trousered leg out and waves at us as though we might know him. Setting down the fuchsias, I walk over to where he's got himself tangled up in his seat-belt. Half in, half out of the car, I notice this man is all argyle golf jumper, milky irises, and ill-fitting-false-teeth smile.

'Ahoy there!' he says.

'Do you need some help?' I reach out to disentangle him from his seatbelt before he garottes himself.

'No, no, dear. There's a knack to it. Hang on . . .' There's a click, a clang of metal, and he suddenly rolls clear of the enormous old car. 'She always submits in the end. Ha ha.'

'Sorry, are you going to be parked up here long?' I say. He does seem familiar, but I can't place him. 'Only you're hemming us in, and we'll be off in about . . .' I turn back to Mike. 'How long do you think we've got left?'

Mike's scrutinising this eccentric visitor with his head cocked to one side. 'Barty Bing?' His eyebrows draw together. Then he smiles uncertainly. 'Barty Bing!'

Of course! This man is a member of the Croydon Diggers and Dibbers, last seen at Dotty G's wake, sitting on the Croydon table with Betty Moule, Neville Studley, and Louise Lampard. Wondering if he's here to cause a scene, I snatch up a hand fork, then feel instantly stupid as the old man salutes Mike.

'Greetings, Michael, greetings! How are those splendid King Edwards of yours?'

Mike sets his plants down, wipes his hands on his trousers, and marches over to Barty Bing. I'm surprised to see he clasps the old man's hand in his and shakes it with gusto, as though they're old friends. There's even a manly clap on Barty's upper arm.

'Captain Barty. It's been a while.'

'Chelsea Flower Show, 2019, we last spoke properly.' Barty claps him back, and then the two men step apart and stand with feet together, seemingly engaged in some formal dance routine that only men of a certain age know the steps to. 'I was driving up to the tennis club to meet a friend when I spotted you and your lady companion, here. I never forget a face.' He flashes me a denture-bright smile and sticks his hand out. 'Pleased to meet you. Bartholomew Bing. And you are?'

I shake his hand. 'Gill. My name's Gill Swanley.'

Barty turns back to Mike, the brilliant smile gone. 'I thought I'd better pull over and have a word.'

I conjure the memory of Seth, lying helpless and wan in that hospital bed. I touch the healing wound on my head. 'I've got news for you, Mr Bing: unless that word is "sorry", I for one don't want to hear it.' I look to Mike. 'This man's pals put one of our number in the hospital. Why are you being so nice to him?'

Mike's face crumples into a pained expression. He turns back to Barty. 'Gill's got a point.' He then stretches himself to his full height so that he's a good few inches taller, and the warmth between the men blows away on a sudden cold gusting breeze. 'I have to say, Barty, it's surprising and . . . actually dispiriting in the extreme to see a man of your moral fibre and good gardening reputation rubbing shoulders with violent thugs and unsportsmanlike fraudsters.'

Barty lifts his head to meet Mike's judgemental gaze. There's contrition in his bloodshot eyes with those milky irises. 'I'm not proud of the way my teammates have behaved.' He looks at me, clasping his hands together behind him, like a counterfeit, not-dead Duke of Edinburgh. He bows slightly. 'And you're quite right to hold me to account . . . er . . .' He blinks hard at me.

'Gill.'

'Gill. Yes.' He snaps his fingers at the successful recall of my name. 'And actually, that's why I stopped to speak to you both.'

'If you want to absolve yourself of guilt,' Mike says, 'I think you'd do better confessing to the police, rather than us.'

Barty Bing smooths his freckled, bald pate with a knobbly hand. 'Look, I am very, *very* sorry about what's gone on and what was done to your friends.' He shakes his head ruefully. 'It's not sportsmanlike at all, and bullying goes against everything I believe in. But the group's never been the same since Luke Cromarty and his rent-a-thug joined, a couple of years back.'

'If it's been so intolerable, why on earth didn't you just ask him to leave?' Mike asks.

'Cromarty had grand plans and he's a brilliant snake-oil salesman.' Barty glances at his Roller. 'He offered "jam tomorrow" if we joined his company's board and invested. Free house renovations and a percentage share of profits from a lucrative project that he said was "in the pipeline".'

'Let me guess: throwing up a luxury housing estate on a certain top-tier golf course, just outside Weybridge?' I say.

He looks heavenwards. 'Betty tried to convince us all to buy into Cromarty's hare-brained scheme. Winning the Golden Trowel so Cromarty could develop on Dorothy Gloucester's real-estate legacy – it was a legitimate ruse, if morally suspect.' His focus returns to our troughs, and he raises his eyebrows and sighs. 'I thought, actually, I don't want to be a part of that. I have a very comfortable retirement. So it may be small recompense, but for my part, I *did* turn him down.'

'None of you ever had an inkling that he'd killed Dotty Gloucester?' I say. 'I find that hard to believe.'

'Absolutely none whatsoever. Not until his arrest. Of course, I'd *never* have given him my tacit support if I'd known he was a cold-blooded killer. I'd have turned him in to the authorities immediately.'

'Well, you're a bit late with noble intentions,' I say, reminded of Colin, who is now treating me like his sister-from-another-mister at work, as if he hasn't made my life a complete misery for months on end. 'The damage is done. And we haven't managed to finish our planting.'

'Ah, well, that's where I thought I could make amends.' Barty's smile returns. 'I'd like to offer you my services.'

'Are you trying some Trojan horse shenanigans?' Mike asks. 'Is this Betty Moule, pulling strings now Cromarty's in a holding cell?'

Barty shakes his head vehemently. 'No, no. Not at all, dear chap. I've already left the Croydon Diggers and Dibbers. I walked out on principle as soon as I heard about you and your young chum with the complicated haircut.'

'His name's Seth.' I wedge a balled fist on my hip.

'I'm sure it is.' Barty rocks back and forth on his heels with his hands now stuffed in the pockets of his Sta Prest slacks. 'Anyway, if you'll have me in your Bromley group, I'm yours.' He bows low.

Mike fixes me with a questioning look. 'What do you think, Gill? Will the others welcome a well-meaning interloper into our ranks?'

I shrug. 'It's not my decision, is it? We'd better ask them first.'

33

'You're coming with me, Mum, and I don't want to hear any more about it.' I'm holding Mum's coat out to her while Zak takes her wheelchair out of the hall storage cupboard.

'No, I'm not.' She pushes past me and heads for the living room. '*Loose Women* is on. I never like to miss that. And then there's *Quincy* later.' She flops into her armchair, snatching up the TV remote control from the tea-stained chair arm.

I stifle the urge to sigh. 'Jack Klugman's been dead over ten years, and you've seen every episode of *Quincy* about a million times.'

Mum scowls and waves me away. She points the remote at the TV, as if Zak and I have evaporated, and presses the power button. *Loose Women* fills the stale, drab living room with daytime-TV-enforced frivolity and colour. 'Fucking gardening, I ask you,' she mutters beneath her breath. 'Like I've got the energy to get on my chips and peas and dig. Dig my own grave!' Finally she turns to me. 'You'd be happy if I did *that*, wouldn't you? Dig my own grave and get in it.'

Don't roll your eyes, Gill. Don't sigh. Keep smiling. Remember what Mandi-with-an-I said about not rising to it. She's looking for a reaction. 'Nobody's asking you to do gardening, Mum.

I just thought the fresh air would do you good, and you can sit and natter with some of the older people when they take a break. There's a retired solicitor called Barty who's just joined. He's very friendly but he's got a bad back, so he takes a lot of breaks.'

My mother eyes me suspiciously and then looks beyond me to Zak. 'Is she trying to get me off with some old ponce?'

Zak grins and shrugs. 'No, Nan. We just want to take you out. It'd be cool for you to see what Mum's been up to all these months.'

'Monkey business. I don't need to leave the house to know she's up to monkey business and meddling.' My mother is pointing emphatically and spitting when she speaks.

'Nan!'

'Okay. That's enough,' I say. I take the remote control from her and switch the television off. 'Coat. Now.' With her coat slung over my shoulder, I hold out my hand to help her out of her armchair. 'Come on, Lily Fielding. You're coming with us, and I won't take no for an answer.'

'But I haven't had a wash.'

A voice comes from the kitchen amid the clanking of pots and pans in the sink. It belongs to Carol. 'Now, you know that's not true, Lily. You've had a shower this morning, and I even shampooed and set your hair for you.' She appears at the threshold to the living room, drying her hands on a hand towel. 'A trip out will do you good.'

Zak pats the back of the wheelchair. 'Come on, Nan. There's gonna be a buffet at one of the ladies' later. Mum's bringing a home-made quiche and a bottle of fizz so we can celebrate my end-of-year exams and my AS exam being over.'

'I don't like quiche. It gives me heartburn.'

'It's tuna and mushroom, Mum,' I say. 'It used to be your favourite. I used extra mature cheddar, just how you like it.'

My mother looks at Zak, switches her focus to me, makes a disgruntled growling noise, and then holds her hand out to Carol to be pulled up. 'Let *her* do it,' she tells me. '*She's* a paid professional. I don't trust you.'

'That's the spirit, Lily,' Carol says, crossing the living room and indicating to me that we should take an arm each. 'The more we get you up and out and mixing with other people your own age, the better you'll feel. That's what the doctor said.'

'You two are in cahoots,' my mother says, pointing at us with narrowed eyes.

Carol winks at me, and I wink back. We manage to extract my mother from her armchair, get her into her coat, and lower her into her wheelchair.

'How long is it since you last went out, Mum?' I ask as Zak pushes her out to the car. I wave to Carol, who is visible at the kitchen window. She waves back and gives me the thumbs up.

'Are you trying to make me look a dickhead in front of the boy?' she asks.

'Mum's just trying to look after you, Nan,' Zak says.

'You can't swear like that in front of the gardening people, Mum,' I say. 'There's a very religious woman who's a member. Swearing makes her uncomfortable.'

My mother twists her head to look up at me, and I notice the mischievous smile playing around her lips. 'Oh yeah? That right?'

I silently chide myself for mentioning Marjorie's intense dislike of 'industrial language', knowing my mother will likely spend the entire afternoon swearing like a sailor just to get a reaction. We bundle Mum into the car and head off to the little green, where we're finishing up the last of our planting.

'I thought you said you'd had trouble with this gardening business,' my mother says.

Through my rearview mirror, I catch sight of her staring out of her window. It is a warm sunny day, and I've deliberately driven us along one of the streets where we've finally managed to finish our glorious hanging baskets. I wonder if she'll notice the racemes of colourful flowers and foliage that cover each lamppost. 'There was a bit of a clash with the Croydon community gardeners, but we've sorted all that out, now. One of them has been arrested for murder and major fraud, would you believe it?'

'Who?'

'Luke Cromarty. The property developer. Didn't I tell you about him?'

Mum nods. 'Oh, that orange, prancing tit? Sunset Pastures? I went to school with his mother. She never washed her fanny, her. "No-knickers Nolan", we used to call her. He he. Not surprised her boy's in trouble with the law. His father fell on his head in 1967.' The car is silent for a few minutes but for Zak's amused snickers. Then, she speaks again. 'Nice hanging baskets round here.'

I allow myself a wide, satisfied smile. 'My gardening group put those hanging baskets up. And we grew all the plants from seed.' Will she praise my efforts? Is there still any nurture or love left in Lily Fielding?

'Why ain't we had hanging baskets on our street? You're busy making it pretty for all and sundry, but you can't doll up your own mother's street? That's nice.'

'You're in housing association, Mum. It's private land. We didn't get permission for that.'

She tuts. But at least she noticed the baskets.

'Do us a favour, Zak, bring all those impatiens over, will you, son?' I point to Seth's borrowed van, which contains the last of the plants for this final grand display.

'What colour?' Zak is sitting cross-legged on the grass next to my mother and Val. He has been tasked with periodically supplying them both with drinks and snacks from the large coolbox Mike brought with him.

I double-check my instructions against the plan Cath printed out. 'Red. The big ones. Please.'

Zak looks relieved to escape the septuagenarian chat, and I am so proud when he returns with exactly the right tray of plants.

'You're learning,' I say, squinting up at him.

He points to the ruby- and lime-coloured decorative foliage I've just been planting. 'Let me guess. Coleus?'

'Excellent. Top marks! You could train to be a horti-culturalist if Chemistry doesn't work out for you!'

'Can I help?' He looks back at his two elderly charges. 'They really don't need a babysitter. They're both full of sausage rolls and cider.' He chuckles. 'I think Val and Nan were separated at birth.'

I widen my eyes. 'Who'da thunk it, eh? Val and your nan? It's like Che Guevara and Goebbels, bonding over swears.'

'Wait, what? Who?' Zak shakes his head, clearly con-fused. Not waiting for an explanation, he sets the tray down and kneels at my side. 'What shall I do?'

'You pass them. I'll plant them. Okay?'

Seth calls out to him and waves. They exchange a greeting, and I smile at how Zak's burgeoning friend-ship with Seth is turning my son from an ADD gaming zombie with low self-esteem into someone far, far hap-pier. Zak has survived his first year of sixth form, partly thanks to Seth's Chemistry tuition and encouragement, and I think, I *think*, my son is starting to believe he can achieve; that the outdoors is an actual place worth ven-turing into. He's swapped his fast-clicking mouse for a trowel! And he's spending more time gawping at Phoebe than his monitor. *That's* got to be a result.

'Are those Mike's kids?' Zak asks, inclining his head towards the younger teen and the tween, helping their father to dig holes for some huge black-leaved canna Tropicannas at the back of the display.

I look up and survey the children I've never met before today. 'Yes. Katie and Hugo. I was beginning to think he'd made them up. But there they are. Real live kids.'

'They look like dorks.'

'They look like nice kids, Zak. Don't go all Lily on me.' I study their faces and wonder how much they look like their mother. Katie looks just like a smaller, feminine version of Mike. Hugo, less so. 'I guess we'll get to meet them properly at Marjorie's buffet.'

'They're dressed like . . . like their dad got them dressed.'

'Their dad's a good man. Don't judge a book by its cover, and all that.'

Zak takes an impatiens out of its pot and passes it to me. 'You like Mike, don't you?'

I turn to my son and scrutinise his face for signs of disappointment or derision or relief. I see only curiosity. 'He's a nice guy.'

'No, but I mean, you *like* him, don't you?'

I shake my head. 'I don't know.' I can feel heat spreading across my face, and it's not just the sun. 'He's just a friend.'

'I don't mind, you know,' Zak says, examining the plant's healthy root system. There's no real conviction in his voice, but there's no hurt, either. 'I understand.'

I see Dave in his eyes. I visualise the tree beneath which my husband's ashes were scattered. My gut tightens into a knot. 'We must go to the tree. Remind me to put it on the calendar again when we get home.'

'Did you hear a word I said, Mum?'

Firming the earth around the impatiens I've just stuck

into the soil, I become aware that my T-shirt has ridden up at the back, exposing a strip of my unprotected skin. 'Must get some cream on. Has Nan got the backpack?' My knees crack as I stand. Beads of sweat are tracking along my hairline beneath my baseball cap, so I take it off and try to rub my scalp with my clean knuckle. I look down at Zak. 'Did you put cream on? You mustn't burn.'

'Yeeeees.'

Making my way over to my mother and Val, who are laughing like drains at some filthy joke Val has been telling, which, mercifully, I only caught the tail end of, I take the sunscreen from the bag and survey our group's handiwork.

'It looks incredible,' I say, taking in the rich jewel colours and myriad textures of the plants we've raised together.

'Best fun you can have with your clothes on, darlin',' Val says.

She and my mother erupt into filthy-sounding cackling for no obvious reason. They are drunk, and for the first time in a while, my mother's mood is on an upwards trajectory.

'Is it those six empty bottles of cider that's so funny?' I ask. 'Or did Marjorie put special filling in those sandwiches?'

Marjorie stalks over to us, wiping her hands on her floral gardening dungarees. Only her chin and mouth are visible beneath the giant, floppy brim of her sun hat. 'Do I hear my name being taken in vain?' The sickly sugary voice she spoke in when I first met her seems to have been replaced by something more natural and less affected. When she lifts the brim to see Val, my mother, and me, the skin around her eyes wrinkles up with what appears to be genuine happiness.

Val lifts the lid on the coolbox at her side and pulls out another bottle of cider. She offers it to Marjorie. 'Get your laughing gear round that, Marj.'

Marjorie titters. 'No, thank you. Not when one's driving. Though one will have a few sherries at the buffet.'

True to her word, as soon as we're installed in Marjorie's house, she pours herself a hi-ball glass of Harvey's Bristol Cream and starts to drink it as if it's orange squash.

'Do help yourselves to the buffet,' she says, waving us all through to the spread she's laid on in the dining room. 'But don't spill crumbs, and make sure you use the coasters provided. I don't want any cup rings on my aspidistra stand or nest of tables.'

I uncover my quiche. 'I brought this.'

Marjorie looks at it and baulks. 'Oh, dear. That looks a little anaemic. Did you blind bake the pastry first?'

My mother pushes me out of the way and grabs the quiche. 'You saying my girl's got a soggy bottom?' She erupts into drunken cackling and starts to make a beeline for the buffet table. 'I've been telling her that for years,' she shouts over her shoulder.

There is more cackling, and it occurs to me that the cider and laughter – mainly the laughter – have enlivened and limbered up my mother's rapidly deteriorating body in a way modern medicine has failed to do in years.

Experience tells me that she is revving up to a bout of exhibitionism and high jinks, which will almost certainly end up with her being an argumentative, negative nightmare to deal with for weeks. Still, Mandi-with-an-I would tell me to be in the moment and appreciate what's in front of me in the here and now.

And what's in front of me is my mother, shunting aside half of Marjorie's 1970s-style buffet fare, Neil's pasta bake, and Cath's bowl of ratatouille, to give my anaemic quiche pride of place. She's leaning over precariously, pulling down on the tablecloth for support. I'm just about to reach out to stop her from dragging the entire buffet onto the floor when Neil appears.

'Lily, love. You go and put your feet up,' he says, manoeuvring my mother away from the table. 'I'll bring you a plate with whatever you want on. What do you fancy? Will you try some of my pasta bake?'

My mother stops to regard Neil, swaying slightly. She looks him up and down. Then grins. 'Hello, sailor. Your lot are good at cooking, aren't you?'

I groan with embarrassment. 'Mum!'

But Neil is unfazed. He merely laughs and starts to dollop pasta onto a plate for her. 'You should see what I can do with a nice meaty sausage, Lily,' he says, completely deadpan, though the skin around his eyes crinkles with mirth.

Hungry from hours of manual labour in the hot sun, we all pile our plates high and sit on the various armchairs, pouffes, and dining chairs that Marjorie has dotted around her through-lounge. Everyone is drinking and chatting. Seth, Phoebe, and Zak are sitting together with Mike's kids, solving the world's ills or perhaps talking about hydroponics, Greta Thunberg, and memes. My mother is happily ensconced with Marjorie, Val, and Barty, pouring scorn on Generation X and Millennials and remembering the 'good old days', which were highly likely bad old days, viewed through a nostalgic, nicotine-stained lens. And here I am, sandwiched between Mike and Neil, talking about the competition with Cath.

Cath raises a large glass of red wine to her ruby-stained lips. The wan complexion and stiff demeanour of an over-worked GP have been replaced by a tan and confident body language as she drapes herself over an armchair. She isn't even wearing grey hiking gear today. 'I think we stand a good chance of winning, now,' she says. She takes out her phone and starts thumbing through. 'Look at what we've achieved in the last couple of weeks.' She turns the phone towards us and flicks through photo after photo of incredible floral colour and form. 'We're geniuses.'

Mike runs a hand over his sunburnt forehead and talks with his mouth full. ''Pends on the competition. I've entered . . .' The older folk have just broken into a tuneless rendition of 'California Dreamin'' by The Mamas & the Papas (even Marjorie, who is undoubtedly blotto on Harvey's) and Mike's response is drowned out. He shouts over the singing. 'I'VE ENTERED THE COMPETITION FIVE TIMES AND SEEN LESSER GROUPS SNATCH THE PRIZE FROM UNDER OUR NOSES. BELIEVE ME, IT'S STILL VERY MUCH ALL TO PLAY FOR.'

34

At 2am I am still awake, telling Dave's photo that today is judging day for the Golden Trowel Award. Then, as if I'm spilling a closely guarded secret to a confidant, I stare at his handsome face, frozen in time, and tell him about the opportunity for change that winning the prize offers.

'I mean, don't laugh, but imagine *me* setting up in business! A flower farmer, out near Weybridge, of all places. What do you think of that? Mad, isn't it?'

Dave doesn't answer. He doesn't answer because he is just a memory and a two-dimensional photograph in a TK Maxx silver frame. He hasn't had input into my working arrangements for ten years because, as I'm all too aware of, I am alone.

I kiss his photo. 'It's a silly idea. I don't know what I'm thinking. Zak's hopefully going to uni when he finishes sixth form, and I'm going to need every penny I can scrape together to keep this house and top up his funding.' I set the frame back down on top of my chest of drawers. 'Go to sleep, you daft cow,' I tell myself.

I fall into a fitful shallow sleep eventually. When I wake, I realise I have overslept. It is 8.27am and we were supposed to meet at eight at the church hall.

'Damn, damn, damn.'

I clamber out of bed and throw on some clothes, spraying my armpits and rubbing a blob of toothpaste around my teeth as an interim hygiene measure. The judges wanted to meet all of us, and here am I, looking like . . . actually, looking like a gardener.

'Calm down, Gill. Deep breaths.'

Creeping past Zak's bedroom door, I can hear him snoring. No need to disturb his beauty sleep. It's a weekend and the summer hols. The kid deserves a lie-in.

I pad down to the kitchen, quickly make him an instant coffee, and put it in a flask. I write a note.

Morning, Zakky. Off to judging day. There's coffee in the hand flask and bread in cupboard. Make yourself some marmite on toast. Back soon. Love Mum. xxxx

The journey to the church hall takes only minutes, since I attack every speed hump as if I'm Steve McQueen, gunning his Mustang GT through San Francisco with the devil at his back. Except, this is my Volvo – reliable at fending off rogue moose on Swedish forest roads, with all the manoeuvrability of a geriatric elephant with lumbago. By the time I arrive, I've given myself mild whiplash and have scraped the underside of the car on at least three humps. Ah, well. At least it appears to have rained heavily overnight. It will have given our plants an invigorating drink and will have washed off any unsightly sap-sucking aphids that might have gathered on the stems and leaves.

I run into the church hall to find the judges poring over our plans.

'Ah! Here she is at last,' Mike says. 'This is Gillian Swanley. The eighth member of our little club, if you count Mr Bing as the ninth addition. Gillian's big in insurance, but a virtuoso pricker-outerer.'

My heartbeat is racing. I stick my hand out to greet the judges, who introduce themselves as being connected to RHS this and contributors to *Gardening Weekly*'s that. The head judge is a woman called Winnie Tadcaster, gardening editor of *Wise* magazine.

'Hello. Hello, I'm Gill. I've got scrubber's hands, because I like to prick-out without gloves on. Ha ha.' Why on earth did I just say that?

Neil snorts at my faux pas. Marjorie tuts. The judges merely look at me as though I'm demented, and even Mike glances down at his Crocs, quite clearly dying inside.

'The judges are just looking at some of the planting schemes you devised, actually,' he says. He turns to Winnie Tadcaster. 'Gillian's relatively new to gardening, and she's brought an unexpectedly refreshing take on colour schemes and sustainability to the group. Very vibrant and pollinator-friendly.'

I search my soul for an intelligent response that will speak to both design and biodiversity. 'I like bees.'

Realising that I need coffee, I sidle off to the coffee urn Marjorie said she'd be laying on. Someone has put out misshapen but yummy-looking homemade cookies too, so that's breakfast sorted. I take one. I am baffled, however, by the sight of plastic cups full of Mike's dandelion beer at nine in the morning.

Neil appears at my side. 'Do you think he's trying to

get them drunk so they'll give us extra marks?' He twirls his Dalí moustache archly.

'It's not a bad idea. Maybe they'll give us extra marks to *not* drink it. Did Marj bake these cookies?' I take a bite of the biscuit and wrinkle my nose. They taste a bit . . . pungent. I pull the collar of my T-shirt over my nose and sniff, to make sure my sense of smell isn't confusing my tastebuds. But I smell fine. 'Didn't get time to shower this morning,' I explain with my mouth full. I then push something fibrous past my teeth with the tip of my tongue and retrieve it with my finger and thumb. A dark green blob. What the hell is it? 'Who made these?'

'Phoebe and Seth.'

I spit the masticated cookie out into an empty cup. 'I don't believe it. They've baked weed into them. They're actually trying to dope the judges into giving us the award.' I gather up the plate of baked wares. 'Quick! We need to get rid of these before we all get disqualified and arrested.'

Neil takes his little straw trilby off. 'In here. I'll bung them in my car. I've got friends coming to dinner tonight and I've made nothing for pudding.'

'Neil!'

'They'll go nice, warmed up with a blob of ice cream.' He shrugs and sweeps the entire plateful into his hat. 'Waste not, want not, darling. You should come. Let your hair down. Eat a few biscuits. Maybe I should invite Marj. She might see Jesus.'

Marjorie has been slowly edging her way back to

the table and now, she's standing by the urn, clearly eavesdropping on our conversation. 'Did one hear you mention the good Lord?' She reaches into Neil's hat and takes a cookie. 'I feel certain he's been watching over our botanical endeavours. One is nowhere closer to God than in the garden.'

Neil takes the cookie from her. 'I sneezed on these, Marj. And Gill's been fingering them. She hasn't had a shower today.'

Marjorie shrinks back, eyeing us both with distaste. 'How very unhygienic. I shall wait in my Jazz.'

Soon the judges have seen all of our plans and are ready to inspect our planting. Piling into Mike's and Marjorie's cars (except Marjorie has refused to take Neil or me because of our lack of basic hygiene), we lead the way to the first display – the street of hanging baskets installed by Val, Cath, and Neil. With frequent rainfall and the bursts of glorious hot sunshine, everything has doubled or tripled in size since we installed the baskets.

Mike brings the car to a standstill and turns to the rest of us. 'You lot wait here. I'll go and play host with the most.'

Neil, Cath, and I watch as Mike ushers the judges to the baskets. His body language is awkward.

'He's talking too much, isn't he?' I say.

'God, don't blow it, Mike,' Cath says. 'Just show them the bloody baskets and get back in the car. They don't need a running commentary over some surfinias.'

The judges walk slowly along the road, looking up at

the tumbling flowers and chatting among themselves. They make notes on an iPad and nod a lot, but remain grim-faced.

'He's coming back,' Neil says.

Mike gets back in the Mondeo, red in the face and flustered, as he tries to put the key into the ignition and misses. 'Right. Widmore Green troughs and hanging baskets, next.'

Neil leans forward from the back seat. 'Do we really have to babysit them like this? It's excruciating.'

'The sites are so scattered. I don't want them mixing up the council's planting or some second-rate neighbourhood amateur display with ours.'

'*We're* amateurs,' Cath says.

Mike kangaroo-jumps away from the kerb, huffing and puffing in indignation. 'I wouldn't say amateurish describes our combined expertise. No, ma'am.' He pushes his glasses up with his middle finger.

The thoughtful, optimistic, enthusiastic Mike I've got to know over the past few months seems to be fading. In his place, I can see a little of the original Mike Potato – the heel-clicking, saluting pedant that I met that first day in the church hall – slipping back into the driver's seat. I realise he's nervous as hell, and that the uptight persona of Mike Potato, King of King Edwards, is his armour. I feel a rush of fondness for him.

We move on to the troughs, which look stunning from the vantage point of the car. We alight and gather around the glorious displays that Seth and I put together (with a little casual labour from my son and some help

344

with finishing off from Mike). This time, Mike asks *me* to give the commentary on our planting choices.

Praying they can't hear the fear in my voice, I name the plants and give our reasoning for the pairings. I don't even mispronounce the Latin names. The judges nod solemnly at me and continue to make notes without betraying their thoughts one iota.

When we retreat a couple of metres to the parking area to allow the judges to discuss the displays out of our earshot, Seth stands next to me and cups his hand to my ear.

'I think we've got a chance, you know,' he whispers.

'How do you know?'

'Look at their body language. Look at that Winnie Doncaster.' He points surreptitiously.

Winnie Tadcaster steps forwards. She steps backwards. She's examining the far trough from all angles. There's nodding and the suggestion of a smile at the sight of all the fat bumblebees bouncing from one bloom to another. Meanwhile, the RHS guy and *Gardening Weekly* magazine woman are taking photographs of the second trough, bending to examine the flowers and chatting among themselves in animated voices.

'They like them,' I say.

Allowing myself a smile, I can feel some of the tension leaving my shoulders. The judges are standing by the far trough, so I walk the few feet over to the trough closest to us, where we'd paired some tomato-red Apache dahlias with the crimson and yellow claws of gloriosa Rothschildiana lilies, contrasted with the cobalt-blue thistles of some eryngium Blue Steel. I gasp when I spot something fluttering by the blooms. I can barely believe what I'm seeing so I move closer.

I point. 'A hummingbird? Hey, Seth! Come and look at this. Is it a mini hummingbird?' The hovering delight is smaller than my thumb.

Seth joins me by the trough. Open-mouthed, he looks at me with delight in his eyes. 'Aw, sick! I reckon that's a hummingbird hawk-moth. I heard about them, but this is the first time I ever seen one.' He calls Cath over. 'Look!' He points to the delightful sight.

'A hummingbird?'

'It's a kind of moth, yo. That's like, well special, right?'

Cath looks at him askance. 'I think you've still got concussion.' She walks back to the car.

Yet the hummingbird hawk-moth, which feels like a little bit of magic on an English summer's day, does not go unappreciated by the judges. They approach the trough.

'Oh, I say. What a lovely little fellow,' Winnie Tadcaster says, studying the moth as it hovers by the eryngium. She turns to me. 'Well, these troughs are alive with bees, butterflies, hoverflies, and now, one of my favourite insects. You really do know how to keep the pollinators happy, Gillian. Good work.'

I grin so hard, my face aches. Is this a sign? A sign that I can finally stop treading water; finally stop worrying that death is coming for me early, as it did for Dave? Is it a sign that I can finally get on with living my life?

35

'Up you get,' I say to my mother on the day of the awards ceremony. I yank back her bedroom curtains and open the window to allow the fresh air and the warmth of the sunshine in. 'We've got a big day ahead of us.'

She pulls the duvet back over her head. 'Leave me alone. I'm not well.'

'What's wrong with you that a nice breakfast and trip out won't rectify?' I can feel dread starting to erode my excitement. Is my mother going to torpedo my big day?

Zak appears at the threshold to her bedroom, holding a tray. 'Morning, Nan. Hope you're hungry.' On the tray is a plate containing a fresh almond croissant – my mother's favourite – a cup of coffee and a freshly plucked pink rosa rugosa Rubra from the communal gardens in a small rose vase.

'Aw, our boy's so thoughtful.' I reach behind my mother's shoulders to help her sit up. 'Look at that, Mum. He's made you a cuppa and brought you a rose. What a little gentleman!'

My mother grimaces at me. 'I'm not hungry. I'm not thirsty and I didn't ask for a rose.' She side-eyes the vase. 'Is that from the gardens? They're bloody thorny as hell. Are you trying to kill me?'

"Course not, Nan,' Zak says. 'They just smell amazing, so I thought I'd –'

'Is that an almond croissant?' she asks.

I nod. 'Fresh from Sainsbury's this morning. She'd just put them out.'

Shunting herself up the bed, she beckons Zak close. 'Give that here, son. You're a good lad.'

I wink at Zak and plump Mum's pillows. 'We've got to be out in half an hour, so get your laughing gear round that pastry, eh?'

Mum shoots me a withering glance, but she's already tucking into the croissant, scattering greasy flakes over the bed. 'That Barty Bing going?' she asks, spitting half-chewed marzipan onto the tray.

'Yes, Mum.'

She regards me momentarily and downs her coffee almost in one gulp. 'Better get my gnashers in.'

By the time the sugar and caffeine have hit her bloodstream, she's a different woman. I haven't managed to get her showered and dressed so fast in quite some time.

'What you dawdling for, boy?' she asks Zak, pushing him out of the way to get to the cupboard. 'Get my wheelchair into your mother's car, will you? It ain't gonna push itself to Wisley.'

'Oh, Gill. I'm so glad to see you,' Mike says when we arrive at the church hall. He's standing out front, wringing his hands – not figuratively, but literally. He looks pale grey and his skin has a clammy sheen to it. He's visibly shivering, though at 9.55am, it's already twenty degrees outside. 'I don't know why, but I've never been this nervous before an awards ceremony. This is worse than when I was up for the DT Brown Trophy for white potatoes at the National Vegetable Society's National Championships. *Much* worse.' He holds his hands up and looks at them askance. 'Why have my fingers gone funny?'

I can't help but laugh at the sight of the King of King Edwards showing me his lily-white fingertips. 'Bad circulation?' I say. 'I shouldn't worry about it, Mike. You just need something to eat and drink. Have you had any brekky?'

He shakes his head.

'Men!' I hasten back to the car, where Zak and my mother are waiting, chatting amiably about the eligibility of Barty Bing, and whether or not Marjorie is genuine competition for his affections. From the back seat, I snatch up the paper bag containing the second pain au chocolat I'd ambitiously earmarked for myself, not realising that nerves would suppress my appetite. From the drinks holder, I retrieve my Thermos full of Mum's Lidl mystery-German-brand coffee. I take both back to Mike and press them into his hands.

'There. Eat this and drink that. Now, where are the others?'

He inclines his head towards the door. His teeth are chattering ever so slightly. 'In there. Everyone's had a sleepless night. Everyone's on edge. Marj and Val have been downing effervescent co-codamol like it's tequila. "For the nerves", they said.'

'Okay.' I link arms with Mike and steer him inside. 'Let's see who's still standing.'

We venture into the hall, which smells more warm and dusty than damp today. I spy my botanical brothers-and sisters-in-arms huddled around Marjorie's coffee urn.

'Morning, all,' I say. 'It's judgement day. Greatness awaits, gang. Are you ready?'

Most are nodding too vehemently, apart from Cath, who yawns like a bored lioness.

Barty Bing seems unaffected. 'Morning, Gillian. Are you bringing the lovely Lily to our big event?' His false teeth start to slip out of his mouth, and he's forced to push them back in.

'Yes, Barty. She's keyed up on sugar and ready to rumble. Looks like we all are. Are we gonna win, guys?!' Suddenly, I feel like some kind of low-rent motivational speaker, like David Brent in *The Office*.

'Who the hell knows?' Neil says, rubbing his eyes. 'Come on. Let's get this over with before we all expire from nerves and sleep deprivation.'

When we arrive in the car park of RHS Wisley, I feel insignificant and out of place. All around me, pot-bellied, male veteran gardeners are shaking hands. There are scores of older women too – all Women's Institute types like Marjorie, who seem to know one another. The odd person smiles Marj's way, but she's not greeted with effusive kisses on both cheeks and carefully choreo-graphed embraces. I observe how the odd person nods to Mike, but again, he seems like an outsider in this niche little world of the semi-professional green-fingered.

Pushing my mother in her wheelchair towards the

single-storey entrance, I glance at our group, walking on ahead. Seth, the weed-farming tradesman, who presents like a roadman but is actually a young carer; Phoebe, the middle-class Extinction Rebel trying so hard to be street-tough; Val, the pensioner punk; Cath, the mousy perma-stressed GP; Neil, the Dalí-moustache-twirling teacher; Mike, the imitation planning officer in his Sunday best Farah slacks and lemon polo shirt, who is actually a single father with Monty Don dreams; and Marjorie, a modern-day Miss Marple type, who is more Peckham market than St Mary Mead. And me. Boring old me, with my guilt and my complex grief and my mommy issues. We are a motley bunch. Perhaps we don't belong here.

Then, when we are assembled inside the enormous glasshouse, where the ceremony is to take place, surrounded by tropical foliage tall enough to caress the lofty glazed ceiling in some places, I spot our rivals on the other side of the reception space. Croydon. There they are – dressed to impress, with Betty Moule at the helm.

'Is she wearing sequins *again*?' Val asks. She nudges Marjorie. 'Oi, Look! Barnacle Betty reckons she's gardening's answer to Joan Collins. Silly old cow.'

Marjorie takes out a pair of glasses. Glancing at Barty and quite clearly deciding that he isn't watching at this moment, she pushes the specs on and gawps at Barnacle Betty. 'Oh, good Lord! One can't believe the inappropriateness of it. She looks like RuPaul.'

'Never had you down as a fan of *Drag Race*, Marj,' I say.

'One isn't.' Marjorie curls her lip. 'And sequins are environmentally disastrous.' She frowns, peering through her X-ray NHS specs at the Croydon team. 'No sign of that horrible orange man, thankfully.'

'He'll be on remand in prison,' I say. 'They won't bail a murderer and major fraudster.'

Seth points to Taylor Jones. 'Well, that mouth-breather, what pushed me off the ladder and nearly knocked your block off, ain't got no shame. I should go over there and . . . I dunno . . . give him a good shove or something.'

I size up Taylor Jones. Today, he is wearing a collared shirt and suit trousers, though his sullen expression and defensive hands in pockets give him more an air of someone about to attend a court appearance than an awards ceremony. I reach over and squeeze Seth's shoulder. 'The wheels of justice grind slow but fine. He'll get his comeuppance. Don't you worry.'

'I ain't so sure. Not while he's got the likes of Betty Moule protecting him. He's hiding behind her being a respectable old biddy, now Cromarty's out of the picture.'

I see that Barnacle Betty is flanked not just by Taylor the thug, but also Louise Lampard, the erotic novelist, and Neville Studley, the disgraced GP. 'What a bunch. If they win, after behaving like such lowlives, there's something wrong with the universe.'

'Well, *I* can't believe Dr Touchy Feely has the temerity to stand there grinning,' Cath says. 'He's the worst of the lot, as far as I'm concerned. Pervert.'

There is the sound of a PA system whistling into life. A red-faced man in a grey expensive-looking tweed suit and bow tie starts to speak. He sounds like King Charles on tramadol but with hair curtains like a 1980s Michael Heseltine. 'My lords, ladies, and gentlemen, thank you for travelling from all over the British Isles today for the fifty-sixth Golden Trowel Gardening Association awards ceremony. I am the Club's chief executive, Sir Timothy Fitzgerald-Smythe.' He opens his arms like a tweedy Messiah. 'Welcome to RHS Wisley.'

The most British-sounding round of polite applause that I have ever heard ripples around the audience.

Sir Timothy Landed-Gentry smiles the toothy smile of an excited, ageing horse being shown sugar lumps. He toys with his bow tie. 'Today, we will announce the runners-up and winner of the Golden Trowel for the "Best Community Gardening Club in Britain" – our most prestigious award.' His happy horse smile fades abruptly. 'First though, let us observe one minute of respectful silence to acknowledge the passing of one of the Golden Trowel Gardening Association's longest-serving patrons, erstwhile "Trowellies" judge and a former worthy contestant, Miss Dorothy Gloucester.'

There is no mention made of Dotty Gloucester dying in suspicious circumstances or Luke Cromarty having been arrested for her murder. But as we stand and pay our respects, I notice the silence is broken by the other hopefuls whispering to one another and staring over at the Croydon group. Presumably gossip travels just as fast on Golden Trowel grapevines as any other, and judging by people's pointed scowls, the grapes are distinctly sour, where Betty Moule and her acolytes are concerned.

When the minute is up, Sir Timothy Landed-Gentry presses the knot of his bow tie as if he's switching himself back on, and the smile returns. 'May Dorothy rest in peace.' Now he's back in full game-show host mode. 'Of course, you'll all have heard that this year's Golden Trowel Award winner will attract the one-off prize of . . . and I can't quite believe this . . . the deeds to Dorothy Gloucester's exclusive Surrey golf club.' He looks around at the audience of gasping, grinning competitors. 'How about that, ladies and gentlemen?'

Members of the audience 'ooooh', even though we are all well aware of what is up for grabs, because it's been covered in all the national newspapers, as well as in the GTG Association's regular e-bulletins.

Not everyone is delighted, however, because I hear the flat Northern twang of another GTG team member saying, not quite beneath her breath, 'Some use that is, if you live in bloody Yorkshire!'

Our host is unaware of any disgruntlement though, or perhaps he simply doesn't care, because he's still baring those teeth in an equine grin. 'You may have read Miss Gloucester's frankly *genius* stipulation that the golf club is to be converted into an organic flower farm by the winners.' He starts to applaud dead Dotty's idea. 'Simply inspired. What a magnificent gardening challenge, *par excellence.*' Now he's wagging his finger. 'But don't forget there will also be a double-page spread in every issue of the widely read *Wise* magazine in the next twelve-month period.'

There is more applause. Somebody makes a wisecrack up near the front, which I can't hear, and it's greeted with nervous laughter.

'It's like sodding *Sale of the Century*,' Mum says to Val. 'Any minute, I'm expecting Nicholas Parsons to come on and reveal a Datsun Cherry with some bikini-clad Barbie sprawled on the bonnet.'

'Nicholas Parsons is dead, Lil,' Val says.

'Exactly.'

They both burst into a fit of cackling, and everybody turns around to stare at us.

'Just behave, will you?' I hiss in my mother's ear, gripping the handles of her wheelchair tightly with frustration. 'You're making a spectacle of us.'

She waves me away. 'Who's the mother here? Me or you?'

'Just pipe down, for God's sake.'

I'm tempted to wheel her into a clump of banana palms, where she won't get up to mischief, but Marjorie treats me to a steely stare and presses her index finger to her lips.

Sir Timothy Landed-Gentry clears his throat. 'Let's begin this glorious British celebration of all things horticultural with a message from our sponsors, *Wise*.'

There is a giant screen at one end of the stage. The image of two insanely attractive older people – George Clooney and Sharon Stone standards of glamour – pops up, and a slick corporate video of them starts to play. The silver foxes play tennis, drink cocktails in a smart bar, and go on a cruise to somewhere far-flung and tropical,

355

looking immaculately coiffed, stylishly dressed, and slim at all times. The film ends with a shot of them wearing pastels while tending flawless roses in the rooftop garden of a ridiculously expensive-looking penthouse, complete with views of the City of London.

An A-list ageing Bond actress does the voiceover: '*Wise* is proud to sponsor the Golden Trowel Awards, because we know the biggest adventure in later life starts in the garden.'

'My life is just like that,' Val says, tongue in cheek. Even for this borderline bling ceremony, she's come dressed in her usual off-gardening-duty uniform of ripped jeans, faded old Sex Pistols T-shirt, and a beat-up black leather biker's jacket.

'Load of bullshit,' my mother says. 'That's how they get away with charging through the nose for their insurance and holidays. They're selling a lie.' She cranes her neck to see beyond the limits of her wheelchair. 'Is there any free booze at this thing?'

'No. Think of your bladder,' I say. 'And shush.'

The prize-giving begins in earnest, as Sir Tim Landed-Gentry announces various winners of lesser prizes – best blooms (roses and dahlias get the biggest applause), best vegetables (Mike insists the guy who wins for top spud is a lousy amateur), best private gardens and allotments (Marjorie pooh-poohs the Brontë-country pensioner who wins as a poor facsimile of a plantswoman, who inherited most of her mature garden intact from a protégé of Gertrude Jekyll). A steady stream of grey-haired, dishevelled types, all looking uncomfortable in their smart clothes, mounts the stage to collect a silver-coloured trowel trophy from some *Wise* bigwig. We all clap and clap and clap and clap, and I start to get terrible flashbacks to Zak's school's prize-giving days, which went on for four hours and always resulted in every child getting an award, and every parent ending up with deep vein thrombosis from sitting on hard seats and repetitive strain injury from applauding.

Eventually, the minor awards have all been given out, and it's time for the main event.

'I'm so nervous, my feet have gone numb,' Mike says. He has gravitated towards me and we are now standing shoulder to shoulder.

'That's not nerves,' I whisper. 'I told you. It's poor circulation. Hardly surprising – we've been hanging around for over an hour.' I study his face, and he's still drained of all colour. It's clear that this award means everything to Mike. Winning would be his 'sign' – a green light to change his life for the better. I take his hand. 'Even if we don't win, you can still do all of those things you were dreaming of. That's what business loans are for.'

'We're not going to win. I can feel it. Croydon's going to get it. Or maybe I've underestimated Harrogate. They're very, very strong this year.'

'Whoever's won, it's already in the bag,' I say. 'The decision is in that envelope the host is holding. Making yourself sick with worry isn't going to achieve any-thing.' Mandi-with-an-I would be proud of me. 'We've either won or we haven't. It's nought or one hundred per cent.'

Zak inserts himself into our little tête-à-tête. 'That's what we call "mum-stats". And she's never wrong.'

Three people walk onto the stage, and I recognise the judges who came to see our planting.

'They're here,' Marjorie says, her eyes shining. 'This is it.' She holds crossed fingers in the air and turns back to the stage.

Sir Tim brandishes the golden envelope and speaks solemnly. 'My lords, ladies, and gentlemen, it's time for the award we've all been waiting for. Who will be the best community gardening club in Britain? Who will win that incredible top prize?'

Neil presses his hands to his mouth. Cath's balling her fists. Seth puts his arm around Phoebe. Val and Marjorie hold hands, and Mike and I stand side by side, our fingers just touching and channelling what feels like a billion volts of nervous electricity. Barty, meanwhile, has been side-tracked by my mother's winsome smile and is grinning back at her like a loon.

'Now, we asked the national treasure, Monty Don from *Gardeners' World*, to present this award, but sadly he had prior commitments. In his place though, I am delighted to announce that presenting this year's award is celebrity gardener lookalike, Donty Mon, from Scott Cezanne lookalikes agency in Scunthorpe.' He puts his hands together and beams at the curly-haired imposter in a leather jerkin and scruffy trousers.

'Donty fucking Mon?' my mother asks. 'Have they been sniffing Gaviscon Advance?'

Donty makes a very short speech in a very strong

regional accent, saying how glad he is to be in the Wisley glasshouse for such a grand occasion. He waves the envelope in the air, and I spot Betty Moule clasping her hands to her glittering chest. 'Before we open this, though, I'm delighted to announce the shortlistees.' He looks at some notes on the lectern.

Mike grabs my hand. His palms are clammy; his finger-tips freezing.

Donty reads aloud: 'First up, the Penrith Growers for their excellent, colourful displays in difficult terrain and weather conditions.'

We all clap. I feel beads of cold sweat roll down my back to my waistband.

'Next, we have those masters and mistresses of formal bedding displays, the Harrogate Horticulturalists.'

Most of the room erupts into rapturous applause. There is even a wolf-whistle. Harrogate is a popular choice. Maybe Mike was right. Maybe they will win.

Donty continues to read his script: 'What would the finalists' list be without the Croydon Diggers and Dibbers, with their awe-inspiring traditional British planting?' He claps for the first time. Maybe even Donty Mon is on Luke Cromarty's payroll, or perhaps he's just a fan of Louise Lampard's saucy books.

'And finally, let's give a round of applause to the Bromley Botanists, who are dazzling this year with tropical-style displays.'

With some flourish, Donty takes the sheet out of the golden envelope. 'And the winner of this year's Golden Trowel Award is . . .'

I sense our entire group collectively inhale sharply and hold their breath. I feel my heart bouncing against my ribcage; the blood rushes in my ears.

Donty Mon nods and smiles. 'The Bromley Botanists' gardeners' club, for their impressive contemporary schemes and pollinator-friendly planting. Well done, folks.'

Mike whoops, lifts me up, and spins me around so hard that I almost knock Mum's wheelchair flying.

'We did it!' Val shouts. She gives a two-fingered salute to Betty Moule and gestures to Taylor Jones that she's got her eye on him. Then she tries and fails to high-five an oblivious Marjorie. 'We only bloody did it.'

Leaving Val hanging, Marjorie is beaming from ear to ear. She looks up to the ceiling of the glasshouse and presses her palms together in supplication. 'The Lord smiles on the righteous. Praise be.'

Neil throws his straw trilby in the air. Cath merely nods, but her eyes are smiling, at least.

Seth, Phoebe, and Zak all hold hands and jump up and down together, screaming with delight.

'Let's welcome Bromley to the stage to receive their award, which will be presented by the CEO of our sponsors, *Wise*,' Sir Tim Landed-Gentry says, clapping furiously.

Zak breaks free from the other youngsters and returns to where I'm standing with Mum and a dazed-looking Barty Bing.

'You did it, Mum,' Zak says. 'I'm so proud of you. Dad would have been so proud of you. Well done.' He enfolds me in a tight bear hug and plants a noisy kiss on my cheek. 'You're brilliant and by far the best mum in the world.'

'I can't believe it,' I say, pressing my hands to the side of my head. 'This is it. *This* is the sign.' I exhale hard and feel almost like I'm letting go of the stress of the last ten years. I look around at my new friends and the cheering crowd and my ecstatic-looking family – even my mother is cheering and punching the air, as if she's been rooting for us all along and this is the best-ever news – and I realise that *this* is the real prize. I haven't just won a share of a farm that I'd own (with restrictive covenants in place and no start-up budget), a trophy, and some publicity. What I've won is far more precious than that. I've won confidence in myself and the companionship of good people. I've won a fresh zeal for living and a new professional path to take. I've won the respect of my mother and the admiration of my son. I've won the trust of others and a giant store of optimism for myself.

Before I consider the ramifications of what I'm about to do, I turn to Mike, grab his big potato head, and plant a kiss on his lips. It's not a lingering kiss. It's a kiss of triumph and celebration. Though maybe there *is* a little bit of tongue involved. When I pull away, I see surprise and delight in his eyes.

'Oh,' he says.

'I'm going to take that redundancy package,' I say. 'Are you ready for what comes next?'

He clicks his heels and salutes. 'At your service, ma'am.'

'Then let's go get our trophy.'

36

'I don't believe it. This is really happening. We won,' I mutter beneath my breath as I make my way through the crowd to the stage at the front.

All around me, our fellow gardeners and their supporters are clapping and smiling. They reach out to pat us on the back as we pass through, as if we're premiership footballers, returning to our team's hometown with the Premier League Trophy. My heartbeat is thunderous, yet I feel barely there – as if I'm walking on clouds. The colours inside the glasshouse are brighter, the chlorophyll smell of the plants stronger.

Marjorie takes the lead, mounting the couple of steps to the stage as though she's marching for Jesus. We follow her, single file, amid the bright flashes of people's cameras, and all I can think of is, *Don't trip up; hold your belly in; I wish Dave could see this.*

We all shake hands with Sir Tim, Donty Mon (who really does look astonishingly like the real deal), and the suit from *Wise*. Well, I say we all shake hands, but Seth and Phoebe insist on fist-bumping them instead, much to the dignitaries' visible bemusement. At the front of the stage, Marjorie is already holding the gleaming golden trowel-shaped trophy, staring into the crowd like the proverbial rabbit caught in headlights. Mike takes his place next to her. He is red in the face and grinning out at the sea of his mainly adoring peers (though there are some sour-looking faces among the smiles, including that of Betty Moule and her co-conspirators). In a fit of magnanimity that I can't quite believe, Marjorie actually holds out the award to Mike, and together, they lift it high into the air.

'Would you like to say a few words?' Sir Tim Landed-Gentry shouts to me over the rapturous applause.

He's. Asking. Me. I swallow hard and become aware that I'm gawping at him, open-mouthed. I will myself to speak. 'Er, I'm not . . .'

'Go on, Gill,' Val says. 'Stand up and be counted, girl.'

Who the hell am I to give the speech? I didn't even join the group until the spring. I'll bet Mike had one prepared and everything, yet the others are all waving me towards the lectern.

I gawp at the microphone, wondering what to say. I've watched Colin accept an award before at an insurance conference. I guess I'll just copy what he did. 'Er, on behalf of the Bromley Botanists, I'd like to thank the judges, the GTG Association, Sir Tim, Donty, and the people at *Wise* for . . . er . . .' I scan the crowd for Zak and my mother. At first, I can't see them. But then, two enormous men part company and I catch sight of my little family, both waving avidly.

Zak gives me the thumbs up and starts shouting, 'Go, Mum! Go, Mum! Go, Mum!' He whoops for good measure.

I feel suddenly like my own skin is too tight and I turn

to Mike. 'Do you want to take over?' I take a step backwards from the mic.

He shakes his head, all smiles. 'Your time to shine, Gill.'

Moving back into the spotlight, I wrack my brains for some witty nuggets of wisdom. 'Thanks to the bees,' is all I come out with.

People are starting to titter. The journalists at the front, holding their little recording devices, are all staring at me as though I've just taken off my bra in public and am wearing the right cup as a hat (and I've honestly not done that since I was twenty-four). *Come on, Gill. Turn the car crash around. Think charismatic thoughts. You weren't always in insurance.*

I clear my throat. 'Thanks to the bees, because they inspired our planting scheme,' I say. I take a deep breath. 'Because for our club, it was never just about flowers. It was also about sustainability and the environment.' Can I find the right words? Yes. I feel them start to flow of their own accord as I see a few of the journalists nodding encouragingly. 'We needed plants that can withstand hotter, drier conditions . . . as well as the odd classic British torrential downpour. We wanted colours that the pollinators and local residents alike would love. Our schemes are about making Bromley beautiful, but also bringing biodiversity back to the suburbs, so that my son can enjoy watching wildlife flourish – the sort of wildlife that was a glorious part of my own 1970s childhood: bees, butterflies, moths, beetles, hedgehogs, lizards, newts, frogs . . . things we thought would never disappear, but which are now dwindling in number terrifyingly quickly.'

People start to applaud. I allow myself a smile that is more than just a nervous rictus grin. 'It's important for you all to know that this award mainly comes off the back of the expertise of our longstanding members, Marjorie Bloom, Val Novak, and Mike Berisford. They have generously passed their knowledge on to the rest of us – Neil, Cath, Seth, Phoebe, and myself – so please put your hands together and give an extra hard clap for them.'

Everyone but the Croydon members are applauding and whistling their appreciation now. Marjorie turns to me, and the happiness seems to radiate from deep within her. Mike's face is so bright red, it looks as though he's made from pure joy, if joy was red and hot and a bit sweaty. Val merely flicks the audience a wry smile and a peace sign.

At my side, Sir Tim makes a move to reclaim the audience's attention, but I find the words haven't finished with me yet.

I hold my hand up and turn back to the audience. 'But actually . . .' There is a squawk of feedback, though I continue undeterred. 'I think it's this mixing of generations and levels of expertise that has allowed us to flourish as a team, despite some quite traumatic ups and downs that didn't only involve slugs and aphid infestation.' I look directly at Betty Moule and then Taylor Jones. 'We've endured systematic acts of vandalism and serious injury that resulted in the hospitalisation of one of our members.'

There is a collective gasp from the crowd.

My righteous fervour has disabled my filter, and I can feel the truth trying to swan-dive off my tongue. 'And it's worth acknowledging that the only reason this year's Golden Trowel Award is worth multimillions is that poor old, extremely generous Dorothy Gloucester unexpectedly had her life snatched from her . . .'

There is a sharp intake of breath from the audience. I look out at a sea of their uncomfortable faces, and realise that not only has Cromarty not been convicted of murder (yet), but it is not my place to ruin this wonderful event for everyone by foisting the grisly truth on them.

'. . . in unfortunate circumstances.' I clear my throat and notice Marjorie in my peripheral vision gesticulating that I should wind things up. 'Poor Dotty loved gardening *so* much that she selflessly decided to pass her passion *and* her considerable fortune on to the next generation of gardeners. I thank her from the bottom of my heart for that.' I look up to the ceiling and put my hand on my chest. 'Dotty, we'll do your memory proud, I promise.'

Have I clawed it back? People are smiling again, albeit with uncertainty etched on their weather-beaten faces.

'So, anyway, if this award is a mark of anything, it's resilience and the sheer bloody-minded will to endure . . . just like Mother Nature. God bless her. Thank you.'

I step back from the lectern, wondering where all that came from. I peer out into the gathered band of gardeners, their friends and families, bigwigs in the gardening industry, and journalists. Even the oldest ones, who have been sitting down, get to their feet and clap. Even *my mother* gets out of her chair and treats me to a deafening wolf-whistle.

'Was that okay?' I ask Neil, giggling nervously.

'It was perfect,' he said. 'Now, let's go back to Bromley and get astonishingly drunk.'

'Back to mine?' Marjorie asks.

'Brilliant.'

'That's three margheritas, two pepperonis, four ham and mushroom . . .' I hold the phone to my chest and shout through to Val. 'What did you ask for again, Val?'

'Four seasons,' she shouts back. 'Marj wants a giardiniera, no cheese, extra anchovies.'

'Did you hear all that?' I ask the waitress on the other end of the phone. I put in the rest of the pizza order for everyone and end the call.

'*One requires a giardiniera, no cheese, extra anchovies.*' My mother is mimicking Marjorie in a high-pitched voice. "Course one does.' She looks borderline sour, though the gin and tonic she's making short shrift of is keeping her on the right side of the line. 'Lady Bountiful can't have something normal, can she?'

'Oh, come on, Mum. I thought you got on with Marj. You're only saying that because Barty opted to sit with them lot in the living room, and you're in here with me and Mike.' I kick the brake off her wheelchair and push her into the hall, towards the living room. 'Come on, Mrs Fielding. Your adoring public requests the pleasure of your company.'

368

Barty gets to his feet immediately on seeing Mum. 'Lily. Why don't you come and sit next to me?'

Mum cracks a smile. 'Oh, Bartholomew. Aren't you the gentleman?' She's putting on her poshest voice – the kind she reserves for handsome doctors when she's admitted to hospital, and any kind of emergency service worker, as long as they look like Stewart Granger.

I make my way back to the kitchen and take my seat next to Mike, who is opening a can of ale.

He pours the billowing amber liquid into a tall glass, sips the foamy head, and frowns. 'Not as good as my dandelion homebrew,' he mutters, setting the glass back down. When he turns to me, the frown is gone. 'So, you were saying about taking voluntary redundancy . . .'

I nod. 'Well, I don't know precisely how much they're offering, because I was just focused on keeping my job. I *think* it's one month's salary for every year of service. I've been there for about fifteen years, so that's . . .' I try to do the maths in my head, but the gin is clouding my calculative capabilities. I try to count on my fingers, to no avail. 'Some money.'

'A decent chunk of change,' Mike says.

'Yep. Maybe enough to scrape by on for eighteen months. But don't forget, I'd still have to pay the mortgage, keep food on the table, keep paying Carol . . . and I don't have any real savings knocking around. The biggest obstacle is us raising the set-up cost for a flower farm of that size. The thought of getting into debt for maybe a couple of hundred thou terrifies me, even if we'd be sharing the liability.'

'Ah, well, I've had some thoughts about that . . .' Mike says, raising his index finger. 'Have you got some paper and a pen?'

Our pizzas arrive. While we eat, Mike draws up some rough expenditure and income projections on a pad Majorie clearly uses for shopping lists.

'There! I think that covers everything,' he says. He drums the pen on his teeth thoughtfully. 'You know, it's not nearly as bad as I thought. Now, we just need the others to commit.'

'No time like the present,' I say. 'Let's sound them out.'

We bring Mike's forecasts to the others in the living room, interrupting the tipsy celebrations with this bitter-sweet little dose of reality.

'I took the liberty of doing quite a bit of research over the last few weeks,' Mike says, sitting on Marjorie's pouffe, his fleeting grin faltering swiftly as he notices the bemused expression on Val's face.

'What the hell for?' she asks. 'We couldn't have known we'd win.'

'Ah, but "If you build it, they will come,"' Mike says. He pushes his glasses up his nose. The grin is back, and he looks at everyone in turn to check his *Field of Dreams* reference lands well. 'I looked at the cost of rent, fertiliser, slug pellets, organic pesticides, seeds, bulbs, corms, tubers, bare root stock, polytunnels, and all the tools and machinery we're short of. And then, in any spare time I had, I went round every florist in South-East London and the Kent borders, asking if they'd be interested in buying from a local grower. Just as a sample.'

Marjorie sets down her last slice of pizza and speaks in her small voice (slurring only slightly). 'Have you figures for which blooms they buy, at what times of the year, and in what quantities?'

'Yes, ma'am. At home, I've drawn up a spreadsheet showing a seasonal breakdown of what sells and when. Valentine's, Easter, seasonal bouquets and gift arrangements, bridal, funeral blooms, Christmas wreaths. I've got a best-guess cost for us producing those, and I've got a median figure for what the florists are currently paying Dutch wholesalers, per stem and per bunch. Obviously, that fluctuates regularly for a variety of reasons.'

Marjorie shakes her head with an air of resignation. 'Well, one can't possibly compete with the Dutch. They grow on such an industrial grand scale that they can afford to pass their economies on to florists.'

He holds his finger up. 'Ah, but what you're not taking into account is that upmarket florists in well-heeled or fashionable areas are willing to pay a bit more for bragging rights to the use of locally grown, organic flowers in their arrangements. They just pass the extra costs on to their wealthy customers.'

'What about making money, man?' Seth asks. 'The small print on Dotty G's estate says we have to run this malarkey as a not-for-profit. I can't live on no rosy glow and fresh air. I got commitments at home, yeah?'

Mike nods. 'Ah, well, there's the huge potential boon of bringing "Berisford's Black Gold" to market. *That* could be a complete game-changer.' He rubs his hands together. 'I've made some excellent distribution contacts while working at Dobbies.' He looks around at our suddenly sober-looking compatriots. 'Come on, guys! We have a golden opportunity here, so why on earth not reach for the stars? The gardening sector is worth billions. All we need to set these wheels in motion is a modest cash injection from each of us and a giant leap of faith.'

'How much?' Neil asks.

Mike then names the sum needed from each of us to fund the start-up.

The others are silent, looking at each other with raised eyebrows.

'Well?' I ask.

Seth stretches out his long legs and crosses his designer-trainer-clad feet. 'Yeah. I wasn't sure at first, but Mike's ideas do sound like they check out, man. I got the cash saved, and at my age, I got nothing to lose. I wanna be my own boss. I don't wanna spend the rest of my working life on no building site, and I think growing flowers would be a nice way to make a living. So, I'm game. Are you, Phoebs?'

Toying with her nose ring, Phoebe nods and smiles. 'My granddad will give me my share of the cash to put in. Better than buying a plot to rewild. At least this way, I'll have a proper career path.'

'Well, count me out,' Val says. 'I ain't got cash to invest. I'm a pensioner.'

'I'm afraid one has the same reservations,' Marjorie

says. 'And Val and I are too old to qualify for a business loan.'

'We'd still be short then,' I say. 'Poor old Dotty's lumbered us with a white elephant. Without enough start-up money, we can't make this work.'

I see the enthusiasm fading in Mike's eyes, like the red light going out in the eyes of Arnold Schwarzenegger's character at the end of *Terminator* 2. I cried at the end of that film, though Dave could never understand why. I'm aware of a lump in my throat right now, at the thought of my freshly forged hopes and dreams being smelted down in a boring, cashflow-prediction furnace. Or something.

'So, that's it, then?' Mike asks. 'Even if I put the lion's share of my tribunal win in, we're dead in the water, despite sitting on land worth tens of millions?' He sighs deeply. 'I guess it's never a bad time to upgrade the kitchen or pay a little extra into the old pension.'

'Jesus, you lot,' my mother says. 'It's like you've all lost a pound and found a penny. Cheer up! You just won a bloody award and a golf club!'

Nobody responds. The air in Marj's living room feels a little stiller and staler.

Barty breaks the uncomfortable silence with a 'Well . . .'

All eyes are on him, now. He puts his veined hands on his bony knees and smiles benignly at us all. 'As you know, I'm a retired solicitor.' He chuckles wistfully. 'One of the top corporate lawyers in London, I was.' He treats us to a brilliant Steradent smile, as his ill-fitting false teeth slip forward slightly. 'It was a rollercoaster of a career alright. I represented some of the top companies in the FTSE 500, over the years. Fought battles that nobody really cared about but that made huge differences to the economy. Some of the time, I was a force for good. Most of the time, I suppose I was a force for bad.' He's still smiling.

Phoebe looks at him aghast, as if she can't decide whether to be actively, vocally angry at Barty for perpetuating the capitalist stranglehold on the common people or not. 'You were one of *them*? You're *The Man*?'

Barty laughs amiably. 'Not really. But I worked for The Man, I suppose. And it paid very well, though it meant I never had time for a family. So, maybe now's the time to put something back. I've certainly got the money, so . . .' He leans towards me and utters the words I so longed to hear through loose-fitting dentures. 'As they say in *Dragon's Den*, "I'm in."'

37

'Well, go on,' I say, staring at the sealed envelope in Zak's hand. 'Aren't you going to open it?' The inside of the car feels too hot, smells too strongly of plastic, and is dusty enough to make my nose tingle. 'Come on, Zak. You're giving me a hot flush.'

My son is gripping the envelope that contains his AS result so tightly that his thumbnails have turned white. 'I don't know if I can do it.' Zak bites his lip. 'What if I've failed?'

I take his face between my hands, relishing the feel of his childishly soft skin. There is a downy moustache above his top lip and the wispy beginnings of a beard on his chin – mine and Dave's very nearly adult son – but he is still my little-big-boy. I can feel the anxiety emanating from his every pore. 'You won't have failed. You're a bright, bright young man. You worked like a Trojan. You'll be fine. Even if it's not what you're hoping for . . . It's only AS Further Maths. It's not the be-all and end-all. You've got another bite of the cherry next year with your A-Levels.'

'Right.' He nods and pulls free of my grasp. 'Okay. This is it.'

'Whatever happens, Zak, I'm proud of you and I love you.'

Tearing the envelope apart, he tweezes out the piece of paper containing his grade. He turns away from me to read it, and when he turns back, he has tears in his eyes.

'Oh, crap. What?' I ask, feeling like my heart is in a vice. 'What did you get?'

The tears give way to a killer smile. 'B, Mum. A bloody B! In Further Maths! I was expecting a D, if I was lucky.'

I throw my arms around my son in that too-tight space, but now it is only cramped because the car is full of love and happiness. 'Congratulations, you little star.' I plant a noisy kiss on his face. 'Okay, tonight, it's whatever you want for dinner, and we're going to go to the tree to tell Dad.'

Zak is now wearing an uncertain half-smile, as if he can't quite believe his own luck. 'It's a deal.'

'Sorry I'm late, everyone,' I say, opening the door to the meeting room. 'AS-Level results day.'

'Ah, here she is at last,' Colin says as I enter. He glances at his watch and starts to slow-clap me. 'Chislehurst Green's answer to Alan Titchmarsh.' He's smiling, but there's derision etched into the lines around his eyes. He smooths his joke tie down – today's theme is *The Simpsons*. 'I saw the double-page spread in my mother's new edition of *Wise* magazine. You're quite the celebrity now. "A moving speech Greta Thunberg would have been proud of," they said.' He strokes Homer Simpson's belly. 'We'll have to make sure you don't start staging sit-ins outside the office. Ha ha.'

Feeling my temperature rise, I peer at my colleagues

from the other regional offices, whom I haven't seen since before the competition win. Happily, they don't seem primed to ridicule my gardening club's achievement. Jess blows me a chef's kiss, Barney gives me the thumbs up, Hardeep, Maisie, Beth, Saima, and Gavin all clap with gusto.

'Thanks, guys.'

'Well done, Gill,' Jess says. 'You can come up to Birmingham and sort my garden out for me, eh? I've been growing nothing but burst footballs and a rusty trampoline for the past five years.'

'Come to Glasgow,' Barney says. 'I'll give you a fifty-pound note to plant in my garden and see if you can't grow me a money tree.'

Beth plonks her handbag onto the meeting table, rummages in it, and then retrieves a die-cast toy BMW that presumably belongs to her young son. 'Here you go. Plant this, Gill. I'll have a 5 Series, please.'

As I take my colleagues' fantasy-gardening orders, I notice Colin looking down at his laptop and clicking away at the mousepad. On the meeting room's whiteboard, a raft of figures appears along with a pie chart.

'Er, can we dispense with the frivolity, please, and get down to the quarterly forecasts?' Colin's lips almost disappear, and one by one, he fixes us all with an accusatory stare, as if we're naughty schoolchildren, disrupting class. He then waits until we're all paying attention, even though we'd already fallen silent.

Jess is writing something down. She tears a page from her notebook and passes me a note beneath the table.

As I unfold the note, Colin starts the meeting. 'There's been a change to targets, you'll all be happy to hear, thanks, in part, to Gill's discovery of a very large fraudulent claim, which has been rejected and is now being prosecuted, along with a separate murder charge.'

I glance down at Jess's note.

If you plant Colin's joke tie, could you grow him a sense of humour?

I stifle the urge to laugh and make every effort not to meet her gaze.

Oblivious to our below-table shenanigans, Colin takes a crisp-looking copy of the *Evening Standard* from his laptop bag and slides it to the middle of the table. He taps on a photo of Luke Cromarty on the front page. 'I for one am very happy to see this daylight robber behind bars, even if he is just awaiting trial.' He raises an eyebrow at me and speaks with an air of conspiracy. 'A little birdie tells me he'll be looking at seven years, for the fraud alone. Life, if he's found guilty of murder too.' Colin rubs Homer Simpson's belly again between his fingers and thumb. 'And my little dickie bird also tells me there might well be group litigation against Sunset Pastures Homes. And maybe, just maybe, my dad will be one of those litigants. Bye bye, rickety walls and black mould, with a bit of luck. Hello again, decent living conditions and . . .' He clears his throat. '. . . my inheritance.'

'Can I borrow that paper, Colin?' I ask. 'I'd quite like to read the article on my break.'

'Sure.'

The meeting drags on in the usual way that regional team meetings always drag on, yet I know everything is about to change – certainly for me. I shift in my seat, unable to get comfortable. The figures in Colin's presentation are a meaningless jumble. Rather than listen to my colleagues' regional updates, I am replaying the last few weeks in my head: the competition win, the newspaper interviews, the research into flower farming, the business plan, my mother's improved behaviour and outlook, Zak's improved focus . . . the couple of evenings out I've had with Mike that might or might not have ended in tentative kissing. I am overwhelmed by a hot flush.

When the team meeting comes to an end, I say my goodbyes to my regional colleagues and hang around, pretending to tidy my paperwork.

Colin is packing away his laptop. He looks up at me. 'Oh, Gill. Still here? I thought you'd be going for lunch with the others.' He reaches over and pushes the *Evening Standard* towards me. 'You can take that. Go on. I don't need it back.'

'Thanks.' I roll up the newspaper and stick it in my bag. I swallow hard and ignore the ice in my gut. 'Actually, Colin, I wanted to speak to you.'

'Oh yes?' He looks at me expectantly.

I take a letter out of my bag and hand it to him. 'This is for you.'

He cocks his head to the side and frowns at the envelope. 'What's this?' He opens the letter and reads it for what seems like an age. Then he holds it out to me. 'I don't want this. Here. Take it. We'll pretend I didn't read it.'

I shake my head and refuse to take back the letter. 'Colin, I want the voluntary redundancy. Honestly, my mind's made up.'

'You're actually taking up professional *hedge-trimming*?' He starts to laugh at his own rapier wit, but then he must notice my thunderous expression, because he stops. 'Oh, you are actually planning to . . . ? Oh, come on, Gillian. You win one community gardening competition and you think you can trade in fifteen years at one of the UK's biggest insurance companies for what? A lawnmower and minimum wage, working in the driving rain and gale force winds? After all I did to save you your job?'

Every spiky, acidic, icy, venomous word I could say in response to his hypocrisy vies for attention in my mind, but I can hear Dave's voice telling me to *play it cool, Gill.* 'You offered, Colin, and I'm accepting. Voluntary redundancy. You have my three months' notice, but I'm happy to take it as paid gardening leave. Ha ha.'

Colin's sharp features tighten, giving him the look of a rodent with ill intent or piles. 'I don't believe I'm hearing this. Of all the cheek! You came begging to me to investigate the Cromarty fraud case in return for wiping the blot off your HR copy book. You *begged* me. And this is how you thank me for getting Janice off your back?'

Suddenly, I don't want to listen to Dave's laid-back-guy advice. I realise I am not Dave. I don't mind conflict and I've become something of a fighter of late. There is more of Lily Fielding in me than I'd previously cared to admit. But that's okay. Having 'Strong Woman™' DNA is a gift, not a curse. Mandi-with-an-I would be whooping and punching the air at my realisation and what I'm about to say next.

I assert my dominance by spreading my hands wide across the tabletop. 'The price has now gone up, Colin. I want what you gave Graham Dawson when he left. A year's salary *as well as* a month's pay for every year I've worked here, else I'll take you to a tribunal, and they can hear all about your attempts to constructively dismiss me, just because I'm a working single mother and a part-time carer for an infirm parent.' I smile sweetly, channelling Marjorie's steel hand in a baby-pink angora glove.

The colour drains from Colin's face, and when he speaks, his voice comes in but a whisper. 'Fine.' I watch his neck tendons stiffen above that idiotic tie. 'Leave it with me. I'll see what I can do.'

'Oh, you won't see what you can do, Colin. You can just damn well do it.'

I make my way to the disabled loo, lock the door behind me, and grin at myself in the mirror. 'You did it,' I tell my reflection. 'You're finally mistress of your own destiny, Gill Swanley. About time, too.'

With almost an hour of free time at my disposal, I cannot face sitting at my desk in that claustrophobic, open-plan hellhole, where Colin is free to glare at me from a distance across the sea of hot desks. I take the newspaper containing the front-page article about Cromarty, pretend that I haven't heard Armpits Alice's offer of correctly stirred coffee, and repair to my Volvo. Outside, I inhale the almost fresh air deeply, feeling as though I've been holding my breath since my showdown with Colin. Maybe I've been holding my breath for the last decade. It certainly feels like it.

Unlocking the car, I climb in, put the key in the ignition and switch the stereo on. Depeche Mode quietly has a 'Black Celebration' in the background, and the lyrics couldn't be more apt. I do feel like celebrating the fact that I've seen the back of another black . . . well, morning, if not yet the entire day. The countdown to freedom has begun.

I set the contents of my lunchbox on the dashboard, crack the windows and start to dig into my foul-smelling egg mayonnaise sandwich.

'Right, Cromarty,' I say, straightening the paper out with my free hand. 'Let's see what we've got here.'

I read the article. No salacious details are revealed beyond him being arrested for murder and major fraud, presumably because it would prejudice his court case. But the image of him being carted off in cuffs to a waiting police van is a satisfying one. I wonder who had been taking photographs at the scene of his arrest? Who disliked Cromarty enough to send photographic evidence of his downfall to the newspaper?

'Not a popular man, are you?' I say to the orange-faced fraudster.

Then I realise that the overhead vantage point gives it

away. 'Aha! One of your builders. Maybe our Seth sent it in. Or maybe he's not the only one who thinks you're a massive turd, Mr Dayglo Trainers. Ha. You reap what you sow, pal.'

Setting the paper on the passenger seat, I finish my lunch, feeling more excited for the future than I have for a long, long time. My egg sandwich has more flavour today. My reusable bottle of squash doesn't even taste of plastic and dishwasher salt. My apple is perfectly crisp and tart.

As I start to tidy my lunchtime mess up, I notice that the breeze blowing into the car has lifted the front page of the newspaper to reveal the stories on pages two and three. Though the screwed-up ball of tinfoil from my sandwich covers the accompanying photos, a headline catches my eye.

New Addington Man Named as Suspect
in Attempted Murder

Feeling the prickle of curiosity tap along my spine, aware that the hairs on my arms are standing to attention, and not just because of the breeze, I read on.

The police search for the suspect who brutally stabbed nineteen-year-old Jordan Tate outside the Eagle's Arms in West Croydon has ended with the arrest of New Addington man, Taylor Jones. Jones, a twenty-year-old apprentice joiner, is listed as a director of Sunset Pastures Homes – the retirement housing company set up by disgraced property developer Luke Cromarty. Detectives working on the case were tipped off when a media appeal for information resulted in them being sent mobile phone recordings of the incident by two members of the public. Jones, recently a finalist in the Golden Trowel Gardening Association's Club of the Year Award, has been denied bail and is being held on remand, awaiting trial for attempted murder.

'Wow, wow, wow.'

Blinking slowly, I re-read the short article. I then lift the ball of foil off the accompanying photos – a photo-fit of Taylor Jones, next to his actual mugshot in which he looks like the dead-eyed, mouth-breathing moron that he is. A cold sweat breaks out on my top lip when I contemplate quite what a nasty piece of work we've had a brush with. I feel instantly guilty that I risked Zak's safety by challenging Cromarty – a man who murdered for money and set his muscle, Taylor Jones, on us. But I hear Mandi-with-an-I's voice saying, *You can't know what you don't know, Gill.* And I could never have known the extent of Jones's violent proclivities. At least my efforts will put Cromarty behind bars. And it seems Taylor Jones has earned karmic payback for his attacks on me and my friends, all by himself.

'Good,' I say, closing the paper emphatically. 'That's that, then.'

38

'Ready?' Mike asks when I open my front door later. 'Your chariot awaits, ma'am.' He points to his car, where Hugo and Katie are sitting in the back seat, looking down, presumably at their phones. Hugo is picking his nose with gusto.

'Hi Mike!' Zak pulls on his coat. 'Did Mum tell you about my result?' His smile lights up his face as if there's a power surge in the National Grid.

Mike holds out his hand to shake. 'She certainly did. Many congratulations, young man.'

As I pull on my trainers, I can't help but sigh with satisfaction at the sight of Zak shaking hands amicably with Mike – my new business partner, my fellow gardener, my friend, and possibly more.

'What a day, eh?' I say.

'A lot to celebrate,' Mike says. 'And tonight's my treat. I've booked the restaurant you mentioned.' He checks his watch. 'We should be there in plenty of time, depending on the traffic.'

Setting the alarm and locking up, I look up at my house and realise it's time to fill it with new memories. I have finished treading water.

In Mike's car, I thumb out a message to Mandi-with-an-I, whom I'm supposed to be seeing tomorrow lunchtime.

Hi Mandi. Sorry to spring this on you last minute, but
I've got to cancel. I'll be in touch. Gill.

I feel a pang of sadness as I send the message, because I
know I will not go back to see Mandi-with-an-I, except
to give her a parting thank-you gift. But as I watch the
Victorian houses of Catford pass me by on the way to
the South Circular, I smile resolutely. I have no more
need of my therapy sessions. I am as healed as I will
ever be. I have started to make good decisions without
Mandi's emotional crutch. I am ready to take the stabilisers off and ride the bike of life on my own.

'Is this it?' Mike asks, pulling up by a copse of trees close
to Arsenal's Emirates Stadium.

I reach back to squeeze Zak's hand. 'Yep. This is it.
We won't be long.'

Zak and I leave Mike in his Mondeo and head for the
tree. Dave's tree. We link arms as we walk.

'Wow, it's got big since last year,' Zak says, gazing up
at the lush canopy and the dangling spiky fruits of the
London plane tree.

'Platanus × hispanica,' I say. 'I didn't know that was
its Latin name, but there you go. Now we both know!' I
run my hand over the mottled bark, which looks to have
been stripped almost bare by the two squirrels that spiral
up the trunk in some kind of kiss-chase for squirrels.
'Your tree's got a fancy name, Dave.'

Zak chuckles and sits on the dry ground that has
been spared the drizzle, thanks to the leaf cover. I sit

next to him, unbothered by any bird-poo stains my jeans might suffer. I put my arm around my son and pull him close.

'What do you want to say to Dad?' I ask, willing a welling tear to subside.

Zak's eyes are dry today. He is still smiling. 'I did amazing in my AS-Level Further Maths, Dad. I'm gonna apply to universities for maybe Chemistry, this coming October.' He looks sideways at me. 'Maybe.'

I throw my head back and laugh. 'Ha! Did you hear that, Dave? *Chemistry*. Your boy's a scientist. After all the bellyaching he did about Chemistry.'

'Maybe Computer Science. Maybe *Plant Science*.' Zak's eyes are wide. He's teasing me, knocking my arm with his shoulder. 'How about that? I could join the new business as your botanist in da house.'

For the first time in ten years of visiting the tree, we laugh and are buoyed by our good news and our brave efforts. I tell my dead husband about the gardeners' club and Cromarty and Taylor Jones and Colin being such a duplicitous arse and the competition win and the flower farm. There is a surfeit of news, after years of having little of note to report beyond the daily grind of work, eat, sleep, repeat. I don't tell Dave about Mike, though, because I feel like I want to keep that – whatever it may be, at this early stage – as something for me.

I am alive, and though I will always love Dave and I will spend my life missing him, I finally accept that the room in my heart is not finite. There is space to love again. Nothing else will ever compare with what I had with Dave. It will be different. It will be fresh and new, like the return of the grass after a drought, when the rains come again. This, I realise, is what life is: the endless cycle of a perennial, which dies in the winter but flourishes anew in the spring.

Slender as a sapling, Zak springs to his feet. 'Bye, Dad. I love you. See you again soon.' He hugs the trunk tightly and then steps back to look up at the tree's green canopy, wiping a solitary tear from his eye.

I spot a spiky round fruit on the ground and pick it up by its stem. Twirling it in my fingers, I smile as an idea occurs to me. 'Hey! Fancy growing a Dad-tree in the back garden?'

Zak links me, and we walk back to Mike's car. 'Only if we can plant it together. In fact, do you think I can help out with the new flower farm during school holidays? I'd really like that.'

'It's a deal,' I say, pausing to kiss him on his forehead. The ground feels softer beneath my feet – I am buoyed by the thought of the many unanticipated riches gardening has brought me – freedom, friendship, and bonus time with my beloved son, before he flies the nest. Today, I feel like the luckiest woman in the world. 'Welcome to the gardeners' club.'

Acknowledgements

The Gardeners' Club started as a very, very different story back in 2010. It began life as a sample called *Not For Profit* – a few funny chapters about a rebellious, drunken dreamer who was miserable in her job, inspired by my time as a professional fundraiser working in London. My friend and erstwhile Puffin publisher, Shannon Cullen, liked it enough to send it to her editor colleague at Michael Joseph back in 2012, but the market at the time wasn't ready for a very early precursor to Fleabag. 2012 was a different country, in literature terms.

I shelved the project for two years, then came back to it in 2014. While I was waiting for my debut crime-fiction deal for *The Girl Who Wouldn't Die* to be negotiated, I rewrote those early sample chapters, transforming them into a full-length contemporary women's novel called *Gardening Leave*, featuring an unhappy conveyancing solicitor (see the theme emerging?!), who finds solace in floristry. My agent, Caspian, couldn't place the novel in an all-but-dead women's market. Still, my main character was growing up with me, and I felt I had something to say about middle-aged misery and horticultural pursuits.

So, scroll forward to 2024 (the year in which I wrote *The Gardeners' Club*), and Penguin Michael Joseph editorial director, Hannah Smith, saw the potential in my latest sample chapters. She bought *The Gardeners' Club*, and under her guidance, I have turned my story about a green-fingered, overstretched middle-aged mother facing existential despair into a novel primarily about gardening and murder most foul. But *The Gardeners' Club* is also about loss, the struggles of the sandwich generation, friendship and renewal. This is perhaps the ultimate example of writing being all about rewriting as well as dogged, bloody-minded persistence. What a journey this story has been on . . . rather like me!

It has been a team effort to get *The Gardeners' Club* off my laptop and onto bookshops' and readers' bookshelves. So I must thank the following people for their support and input in that lengthy process. Thank you:

To my darling family, Christian, Natalie and Adam, for putting up with me when I'm 'in the tunnel' and chained to my laptop seven days a week, week in, week out, during the penning of a first draft. Their encouragement spurs me on to keep writing, and they will always laugh at my shocking jokes where others merely stare at me in disbelief.

To my literary agent, Caspian Dennis, for being my biggest champion as well as a terrific friend, with the best-kept facial hair in publishing. He also wins points for laughing at my shocking jokes. Caspian has stuck with this story, in its various iterations, for ten years. We got there in the end, kiddo! Thanks also to all the others in the crack team at Abner Stein – especially Sandy, Jasmine, Rebecca, Tom and Ray.

To my editor, Hannah Smith, and the excellent team at Penguin Michael Joseph. Thinking back to how this book came into being, it is surely destiny that PMJ should be *The Gardeners' Club*'s home. Thank you for loving Gill, Mike Potato, Marj and pals as much I do! Thanks for 'getting' my gardening obsession and love of oddball characters and daft names.

This first book wouldn't be the funny, page-turning read it is without the additional editorial machinations of Katya Browne and Fiona Brown.

Thanks to Phillipa Walker for looking after the pre-publication stage. Thanks also to the sales, PR and rights people at Penguin (whom I haven't even met yet at the time of writing these acknowledgements!) for their role in getting *The Gardeners' Club* into shops and into the hands of readers. Teamwork really does make the dream work.

To Shannon Cullen, publisher extraordinaire. When she read my original sample of *Not For Profit* in 2012, her encouragement planted a seed in my stubborn little brain that eventually grew into *The Gardeners' Club*. She is the very definition of a champion of good writing.

To the lovely librarians who will buy copies of *The Gardeners' Club* in for their crime-fiction-loving readers, and to the book bloggers who read early copies and champion the Bromley Botanists on social media.

To my amazing readers: those who have enjoyed my writing since my debut, *The Girl Who Wouldn't Die*, published in 2015, and those who are only now discovering my writing through the criminally daft exploits of my all-new cast of green-fingered characters. I hope you'll all enjoy the Bromley Botanists' *next* adventures in compost and crime as much as this first book in the series. Spread the word to your friends and family! And if you haven't read them already, I hope you'll get stuck into my backlist titles.